A ROMAN PEACE IN BRITON
Blood on the Stone

Joe Tackett

This book is dedicated to my wife, Krystal, and daughters, Kelsea and Abigail Joy. Their faithfulness and understanding while I worked full-time in the law and spent my spare-time wrapped up in creating this novel inspire me to this day. Thank you and love ever-lasting.

CONTENTS

ACKNOWLEDGMENTS

There were a lot of people who put their two cents worth into the making of "A Roman Peace in Briton: Blood on the Stone". Whether it was suggested threads of research or character and plot evaluation, a set of valued friends and family humored and encouraged me as this novel took form. I thank all of you. Further thanks to Amy Richards, whose sharp eye caught many a punctuation snafu and edited out countless superfluous words. And to Jordan Ladikos, the gifted artist who managed to capture the book's essence and express it through the cover art's design.

I would also like to thank the many historical novelists who first inspired my interest in the genre. Bernard Cornwell, Robert Graves, Colleen McCullough, Mary Renualt, and countless others have held me in the grip of one great historical read after another. I would also be remiss if I did not thank Gaius Julius Caesar. His Commentaries were an excellent resource and a joy to read with its clear and concise style. Many other ancient historians and their works such as Herodotus, Tacitus, Livy, Plutarch and Strabo were studied and their insights and recordings shamelessly looted in an attempt to draw historical perspective. Finally, I thank my family, whom in the Lord bestowed great patience while I spent numerous hours with my nose buried in reference books, scratching out notes or hunched over the laptop working on a redraft.

LIST OF PRIMARY CHARACTERS

The characters marked with an asterisk actually existed. The others may have.

* **Gaius Julius Caesar**: born 100/101 b.c. and died on The Ides of March 44 b.c. Son of an ancient family of noble and patrician roots, Caesar was a brilliant general and politician allied with the populares. Conqueror of Gaul, Egypt and Britannia and ultimately the Republic of Rome, he served as Rome's dictator and first de facto emperor until assassinated.

Cussius Caesar: An ambitious Legate and distant junior cousin to Gaius Julius Caesar.

Marcus: a senior centurion and double decade veteran of the legion, who first served with Caesar in Further Spain and then in the Gallic Wars.

Leko: Born a free Gaul but enslaved as a result of his tribe's defeat by Caesar, taken as loot by Marcus and tasked as the centurion's orderly.

Jayas: A young Celtic nobleman and warrior, and son of Lord Toge and nephew to King Tagerix of the Coritani tribe.

Rhu: An ageless Druid priest and spiritual center of Celtic resistance to the Romans.

Gymm: Son of King Tagerix and cousin to Jayas.

Thara: niece to Rhu and younger sister of Lana.

Lana: niece to Rhu and older sister of Thara.

*Mandubrac: leading noble of the Trinovante, enemy to Cassivellaunus and allied to Rome.

*Cassivellaunus: Celtic warlord who led a confederation of tribes against Julius Caesar's second expedition in Britannia. Defeated in battle by Caesar near modern-day Hertfordshire, England.

Kegan: Clan chief of the Bibroci, a minor Celtic tribe in Britannia allied to Rome.

PREFACE
54 B.C. Interior of Britannia

Blisters covered his feet, but he forgot the pain and exhaustion and managed to keep going. Despite admonitions from his master to stay back with the pack animals and supply, he would not miss this for the world. For a few minutes, Leko ran among the trees and underbrush, stumbling, falling and picking himself up, scratching his face and hands on thorns till the blood ran.

He stopped and gave up the chase, his right hand clutching the battered short sword, his left resting on his hip. He was panting heavily. His heart beat rapidly and the sweat clung to his body like an extra set of clothing. Darkness was falling with the weakening sun, the forest silent as if nature could sense the deadly tension threatening to unfold. He emerged from the forest and sat on a stony outcrop overlooking a large clearing ringed with trees and marsh. Beyond, he could barely make out a walled enclosure snuggled tightly among wooded hills. He sensed movement in the far reaches of the wood but it was too far to be sure. From atop the bluff he could see the Roman forces muster at the edge of the river.

His mouth was dry but for the gummy residue that clung to his palate like a freshly glued bow. He wished he'd brought a water bag but shrugged off the inconvenience and shuttered his thirst into a faint corner of his mind to keep his aching feet company. Dimly, Leko thought he could see his master and imagined he could make out the stern orders that tightly controlled the practiced movements of the legions. He swallowed hard and muttered a silent prayer that his master would come through unscathed.

UNDER THE COVER of mist and darkness, Caesar had led forty cohorts and close to two thousand cavalry into the forbidding interior of the mysterious, green lands the Romans called Britannia. Guided by their native allies they had covered twelve miles, good progress for a night march. The mist receded, and dawn revealed bands of Celts waiting behind a twisting line of felled trees and shallow earthen trenches. Now, late in the day, small parties of cavalry and chariots periodically swooped down upon the Roman flanks, but they had joined no major battle.

Legate Cussius Caesar sat motionless atop his horse, alert, his ears attentive to every sound. The noises, however, were the same-- the metallic clink and creak of leather and armor when a legionary shifted in the saddle, the smacking suction noise of hooves in muddy ground. He was aware of these sounds in the fringes of his consciousness, but something shook him from his indifference. He realized it was the unnatural silence in the Celt positions. He perked up. Cussius watched with intense interest as another bunch of charging Celt skirmishers dashed forward from the rudimentary fortifications to hurl missiles and slink back to cover. His gaze followed the graceful arc the spears traveled, and he exhaled slightly as they fell well short of their mark, splashing harmlessly in the shallow, brown river. He admired the warriors' dash and bravery but frowned at their typical lack of discipline. Barbarians, he sighed. They did not have the sense to know when they were bested. At the very least, they made a good show of it. He had an eye and talent for horsemanship and reveled in watching the native warriors dash to and fro with great agility, their legs guiding their mounts while they loosed spears with their arms.

Cussius was less than impressed with the breed of their mounts. Their horses were shaggy-coated and unkempt, but sturdily built with big hooves and flowing forelocks that fell over bulging eyes. No saddles were evident, and many of the riders wore helmets, rimless and pot-shaped, adorned with goat or stag horns, some fashioned to resemble hideous birds or asps with gaping jaws and elongated fangs. The metallic ornaments contrasted marvelously with the blue paint liberally slathered on the exposed areas of their bodies. Those who scorned helmets had their long hair spiked stiff with lime that glowed preternaturally in the gleam of the fading sky.

Cussius leaned forward in his saddle, anticipation tingling the fine hairs on the back of his neck. He turned impatiently and patted his snorting mount on the neck.

"Not yet," he murmured to the anxious horse. He wheeled and rode down the length of his troops. All of them had the steely-eyed look that only men who had survived the ravages and savagery of combat could wear.

"Almost, men! Hold the line and on my command!" Cussius yelled. He reined in next to Antonius.

"Any minute now, sir." Antonius kept his eyes on the hill while yanking his sword from its scabbard.

Cussius grinned widely and nodded, pulling his own blade free in the process. They waited for the signal.

CAESAR STARED ACROSS the divide. It was an hour before dusk, and the fading light clung desperately to the darkening hills. Somewhere in the dark, towering forest bordering the river on either side, he knew the bulk of warriors of Cassivellaunus and his confederated tribes lurked. The cagey warlord had not expected to be followed this deep into his lair, and Caesar meant to press the advantage. A bit weary, Caesar clenched his teeth, his mouth a tightly compressed line. History favors the victors, he thought as his mind wandered to his writings. Posterity be damned. He unclenched his teeth and relaxed in the focus of the moment. The here and now demanded his attention.

He looked over at his tribune and nodded. The officer swung a banner in a neat, crisp pattern, the pennant flapping loudly. Other banners picked up the cadence, signaling orders left and right, tight shouts cascading up and down the ranks in tandem with trumpet calls. Staring across the river, Caesar maintained his stony demeanor as his legions surged forward.

"FOLLOW ME!" Cussius screamed. He kicked his mount and splashed through the ford of the river, the brown spray soaking his legs and drenching his horse's stomach. Vaguely he made out slender black shafts zinging by his head and striking the water with a snap, but his attention was glued ahead. He spurred harder and made the bank, his horse easily maneuvering up the grassy incline. Ahead and slightly west he could see the Roman line collide with the Celts. The loud clash of sword on shield, body on body, the anguished shrieks and screams of the dying, and the triumphant howls of the living mixed without prejudice. In the fading light, he saw more blue-skinned warriors erupt from the green of the forest in a screaming wave.

Chariots swooped down in which warriors armed with javelins fired spear after spear into the Roman lines. The chariots barely slowed as nimble warriors balanced and leaped from the fighting platforms at a run to join the fray. Now empty of cargo, the chariots looped back to safety, their wheels rumbling. From the corner of his eye he saw a blue-painted warrior tear down the slope and heave a spear before he stopped short and threw up his arms with a yelp. A Roman javelin tore through his chest and protruded from his back. The man collapsed and slid a short distance before coming to a stop against a ragged tree stump.

Cussius spurred his horse harder and leaned over its neck. He could hear thundering hooves behind and to the side of him and knew his men followed close. He made for the Celtic flank where more savages mustered to reinforce their forces engaged with the Roman legionaries.

"Ride! Attack!" he shouted. He knew the battle could turn here, and he was determined not to let the Roman foot-soldiers claim all the glory. Beside him a horse surged, and he watched Antonius be the first to smash into and through the milling Celts, the impact of his steed sending one warrior down in a heap while a second scrambled away from the kicking hooves, dragging a crooked and useless leg behind him.

Cussius saw a cavalryman go down, hurled from his mount. He watched a tall, bare-chested warrior leap from his black horse and charge the fallen Roman, his long sword already swinging in a deadly arc.

"Forward!" Cussius screamed as he stormed the remaining distance and sped into the hottest part of the melee. The wet smack of horse colliding with the frailties of man met his ears. He swung his sword from side to side, the blade slicing and cutting through flesh before emerging slimy and red. He struggled to keep the maddened barbarians at bay, kneeing his horse forward and whirling it about, using its muscled chest and rump as battering rams. Strong hands gripped his leg, and he kicked wildly trying to loosen the hold but the iron grip did not weaken and he slid from the saddle and went to the ground. He felt the jolt of a fist glance off his head, and he rolled out of the way before struggling to his feet. Blue warriors came at him like a pack of snapping dogs, but Cussius countered their searching blows and slashed at his tormentors while Antonius and others fought their way to him. He sprang free from the press of men and the rise and fall of barbarian iron. He whirled around and gained his bearings.

Panting, his mouth and nose dribbling blood, Cussius found himself faced by a young warrior who was short and squat with a barrel chest and thick arms. The warrior's face was painted in a sneer and his right hand held a bloody sword at eye level, the slits of his eyes feral and deadly. Cussius leaped forward and locked his grip with the warrior, but the man was strong and managed to get a hand around Cussius' neck. His eyes gleamed evilly and his hot breath was sour and dank like rotted cabbage, making Cussius nauseas as he struggled to breathe. Desperate, he brought his knee into the warrior's groin and felt the vise-like grip around his throat lessen. He struck out viciously with his helmeted head and heard a dull crunch. The warrior's body slid heavily to the earth, unconscious and convulsing. Cussius unleashed a fury of strokes that splattered blood like rain until the warrior moved no more. With a shout and wave of his sword, Cussius led his troops deeper into the sagging Celt flank.

BLAZING A PATH overhead, flaming arrows made fiery trails against the shadowy hills. Marcus grinned, imagining the devilish work the flaming projectiles would wreak upon the Celts. The more damage the barrage inflicted upon the enemy, the better off his troops would be, but he did not have long to wonder. All too suddenly the barbarous horde was upon them. The Celts screamed wildly in their foreign tongue, their bodies and faces painted in fearsome displays, their arms and legs pumping and covering the flattened ground in bounds. Marcus felt the rush of the enemy tribesmen as they collided pell-mell with his line, which did not budge.

"Push!" he screamed as the excitement surged and the blood swelled. Marcus thrust his broad frame into a hole in the line created when a legionary sagged to the ground, his arm dangling tenuously from a cleaved shoulder. Another legionary staggered from the line, his face a mask of blood, a red, jagged gash splitting his mouth and nose all the way through his brow revealing gleaming white bone.

A leaping Celt cleared a pile of tumbled bodies and raised his sword. Marcus slapped the blade away with his shield and stepped in, fending off the attempt to bludgeon him with a well placed thrust of his gladius. The warrior sagged to the earth, dead before he hit the muddy soil. Marcus and his men pushed over a pile of fallen bodies, Celt and Roman alike. Forward and to his right, Marcus saw the swirling of many horses.

The sharp whinnies and screams of dying horses and the muffled groans of trampled men announced the arrival of the Roman cavalry. Marcus knew to push through and redoubled his efforts, exhorting his men forward. If they pushed through and met up with the cavalry, the barbarian force would be split in two and nothing would stand in their way of assailing the cleverly concealed hill fort.

"Wheel left and push! Fight!" he screamed. His men rallied around his silver figure, and with a roar, the line surged forward. Marcus noticed that fewer and fewer Celts stepped into the fray. The remainder, unsure of reinforcements, cast fearful glances over their shoulders. This momentary lapse would cost them their lives. The Romans rushed at them with savage fury, cleaving and impaling helmeted heads and bared chests with brutal efficiency. The angry roar of the raging battle on all sides of the blue-skinned warriors unnerved them, and their confidence wilted like a flame in a harsh wind. For the first time, Marcus could see fear in the eyes of these painted brutes.

A horn sounded, and in response, the tribesmen slithered away. Many threw down their weapons where they were and sat down, dejected and deflated, their heads upon folded arms. Others made for the cover of the forest, madly leaping downed trees and fallen comrades alike. In stumbling, chaotic fashion, the blue streaks melted into the safety of the woods. The field was left to the Roman invaders.

CAESAR DISMOUNTED AND stood upon the killing field as night moved in and dark clouds draped the feeble starlight, pressing shadow upon shadow until all was dim under the dull moon. He was weary and lost in his thoughts, but he was keenly aware that he was not alone. The screams of the dying and wounded cascaded across the battlefield and kept step with his pacing. From the darkness came croaked cries for water from chapped and burned lips. All around, his men waited and watched, their faces smudged and bodies battered and bloody.

Caesar fiddled with the torc as he walked. The gold felt cool and smooth under his touch, and by gently stroking it with his fingertips, he could feel the delicate carvings. In his hands he held the symbol of Cassivellaunus's power. Caesar's acceptance of the torc brought the hostilities to an end. All that remained were the formalities. He sighed and was glad the sound was carried away by a passing wind and lost amongst the swish of the trees. The parley where terms would be enforced was forthcoming, and Caesar wondered from what well he would summon the energy to forge on. Officers, orderlies and legates gathered around him, anxiously awaiting his final word.

CHAPTER ONE

It was three crows of the rooster before dawn. The camp was mostly silent, aside from the roving guards and posted sentries. Fires had long ago burned down to smoky gray layers of ash simmering atop orange glowing coals. In the distance, shrouded by the moving blankets of mist, night birds joined in song. Yipping foxes added their voices to the late-night serenade, their shrill barks carrying across the plain from the towering dark forest that bordered the camp.

Inside the largest of the camp tents, a small oil lamp cast long flickering shadows along the walls. Caesar sat hunched over a desk, his head unmoving, his eyes squinted and roving over the fine black lettering on the papyrus scroll he held in his hands. He struggled to capture the small glow of light atop the thin surface. Finally, he set the scroll down and leaned back in his chair. He cracked his knuckles loudly, and then he tried to stretch while seated but was unsuccessful. The pain in his lower back was acute despite the best efforts of his Greek physician. The Greek was more a surgeon by trade but his abilities to heal were unmatched. In fact, the man's talents were rare and irreplaceable.

The summer campaign against the Celts of Britannia had been hotly contested and left insufficient time to heal properly. His eyes hurt, and he sighed as he rubbed his temples. His head throbbed, but he did not feel any of the tremors that portended one of his fits.

He looked forward to daybreak and breakfast. He glanced at the bowl of olives on the corner of the cluttered desk. He bit into one and winced at the saltiness as he spat the pit out. He thought about calling for the Greek. The potion the physician prepared for him daily energized and soothed the pressure in his head. Its only drawback was the chalky film it left in his mouth, which was difficult, if not impossible, to purge. A small sacrifice for the rich health benefits, he thought.

"Procillus," Caesar called. With his head hurting the way it was, it was better to have Procillus read the remainder of the papyrus to him. He looked around for his slave, who was usually underfoot, attending to some task or another. "Procillus," he repeated. To the consternation of his army and subordinates, time of day or night was of no concern to him. Caesar drove himself hard and expected the same of others.

His trusted scribe and slave, Procillus, sat on the ground, his legs splayed before him and his back propped up by the proconsul's voluminous correspondence, which was stacked in neat little bundles tied with cord. His arm lay under his head and his curly gray beard lay tucked against his shoulder. He snored loudly as his chest rose and fell.

Caesar decided to let the slave squeeze in a few more moments of sleep, and he picked up the papyrus again, careful not to fold or crease the scroll. He was fastidious with correspondence and manuscripts, for the written word was worthy of respectful handling. With a grimace, Caesar finished reading the correspondence from Labienus, which had arrived late yesterday. The news was grim.

"Procillus!" he shouted. The slave sprang up, looking around wildly before hustling to his master in short shuffling steps. A sentry stuck his head in to make sure all was well and Caesar waved him off.

Yawning, the slave stood ready. "Yes, Master," he calmly said in clear and learned Latin with just the slightest hint of an accent. He sounded more like an Italian country squire than a learned Greek slave tasked with keeping up with Caesar, whose own father had paid for the man's services many years earlier. After Caesar's father was killed, the old Greek stayed on with Caesar, who had always known him as Procillus, his given Roman name. When Caesar thought about it he had no idea what name the man received from his parents on the faraway stony farm where he was whelped.

Caesar sat with his hands in front of him, deep in thought. He picked up a pen, a raven quill with a sharp bronze tip, and twirled it in his fingers, the quill stem rolling along his knuckles. There was trouble across the channel in Gaul, the kind of trouble that could serve as the fodder for his many enemies in the Senate to issue a recall, the kind of trouble that could derail a career, which he could not allow to happen. Many had opposed his second expedition to Britannia, calling it folly and him vain.

He knew of the rumors, the gossip, of which his agent in Rome kept him well informed. That same agent also kept Caesar's name on the lips of the powerful senators, merchants, magistrates and other ranking members of Rome's complex and ponderous government. Of course, Caesar paid the man handsomely for his work. He also kept the man in ready coin and drafts to secure the loyalty of certain influential figures, which was the best he could do, being thousands of miles from Rome, to keep his position secure. Well, not the best. Victory after victory was immensely helpful, as well.

Despite the outpouring of coin and gratuities, however, Caesar was aware that many forces sought his demise. According to his man, powerful factions within the Senate were whispering that Caesar had breached his mandate in making war on Britannia. They would ask, "Where is the threat to Rome?" Off the Senate floor, they worriedly wondered of his intentions, even as his fame, glory, and generosity grew with each victory and newly claimed territory.

Caesar knew this response was purely a product of envy and fear, but nonetheless, the troublesome Gauls once again complicated matters. He put the pen down. He was loath to leave. He felt a strong urge to further explore this island, the same tug and pull that propelled him through life. The thought of unfulfilled potential plucked at his mind. He felt as if he had barely scratched the surface of this place and was eager to explore the land and secure more glories.

"Victories and momentary lapses," he mumbled out loud without meaning to. He did not look at his scribe.

"Indeed. You have many of those, master. Victories, I mean," Procillus said wanly, wiping the sleep from his rheumy eyes.

"They are fleeting, though," Caesar added in distaste. "The Senate and the people of Rome are concerned about now." He stared at the flickering flame of the lamp, momentarily lost in thought.

Procillus moved closer to the light. "Governor-General. You need some sleep. This can be done first thing in the morn, after you have rested and eaten something more than the stale bread and olives you somehow manage to thrive on. Besides, you would be much more effective after a brief respite."

Caesar looked at the slave as if he had just suggested that he capitulate to the Celts and return the document that sealed the cessation of hostilities. "I am quite capable, thank you very much, to determine when and under what circumstances I take my rest," Caesar snapped. He regretted it. He knew the old scribe meant well. And for that matter, the whites of Caesar's eyes tended to agree, streaked as they were with veins of red under the dark, hollow pockets of his wrinkling skin. Even the great Caesar needed rest.

The wind blew through the tent flap and the flame bent low and then burst back up. A glint in the corner drew Caesar's attention. A Celtic shield rested against the tent wall. Cassivellaunus had given it to him. A symbol of his goodwill, he had said. The shield was beautifully designed, intricately decorated with a round boss containing a delicate carving of a wolf outlined in gold. It brought him back to the recently ended hostilities. There never seems an end to problems, he thought. He had made his decision.

"Procillus, we have a few hours until first light. Have the orderlies notify First Centurion Marcus Rulus and my dear younger cousin, Cussius that I wish to see them at dawn. Go on," he ordered.

Procillus raised his eyes and only nodded. He turned and walked out of the tent, letting in a gust of cool night air with his exit. Caesar could hear him waking the orderlies and relaying the orders. Yawning, Caesar stood stiffly and walked to his cot, which contained a single thin woolen blanket. He removed his sandals and swung his body onto the bed. He felt the tension begin to drain as he stared at the top of the tent and let his thoughts work around the many issues still to be resolved. A queer smile played at his lips as he closed his eyes. The little sun inside his head grew dimmer and dimmer, and finally, he could sleep.

CHAPTER TWO

THE MOURNFUL SOUNDS of the legion bugles beckoned the soldiers from their exhausted slumbers and rudely announced a fresh day. In concert with that somber howl, Marcus rolled off the worn thatched pallet of crossed wool with practiced ease. Outside, he could hear his orderly singing one of those strange Gallic tunes that always left him a bit gloomy, not the melody he needed to start the day. His rest had been needlessly interrupted by Caesar's orderly, and now his head ached and his mood was on the sour side.

He groaned as he stood. His body hurt with bruises and knotted muscles. For close to twenty years he had answered the call of the bugle and the routine of the legion was in many ways as second nature to him as walking or eating. The rhythm of the legion beat within his chest as regular as the tide of the sea that brought him to this strange land filled with wild and savage blue-skinned inhabitants. That didn't make rising in the morn any easier, though.

Rolling his massive head on his thick neck, he worked out the nighttime kinks and emitted a satisfied sigh with the cracking of his vertebrae. Dawn was just breaking and curious streaks of light were beginning to emerge on the swelling blue of the gentle sea. The familiar rustling of thousands of men and beasts stirring met his level gaze as he stepped out of the shadow of his tent. Pausing, he took a moment to yawn and wipe the sleep from his eyes. He breathed deeply, filling his lungs with the land's scent, the stiff ocean breeze mixed with the pungent aroma of animal sweat, coppery blood, smoke, and refuse inherent to a legion camp. The fact that he found this a most familiar and comfortable scent marked him as a warrior of Rome.

With practiced precision, he began stretching his thick arms outward as he rotated his stiff limbs. As part of his daily routine, he deliberately mimed the swordplay that defined his career and with which he had carved out a place he called his home. He grimaced and stretched his back until he heard it crack. Next, he stretched his legs and jogged in place for a moment, trying not only to loosen up but to get some blood flowing. His muscles were stiff from the short night's rest, and his old wounds tended to smart in the morning.

"Good morning, Master. Something to eat?" his orderly asked, surprisingly cheery, considering his own lack of sleep. He spoke passable Latin but peppered his phrases with Gallic words. Marcus usually caught three-quarters of what he said.

Marcus grunted in return. Last night's wine ration did not sit well in this morning's stomach and he pushed away the stale bread crust hurriedly offered by his orderly, but took the cheese. He sniffed the moldy goat cheese wrapped in musty burlap and decided caution was the better part of valor. He wanted wine. A good Roman wine would clear his head and settle his stomach. Instead, he gulped half a flask of tepid water, rinsing the grime and filth out of his mouth, spitting the remainder on the trampled soil. The water had an iron taste to it and left his mouth tangy.

Leko placed a wooden bucket in front of him, and Marcus took a moment to splash some brine on his face. "Thanks," he gruffly said. He held out his hand and took the razor the boy had sharpened. With quick, brisk strokes, his face was scraped clean by the thin blade. Nodding his thanks, he handed the razor back.

"If you are half as quick with the sword as you are with that cheese and razor, you just might end up a suitable soldier in my legion," Marcus said, teasing the eager youngster. The youth smiled quickly, his teeth flashing white against his sun-darkened skin.

The orderly was a young Gaul orphaned by one of the many battles that had raged across the continent the past few years. He claimed to be the son of a Gallic king who had met his end at the hands of Julius Caesar and his unbreakable legions, but Marcus knew that almost every slave claimed to be the progeny of some forgotten chieftain. Marcus had taken the young Gaul and a couple dozen others as spoils from the last large battle on that soil before they made the dangerous and very uncomfortable crossing of the channel. Keeping the boy he sold the others on consignment to an honest Roman merchant named Sambinius, hoping to realize a fair profit upon his return to Rome.

Marcus preferred to call the boy by his pet name, Leko, a shortened version of some accursed, unpronounceable Gallic label that he was loath to memorize. The young man wore his long blond hair plaited in the style favored by the vain barbarians. Though not yet sixteen years of age, it had not reached its full zenith as worn by the more mature Gallic warriors. Steadfast and not prone to complaints, the youngster made an able orderly and more than earned his meager keep.

Leko followed Marcus around like a pup would his mum, mirroring his movements and eager to help. "And if you gave me a chance I'd show you that I can fight," he playfully growled with a respectful determination that belied his youthful stature. He practiced daily with the tarnished short sword and battered shield that Marcus allowed him. Enduring these grueling sessions with Marcus had made Leko nimble and true, and he warmed to the regimen with youthful zeal and dedication. The shorter Roman gladius was different than the long sword customarily used by his people, but it still strengthened his arms and shoulders and he grew into it ably.

Marcus nodded, fairly amused at the boy's persistent pestering. "All in good time, Leko. I have to see the General, and no, you cannot come with me. Tend to my horse. Find him some forage and water. I'm sure he could use the attention." He left the boy and stalked the short distance to his pack roll where he kept his crested helmet and medallioned cuirass. Like other centurions, he was distinguishable by his polished silver armor that ran from shin to neck. He wore his sword on his left, as was customary, and his dagger on his right, and of course, he still carried his shield. Conspicuously missing from the standard uniform was his *vitis*, a traditional vine cane often used to mete out ferocious beatings to loafing legionaries. It was unnecessary for him to carry one, as he was Senior Centurion or Primi Ordines of the first rank, and no legionaries under his command dared shirk a task with him at the helm. He had not carried the *vitis* for the past two years, and if things transpired as they should, there would be no need to unpack it now.

Having gathered himself, Marcus ambled off in the direction of his commanding general's quarters. With imposing and well-guarded blockhouses securing its periphery, the camp was huge and functioned like a miniature city. Yet despite its size, navigating the camp was easy. Marcus found it comforting that this camp would look no different than one erected on the Campus Martius outside the walls of Rome, or in Parthia or Africa for that matter. Two main streets running north-south and east-west, the *Via Principia* and the *Via Praetoria*, led into the camp. Both of these main camp passages converged upon the camp's headquarters: Caesar's command tent. Halfway along, he spotted his considerably younger, more connected rival and fellow officer, Cussius Caesar, also headed toward Caesar's doorway. He girded himself for the inevitable confrontation that accompanied these encounters.

"Good morning my dearest of Centurions. Pressing business this morning?" quipped Cussius in the furiously mocking tone that seemed to partner with every syllable he ever uttered. Cussius Caesar, commanded a cohort of cavalry that rivaled his own legionaries in terms of accomplishment. If he were not so capable, Marcus's loathing of the man's personality, or lack thereof, would have already culminated with Cussius skewered on the tip of his gladius. As it were, Marcus sated himself with a verbal joust of his own.

"Good morning, sir. Late night? I hear tell this foggy island is filled with enough supple boys to make a proper Greek such as yourself blush like a fair maiden," laughed Marcus, his mouth smiling but his eyes chipped flint. Cussius smiled in return, but if looks could maim or kill, it would have been a funeral pyre rather than a cooking fire that Leko was building for his master.

While Marcus was of medium height, as Romans tend to be, Cussius ranged taller, calling into question his mixed heritage. While Marcus resembled a mature oak able to withstand nature's fury, Cussius was more like a willow, yielding and flowing with what nature begat. Wherein Marcus was thick, barrel-chested and broad across the shoulders, Cussius was of slender build, speaking to his natural ease and agility with the horse.

The shared qualities that bridged the class and generational gap between the two were their mutual infatuation with, and indeed their sheer admiration for combat. Both had distinguished themselves through their tenacity and willingness to innovate before the enemy. Such qualities had long ago garnered the attention of their mutual benefactor, Gaius Julius Caesar, Proconsul Governor-General.

Marcus absentmindedly arranged the flowing red tunic so that it folded over his shoulders. Glancing over at Cussius, he was not surprised to see that his uniform gleamed, all spit and polish, appearing as if its wearer were on parade in the center of Rome rather than standing in the muck and grime of the fields of Britannia.

Before they could announce themselves to the sentries, their commander strode from the pillared façade of Caesar's tented headquarters. He stood an inch or so taller than Marcus yet shorter than Cussius. Even at this early hour he appeared alert and composed. His stride bespoke purpose and determination, and his piercing dark eyes expertly surveyed the two with a knowing and measured look that left Marcus with a feeling that he was found wanting in some fashion.

Simultaneously, the two stopped and clapped their clenched right fists to their chests and then skyward with the standard legion cry of "Salute!"

Caesar returned their salutes and then gestured for them to follow. "I feel like walking," Caesar clipped evenly. His dark hair cropped short, Caesar, known to be preoccupied with his coif, methodically flipped at his hair as he ran his hand backward. Marcus sensed that Caesar had barely slept three hours a night for the past month, and as a result, dark circles were beginning to form around the hollow edges of his eyes.

"I appreciate your timeliness at this early hour," Caesar said, his eyes focused on the unfolding bustle as docked transport ships were being rolled into the water with a splash. "I have a task for the two of you. Indeed, Rome has a task for the two of you, and we trust that Rome can count on your obedience in this matter to the utmost of your considerable abilities." Caesar quickened his pace, and Marcus and Cussius hustled to stay up. "While we have been pursuing our rights to this island, the seeds of rebellion have been nurtured in Gaul. It seems that a certain two brothers have caused quite a stir across the channel and have the tribes in an uproar. One of them actually had the temerity to pronounce himself to be King of the Gauls." Caesar said this as if no other notion in the known universe was ever more preposterous.

Caesar stopped suddenly and turned to Marcus, snorting in disdain. "Worse still, many Gauls are acknowledging him as such. As we very well know, our intolerance of this issue is incontrovertible. It's quite obvious that I cannot, and by that I mean, Rome cannot, allow this rebellion to fester, and I am to be the cleansing instrument of Mars. I shall do what is necessary to quell this Gaul once and for all. Do not doubt that for a moment. Rome is sovereign and these Gauls will yield." Though his eyes were ablaze with a scorching intensity, his tone never ventured beyond the usual confines of a casual conversation. From afar, one could very well guess the three were discussing the bi-monthly grain shipment due Narbo and not the pending counterattack Caesar planned for Gaul.

Always alert to the possibility of forwarding his fortune, Cussius could barely contain his eagerness. "Commander, my allegiance to Rome and your generalship is unquestioned. Just point and your will be done." To underscore this point, he raised himself to his greatest height, shoulders back, patrician chin and nose slightly raised as if the mere thought of being taken at less than his word were unthinkable. Marcus fought the urge to roll his eyes.

"I have no such doubts at all, and that is why I have summoned the two of you," Caesar said with a wolfish grin. Pivoting quickly, he gestured toward the rolling green field that swept from the towering, chalky, white cliff beaches to the lofty ancient forests stretching west and north.

He continued his stroll. "For the time being, we have subdued the local resistance and have entered into alliances with a few of the weaker local Celtic chieftains; and with Gaul in flames, we must not tarry here lest we return to Gaul in the time of hunger." The mention of Gaul and hunger put the three in mind of past campaigns. Experience had taught them all that the struggle to survive hinged as much on the means to eat as it did on the legion's ability to fight, but all were also keenly aware that a hungry legion made for a motivated legion.

"Be that as it may, you two shall not be making the crossing back to Gaul with the rest of the legions." He paused long enough to drink in the questioning looks hastily exchanged between Marcus and Cussius, and it was evident that he thoroughly enjoyed the confusion he had so easily sown with one casually uttered sentence.

Marcus noted the flicker of amusement in his commander's eyes, and his eyes narrowed with suspicion as he wondered what Caesar was up to. Finally, he could contain himself no longer, cleared his throat and plowed ahead with the same incisive perspective that marked his style of command.

"Governor-General, may I respectfully inquire as to what earthly benefit would accrue to Rome with Cussius and myself confined to this miserable island with its hostile populace at our throats?" asked Marcus in his slightly accented Latin.

Not to be outflanked by Marcus, Cussius deftly maneuvered himself back into the dialogue as well. "Ironically, I find myself agreeing with my more reserved compatriot. It would seem that Rome could use our swords in dealing with our stubborn Gallic subjects." Pleased with his contribution to the conversation and sure of Rome's need for his military prowess, Cussius contentedly left the statement lingering in the air as he waited his commander's reply.

Caesar, as astute a diplomat as he was a warrior, would not brook the slightest hint of discontent for his authority or judgment. A clear, icy coolness replaced his smiling warmth.

"You both serve at my whim and pleasure. So, in essence, you serve at the whim and pleasure of Rome. Take a look around, soldiers of Rome. We are not in the forum of the Senate, and this is not an issue that is subject to debate," he said, the veiled nature of his statement not lost upon his subordinates. "You owe your respective commands as much to my generosity as to your own abilities. Never think for a moment there are not dozens of ambitious young Roman nobles who would love to be handed the reins to your cohorts. I doubt they would pause to challenge the wisdom of how I opt to deploy my legions," said Caesar with just a hint of sarcasm and punctuated by the soft jabbing of his index finger in the light morning mist peculiar to this region of the world.

Satisfied with the stony silence greeting his latest admonishment, Caesar moved on as if there were never any doubt as to the efficacy of his plans. He pointed beyond the great swath of forest. "A garrison is to be established at the confluence of the two rivers seven days hard march to the north. Our local allies have informed me that north and hinterland conceals the true wealth of this island. Your task shall be a simple one: divine the nature and extent of the wealth of this region, and as we do with every territory, devise the means to extort and export its wealth to Rome," said Caesar with his knowing smile. "Of just as much importance is the need to ensure that Cassivellaunus complies with the terms of the truce. In particular, you will need to secure the tribute owed Rome. This is important. I am depending on that tribute payment to help finance the newest campaign in Gaul. Additionally, these Celts need to understand that, just because I'm over on the continent it does not mean they are relieved of their obligations under the truce agreement." Unsure that the two fully grasped the situation, Caesar continued the lecture.

"At the risk of boring two hard-charging soldiers such as yourselves, keep in mind that the politics of Rome must always be a consideration in our actions as soldiers. As you well know, Rome's coffers must be kept brimming with newly acquired gold, and slaves must be continually imported lest the noble senators believe me to be withholding their fair due. Besides, what good is conquering new lands if they are deprived the benefit of Roman civilization? In exchange for our civilizing influence, is it too much to expect a bit of recompense from our newly acquired barbarian subjects?" Pausing for effect, Caesar reached for a weathered, leather-bound Etruscan pouch emblazoned with the symbol of Jupiter. The leather appeared as if it had been reworked and kneaded with oil, retaining a bit of suppleness despite its apparent age.

Before Caesar could expose its contents, Cussius could refrain no longer. "General, may I inquire," he asked in his patrician Latin, "as to whom would wield overall command of this garrison?"

Caesar sighed slowly before he continued. "Patience being a virtue, your blessings are abundant in other capacities, young Cussius," quipped Caesar in his patronizing manner. "To that end, you are dismissed. You will receive further orders on this matter. For now, I wish to speak with an old friend." It was apparent this was no request, and Cussius hastened to comply, rather shocked that he was being summarily dismissed on the heels of his valid inquiry. Cussius and his wounded ego retreated from his commander's stern gaze.

Caesar approached Marcus with genuine warmth evident in his eyes. "Ah, Marcus, my dear old friend," he said as he clasped the old warhorse in the standard Roman embrace. Years of service with his commander had conditioned Marcus to expect the unexpected with Caesar. His unpredictability, force of will, and fierce determination remained key factors in his successes, be they military or the adroit political manipulations necessitated by his life as a Roman noble.

Never one to pontificate unnecessarily, Marcus returned Caesar's familiar embrace with a nod of his boulder-like head. "Sir, of course you may count on me. My allegiance to you, to Rome, is steadfast"

Smiling, Caesar kept his hand cupped on Marcus' rounded shoulder. "I know, and that is precisely why Cussius is to assume overall command of the garrison and Roman Briton during my absence," he said evenly, the look of genuine affection never retreating from his eyes despite the statement relayed to his friend and subordinate.

Marcus groaned but quickly regained his composure. "Yes, Caesar."

CHAPTER THREE

IT WAS A CLOUDLESS day and the sun shone brightly on the sweating combatants as they circled each other, one feinting left and slashing under the guard of the other. Instantly, Jayas brought the course leather-wrapped hilt of the blunted wooden sword crashing into the exposed lower jaw of his cousin and fellow tribesman, Gymm, with a nasty upward thrust and twist of his right arm. Blood oozed from the gash opened on Gymm's square chin, and a crimson puddle formed on the muddy and trampled ground churned over by the furious movement of the two combatants. A chorus of raucous cheers rose from the sixty or so young warriors grouped around to watch two of their stouter companions wage their battle. A louder shout of pained indignation joined the chorus as Gymm bellowed in rage, lowered his head and attempted to drive Jayas into the ground with sheer brute force.

Attempted on any other warrior, such a tactic would have certainly borne fruit, as Gymm was a bull of a man and few could withstand his determined assault. Not quite twenty-one summers of age, he was proving to be an exceptional warrior. Still, his expansive physical proportions were not outmatched by his courage.

Laughing deeply, Jayas sidestepped his charging cousin, thrusting out his left shin and tripping Gymm to the ground with a resounding thud. He shook his head and bent over at the waist, his left arm resting on his thigh, his breathing fast and deep. "Enough

for today," he said, slightly panting while chuckling at the determination once again displayed by the stubbornly aggressive Gymm.
"There will be plenty of real battle and glory to be had when we
raid south in the coming weeks."

Jayas felt a surge of excitement course through his broad chest
at the thought of the riches to be had through the raids he and his
clansmen were to wreak soon. He and his warriors were eager and
willing, and the excitement in the air was palpable. Little else was
spoken of these days. Even as they rode and drank and ate, the talk
centered on the upcoming season's raiding or speculation about the
other tribes' battles with an invader from across the sea. These were
exciting times.

Jayas was satisfied with the day's training. The daily regimen
he and his clansmen had subjected themselves to was legendary, at
least in their own minds. Since the young men were old enough to
pick up sticks, the elders had encouraged them in horsemanship
and swordplay, spurring on their boldness and bravery. They had
learned the ways of the hunters while still boys, their games demanding patience, silence, and stealth. They learned of the fierce joy
of a charge on horseback, and although self-sufficiency was valued,
dedication to each other reigned unquestioned.

Returning the blunted training sword to the worn leather and
fox fur sheath attached to the wide belt clasped to his waist, Jayas
extended his broad left hand to the seated Gymm and hefted him to
his feet in one effortless motion. "Come with me, cousin. You need
to have that looked at, and perhaps sewn together. It's not the first
time either one of us has been cut, the gods know." He was cutting a
sign into the ground in an effort to ward off the evil eye. A silly notion, he was sure, but he thought it better to err on the side of
caution when dealing with the spirits. If they existed, that is. Grinning to himself, and happy to have been on the delivering end of
this exchange with Gymm, he looked his comrade in the eye, marveling at their similarities.

When they were walking side by side, a stranger to the tribe
would believe the two young men to be brothers. Both were tall,
considerably so, even by Celtic standards. Each sprouted untamed

hair over their top lips but their faces were scraped clean otherwise. Both wore their hair long in the fashion favored by the majority of the Celtic men folk, though Jayas' hair resembled the yellow of a midday sun while Gymm' retained a lighter brown that streaked yellow during the humid summer months.

Large and muscular from years of training for battle and a sound diet strong in the flesh of cattle, sheep and swine, their bodies were inured to hardship and built for punishment. Tribal tradition held that Gymm was to eventually ascend to the position of tribal headman once the requisite number of years had passed and sufficient wisdom had been obtained, but merit dictated that he defer until then to his friend and cousin, Jayas, in most matters.

"Next time, Jayas," croaked Gymm from between swollen lips. His pride was cause for more pain than any visible injuries. He winced as he ran his calloused hand over his cut and bruised face, but otherwise he withstood the pain and discomfort with characteristic Coritani fortitude.

"From here on out we save our strength for our enemies," Jayas said as he turned and walked onto the firmer ground of the village's crowded main artery. Young children ran up to him, their eyes full of wonder and worship, and their shouts of joy warming his heart. He tousled their hair and growled playfully, making ugly faces and chasing about like an overgrown puppy until the children returned to the calls of their mothers and sisters. They took a shortcut through the village market, pausing a moment to haggle with a peasant farmer too fond of his hogs to strike a fair bargain.

"Your loss," Jayas told the tightfisted peasant.

"Maybe the next buyer will offer more," the farmer said with a shrug.

"I hunt for mine, but your stock is safe enough. Too scrawny for my spear," Gymm said.

Shedding thoughts of fresh pork Jayas' active mind strayed into familiar territory as he caught a glimpse of Thara busily moving loose wool, ready for spinning, into hollowed wooden stumps. Beautiful, with long, dark hair tending to curl when caught in the rain, she was now eighteen summers of age. She went about her work with languid grace, unhurried but determined, and her profile made him catch his breath. Possessing the sharp wit of her successful tradesman father and the even sharper tongue of her whippish mother, Thara drew the attention of all the young warriors, but she had Jayas' attention in particular. Her older sister, Lana, was just as beautiful and alluring, but Jayas had never warmed to her as he did Thara. Besides, Lana had married and moved south with her new husband a summer or two ago, and had been rarely seen since.

Gymm lagged behind as Jayas walked up to where Thara worked and stood silently, waiting for her to finish moving the wool. As usual whenever Jayas was around pretty women, his left hand self-consciously traced the lengthy scar running from the corner of his left eye, curving down his jaw line. The scar did little to detract from his looks, and if anything, added to his mystique as a warrior. Either way, it was of no concern to him. The scar came courtesy of an arrow flung by a panicking Bibroci warrior as Jayas thundered down upon him. The raid netted much booty, including his favorite warhorse, which he rode to this day. It was his first foray as a warrior, and he acquitted himself well, and the scar merely bore witness to that fact. The same could not be said for the offending Bibroci warrior — that was the last arrow he would ever launch. He cleared his throat. She looked up at him.

"Yes?"

He never really could tell if she was warming up to his clumsy flirtations, but that did little to stop him from trying. "How's my wife on this fine day?" mumbled Jayas in a tentative tone to which he was unaccustomed. A fury in battle and a scourge to the tribe's enemies, one look from Thara was enough to weaken his knees.

"When I see her, I will ask her," came the bold retort, springing from Thara's petulant mouth at the speed of a diving sparrow. Her reply elicited the hiccupping giggles of the other unattached young women who were busily spinning the mounds of wool into more manageable bolts of cloth that would then be sold at the village market or traded down south. Much of the wool these women wove, as well as the cattle the men drove, was bartered in the southwest to the tribes that maintained a tight hold on the region's tin deposits and copper mines. More extensive trading involved cross-ing the sea, a long and rare journey, to obtain weapons crafted by the Spaniards, their fire-scorched iron highly valued by the warrior culture. Of course, this made for stronger weapons and better tools, which were highly valued amongst all the neighboring tribes too, some friendly and some not.

Jayas smiled. "That would be kind of you. And please let my wife know that her husband desires more time together."

Thara's jibe elicited a rare comment from Gymm when they were out of earshot of the women. "How does she know your wife when you're not even married?" mused Gymm aloud in thoughtful consternation as he strode on the right of Jayas.

His brows cinched together and chin still bloody, the puzzled look remained until Jayas laughed heartily and thumped a ham-sized fist on Gymm's bare shoulder. "The ways of women are unknown to simple warriors such as us. The day will come though when I will ride through the southern gate with a herd of horses, a pile of gold and the heads of our enemies as tribute for her hand. Then her father will know that I am worthy to be her husband." With that bit of prophecy expended, he let the idea drop off as he thought of things to come.

With one last furtive glance back toward Thara, the two casu-ally strode into the great room of the center lodge. Jayas grabbed a rag and tossed it to his cousin. "Now go wash that wound on your chin. We don't need it to swell up with illness. Your head is large enough as it is. And have Wynn apply a poultice. That should do it," said Jayas in a lighthearted fashion, wanting to make sure that all was still well between him and Gymm.

Gymm clapped him on the shoulder. "Next time, cousin Jayas, you will need the poultice. But it's good training," Gymm said, breaking into a grin, "And so is hunting boar. Tomorrow," reminded Gymm as he ducked out the awning and back into the daylight.

Catching the scent of roasted lamb and oat bread, Jayas ambled next to the hearth and draped his large body down on one of the rough-hewn, thickly constructed oak stools typically reserved for his father. He grasped a steaming piece of lamb and hungrily tore at the flesh with even, white teeth. He hardly paused before chasing it down with a rolled up chunk of bread dipped in thickened gravy made of melted lamb fat, sea salt and milk. His throat still parched from the morning exertions, he filled a tin cup to brimming with freshly drawn goat's milk and threw it back with relish. Sated, he belched loudly and stood to greet his father, who could be heard nearing the lodge steeped in muted conversation with other elders of the tribe.

With joy and pride on his face, Jayas' father met his firstborn son with a roared greeting. Always respectful to his elders and in particular to his father, Jayas shook his head in greeting and ac-knowledged all present. Jayas alertly noticed that one of the men accompanying his father was a nobleman loyal to Chief Cassivel-launus, a long time rival of the tribe who had recently been at war with the Romans. To Jayas' frustration, no warriors from Jayas' tribe were granted leave to join in the battles against the Romans. In-stead, he and his companies were relegated to escorting the drovers and a herd of beef to Cassivellaunus as the tribe's contribution to their efforts against the invaders. Though not on friendly terms with Cassivellaunus's people, Jayas' pride burned hot at the thought of not joining in the fight. He and the other young warriors yearned to test their battle skills against a new enemy instead of conducting raids against the same belligerent neighboring tribes. His heart quickening in excited anticipation, Jayas eagerly awaited his father's words.

"I saw Gymm. I trust the morn's training went well?" asked his father after his eyes had adjusted to the dimly lit interior of the lodge that housed twenty or so members of Jayas' close knit family. Tall and broad, the battle-scarred Toge cut an imposing figure wherever he stood. In the confines of the lodge, his figure tended to grow with the shadows, adding layers to his already considerable bulk. As the golden torc hanging around his muscled neck attested, Jayas' father, village chieftain and lord of vast holdings, was of noble lineage and was much respected by allies and foes alike. Lord Toge owed allegiance to his older brother, King Tagerix, who was widely considered to be the leading noble of their particular tribe of Celts.

Greetings exchanged, Lord Toge beckoned his guests to gather around the large sturdy oak table. Grabbing a polished, ornately sketched tin mug and urging his guests to do the same, he dipped it into a cavernous bucket of ale set upon the table. He slaked his thirst, wiping stray drips of the stout ale from his bushy moustache and chin with a brawny fist. Not one to engage in further niceties, Lord Toge addressed Jayas.

"Assemble your men. You are heading southeast two weeks from now. Cassivellaunus has been defeated by the Romans. Their war leader, Caesar, returns to Gaul to do combat with our brothers across the sea. Cassivellaunus has now made peace and will not join in our raids against the Romans' Celtic allies. This Caesar has taken his family hostage, and if he makes war on those tribes, they are as good as sacrificed to the gods. If the truth be known, he's also probably angry that we did not send our warriors to support him against the foreigners." Lord Toge said this last bit with the slightest insinuation of resentment cutting into his deep voice. That was as far as he would go in questioning the King's decision to forego laying aside old rivalries for the time being in order to confront what Toge saw as a bigger mutual threat, the Romans.

His broad, angular face inscrutable, Lord Toge cut a stern figure as he continued. "We were not at war with these Roman invaders, nor do we desire to be at war with them at this point. You and your two companies may raid any of our traditional enemies of the Cenerimagni, Trinovante, Ancalites, Bibroci and Cassi tribes as usual. Raid their cattle and other livestock, kill any men they send against you, and learn what you can of these Romans. Test their commitment to the tribes you raid, but if possible, avoid directly confronting them," declared Toge in the serious tone he reserved for those matters affecting the tribe's welfare.

Revolted at the thought of avoiding warfare with anyone, Jayas suppressed his combative nature and stifled the urge to argue with his father about fighting the Romans. He knew his place and would defer to the leadership of his father — Jayas fully knew what was expected.

"Father, we are ready. Your orders are clear and I will do my best to follow them and to bring honor to my family and my tribe," Jayas said, maintaining eye contact with his father. Inwardly whooping with joy but outwardly stoic, Jayas buzzed at the prospect of leading his horsemen into battle earlier in the year than expected, and upon taking his leave, Jayas hastened to assemble his warriors.

CHAPTER FOUR

JULIUS CAESAR STOOD ON the finished deck of the hastily built flat-bottomed boat. Designed on a Gallic model and made entirely of oak, the boat had a high bow and stern which protected it from heavy seas and violent storms and allowed it to be adroitly maneuvered in the dangerous and unpredictable coastal waters. Looking up at the midday sun, he noted the craftsmanship evident of the rawhide sail as it snagged the swirling gusts of stinging wind. His legs were spread shoulder-width apart to keep his balance with the swell of the breaks. He stared at the bubbling cut of the water, the boat's wake leaving a foam of white on the choppy surface, evidence of his passage. His tranquility vanished at the voice of his *Praefectus* rising above the wind and the sounds cast by the fluttering sails.

"Governor-General, do you really trust your cousin Cussius to do as you say, and indeed, if he does attempt to carry out your directive, what measure of success could he possibly obtain with an island full of savage bandit chiefs? Cassivellaunus is one cunning barbarian; and our main ally, Mandubrac, is little better than a brigand warlord himself. And what of all the other wild tribes with which we have not yet contended?" Trippio shouted above the wind, his usually tanned face taking on a pallid hue. Trippio never sailed well and spent the majority of any sea voyage below deck, orderly by his side with bucket and cloth. Involuntary spasms of his stomach continued to wreak havoc on the man as the sea swelled and dipped the transport ship.

"It's been considered, Praefect Trippio, and my decision was premised upon those precise considerations," Caesar said, who was fond of simple logic finding use in complex examinations. Besides, he was really not in the mood to discuss the topic and hoped the concise explanation sufficed. His mind was focused on the trouble on the mainland and how best to snuff it out. He sighed and decided to humor Trippio.

"Moreover, why worry about the past when the future holds many unresolved challenges?" he asked the prying Trippio while scanning the skies for any sign that might portend a storm.

Trippio, undaunted, clung to the swaying deck like a novice rider on a spirited mount. "Are you not worried about the tribute? What about the gold, slaves, wool and timber you demanded?" asked Trippio, a little green around the eyes from his battle with the sea.

Battle was where Trippio was most comfortable, and he usually found the inner workings of legion politics to be a tiresome affair, but he sensed subterfuge afoot and hoped his old friend would reveal the inner workings of whatever plan he had set in motion. "With all due respect, sir, why leave Cussius in command of such a sensitive and demanding detail? He is a fine soldier, I'll admit, but he is also cunning, greedy and singularly ambitious. Might I add that he is dangerous, sir? The barbarians are just as likely to slit his throat as hand the tribute over, for he inspires that in others."

Caesar took a deep breath of salty air. "And?" he asked, one eyebrow arched in question. "Indeed. What a tragedy it would be for a conniving, greedy and singularly ambitious young nobleman to meet his due at the hands of wild savages. Indeed, it would be a proper tragedy. Of course, I would have to write his mother and relate that he died bravely carrying out orders in Rome's quest to bring civilization to savages. The greatest tragedy of all is that Rome would never know how great he could become. Of course, he could prove himself to be the effective, innovative leader of men I believe him to be, and return to Gaul with tribute in hand. And if that comes to fruition, then Cussius will be rewarded with greater responsibilities, a step up on the course of honor," Caesar explained.

Caesar's explanation seemed to have little of the desired effect and Trippio looked as confused as before. "But what about First Centurion Marcus Rulus? I believed you quite fond of him?"

"I am. But Cussius' brashness is best tempered by Marcus' experience. Let us speak no more of it. For them, they are now in the hands of the gods," Caesar said with one last backward glance at the mysterious island slowly disappearing from sight.

CHAPTER FIVE

Cussius could barely contain the excitement fluttering through his chest. From the pebble-strewn beach, he had watched the proconsul Julius Caesar sail eastward with the vast majority of the legionaries in tow. Now, however, the enormity of the situation was beginning to settle upon Cussius. He realized that he was in command of a measly thousand legionaries and expected to maintain a Roman presence in this hostile land, all while Caesar rampaged across Gaul once again. Convinced his was a backwater assignment and a punishment of sorts, Cussius was nevertheless determined to make the best of the situation and extract a severe toll on the surrounding Celts. Allies and hostiles would feel his wrath without exception. Chuckling to himself, he kicked his mount and yanked the reins hard to the left, whirling horse and rider in the direction of the primary Bibroci village he was to occupy.

His pace was unhurried, and his mind wandered to the many things he had to do. He was anxious to impose his will on the chieftain of this village, even though the Celt had already attached himself to Rome through his allegiance with Caesar in the most recent fighting against Cassivellaunus. That alliance came at a price, however, and Cussius meant to collect, to maybe even work some profit for himself. The spoils are said to belong to the victors, and as Rome's representative here in this wretched country, he would enrich his family as well as his own name. He would not allow his ambition to go unchecked by this foggy and wild land filled with blue-painted savages.

He glanced at his brooding companion and wondered what he was thinking. He is probably dreaming of cheap whores and sour wine, Cussius mused. He wasn't quite sure Marcus grasped the situation, but he thought eventually he would come to understand. But no matter if he did not. If he didn't have the head to grasp this as an opportunity, he would be dealt with accordingly.

"I think we must be sure that our friendly Bibroci deliver the allotment of beef and wheat by midday or we may have to painfully remind them. I also believe they are due to supply half a talent of gold and silver," Cussius said for the benefit of Marcus. So far, the man had not offered much in the way of conversation. He was sure Marcus grated at being under his command, as he was nine years his senior and had served much longer under cousin Caesar than had Cussius. Marcus surprised him with the content and breadth of his answer.

"I believe a less heavy hand may better serve our endeavors at this time," Marcus said thoughtfully, squinting his eyes against the sun. "If you have forgotten so quickly, let me remind you, sir, that we are vastly outnumbered here and will depend heavily on the cooperation and mutual goodwill we establish with our allies. The Bibroci, in particular, have been quite helpful, despite the fact that they initially resisted an alliance. It's a delicate balance that we find ourselves maintaining. Even an old soldier like me can see that," Marcus said matter-of-factly, all the while slowly moving his eyes to and fro as he surveyed the scene before him. He knew that keeping the impetuous Cussius from upsetting a delicate situation might well be beyond his abilities. A part of him secretly wished for the man to fail miserably, for his command to be an utter disaster. Then maybe Caesar would see what his oversight had cost him. But no, that would not do, he thought with a frown. If Cussius failed in a spectacular fashion, the Roman body count would be too high, maybe even disastrous. Such an outcome was intolerable to Marcus despite his misgivings about the man. He suppressed a scowl. Marcus was an extremely brutal and competent soldier and leader of men, but the political subtleties incumbent within his instructions from Caesar were a challenge he did not relish. He knew the young man riding next to him would prove to be much trouble and wondered why his commander had thus sentenced him,

Before Cussius could respond, Marcus continued the thought. "Sir, you are correct in that we are going to need to procure food locally, as our supplies have dwindled. Obviously, we cannot expect resupply from Caesar if he is fighting the Gauls. At the same time, we can't exhaust our allies too much or they will turn on us and it would be a hard way to go with just our cohorts."

Jaw set firmly, Cussius grudgingly allowed a small cold smile to sneak onto his face. Fighting down his rising temper at what he considered impudent and overly gratuitous advice from Marcus, he settled for growling back. "The next time I seek counsel on matters of diplomacy with the local savages and requisition, I'll be sure to consider your most articulately defined opinion. Now, shall we pay a visit to this sorry excuse for a village? Maybe the chief would be so kind as to accompany us on a scouting and foraging mission in the countryside, if he could be so persuaded, of course," said Cussius in the most facetious tone he could muster. Having suffered enough conversation with the rigidly unimaginative Marcus, he set his stony stare on the broken gate greeting the column.

The Bibroci village was a sad, savage place. It was continuously subjected to competing raids from Cassivellaunus and other wild Celtic tribes, and yet, through it all they still managed to survive, even to thrive by their own limited standards. Now, dwindling cattle herds from the constant tribal raiding were to be compounded, as the Romans had demanded a king's ransom in livestock, a precious resource that the tribe could scarcely afford to part with. Thankfully, the Bibroci were also prolific growers of wheat and rye or starvation would have been an imminent threat.

As the Roman column trotted through the gate, the light of the swollen sun broke on the many folk ringing the primary village path. Unpainted Bibroci warriors gathered in bunches, mixing in with the women and children, but shooting nothing more deadly at the Romans than the sullen looks of men forced into an uneasy alliance.

Dogs of all sizes ran free, trotting alongside the column, growling and barking in excitement at the strange sight and smells of the Romans. Marcus ignored the dogs but the throng of unruly Celts made him nervous, even though he was quite sure that his men could handle anything that should arise. The women and children among the warriors lessened the odds of an armed confrontation and provided a small sense that calm would ultimately prevail. After all, he reasoned, the scene was not much different from those he had witnessed in España and Gaul. The small hands of surprisingly clean children wearing colorful fleece trousers were cupped in the nervous hands of their mothers. Their wide eyes stared in fear and wonder at the sight of the battle-hardened Roman troops tramping in step, sending up small clouds of fine red dust on their way through the village. The youngest of the warriors openly glared at the legionaries but wisely offered no challenge to the Roman column.

As the column rode past the village market, Marcus noted how few stalls were occupied, which was either a ruse to fool the Romans and safeguard their goods or this village was truly undergoing hard times. Most likely the latter, Marcus thought, as he caught smell and then sight of a butcher and his wares. A whole beef stripped bare of its skin hung dolefully alone from iron hooks set into the rough rafters of the butcher's simple workspace. It was the end of summer, and so large black flies excitedly buzzed about the carcass. Pausing from his labors, the butcher delayed long enough to stare back at the Romans before continuing his expert hacking of the beast while fanning away the horde of flies with his other hand.

Not too far ahead, two more dirt-packed trails converged at a rather large round building made of timber with walls of wattle and daub and a thatched roof of grasses, reeds, and straw. Of simple and practical design, the building had cut-in windows with lamb's stomach tightly stretched over to allow in light and keep out rain. Attached to the home was a sizable corral containing a dozen or so of the peculiarly sturdy Celtic horses native to this island. With such evident wealth on display, Marcus knew this to be the home of one of the village nobles.

CHAPTER SIX

IT HAD RAINED hard all night and Jayas wondered if this was a sign of things to come. Thunder and lightning had burst upon the valley, bringing sheets of rain that at times appeared to be moving across the sky instead of downward. Outside, young trees and crops bent low to the ground under the wind. Livestock huddled together, defending themselves against the storm. Other animals sought refuge in the thick hazel shrub that stubbornly resisted the slashing wind and rain. Thankfully, by the time the roosters began to crow, the storm had moved beyond the valley and onto the plain beyond.

At midday Jayas set out on the muddy road, his horse's hooves making a great, wet sucking sound with each step. The farmers and merchants who moved their goods by foot, horse and cart made way at his approach by crowding to one side of the uneven and rutted roadway. Children sitting in the back of frail straw-strewn carts drawn by their parents stared in envy at the fierce-looking warrior seated atop his gray dun. Being free born but poor, they would be foot soldiers or farmers when they grew old enough to carry a spear or hoe, depending.

Leaving the traffic behind, Jayas guided his mount toward the hills ringing the valley in which his village sat. The hills were a beautiful sight, forest-covered, but yielding large clearings where his people had harvested oak, ash, elm and beech. Nothing had gone to waste. The lumber was put to good use providing sturdy building material and warmth in the long winter months. The farmers planted wheat, barley and rye in the fertile soil of much of the cleared land, and other portions were converted to pasture where shepherds minded herds of cattle, sheep and swine in carefully managed plots.

He veered from the track and onto the path in the forest, which was surprisingly dry. The way was wide enough for two horses abreast, but the massive oaks provided a natural canopy that shielded the path, keeping it relatively dry and bringing the familiar clop of his mount's walk to his ears. In the distance, Jayas caught the briefest flicker of something blue contrasting with the leafy greens and browns of the foliage. Curious, he slowed his mount, nudging it off the trail, and stealthily approached the area where he had glimpsed the blue.

THARA HUMMED TO herself as she deftly plucked the plump gooseberries from their perch and placed them in the fur-lined leather pouch strung about her waist. Above her, a dozen or so birds sang to one another as they bounded through leaves and beat their wings while balancing on limbs. Their clear trilling notes lilted through the forest and provided harmony to her silent lyrics. Stopping her harvesting for a second, she scanned the trees and listened. To her right, a squirrel rustled about, stood up on its hind legs and looked at her, its dark eyes glittering. Though not frightened, she respected the forest. Thara knew that wolves had their dens here. At night, she could hear their plaintive howls, the guttural chorus that never failed to send a primal shudder through her heart. Wild boars were also known to lurk about, and Thara kept an alert eye on the underbrush, especially scanning the thick brush lining the well-traveled path which cut through an untended field. But wild animals were not the only predators inhabiting the forest; unscrupulous men were also known to haunt these woods.

Adding to her sense of calm, however, was the bow made of yew and strung with sinew she carried. Her doting father had taught her from a young age how to draw and release an arrow, how to hit her target at a distance many young men would admire.

She quite often brought home a rabbit or two when she went to the forest. She enjoyed the time to herself and relished the break it afforded her from her mundane household duties. Hearing the rustling of leaves and the cracking of twigs echoing in the quiet of the forest like distant cracks of thunder, Thara whirled about in alarm. She cautiously grasped her bow, the feel of its polished wood reassuring her as she smoothly reached behind her neck for one of the slender ash-shaft arrows bundled in the finely crafted leather quiver. She nocked an arrow and calmly drew the bow's string to the corner of her mouth. Steadying her breathing into a controlled rhythm, she aimed the sleek iron pointed arrow in the direction of the noise.

"I know you're out there, so you might as well come out and show yourself," she stated, licking her lips anxiously as she awaited a response. She prayed it was only a frightened buck bolting through the small isolated clearing at the sound of her challenge or that of a herdsman searching for a wayward calf, but she suspected that it was neither.

"How do I know you won't send that arrow my direction even if I do as you say?" asked a husky voice from the deep cover of the tangled and overgrown edge of the field.

"Who is to say I won't let it go if you don't," Thara snapped in reply. As the sun suddenly broke through the thick cover of clouds she could more clearly make out the outline of a man in the foliage. "Well, I don't have all day to dawdle. It's a big forest. Room enough for both of us, I suppose. Either announce yourself or be on your way. It matters little to me." Thara decided that if he meant her harm from afar he could have already done so, and she cautiously allowed the taut string to return to its undrawn state but kept the lethal arrow nocked just in case she had to swiftly bring it to bear.

In response to her challenge, the mulberry bushes that encroached against the tightly grown strand of young maple trees parted and a familiar figure emerged from the tree line. He was expertly leading a strongly proportioned horse by a rawhide tether. A wide grin splitting his broad face, Jayas touched the ridge of scar tissue that puckered on his jaw in a sort of salute.

"That's no way to greet your husband, woman. Now how would you explain to the sons you are going to bear that you plugged their father with an arrow?" Jayas joked as he silently thanked the gods of the forests for this wonderful stroke of luck. Thara's long dark hair lay unbound in the traditional fashion of un-wed women, and around her shoulders she wore a fleece shawl of high quality dyed the brilliant blue favored by the women of the tribe. He noted that the color complemented her eyes. Jayas noticed a slight flush on her cheeks, which served to accentuate her high cheekbones. Her green eyes disapprovingly met his appraising gaze. Suddenly sheepish, he averted his eyes and searched for something clever to say, but his usually reliable wit had wilted in the face of her disapproval. To his eternal thankfulness, his horse whinnied and broke the awkward stalemate his clumsy attempt at flirtation had brought.

"Were you talking to me or to them?" Jayas asked Thara as he nodded to the west.

Thara had just begun to enjoy the look of discomfort she had caused him when she turned her attention to the direction he poin-ted. Emerging from the trees at a trot from no more than a javelin's throw were three armed men on foot. Thara did not recognize any of them, but Lord Toge' holdings were large and many people lived, worked and traded in his realm.

A short, stocky man with dark untamed hair that hung greasily around his blocky face was in the lead. His eyes had the hard look of a man accustomed to taking what he wanted. His unkempt beard was in desperate need of attention and curled about wildly. His long hairy arms seemed out of place with his squat body, but the way he held the mean-looking sword suggested he did not agree. His brow was tattooed with a criss-crossing blue pattern that had lost some of its luster with age and the elements. From the bridge of his nose and around his eyes, the same intricate blue pattern dominated his face. The other two, younger and carrying spears and short axes, were mean looking too. They had thinner beards than their leader, and only their cheeks were marked as his. The youngest of the three, probably no more than seventeen summers, had quick, nervous eyes that darted back and forth between Thara and the rapidly approaching Jayas. Slowing within fifty or so steps of her, the leader eyed her like a man determining the value of a mare.

His smile was ugly. "Hey girl, quit playing with that bow like you know what it's for. That's a warrior's weapon you got in your hand. Come to think of it, I could use a fancy bow such as that. Truth is, I could use a fancy girl too. You would make a fine wife, or better yet, you would fetch a good price up north. What do you think, boys?" Thara recognized the man's rough drawl as belonging to the Brigante tribe who lived in the west, near the coast. The Brigante rarely drifted this far south or east since suffering a large defeat at the hands of Lord Toge fifteen summers ago. When they did, it was usually to steal whatever they could, as their land was a rough, hilly country that grudgingly yielded its fare. Brigante raiders usually stayed way out on the fringes of Coritani lands, raiding the more isolated farmsteads and driving the stock back to their rocky enclaves. If in large enough numbers, they would kill the men and take the women and children as slaves to keep or barter. Obviously, these had eluded the patrols of Jayas' men and had remained undiscovered by the local farmers and herdsman. Until now.

"I've got archers in the trees. If you don't drop the bow, you will die and I will still have your bow. You too!" the Brigante loudly shouted for Jayas' benefit. "Take off that belt and drop the sword. We will have the horse, and if you refuse, you too will die and we still get the sword and horse," he growled threateningly while stabbing the air with the point of his sword. Taking their cue, the other two Brigante warriors fanned out, grim expressions contorting their faces as they gripped their spears in nervous anticipation.

Furious, Thara drew back and released her three fingered grip on the string of her bow sending the arrow streaking toward the lead Brigante and striking right below the reach of the man's dry and cracked leather armor. It tore through the flesh of his stomach, boring through layers of fat and muscle, tearing his liver before lodging itself in the bone of his back. Shocked, the man stared down at the protruding shaft, the hawk-feathered fletching still vibrating from the arrow's impact on his body. Once strong legs buckled as the man grasped frantically at the shaft with one hand, but the arrow stubbornly refused to retreat.

Jayas' scar was pulled up and forward as the muscles in his jaw curled his lips into a wolfish sneer. He unsheathed his broadsword and bounded across the field, dodging small bushes and footfalls. He did not slow as he closed on the wounded man. With a massive swing of his great sword he struck downward at a slight angle as if chopping wood. His sword was made of the strongest iron and by his village's best swordsmith, a crusty old Spaniard who came to the tribe years before Jayas was born. The blade was long and heavy, a weapon meant for slashing, with fire hardened edges that tore through the muscle, sinew and bone of the man's neck.

With a screech and a grunted heave, the closest Brigante warrior threw his spear at Jayas, the projectile hissing as its angular head cut a swath toward its target. Dodging left, the missile harmlessly sailed wide right as Jayas continued his attack. Eyes wide in panicked disbelief, the Brigante warrior unslung his war axe, a brutal weapon with a handle made of strong oak and a sharpened iron head capable of shattering bone. Shouting more in terror than from any sense of imminent victory, the inexperienced Brigante stood rooted with the axe held aloft in an effort to ward off Jayas' blow — to no avail.

Jayas brought his own broad-bladed thrusting spear in a malicious lunge at the chest of the Brigante. Serrated and flame-shaped, the hollow-ground blade burst through the flimsy armor, penetrating muscle and breaking through the breastbone to the soft and vulnerable vitals. Jayas then ripped the blade out of the warrior's chest and turned to the last Brigante, who was now sprinting away like a wild hare with a pack of hunting dogs on its scent.

The rush of energy now coming back under control as the initial flash of battle began to wane, Jayas shouted, "Coward!" at the back of his escaping enemy. Still incensed at the unprovoked trespass of his lands and their malicious intentions toward Thara, he craved the death of the fleeing Brigante and headed back to grab his horse, kicking the head of the Brigante he had impaled with his spear on the way by.

"Let him go," Thara said just loudly enough for Jayas to pick up as he leapt upon his horse. Baffled by this turn of attitude, he brought his horse to a stop with the squeeze of his knees and a slight tug of the reins.

"Let him go? Let an enemy who insults my woman, trespasses on my land, threatens to kill me, go? Are you mad? That is why men fight the battles and make decisions about war. Do you think they were going to let us go if we did as they demanded?" he asked, his tone of voice incredulous and rising with the argument.

"Men fight battles? Yes, that's true enough. Though I do recall that I was defending myself quite well before you charged in," she said defiantly, bow in one hand and her other hand on her hip. "Battles are good and full of glory for those who fight them when the fight is necessary. This fight is over, and by the gods, we have prevailed. Let him go. He may remember your mercy and speak highly of you to others. And by the way, I'm not your woman," she said with a jaunty shake of her head and just the slightest of smiles.

Jayas stammered, "Remember my mercy? Speak highly of me to others? The tale he will tell is of outfoxing and outfighting Jayas. He will tell others that he trespassed on my land, that he met me face to face, hurled the greatest of insults and made a magical escape. He will tell all that he bettered me and bring shame to our tribe and my father. It cannot stand," he said indignantly. "Letting him go will only embolden others of his kind and their raids will get worse. The Catuvellauni would learn of it and raid our cattle and steal our women. They only respect our strength. You know this to be true," Jayas said, sure in his convictions.

Thara's face softened. "Maybe they only respect our strength of sword because that is all we have given them to respect."

Flustered at the argument, Jayas' cheeks burned with his desire to have listened more carefully to the old Druid tutor who was charged with his education. The Druid would spin riddles and puzzles and word games relating tales of times past that always contained a cleverly worded morality tale. Then, as now, he found himself flummoxed with the circular quality of it all.

"By the gods, woman! They were about to give us sword, spear and axe as their tokens of friendship. It is right they were to be put to the sword," Jayas stammered defensively. Meanwhile, he regretfully watched the Brigante warrior hurdle a hazel bush. The warrior clumsily caught his boot in a tangle, falling awkwardly and losing his javelin in the tall grass. Scrambling to his feet, legs and arms pumping, he made the shade of the forest and disappeared into its depths.

Jayas considered charging off after the man and lancing him through, but the thought that there might be others about who could threaten Thara made his decision easy.

"I will ride back with you then," Jayas said to the delighted surprise of Thara.

CHAPTER SEVEN

The sun lazily sat at its zenith, bringing its warmth and life-giving light to the plants and creatures that inhabited the meadow. Tangled piles of fallen timbers offered themselves to the foxes and ravens as havens of refuge. Larger creatures, such as the bear, the boar and roe deer, paid tribute to the field by their frequent visits to graze on the herbs and sweet grasses that flourished around a copse of ancient oaks. Warbles and robins shot to and fro among the ash trees, feasting on the berries.

A stream cut its course determinedly between two hills in its push to the sea. Otters dove playfully through the surface, taking occasional breaks to float on their backs and go with the current. Blackbirds touched down amongst the heather to take their fair share of the ripened berries hanging fatly from their bowed stems. High above, hawks patiently circled, constantly on the lookout for the careless stoat or shrew to scurry on its way, blissfully ignorant of the threat in the sky.

Rhu saw all of this and more. He understood the cycle of life as it had been studied for a thousand years and given to generation after generation. His was a proud tradition, one of seminal importance amongst the people. As he watched the hummingbirds hover in their quest for the nectar of the sweetest flowers, Rhu felt the earth shift ever so slightly. Birds squawked and flapped their wings in wild confusion, finally seeking sojourn in the air. Red deer nervously stamped their hooves, their tails and necks erect with un-certainty at this interruption. Previously undiscovered red grouse erupted in flight to escape the unsettling effect.

While Rhu's legs lightly shuddered, his toes spread to claw a better grip into the rough floor of the forest. Feeling the anger of the earth spirits, he chanted a quick prayer of atonement then reached for a beech sapling, using its solidity to keep him steady. Finally, the tremors stopped and the ground settled into an uneasy silence that was oddly out of rhythm with the place.

Rhu knew the moment the earth moved that nothing would ever be the same. The earthquake came on the heels of a fitful night of sleep dominated by strange dreams filled with odd signs. The druid welcomed the dreams, which were a portal to the future, if one knew how to interpret them, and he did. The omens foretold of great upheaval and dark years ahead for his people. His dreams in-cluded great roads of bloody stone traversing the island from east to west. Earlier druids had abandoned the great stone temples of their ancestors, and now he foresaw a time when the people would ig-nore the old gods altogether. First they would slack in their sacrifices and offerings, and then they would turn to the ways of a people from across the sea. The springs and groves where the druids held their rituals and communed with the spirits would lie barren from neglect. If the folk abandoned their duty to the gods, surely the gods would ignore the plight of the people. The earth spirit had spoken and Rhu had listened.

Rhu stoically accepted his duty as spiritual keeper of the people. Twenty years of intense study and memorization at the knee of his mentor had yielded mastery of the ancient knowledge. In turn, he had tutored many of the young nobles, as well as those who were now aged and wrinkled or gone to earth. He was a keeper of the law and diviner of celestial intent, but he had also arbitrated many disputes between warring factions and had blessed scores of warriors who sought guidance on the cusp of battle. His knowledge of plants and herbs was renowned, and his skills as a healer were much sought after throughout the land. He did not owe allegiance to any singular tribe, chief, or king, and thus unencumbered by entangling associations, he freely traveled to and fro across the land of his birth, teaching, healing and settling disputes according to druidic dictates. One thing was certain. His words carried the weight of a king's.

As he carefully picked his way along the forest path that paralleled the stream, he listened to the sound of the water flowing over rocks worn smooth by its constant rushing. The gurgled hum as it swirled around and over fallen tree limbs comforted him. He knew what had to be done and set upon his course.

CHAPTER EIGHT

THE SURPRISINGLY LARGE and spacious center room of the Trinovante noble's roundhouse accommodated more people than Cussius originally thought possible. Spacious, it had large upright poles set firmly in the ground to provide support for the roof. The walls were made of wattle and daub and whitewashed with lime. Cussius had witnessed the building of one of these structures, and it fascinated him how rudimentary but effective the design proved to be. Expedient too. Much like Gaul, few of the buildings or villages on this land came within a whiff of the grand and complex architecture of his beloved native city. Romans built with a sense of time and space, their structures designed and constructed heartily with stone, concrete and wood. A sense of permanence accompanied Roman construction while these Celts seemed content with more flimsy material that necessitated constant maintenance. "It is a state of flux they seem to embrace," he murmured to himself.

The din of voices and reed flutes bombarded his ears as he drank in the scene. Trinovante nobles filled its murky interior, the stale scent of sweat and body odor mixing with the smell of boiled corn, smoke and roasted meat. Gratuitous amounts of mead were passed around and greedily swilled between the swapping of tales and bragging of exploits. In general, the Celts seemed in high spirits as they laughed, exchanged bawdy jokes and groped willing servant girls who gave as good as they got.

He and Marcus were sandwiched between four noblemen who reeked of sweaty leather and were loud and lewd of tongue. He noted their propensity for alcohol and fortified mead, and he maintained his guard. For his first libation, he opted for wine mixed with equal parts water to ensure his head remained clear. Marcus had no such reservations and helped himself to hearty swigs of the free-flowing spirits, while the Trinovante were enthusiastically indulging the same. Cussius kept a wary watch. When filled with Roman wine, they were quarrelsome, boastful and ever ready for a fight, and Cussius found the Celts of Britannia to be as fractious and quick to battle as their Gallic cousins — maybe even a bit quicker to fisticuffs and drawn daggers.

Through the smoky shadows of the room, the more reserved Marcus keenly studied the chieftain of the Trinovante. He appeared to be close to forty years of age and had a hard, confident face. Like all Celtic men, his hair grew long, halting below his sturdy shoulders. The deep-set brown eyes peered out from a prominent brow, giving him a brutish quality, and his clothes were simple but well made. On his thick legs he wore clean trousers fashioned of softened bull's hide. Tucked into his calf-skin boots, the bulge of a thin-bladed, bone handled dagger rested. A colorful, loose-fitting shirt covered his chest but left exposed the silver and gold torc, symbolic of his wealth and prestige in the tribe, worn around his neck. Around his ample waist was a leather belt interlaced with iron, and from it hung a richly worked and ornamented sword. Inlaid with enamel and decorated with red coral, it was an object to admire. A beautiful young woman knelt at the chief's side and refilled his cup from a copper pitcher.

Seated at the place of honor, King Mandubrac of the Trinovante sized up his two erstwhile allies with the eye of a man accustomed to the treacherous tribal politics and warfare constantly waged on the island. He was familiar with the Romans and their propensity for war and brutal subjugation of the conquered. In one form or another, they had been engaged in conflict with Celts for the past three centuries. His own grandfather's father had fled the continent with half the tribe and made the short, choppy voyage through the mist-laden sea because of the constant push and press caused by tribal conflict and the confrontations with expansionist Germanic tribes and an outward looking Rome that left the tribe with little other recourse.

Desperate and warlike, his tribe had tenaciously gained a foothold on the coastal region of Briton In spite of steady raiding by their enemies, with dogged determination they even managed to expand their lands. Now, as the fourth generation of his clan to lead his people, he had forged a loose confederation with other harried tribes in an effort to ward off the ambitious warlord Cassivellaunus, who had killed Mandubrac's father in a territorial grab, and thus earning Mandubrac' eternal enmity. After initial token resistance to the Romans, he had sued for peace and aligned himself and the tribe's fortunes with the invading Romans, and in truth, the Romans owed their swift conquest of Cassivellaunus to Mandubrac's intense hatred of the man. When Cassivellaunus fled deep into his territory, he took refuge in a remote fortress concealed amongst the woods and marshes. Sealing the alliance with Caesar in one lethal stroke, Mandubrac revealed the location of the stronghold, and the besieging Roman legions quickly broke all resistance.

Setting down his cup of mead, Mandubrac wiped errant beads of brew from his drooping red moustache and grunted something in Celt to a waiting retainer. "Silence! Your king has the floor!" the red-faced man exclaimed. As the revelry and feasting stopped, Mandubrac rose and addressed the expectant Romans.

"I am honored to have your presence in my humble lands. We have suffered much in the past fighting, but the gods saw us through and brought us warriors from across the sea. With the aid of our Roman brothers, we have triumphed." A dozen heads nodded but his eyes sought the Romans. "I hope you find our hospitality to be generous and I wish you many blessings. May your lives be as long as that of the stars," he said in heavily accented Latin. He had gleaned his vocabulary from Roman merchants who plied the trading waters between the continent and the island. Gathering steam, he ploughed on.

"I thank the stars, the sun, and the moon for the peace your presence has brought. Our alliance is good and should continue for as long as our peoples dwell on this earth. May our children's children know no enmity." Mandubrac brought his replenished cup back to his lips and drank deeply in salute to his guests. He then raised the now empty cup heavenward in a gesture of respect and honor. His motions were mimicked by the other Trinovante warriors, and they shouted their own words of praise and honor, their rough voices reverberating within the walls.

Order gradually returned, the rowdy nobles quieting down under the glare of their chieftain. "But I'm afraid you underestimate the nature of our enemies. Our alliance has brought the arrogant Catuvellauni to heel, but they are a vicious and dishonorable people, worthy of little trust and not prone to peace. Cassivellaunus will break this truce as soon as he regains his strength. My spies tell me he uses this treaty to rebuild his forces and seek new alliances with other tribes," Mandubrac said as he studied the implacable faces of the two Romans.

In truth, he really wanted the Romans to leave as soon as possible. Though fertile, his lands had suffered from the recent battles with Cassivellaunus, who had scorched the surrounding lands as he retreated in an effort to deprive the Romans of foodstuffs and resources. The losses were temporary, and Mandubrac considered them insignificant if only he could persuade the Romans to continue the war against his enemies, but he found that unlikely and these invaders had to leave. Warring on the island had its own flavor. Even if one tribe devastated another's land and did great harm, in the end, the enemy left the populace with their own laws and land. These Romans were different, and those differences flummoxed him. They want to settle on our land and amongst our tribes, to bind us in slavery forever, he thought. He would do what it took to protect his people and expand his holdings, and so he had made this truce, but he would have to find a way to rid the invaders one day.

He paused a moment to study the younger of the two Romans, who had a way of looking at a man as if he could draw his thoughts out of him, whether or not the man intended to say anything. The young warrior was tall and lean and cut a noble visage with a wide, clear forehead above full eyebrows shadowing penetrating grey eyes. It was not only his appearance that attracted attention, but also his attitude, aloof yet alert. Thus far, he had been more observer than participant, and Mandubrac' words were met with silence. He took a new tack.

"As friends of Rome, how can we be of further help to you? I understand you will be leaving my territory to establish a stronghold further north between the land of the Catuvellauni and that of the Coritani. My warriors are eager to continue the battle against our enemies and would be willing to accompany you," he said, curious to see if this bit of information fazed the silent Romans. His only reward was the raised eyebrow of Cussius. The other Roman, the one called Marcus, appeared as if he might have wanted to respond but sat silent instead, grudgingly deferring to his younger counterpart.

Then, before the chief could continue, Cussius interrupted. "You are a wise chief and a great leader in war, and under your leadership, your people are sure to prosper. We are honored to be feasting at your table. Your warriors are praiseworthy and your women are beautiful, surely the envy of all of Britannia." Cussius then diplomatically tilted his own cup to his lips. At his side, Marcus mimicked the toast with loud slurps.

Cussius continued. "Chief Mandubrac, please tell me something." He pushed his empty platter toward the center of the smooth-topped table and leaned back in his chair. "What benefit would accrue to Rome if we were to, ah, assist you against your enemies? Isn't that the question you want answered?" asked Cussius while using the tip of his little finger to pick at a wayward scrap of pork wedged between his teeth. Unsuccessful, he gulped a swig of his drink, swirling the amber liquid about his mouth in an effort to tumble the bit of meat from its stubborn perch. Satisfied with the result, he forged ahead.

"It is no small matter to risk Roman lives in support of your proposed undertakings," Cussius said seriously. "Cassivellaunus has made his peace with Rome. Having made his peace with Rome, he has made his peace with you. He understands the terms he must meet. First, which is more our concern than yours, is his payment of tribute. Second, he has rendered the requisite number of hostages of appropriate noble rank. They are with Caesar. The third term of the peace?" he asked while holding up three fingers. He had the room's attention. The only sound was that of the servants clearing the table and refilling cups. "He is forbidden to molest any of our allies who opposed him, which would include the Trinovante. That provision was made with your interests in mind and accrued to your direct benefit. Until further notice, the status quo will be maintained."

The terms dictated by Caesar and readily accepted by Cassivellaunus were too generous in Cussius' estimation. He thought the wily old Celt much wealthier than earlier believed, and able to pay more tribute than Caesar had demanded. Though it grated on him to ease his foot off the neck of a vanquished foe, he knew he could not openly defy Caesar's directive without the insufferably disciplined Marcus taking offense.

"If he breaks those terms, rest assured he will not do so again," Cussius glibly said as he ogled the comely Celt servant girl refilling his cup with the sweetened beverage made of wheat and honey. He still preferred a good, strong red wine to this thick concoction, but the settling effect and slow rush of warmth it brought to his face were familiar enough. He winked an unfamiliar gesture of thanks to the servant, and she smiled provocatively in return and dashed away to fill another warrior's cup, her hips swaying to further draw Cussius' lusty admiration. Not a man of restraint, he would take his liberties by might or by right. He smelled opportunity here and knew that the unpredictable Celts, always scheming and shifting allegiances, would ultimately set off the war that he himself could not.

CHAPTER NINE

THE NEXT FEW days passed in a flurry of motion. Marcus initiated orders and intimidated his subordinates, readying his full strength cohort of five hundred legionaries. Though none too happy at being stuck on this island under orders from Caesar, they were good, strong, loyal men. They had made him proud, fighting the Gauls to defeat and mauling the fierce and savage Germanic hordes that surrounded Gaul before invading Britannia. His men had earned their deadly reputation. They had once marched fifty miles in one day, taking meals and drink on the road, no small feat, given the weight the Roman soldiers humped every step of the way. With no rest, they did not complain when they were ordered to close ranks, wheel left and close with the enemy.

As dawn approached, the sky gleamed. Today, Marcus shunned his mount and handed the reins of the bay mare to his orderly. His head thrummed dully and his mouth was dry and tacky. His eyes burned from too little sleep and a lack of quality from the sleep he managed to steal. Any rest he had of late came at the bottom of a drained cup of ale or swilled from the spirits bag he pilfered from a Bibroci trader. Despite his aches and misgivings, he wanted to stretch his legs and opted to march at the head of his men with Leko leading the bay. The boy's steed was a lop-eared old mule with one eye that begrudged every step he was forced to make, but he seemed appeased when Leko dismounted and the bay settled in beside him. As for Marcus, he had earned the right to ride at the front of his men, but being too long in the saddle did not suit him. Besides, Marcus thought to himself, he had earned these calloused feet and strong legs by many miles of marching.

As he sweated and drank water his head cleared and the aching ceased, but the burning in his legs began ten miles into the march. Marcus cursed all the time he spent in the saddle and every extra piece of meat and the added drink in which he had indulged in the last few weeks. Glancing to his left, he noticed that Leko showed no signs of fatigue or discomfort, and he smiled at the boy's youthful determination. Thankfully, the road traversed an elevated plain and the chalky soil furnished a dry and open road, much easier marching than the swamps and forests of the lower ground.

The pack dug comfortably into his strong shoulders as Marcus settled into the march, the skin rubbed course from years of the same pull and tug of the leather straps. Like every Roman foot soldier, he carried a full load consisting of a wool cover, three days rations, a canteen of water, a bucket and axe, together with a leather strap, a sickle and a chain. His *caligae*, or sandals, were broken in and conformed snugly to his feet, and the two thick layers of leather held together with iron nails that were the soles adequately absorbed the pounding his feet endured. Any needed repairs were easily done by swapping out the worn leather soles for fresh strips.

Toward sundown, a rider assigned to the supply train rode up. The weary rider dismounted, his face dark with day-old stubble and hefty doses of dust and grime, and updated his commander.

"Sir, Legionary Tuno reporting with a message from second officer, " he managed, his voice cracking midway through, the lack of moisture in his mouth magnified by his nervousness. Clearing his dry and itchy throat, he gathered himself and continued. "Two of the supply wagons are down, sir. The wheels need repairing. I'm told it will take two to three hours to fix. We're only two hours behind you as it is. Catching up won't be a problem if you want us to double time it." Finished with his task, the soldier remained stock still, watching the creeping color rise in his commander's sundarkened face.

Marcus did not like having his supply line stretched out in hostile territory. They had marched twenty miles since leaving the camp near the stronghold of Chief Mandubrac, but he would have preferred thirty. In one month's time, he and Cussius were to meet the Catuvellauni on the most northern bend of the Temes River. They were then to escort the tribute to the coast for shipment to Caesar in Gaul. So terribly simple, in theory, he thought, but realities on the ground always prove otherwise. Marcus knew this would not be the only cause for delay they would invariably meet during the course of the mission.

"Sound the halt!" Marcus screamed. "Strike camp here," he bellowed to the smiling ranks of legionaries. At his directive, the *cornicen* blew into his horn, relaying the orders to the cohort. Grateful to a man for the premature halt to the march, they methodically set upon their duties.

"Leko!" he shouted, turning around impatiently. "Bring me my horse. Unload that ugly packhorse and climb on. You're a wild Gaul. It'll feel like old times. You're coming with," he said irritably as a large grin split the face of the slave in response. He knew he had to send a messenger to Cussius advising him of the delay. All day he hadn't seen his commanding officer, whom he thought was leading foraging missions in the countryside. Now, where to find him, he groused to himself.

THE SMALL VILLAGE situated next to a backwater pond did not consist of much, four or five small roundhouses and a few huts built on a slight rise, all of it shrouded in mist. The villagers eked out a subsistence of millet, cattle and milk; but trading furs up and down the river was their primary pursuit when not engaged in some minor dispute with neighboring clans.

Leading a foraging mission with the help of a troop of Trinovante riders, Cussius had found the settlement woefully unprepared when he swept through on horseback. The ensuing battle was brief but fierce. Screaming in rage and dressed in little better than skins and furs, the brave village men fought desperately to save their loved ones, but in the end, they were overborne with numbers and a dozen bodies littered the ground in a grotesque embrace of death. Trinovante warriors climbed amongst the mass of tangled and bruised limbs where the ground was slick with blood and filth. Undaunted, they pressed on in their frenzy whooping with joy. The warriors hacked at the necks of their enemies to loosen their heads before finally ripping them free from their owners' bodies with a violent yank of the hair. The heads would find their way to Trinovante villages and ultimately hang from their huts as trophies and a grisly warning to their enemies.

Cussius was enjoying the right of conquest to its fullest degree. He had cornered a dark-haired beauty in the village headman's pitiful excuse of a home. Pressed against the wall she made no pleas for mercy or clemency as she held her head high, her shapely bosom heaving in quick even gasps. He followed her eyes as they desperately searched for possible avenues of escape. Her eyes darted to the left where a short wood-handled blade lay atop an overturned barrel. She dove for it but he was quicker. He gripped her arm tightly, increasing the pressure with the strength of a horseman. As he locked onto her dark, smoldering eyes, Cussius could sense she possessed an inner strength of which few men could boast. Finally, the crude blade fell to the hard-packed floor with a *clank.* The woman struggled mightily, swinging her clawed hands and tearing at his leather breastplate but she was no match for his strength. As she squirmed under him, the girl's fine features contorted in pain, her cries reduced to whimpers. Her eyes were unrelenting in their anger and hate, but her flesh lacked the strength of her spirit. His rough, calloused hands groped her body, pinching and prodding; the symbol of his uninvited passage exposed by the purple, mottled splotches left on the side of her bare thighs. He could hear screams mixing with the guttural laughter of crude men, and the stinging smell of burning thatch and flesh was strong in his nostrils. Grayblack smoke trailed a lazy pattern with shards of greasy ash drifting slowly to earth. Not what I expected, but not a bad start to things, considering the land and its backward people, he thought to himself.

Climbing off the girl, he motioned to his sergeant. Leering, the soldier approached, offering the lead of Cussius' horse to his waiting commander. Mounting, Cussius swore to himself. The shattered village had proven poor, with only a few cattle and a small amount of gold. They discovered the gold only after Cussius had the headman flogged to death. Rather than die in such an inglorious fashion themselves, less stalwart kin revealed the location of the gold.

Panting a bit from his frenzied exertion with the exquisite creature, he pointed at the young woman, who was now calmly pulling on her dress and tunic. "Take that tasty little barbarian bitch and mark her as mine. I don't want these savages touching my property," he snarled at the waiting legionary. "And secure that gold. It's not a fortune but I want every coin accounted for. You understand me?" Cussius' gray eyes were hard like granite and his bearing forceful.

"Yes sir!" the soldier boomed, disappointment edging his voice.

"It's time to leave. Send a rider to Marcus. Tell him that we are heading parallel to the river and will make camp five miles ahead." Cussius stared past the soldier at the spectacle unfolding at the end of the village.

"Very well, sir." Tired and hungry, the soldier kicked his mount to a gallop, and Cussius mounted his bay to confront his so-called allies.

The women and children were being pushed and shoved into an enclosure with the cattle where Kren busily directed the division of spoils. The Trinovante would sell them to Iceni slavers or trade them amongst each other. "Kren," Cussius said, badly butchering the Trinovante noble's name as he reigned in beside the Trinovante chieftain, his horse snorting and eager to be clear of the smoke. He leaned down and addressed the wily chief.

"The cattle feed the troops. Drive this livestock to Marcus and add it to the supply line. A third of the slaves belong to me. Sell them and return my share in accordance. That is the agreement and you know it." Cussius watched Kren receive this news. As far as barbarians went, Cussius thought he wasn't too bad. He was prone to guile and avarice, but Cussius had seen many a similar man in the streets of Rome and in the forum debating. Kren and the other barbarians were not as dignified or educated in the classical fashion, but they were just as mean tempered and savvy as any, and Cussius knew that meant he could be dealt with.

"My man will make the selection," Cussius said, "and the raven-haired wench is coming with me." He pointed at the girl he had earlier marked as his own. At his signal, two legionaries assigned to his personal guard strode toward where the girl sat. Her legs crossed, she did not say a word when they gripped her by her thin arms and yanked her to her feet. Her only reaction was to stare unblinkingly at the unmoving groups of cavalry.

The barbarian auxiliaries stood aloof and did not interfere, though strangely they forked two of their fingers and spit between them at mention of the girl. His lips parting to reveal a row of crooked, blackened teeth, Kren answered. "As you wish, my Lord. You receive first selection." A nobleman by his own right of arms, Kren understood the unwritten code of honor very well. He had two heads hanging from the twisted mane of his mount, and he planned on adding some slaves to his plunder. The young warriors accompanying him were more interested in the heads as opposed to the slaves. Their minds were already filling with the songs that would be sung in their honor and the half-truths they would share around the council fire.

"As is my right," Cussius said, "and I intend to exercise it vigorously. Now onward we go. There will be time for sleep and good eating later." Cussius' gruff tone left no doubt who commanded. He understood the barbarians valued toughness and respected might. They were fond of strength and took what they would without hesitation. Weakness existed for the strong to exploit, a concept he grasped with clarity of vision. In his estimation, he had quantities of both clarity and vision and he wondered how he could parley that into what he really wanted. Being so far removed from Rome and more important, away from Caesar, had its advantages.

Suddenly inspired, he trotted out in front of his assembled men and addressed them. "Men! Warriors and soldiers of Rome!" he shouted loudly so that the barbarians could hear as well. "The road ahead contains glory and riches belonging to those strong enough to take it. There is enough gold, cattle, and slaves for the taking. We will all be rich beyond measure. Women will sing our praises and invite us into their huts," he yelled with a wink to the expectant warriors. "Your enemies will learn to fear you. They will send you slaves and gold and quake at the thought of your anger." Cussius was pleased to see the message was well received. His auxiliaries huddled in groups, horses nervously close to one another as their riders excitedly talked amongst themselves, an obvious consensus in the making.

"To my Roman brothers," he said while turning slightly in the saddle, "we are thousands of miles away from home. Rome has forgotten about us. They know not the sacrifices you have made with so few complaints and so little in return. As a matter of fact, most of Rome refuses to believe this island really even exists, but then many of you refused to believe it existed until we landed on that rocky beach."

"Look around, men. Who is here with you? Caesar has abandoned us here to look after ourselves the best we can," he said, knowing full well this was an easy sentiment to play upon. The troops were veterans who had been campaigning for at least the last five years. They had heard Caesar promise the legions plots of land to settle and plenty of gold to fill their lagging sacks in return for their service, but there was always one more battle, one more campaign, and only the promise of furlough and home, which never materialized.

"He left us here while he goes to Gaul to strip it of its wealth, to fatten his purse and hoard the loot paid for with the blood of our brothers. He left us here while he bangs the drums of war, kills the enemy, and takes what he wants. He has forgotten us." He sneered, his voice grave and tinged with sadness. "But we have not forgotten our duty to one another. I will never forget your sacrifice, and all men who follow me will be handsomely rewarded and receive their just due." Though solidly loyal to Cussius, the thought of direct disobedience to Caesar was an uneasy prospect. Treason was punishable by crucifixion, and an air of uncertain nervousness surrounded his troopers. Many had witnessed this cruel death and none wished to hang on the wooden beams.

Some of the men looked down at the ground while others stared at their commander in tentative agreement. Nervous silence met his words until the clanging of shields shattered the air. Excited with the prospect of loot and glory, the Trinovante warriors pierced the air with their war whoops and beat their swords against their shields in a rhythmic cadence. Caught up in the moment, a few of the legionaries picked up the chant, and then the rest, their initial reluctance giving way to the mounting excitement, joined in as well.

"Count me as persuaded, my Lord," said a grinning Kren, spurring his mount to come abreast the strutting steps of Cussius' horse. "I pledge my sword and those of my men to follow where you lead," he said emphatically to the welcome roar of his men. They jabbed the air with their swords, yelping loudly, their eyes greedy and minds already tallying the heads they would collect and the riches to be obtained.

Smiling wildly and eyes ablaze, Cussius grew into the moment. Muscling the dancing beast in a slow circle, he surveyed his now eager men. "By right of strength we shall prevail!" He then kicked his horse into a sprint. "Let's go!" he shouted as warriors roughly jostled their new slaves into a ragged column. This is the beginning of my time, Cussius thought as he rode to the front of the ranks.

"This is my time," he muttered to himself, "my time."

CHAPTER TEN

RHU SMELLED THE rotten scent of death and decay before he actually sighted the small village. He was not surprised. The palisade surrounding the tiny hamlet had not provided any protection from the raiders and lay torn apart, along with the fencing that had bordered the livestock enclosures. Immense sadness filled his being. The village had been one of his favorites, and he often stopped to visit with the chief who had married his great-niece. A pity, he thought as he slowly walked through the smoking remains of the small village. He was careful not to disturb the spirits who still lingered, trapped beside their unburied hosts, not yet having found their celestial outlet.

His outrage and sadness increased as he circled the hamlet. There were no women and children rushing out of their huts to greet him with wide grins and warm bread. Absent were the familiar sounds of cattle mooing and goats bleating to one another amid the animated laughter of the children. They were all gone, spirited away by the same force that had annihilated the unsuspecting village. Now they were but a whispering memory.

He gritted his few teeth until his gums hurt. This was not the first time he had witnessed the carnage of raiding, but something about this carnage did not seem the same as those other times. Rhu sensed this could only be connected to the earth's imbalance. The island was out of rhythm, and death and destruction would reign as long as it was so. Glancing at the sky, he calculated the number of nights until the full moon. He still had at least twenty days to prepare.

After saying a few prayers for the dead, Rhu went about the business of seeing to the naked corpses. He would not leave the bodies of these brave men exposed to the appetites of crows and feral dogs. Though it took him half the day, he dragged all the bodies into a half-burned hut before ritually blessing it with a cleansing ointment, and then, satisfied that the souls of the dead would be released, soaked the putrid bodies in mutton fat before tossing a burning ember atop the limp mass. Before the nauseating stench of burning flesh overwhelmed him, he tiredly set off again in search of the one who could fend off this descent into darkness and stand against the swelling tide of fate.

CHAPTER ELEVEN

THE NIGHT PASSED without incident, and the column was hastening to meet the two cohorts of cavalry. The messenger sent by Cussius had reached Marcus as the sun dipped below the hilly horizon. He had not been happy to be without Roman cavalry, but he made do with a doubling of the sentries, and as a further precaution, kept the bulk of the hundred Bibroci scouts close in with his men. The remainder ranged around the camp on horseback looking for signs of hostiles.

Aside from a few honking geese and skittish deer, their patrols had scared nothing up, and that was fine with Marcus. Now midday, the late summer sun unmercifully burned through a thin haze of clouds, as good a time as any to halt and rest the troops.

"Half the men to rest, the remainder ready at arms!" he shouted, his instructions taken up and passed down the line by horn and the bellow of his officers. Surveying the terrain, he let his gaze settle upon a father and son busily clearing the rhododendron scrub from a wood of mature hornbeam and ash. They were too absorbed in their labors to pay the soldiers much attention. Some birds that had been scratching around for insects in the scrub grass took to air, disappearing behind a wooded hill.

Marcus wiped the sweat from his brow and the back of his neck. "Leko, why are they not running away or paying us any mind?" he asked the youth. He considered Leko perhaps the closest thing to an expert on the Celts, for Gauls and Celts were all the same to Marcus, barbarians but clever and cunning and masters of tribal politics. And besides, he thought, they all speak variations of the same language. A quick study, he had been working on this language with the help of Leko, and he was rapidly gaining some semblance of proficiency.

Pride swelling at the attention he had garnered of late from his master, Leko responded in a hopeful tone. "They're weary of the fighting," he said thoughtfully. "Maybe so much fighting has left little time for planting and tending to the fields. It's late in the harvest season and crops must be gathered and the fields turned over." For a moment, he thought of home and of earlier times when he and the other boys would work the fields at this time of year. It only made sense that the Celts would be doing the same. Nonetheless, Leko was beginning to get a good feel for the land and its people. Even before his capture by the Romans, he knew of the Celts who lived on this island. Trade lines had been established generations before his birth, and Celtic traders were known in the land of his father.

"They might not even be farmers for that matter," Leko said, his unpracticed eyes critically eyeing the two from the distance. Suddenly, his imagination began to run amok as every bush and tree could conceal lurking enemies with ill intentions. "They could be scouts, of course." He shrugged. As punctuation, an audible grumble emanated from his stomach. He was hungry and thirsty, but he was determined not to take a drink or eat food until Marcus did.

"Scouts for whom?" Marcus asked, but he knew that it really didn't matter for, if there were scouts or riders about, it could be safely assumed they were hostile. The Romans were a foreign force marching around in a hostile land that knew constant raiding, which meant the locals were vigilant and used to the ways of war. His own training and experience kept him on edge and demanded a heightened sense of vigilance, a habit formed over a lifetime of campaigning, and he alertly scanned the trees on the edge of the field, seeking a blur of movement or shadows that seemed out of place in the foliage. The thought of undetected eyes boring into him made the center of his shoulder blades burn uncomfortably. He shifted around in the saddle, but the itchy sensation stubbornly remained.

"Look over there!" Leko said, pointing to the northwest.

Marcus cupped his hand over his eyes so he could better see the riders closing in at a measured gallop, a group of Bibroci scouts, their sturdy little mounts effortlessly scaling the gentle sways and rises of the tree-lined ridge. Marcus was surprised to note that only two of the seventeen riders carried bows. The majority wore thick leather armor vests and carried two javelins to complement the long swords swinging from fixed, bronze scabbards.

When the riders approached, the leader of the band of Bibroci scouts, who was thin but wide of shoulder, dismounted evenly and quickly strode toward Marcus. Marcus silently wondered how the man so effortlessly supported the chainmail he found himself admiring. The coat of mail was totally flexible, and the chieftain moved easily within it as if he were born to it. It was of good quality, a testament to the high level of metalworking attained by the Celts of Britannia and a far cry from the usual leather armor worn by the bulk of warriors he had seen so far.

Leko was the first to greet Kegan, but to his dismay, he was brusquely brushed aside by the intently walking clan leader. This rude behavior was not the norm for Kegan, who was usually friendly and affable, and he had become a favorite of the Romans with his ready wit and quick smile. His current demeanor did not sit well with Marcus.

"*Salve*, Kegan," he greeted. Gesturing toward the group of lathered horses, he continued. "Your mounts look as if they've been ridden hard. Are you hungry? Chow isn't ready, but I'm sure we could scrounge something up. Do you bring me news?"

Customarily, Marcus would have waited for the Celt to announce himself and then readied a reply. As the officer in charge of the cohort and the attached Bibroci auxiliaries, military doctrine mandated it. On the other hand, he reasoned, when dealing with the Celts, it was sometimes better just to ask.

"Greetings," Kegan said, finally allowing a brief flash of smile. Acknowledging Leko with a quick glance, he continued, "We looped ahead as you ordered and came upon our allies heading southeast. Your commander has been very busy. I do not think that eating will be a problem for the men."

"Go on," Marcus urged. He didn't want to sit here in the punishing sun, especially if they were about to be attacked. "Continue."

"A few dozen slaves and a small herd of cattle should intercept us a half-day's ride from here," Kegan said carefully, a slight hint of exasperation in his tone.

"That's not a bad thing," Marcus said quickly. "An army marches on its stomach." He would take provisions at any and all times. Experience had taught him that it paid to be prepared, and key to being prepared was maintaining a supply line. He was beginning to realize that the chances of getting back to Gaul to meet up with Caesar would not happen this year. By the time they received the tribute and brought it to the coast, it would be late fall and the channel would be too rough to cross. If they found themselves in a tight spot, the tribes would do all they could to prevent them from securing food for the men and forage for the horses. Kicking the enemy in the stomach, he thought, was a formidable tool of warfare in and of itself.

"That is true enough," Kegan countered, "but it also marches for glory and riches."

Marcus knew that Kegan had a dilemma on his hands. As acting chief and warlord of the Bibroci, he only secured the loyalty of his retinue by regular warfare and raiding. His tribe had aligned with the victorious Romans, but they had lost some political liberty with that allegiance. The peace between Rome and his enemies had curbed his freedom to raid, to take the heads and the cattle of rancorous neighboring tribesmen. It was difficult to keep a following of warriors without regular raiding, and his status was now at risk.

"As far back as I can remember, we have always raided our enemies at this time of year, before the winter returns and sends us to the warmth of our lodges. But now, my warriors have no tales to tell and no meat to feed their wives and children over the long, cold moons ahead. Look for yourself." He pointed at his waiting retainers. "Their blades are clean and they have no cattle or gold. Meanwhile, our Trinovante allies are getting rich. Already they brag to us of the heads and slaves they have taken. My warriors are brave fighters but have nothing to show for it," Kegan said with a classic Gallic shrug of his shoulders.

Marcus allowed a sigh to escape his pressed lips while he wearily watched the Bibroci chieftain. He knew that he was in an awkward position, just as dependent on his local allies as they were of him — if not more. He needed the screen of Bibroci horseman out on his flanks, and he relied upon them for their intimate knowledge of the area and its people as well as to provide him with advance warning of ambush. Keeping them happy was going to be a chore, one that he didn't relish. If what Kegan said was true, then Cussius' foraging mission had already taken a turn fraught with risk.

"There must be more cattle in this area," he said, pointing toward the northwest horizon. "Feel free to appropriate the beasts to add to our supply line. You can have half the cattle and the remainder feeds the army." Marcus' tone was stern, and he hastened to add, "Remember, you and your warriors will receive a fair portion of the tribute expected from Cassivellaunus in return for your services to Rome. Your women and children will have a fine winter and your people will sing your praises for the windfall of loot you will bring them." He really hoped Kegan would accept the terms but do so with some restraint. Wanton killing of the locals would not serve to endear them to Rome, and he thus cautioned Kegan.

A smile erupted on Kegan' face. "You are a wise man. My warriors will not disappoint. You will find us brave and prosperous," he boasted as he turned and clapped a smiling Leko on the shoulder. He leapt onto his horse, spurring it into a gallop with his enthused warriors in tow, their yelps and whoops echoing hoarsely off the hills and hollows of the green landscape.

CHAPTER TWELVE

Twelve times the moon had traversed the night sky since the battle in the forest with the Brigante. Three heads now adorned Jayas' saddle, their sightless eyes grim testament to the keenness of his blade and the unerring eye of Thara. After seeing Thara safe to the hillfort, Jayas and Gymm had gathered some warriors and set off in pursuit of the marauding Brigante, but they were unsuccessful. They noted the ford the Brigante war party used to flee across the river, the retreating hooves leaving impressions as discernable as the stars in the sky.

Jostling her way through the gawking crowd, Thara witnessed the pitiful procession struggling its way through the village. The expedition had not been a complete failure, as evidenced by the gathering in the village's center. The people's lust for retribution had found an outlet in the form of a dozen head of cattle and some women and children who lucklessly found themselves in the path of the vengeful Coritani warriors. Amidst the shouts of scorn and insults, her heart went out to the exhausted captives who stumbled behind the mounted warriors. Heads down and eyes averted, they had already been carefully searched and stripped of anything of value. Thara could see that their hands were bound tight with rough-cut leather strips that rendered the hands numb and useless. She winced as one woman desperately clutched an infant to her breast as she stumbled on the muddy incline, barely breaking her fall with her elbows but keeping the baby unscathed. She shared the woman's small victory over humiliation and told herself she would be sure that the slave and infant received a hearty portion of food.

She did not care to linger with the other gawkers and turned for home. The taking of slaves among conquered peoples did not swell her heart with pride as it did the majority of her folk. She felt no joy, only sorrow for the slaves who had to truckle to their harsh new masters or suffer beatings for their insolence.

A cry and a shout from the watchman atop the ramparts drew Thara's attention, and she rushed over with part of the crowd to see what the commotion was about. Outside the palisade walls, armed riders she did not recognize rode up to the gate on panting and snorting horses.

Obviously in a hurry, the eldest of the strangers shouted, "I am Bran, a distant clansman of Lord Toge, and I seek an audience with him as well as his protection." This last part he did not say with the same vigor with which he had announced his name and clan, but it was clear enough for all to hear, and the tenor of his voice did not go unnoticed.

Thara's stomach clenched tight with uncertainty. She and some of the other women had picked up bits and pieces of rumors and whispered gossip from traveling merchants the past few days. She thought the news had been just that, rumors and gossip, but now the small pit of worry in her stomach began to spread like unwelcome ivy. A couple of nights ago, she overheard her father and mother worriedly discussing her sister's absence. Lana and her husband, clan chief of a small farmstead on the far edges of Coritani territory, were expected two days ago but had yet to arrive, and no word or reason for the delay had been forthcoming. Her father had wrung his hands with worry and imagined the worst, while her mother prayed and refused to believe that all was not well. All things considered, Thara thought, there had to be a grain of truth to all this chatter.

Murmurs of unfounded conjecture broke out amongst the gathered crowd, a nervous excitement replacing the earlier jubilation. Thara looked around for Jayas and spotted him hurriedly speaking with his father. He paused long enough to return her stare with a nod, his handsome face causing her to blush and look away; but instantly regaining her composure, she listened to the presumptions and off-kilter suppositions exchanged by the onlookers.

Thara frowned. "Quiet down," she scolded the wildly speculating women. "The arrival of these strangers could mean anything — it could mean nothing. No use in throwing around wild rumors when not one of you would know the truth if it rose and set with the sun. Have patience and stop your rumor-mongering. The truth will be known soon enough," she said, a bit more forcefully than she intended. She knew her own uncertainty to be the source of her unease, but that knowledge did nothing to allay her fears.

"But Thara, isn't it fun to just wonder about what it all might mean?" asked one of the younger women who nervously smoothed the front of her dyed and embroidered dress. Thara recognized her as one who fawned over all the young warriors, encouraging their boasts and flirting unabashedly. She was of marrying age and more than ready to leave the home of her parents. "If this means raiding, the more likely our husbands-to-be will have cattle and land for us," she stated hopefully. "I certainly don't want to marry a poor swineherd." The other unattached women murmured their agreement, and their eyes flared hot with thoughts of brave suitors risking life and limb to secure the tribe riches and ensure ample offerings for the hands of the maidens.

"That may be," Thara said, a pang of worry creasing her otherwise smooth brow, "but it could be just as likely that some of our 'husbands-to-be' may not return at all." In truth, she understood that tribal raiding was a part of life and as regular as the four seasons, but that did not make it any more palatable. Catching another glimpse of Jayas walking with a group of warriors, a small part of her mind conceded that her worries might have something to do with the swaggering young noble who walked out to greet the strangers.

His presence impossible to ignore, a hush of silence fell upon the crowd as they quieted long enough to hear Jayas out. His voice was firm, calm, and unconcerned. "Bran, you and your men are welcome in my father's house. You are under our protection and no harm will befall you within these walls. Your horses look hungry and thirsty," he said, motioning for a couple of servants to take the reins. "Allow me to see that they are fed and watered. My father agrees to your request and grants the audience you seek. He is eager to hear your words and discover what it is you desire of him." Then Jayas raised his voice for all to hear. "And the council convenes to-night."

THE INSIDE OF THE central meetinghouse was crowded and Jayas yearned to be on the back of his horse with a fresh wind in his face. He scorned politics and avoided the council meetings whenever possible, unless he was sure that some action would result from the gathering. A greater than usual number of nobles and their retainers pressed into its tight interior, raising the temperature of the room and causing a slick film of sweat to form on his skin. The sudden appearance of Bran and his men, coupled with the unexpected arrival of the Druid named Rhu, had stirred up a lot of excitement, and many nobles and wealthy landowners had flocked to the council in anticipation.

In honor of the sudden arrival of Rhu, Lord Toge had ordered a great feast be prepared, and the selection was impressive. The servants had roasted a whole boar stuffed with thrushes, which the assembled Coritani hungrily gobbled, their hands greasy with fat. When the boar was plucked clean, attentive servants brought a second serving consisting of geese and ducks boiled in a broth and served with parsnips. Between great mouthfuls of food, the council excitedly talked, mulling over what they had learned from Bran and his men. Jayas was soon bored with them all and barely bothered with the animated conversations, his attention drawn to their guest of honor.

He was fascinated by Rhu, and he enjoyed watching the Druid pick at the Celtic beans and fat hen that he selected for his simple meal, choosing to abstain from the rich offerings of meat and delicate birds prepared in his honor. His moustache acted like a sieve, trapping errant particles of food, and occasionally, he would pull back on some wayward strands of the wild and tangled hair as he shoveled in another mouthful of beans.

"How old is he," Jayas wondered under his breath. The holy man looked ancient. His hair was pure white and his unruly beard and moustache were peppered with streaks of silver. His eyes held a fierce intensity that burned with intelligence and softened with the ebb and flow of his quiet conversation with Lord Toge. He was whip thin but not gaunt, and he had an air of dignity about him that Jayas found settling. His angular face and neck and his hands and arms retained a soiled look from a combination of soot, dirt, smoke and sweat. Somehow, the unkempt appearance did nothing to detract from the man's regal bearing.

Gymm shook his head at Jayas' softly spoken query. "I don't know. Twice the age of your father at least," he said between hurried mouthfuls of juicy duck. "I'd wager that for sure."

All his life Jayas had heard tales of the Druid called Rhu, who was known as a seer and a healer, but rumors abounded concerning his mastery of other secrets. Some folk swore he could change forms, into a fox or stag and back to a man. Others whispered behind cupped hands that his spirit was more ancient than his flesh and sought a new body, and if you stared into his eyes too long, his spirit would enter you and yours would wither. All Jayas saw was an old man who understood the spirit world. That was enough for him.

Jayas chuckled at Gymm. "You have no business wagering on anything. He could be 100 or he could be 50," he said. The last time they had a wager and he won, Gymm pestered him about the knife he had lost until Jayas relented and gave it back. "Well, I'll bet that bone-handled knife of yours against my sword that he's at least twice the age of father but no older than the combined ages of all our uncles," Jayas said to the bewilderment of Gymm. "In fact, why don't you just go over and ask him," Jayas urged his old friend with a slap on the arm. "I'm sure he won't bite." Jayas could see that Gymm was thinking awfully hard about the proposition, silently mumbling, his eyes scrunched up in concentrated thought, even his food momentarily forgotten so great was his focus.

"It's possible but not probable." Silence returned to the room with the words spoken by Rhu. A giant blanket seemed to have descended upon the chatter. Seconds before, the air was thick with men hungrily feasting and peals of laughter from the bellies of tough warriors; now, even the slight breeze afforded by the open doors had halted its journey.

Discreetly, the warriors smiled to one another, meaty elbows fighting for space amidst the platters and cups. All Celts enjoyed a good riddle and valued the outwitting of another as much as they took pleasure in a good battle. The Druids were renowned for their cleverness, and most just accepted that fact as part of their mystique. Jayas, on the other hand, wondered how Rhu could have heard what they were talking about. He had no wish to be made a fool of in front of men he led in battle and desperately prayed that Rhu was talking to Gymm and not to him.

He swallowed hard. To his relief and the collective disappointment of the older warriors who would have enjoyed seeing Jayas humbled by the Druid, Rhu addressed the young warrior. "Seasons come and seasons go. Let it suffice to know, young Jayas, that I was old when you were a suckling babe clinging to your mum's tit." Rhu's retort brought forth laughter from the men. "The age of my body is of no consequence, as my mind is sharp and the visions I see are as clear and true as the dawn of a new day." Standing with an agility that belied his age, the Druid excused himself, and with a bony hand, beckoned Jayas to follow. Behind them, a clamor arose as people began shouting at once.

CHAPTER THIRTEEN

THE NIGHT AIR smelled clean, and the cooling breeze provided a welcome respite from the rank humidity of the lodge house. The sky was packed with glittering stars and the moon shined its muted beams upon the village and surrounding countryside, casting deformed shadows. Jayas could hear the hungry squall of a young child and the soothing voice of its mother coming from within one of the huts arrayed along the street. Not too far off, a dog barked, earning a rebuke filled with curses from a sleepy warrior. Not knowing what to say to his aged companion, Jayas took a deep nervous gulp of the sweet autumn air as he walked in silence, the strange priest by his side. He waved off a retainer pulling watch and continued to follow the meandering steps of the old priest as they passed outside the gates.

Suddenly, Rhu felt like speaking. "I remember the night you were born into this world like it was yesterday. The moon was full, beautiful and mighty, but it struggled with the night to light the land of our fathers," he said, sweeping his arm to encompass the surroundings. "But a rare event took place that night," he said, pausing to finger the amber pendent that hung loosely from his thin neck, "a rare event portending great changes for our people's future."

His vivid imagination afire, Jayas wondered what event he could be referring to. "The birth of one male child could hardly be called a rare event," he managed, his tone humble.

The priest scowled in disapproval. "The birth of any child is cause for celebration," Rhu scolded. "Do we not celebrate the continued health and vitality of the people?" he asked instructively. "Without our children, we have no future. Who would defend our folk and carry on our ancient traditions that have seen us through so many trying times? Who would keep the rites, the laws, and satisfy the sacrifices that are necessary for our sustenance?" he asked incredulously.

"You have a good point," Jayas conceded, "but I merely meant that the birth of one child can't possibly have that big an impact."

"You apparently lack imagination, so just listen. As I said earlier, the night you were born, the moon was full and happy with the people. You entered this world at the exact time the moon reached the pinnacle of its nightly climb. Free from your mother's womb, you screamed your challenge to the world; and it was heard, for the sky turned black as the moon retreated. Such an omen would usually have been answered with a sacrifice, and the people shouted, 'The gods must be angry. Why do the gods curse us?' they cried. The people were frightened and other priests clamored for the blood token of repentance. Only I could truly see." The old Druid had a fiercely defiant glint in his eye and his stride seemed to lengthen with the telling of the story. Jayas wanted more and listened carefully. He could have heard a straw hit the ground so great was his concentration on what the old man was saying.

"Was the sacrifice made?" asked Jayas. "I mean, something had to have happened. See?" He pointed skyward. "The moon is still here and all is well." He confidently patted the hilt of his sword.

Rhu shot him an irritated glance. "Wake up!" he shouted. "Our land is under attack from a godless people who respect nothing of our ways." His surprisingly strong hands gripped Jayas' arms. "The signs are clear. I have seen the signs as clear as I see you here before me. A scourge stalks our land, spreads like a fungus on wheat, corrupting, weakening, stealing from its host until all that is left is death and famine." Rhu released his grip on Jayas's arms, the light in his eyes fading a bit.

They followed a stream that led to a pond set back in the far corner of a farmer's field. In the distance, a dog's deep, challenging bark was answered by the questioning hoot of a night owl. The moon reflected a ghostly white orb on the calm surface of the pond, the buzz and bites of gnats a counterpoint to the beauty.

"Our land is out of balance, its rhythm disrupted. Can't you feel that?" he asked, his ear cocked toward the ground, face frozen in concentration. "No matter if you don't. I do," he said wearily. Suddenly, he was animated again, arms waving, caught up in the fervor of the moment. "Do you trust me?"

"Do I have a choice?" asked Jayas. He had no issue with going to battle. His whole life had been dedicated to being a warrior. It was expected of him and he knew how to do that well. "I will battle these invaders and they will learn to fear my name," he boasted loudly, chest swelling.

Rhu sighed and shook his head in resignation. "Of course you will. To offer your body as a living sacrifice is the final act of worship, but your mind must be free of pride. When you accept this truth, your spirit will be unfettered. The patterns of the world about you will begin to fade, but your mind and spirit shall be rejuvenated and you shall belong to the whole." His voice took on a forceful pleading quality, quivering with intensity.

"Submit your warrior's heart to that which is greater. Consider yourself not alone in this matter — for all your folk are with you. Be wise and exercise sober judgment. Value the talents and gifts of those around you. If one is of aggressive spirit, let him be aggressive; if he is a warrior, let him be a warrior. If a man gathers sheep well, let him herd sheep. But remember one thing. You, Jayas, are your people's shepherd; and rabid wolves are nipping at the heels of your flock." The old man then turned and walked toward the edge of the forest, disappearing into its shadowy depths, leaving Jayas alone and confused.

CHAPTER FOURTEEN

A FEWS HOURS brisk ride south of the village, Thara lingered on the leafy banks of a clear-flowing stream. Seated on a mossy log in the thicket, she stared at the vast canopy of oaks and black alder trees that crept to the edge of the water. Through the expanse of the scattered green foliage, the rays of the sun grew stronger, coloring the current a lighter hue and revealing minnows an inch long darting around the slippery rocks, wheeling in unison in shiny silvery groups. She breathed in the cool vapors of the dissipating mist that stubbornly wafted above her leafy hide. A warm peaceful feeling settled over her as she breathed the fresh scent of oak, hundreds of green acorns ripening in the branches. She enjoyed the seclusion and soaked in the chirps of the foraging chipmunks, the occasional stir of leaves as squirrels sought acorns and the steady hum of a faraway waterfall. Disrupting the familiar sounds, the low hum of men's voices and the distinct slap of unshod hooves assailed her ears. She glimpsed the riders through the branches, and the young woman smiled to herself. "Right on time," she murmured.

A small group of horsemen, outriders probably, rode at an alert trot but slowed as they approached. Studying the ground before them, they paused at the muddy ford and turned their eyes suspiciously, scanning the bank and focusing on the thicket that concealed her. The closest scout was quick and keen, and he brought his horse to a slow walk and paralleled the brushy undergrowth of the bank. His eyes roved on every side of him, finally penetrating the mottled barrier and locking onto hers.

She stood up with a laugh, arms spread wide in a gesture of welcome. "Hello," she shouted, her unmistakably female form silhouetted against the brushy incline. The warriors spurred their mounts into a run and splashed through the stream.

The riders exchanged puzzled looks. "What are you doing here?" The quick one gave her a severe look. "You're about 10 miles from the village," he said, stating the obvious. "How did you get here?" he then asked, his tone indicating genuine interest.

"Well, let me see. On the wings of a hawk of course," she said sarcastically. "No, I borrowed one of my father's mares. I ride quite well, you know." She walked the short distance into the wood and untethered the patiently waiting mare, a mature and gentle beast. Thara would prefer a more spirited mount, but the old horse was reliable and not skittish in the least. More important, she gathered her sturdy yew bow and the quiver full of arrows she had painstakingly selected. After her brush with the Brigante, she had set to practicing on a more earnest basis. Her father did not object, and he even joined her on occasion. They would shoot arrow after arrow into fence posts and trees.

"Shall we go," she asked matter-of-factly to the open-mouthed amazement of the men.

"Go where?" a few voices questioned in unison. "We're going raiding, and it's no place for a woman," said one with a slight stutter. "As a matter of fact, it's too dangerous for you to be out this far by yourself. I know you've heard of what's been going on, so don't play coy. If we happened to have been some heathen Roman or enemy tribesmen, you could get hurt, or even worse." The speaker greedily eyed her comely figure, obviously thinking of the spoils of battle that lay ahead.

Undeterred, she leapt onto her mount in one smooth motion. "Then thank the gods I'm not alone," she said pointedly. "I'm with men of my tribe, honorable and brave men who are dedicated to their people." Thara knew it never hurt to appeal to a man's ego and sense of chivalry. Her efforts did not go unrewarded. The men sat straighter in the saddle and the lustful gleam in their eyes dimmed a tad at her words. They looked around at one another and simply shrugged, some indifferent but others suspicious and not knowing what to think of this boldness.

Finally, one had the sense to ask, "You actually expect to go to battle with us?" Some of the scouts snickered at this notion until she fixed them with a glare, freezing their mocking bursts of laughter mid-throat.

She sighed in exasperation. "Just take me to your commander," she said, "I think he is the one to make this call. Not you, not me." They conceded her point.

"The rest are not too far away. We're just scouting ahead. You can ride back with Lann when he reports," the scout who had discovered her said, pointing to a sullen blue-painted youth on a small pony. "Or you can wait here. It's your decision, but I'd prefer you stayed with one of us. There are foreigners out plundering, raping and slaving; they would love to capture you." Thara smiled at the man's friendliness. She was well acquainted with the risks, but she appreciated his protective gesture. She could sense the gates of fate beginning to open and she intended to run through them.

THE FIRST NEWS that the Romans had crossed the river arrived quickly, and Lord Toge sent riders with orders for the warriors to amass at the hillfort. Reports put the Romans strength at around twelve hundred mixed foot and horse soldiers, and there were almost a thousand Bibroci and Trinovante warriors with them. Envoys were dispatched to neighboring tribes seeking aid to deal with this new threat to their survival. As expected, ambassadors to those tribes allied with Cassivellaunus returned with nothing to show for their efforts. The old warlord's memory of his recent defeat was still too strong in his mind to defy his allegiance.

Lord Toge and the council determined that a direct confrontation with the mass of Romans should not be risked. Scouts and messengers were dispatched to gather intelligence and apprise Jayas of the movement of the enemy. He then moved out with his command of horsemen to harass, ambush and otherwise delay the

Romans as long as possible. He intended to follow those orders, but he would do much, much, more. He grinned to himself at the thought, his canines bared, which gave him a wolfish sneer that chilled the blood of most men.

Jayas was infuriated upon discovering that Thara had traveled ahead, and more so that she correctly guessed their route of march. His first impulse upon finding her among the advance patrol was to detach a couple of men to escort her safely home, but a part of him wanted her company. The determination and grit she displayed was something to marvel at, he admitted to himself. She had an air about her that made men seek her approval, and that made him feel uncomfortable, but she could also prove to be a distraction in more ways than one. He shared a private laugh to himself. Sitting there on her disinterested brown mare, she looked as much a warrior as he did a goat herder.

"You, of all people," she said accusingly, "should know that I can fight." Her eyes held his without a hint of yielding in them, her head and neck angled in an obstinate pose.

Jayas snacked on a piece of cold mutton as they moved farther south of the stream and deeper into the forest. The cool shade of the forest provided a welcome respite from the uncharacteristic heat and humidity of the season as they rode, and the trees a natural barrier from those interested in the nature and tenor of the conversation. He still had major reservations.

"I never said you couldn't fight," he said, his frustration rising. "I've seen you kill before, but still, you are not a warrior, and we are about warriors' business. Our people face a great challenge and our mission is very dangerous." His eyes narrowed menacingly at the mention of the threat arrayed against his folk. "Besides, you could be more useful organizing and whatnot back home. There's much that has to be done and a solid hand like yours would be awfully welcome in keeping the other women and children steady. Not to mention you would be out of harm's way."

Her face tightened, the color quickly rising to fill her fine cheekbones. Thara' voice was now rising in intensity. "Is it only the men who face this great challenge? Do we women have anything less to lose? Are not our futures one and the same?" She paused for a second to examine the giant young man, confident in her ability to persuade him to do the right thing. "Are we not one people? In the olden times, the women fought beside the men, tooth, hand, foot and club. You know the stories as well as I do. Our women have a tradition, and dare I say an obligation to take up arms against those who would destroy us. I, for one, will not stand by idly to merely await what the gods would have done. Besides, I can heal too," she said firmly, her voice thick with conviction. "Our family has a tradition of being healers. My own mother stitched Gymm up not long ago, remember? And I was there when she set your broken arm. Everyone in the village comes to her when they get injured. Her great-uncle Rhu taught her when she was my age. I have watched and helped her, and I have learned much from both of them." She paused and held up the leather pouch tethered to her waist by a hemp rope. "I've brought the herbs and mosses that can staunch bleeding and lessen pain. I can close and stitch wounds and keep them clean."

Jayas paused and chewed at his moustache, his will to deny her what she wanted wilting in the face of her beatific plea. All that she said was true. The women had much to lose. If the warriors were defeated then the women and young faced a brutal future of rape and slavery. The thought of such a future for Thara cooled Jayas' bones to the marrow and filled him with a stony resolve harder than the iron blade hanging from his belt. Staring at the beautiful face he had known since childhood, he knew he would prefer death than to see her subjected to such a fate at the hands of these men from across the sea, at anyone's hands. Her courage and dedication to her tribe stirred something within, but he also knew the argument was a lost cause. At the very least, he thought, she could lend aid and comfort to the wounded. Wounds, when untended and left to fester, led to an agonizing death. He knew that Thara' knowledge as a healer could prove invaluable. The added benefit of her skill as an archer would not go unused either, he promised himself.

He held up a hand and waved squads of warriors off to cover the right and left flanks as they paused at the edge of a clearing that sloped gently downward, affording him a view of a small farm-stead, home to a single clan of three or four families. A sea of dried up bluebells was spread on the pastureland where sheep and cattle grazed peacefully in the field, and a shepherd and a small boy raised their hands in greeting, humble grins adorning their faces. These families were related to Jayas and loyal to Lord Toge. Their land lay on the border, so it was a matter of time before marauding Romans and their pet tribesmen picked it as an easy target to raid. The clansmen were grateful for the presence of these riders, but Jay-as waved them off. He wanted the raiders to come to him and wanted no trace of his presence revealed.

"And if one can use a bow, let them use the bow; and if one can heal, let them heal," he said softly, chuckling to himself.

Thara's face clouded with anger. "Does my offer of service make you laugh?" she snapped.

His mind made up, he shrugged off the accusation. "You must submit to my leadership. While under arms, my command is to be followed without question. Your oath of fealty to me is required. All retainers must make the pledge." That was true enough. On this ex-pedition he had a hundred and fifty warriors, all freeborn and well mounted, and to a man they had taken the pledge and were sworn to him personally. In return, they were fed well and shared equally in the plunder. They had ridden as one since childhood and drew their first blood together, fighting both the Cassi and the Bibroci, and all of them had been blooded. Though relatively young, they were all veterans of raids and reprisals, born to violence whereby iron was answered with steel. Aside from Lord Toge's veteran chari-oteers, this small but lethal cavalry unit was the pride of the tribe's army.

Her pretty face fixed him with a sneer, which gradually melted into a charmed smile. "My loyalty is to you, Jayas, so long as your loyalty is that of the people above all else," she said with a bow of her head and a bend of her tiny waist. "Now what?" she asked, wondering what strategy he had in mind.

"Now we wait, and you stay near me. I don't want to have to worry about you when the battle begins." He immediately summoned his officers and ordered scouts out to make sure the enemy was in the vicinity. If all went well, he could get the Romans and their vassal tribesmen interested in the villagers well-tended flocks and then pounce like a wolf on a calf.

CHAPTER FIFTEEN

A BILLOWING CLOUD of dust marked the scouts' long awaited return to the steadily moving column. They had traveled a few days and were now bordering lands disputed by several belligerent tribes. In this no-man's territory, loyalty was obtained by the hand of the sword strong enough to wield it.

Marcus had allowed Leko to ride with the scouts and was glad of it. It was better to have a second opinion of the scouts' information, no matter how unorthodox the means or how youthful the source. The report they gave Marcus sounded promising, he had to admit, and Leko confirmed there could be no more than two dozen villagers in the enclave ahead. A tiny hamlet would be a more apt description, but it was thick with cattle and sheep — an easy target to fatten the supply wagon and an opportunity to let the Bibroci plunder a little. Marcus decided to personally lead the raiding party, and he selected a century of legionaries to accompany him and the same number of Bibroci scouts. They were told to be prepared to leave in half an hour.

Marcus stowed his gear and arranged his armor, checking that the leather fastenings of his breastplate had not rotted or been too weakened by the constant strain demanded of them. Leko had a forlorn look of disappointment on his beardless face, and his shoulders slumped forward slightly as he watched Marcus go about his preparations. He took a bite of sun-dried beef, rolling it in his mouth to soften it before chewing and swallowing the fleshy lump, his eyes silently beseeching Marcus for acknowledgment. Irritated at the youth's silent sulking, Marcus finally stated, "Prepare your things as well, and bring me your sword and shield."

An excited smile lit up Leko' face as he handed over the sword for Marcus' inspection. "Master, I will make you proud," he said with youthful exuberance mixed with a newfound, manly determination.

Marcus palmed the hilt of the lad's sword, thrusting it forward to feel its balance and looking down the blade. Noting the keen edge Leko maintained on it, he grunted in approval before handing it back. Then he took the youth's shield and thumped it with his sword, listening and then looking for a crack, but he found none. Next, he inspected the boy's leather armor and was pleased to note that it was oiled and void of tears or other deficiencies. "You will make me proud if you listen to my orders and stay alive. Men and boys," he said poignantly, "regularly die for want of listening. If we have to fight, stay near me and do exactly as I say and as I do. Don't tighten up, but let the sword move you. Action is always faster than thinking of it and then remembering to do it. Keep your shield up and thrust like we have trained. Trust the men on your left and right just as they trust that you will be there. Do not stray from our line or rank no matter what happens. Forget about individual glory, as our strength lies in our ability to fight as a unit. As you well know, lone wolves are easier to kill without the strength and cunning of the pack." He then gave Leko a paternal slap on the back, earning the boy's gratitude for the show of familiarity.

Cocksure and proud at being allowed to go on the mission, Leko snapped to attention as he had seen the legionaries do, throwing up a suitable caricature of a salute. "Yes sir. You don't have to worry about me, Commander. I've seen it done a hundred times. And you know me, I'm all eyes, ears and fierceness," Leko said in a half-growl as he conjured up the most maniacal grin he could muster. It struck a chord in the chest of Marcus as he wondered how he himself must have looked as a youngster, chomping at the bit to have a taste of battle. He wondered if he had looked as vulnerable as Leko, full of eagerness to play a warrior's game, yearning to test his mettle and declare himself a man.

Marcus briefed his officers and left orders with the remaining cohort to erect a marching camp and safeguard the supply wagons until his return. Setting out on the trail, Marcus could feel the familiar tug of flutters in his chest when battle was anticipated, a feeling of elation that always made him feel more alive.

The route lay across swelling plains and frequent hills with corresponding valleys. In the distance, Marcus could see a mass of white and gray clouds piled above the hilly western horizon. The Bibroci took the lead and set a brisk pace, keeping to the edges of overgrown fields where possible and avoiding the imposing forest. They had covered seven miles, and Marcus was beginning to wonder where the scouts were leading them.

"Leko, why do they avoid riding in the forest," he asked, already knowing the answer but wanting to keep the boy's nerves from fraying.

Leko just shrugged. "They believe evil lurks in the forest, and so it is better to stay in the open and out of the depths," he said as if no further explanation was really necessary, as if the answer were already too obvious and warranted no further mention.

Marcus looked over at Leko, his eyes questioning and his patience running thin. "How much further?" he hissed between clenched teeth.

Leko snapped his head toward Marcus and nodded in the direction of the dismounting Bibroci. "Not far," he whispered knowingly.

The Bibroci scouts were tying the horses' bridles to small trees and whispering into their mounts ears, calming them down. Marcus now saw why and followed suit. The tiny village was situated atop a hill and commanded a dominant view of the valley. Behind the village, gently flowing fields containing their livestock bordered a thick forest, almost black in its shadows with the sun stooping beyond its outline. Marcus divided the men. Half were to go to the village with orders to procure grains and other valuables and the other half he would lead to gather the cattle and sheep from the fields. They waited for darkness. If his legionnaires met resistance, they were to deal with it, but no unnecessary killing was the standing order.

Night finally set in and the clouded moon made the path somber and forbidding. The same darkness that protected their maneuvers now protracted their march as they stopped at the edge of the field next to a tree-lined hill. It was too quiet, and Marcus thought of the farms they passed along the way. They too were barren. No one had come out to greet them. Somebody would usually be stirring around on a farm — chopping wood, milking goats and slopping the hogs or drawing water. But not even dogs barked at them. The same thing was happening here, as the small cluster of farms and lodges were eerily quiet.

The night birds had grown silent. No foxes yipped and no owls hooted. Without warning, a huge, blue-painted warrior with a large leather-covered wooden shield stepped from behind a giant oak straddling the edge of the forest. Armed with a javelin, he sprang into the field. Shield up, he hurled the spear with great strength and a legionary collapsed, vomiting blood. The giant warrior leapt back into the depths of the forest in a couple of bounds. From the darkened edges of the forest, ferocious growls and guttural war cries pierced the air like the screaming of banshees. The whistling zing of arrows hitting shields and armor contributed to the rising din, adding a profane elegance to the violence.

On command, the legionaries brought their own shields to the fore. With their swords up, they looked around levelly and instinctively closed ranks. "On me!" Marcus yelled, grabbing the wild-eyed Leko by the collar of his leather breastplate and jerking him toward the center of the line. On instinct, the men formed three ranks of fifteen, as wild bunches of screaming tribesmen burst from the bushes, hurling javelins under the protection of a volley of arrows and stones.

As if a swarm of angry bees rode the air, a deadly torrent of iron-pointed spears, arrows and stones whooshed toward the confused Roman line. Random projectiles wreaked havoc, the iron and bone arrowheads gashing exposed Roman flesh.

"Hold!" Marcus urged his flagging men. Gaps appeared in the ranks as legionaries crumpled to the ground, well-aimed stones smashing bronze helmets and cleaving skulls. "Back-step, march!" he shouted above the din. "To the village!" The decision was easy as he watched the ground suddenly fill with blue apparitions. He hoped his men in the village were not too busy plundering to notice that they were under attack. He risked a look behind him and could see some Bibroci scouts racing their mounts up the hill, the other half century of legionaries scrambling behind them anxious to get into the fray and lend support against the fiercely charging enemy.

In the front rank, Legionary Tuno staggered and then fell to the ground. His hands fruitlessly searched the cause of his agony and found his body riddled with wounds from arrow and spear. The soldier to his left raised his shield to protect his comrade from further agony, but he too fell to the blood-soaked ground, an arrow lodged in the base of his neck.

They were within fifty meters of the village when their torn and battered ranks were finally fortified by the remaining scouts and legionaries. The Romans regrouped in a hurry, concentrating the thrust of their push in the center of the charging mass. A stone flung from a sling struck Marcus' shield arm and he lost his grip. He was exposed. A snarling Celt heaved a javelin, creasing his unprotected side, and a mask of pain gripped his features. In a spurt of fury, Marcus re-gripped the fallen shield and smashed the exposed head of the warrior with the iron boss, shattering his skull. On his flank, he spotted a huge warrior leading a pack of snarling Celts, cutting and slashing unmercifully as the forces collided.

"Kill him!" Marcus shouted at the top of his lungs, snarling back at the furiously swinging warrior. If the man succeeded and cut his way through, it would roll up his thinly spread line and a massacre would ensue. He had to close that gap or all was lost.

He grabbed Leko and a few dismounted Bibroci horsemen and thrust them into the sagging flank. They locked shields and roared defiantly, stomping to meet the reckless, headlong charge of the barbarians. Never faltering for a second, Leko doggedly kept his shield up and was thrusting at anything that came within reach. He added his shoulder and arm to the line, cutting and thrusting until he did not think he could continue.

WITH A ROAR, Jayas charged the Roman formation like an enraged bear, a dozen or so warriors hotly following his lead. A lanky legionary stepped from the ranks to meet his charge, his shield up and sword at the ready. The soldier's eyes were narrowed and beady with lethal determination. Jayas beat the man's shield down with powerful hacking blows of his sword, and with a powerful thrust of his javelin, skewered the shrieking Roman. He barreled over a cursing soldier with his shoulder, the curse ending in a cry of pain as the point of a spear sliced through his gurgling throat. Jayas madly chopped down another soldier who stepped into his place. Swinging the javelin like a stick, he shattered the spear on the helmeted head of the Roman, finishing the man with a backhanded swipe of his blade. He continued to madly hack at the Roman flank, almost single-handedly breaking through to the center and cleaving their forces in two before a Roman officer and some Bibroci scouts filled the gap and covered the Romans' retreat into the village.

"Halt!" Jayas shouted at the top of his lungs. In the wooded defilade, Thara heard his order and signaled the herald, who brought the boar-headed *carnyx*, or war horn, to his fat lips and blew loudly, its deep bellow eerily emphasizing the command. The warriors slowed their advance, some saluting him, some cursing him for showing restraint, but all were impressed by his limitless resolve. Exhausted, Jayas gave the order to retreat, his bloodied but exultant warriors hurriedly falling back to the protection of the wooded hill where they had their mounts waiting. The likelihood of a counterattack by the Romans was essentially nil, but Jayas ordered two squads of twenty to maintain harassing contact with the enemy.

The victorious war party moved swiftly south down the moonlit forest path, leaving the bodies of the dead Romans to fester and putrefy during the night. If the Romans sent out details to police up the battlefield or gather their dead, a roving warrior or two would make it a risky endeavor. Along the trail, Gymm caught up with

Jayas, who was glad to see the look of savage triumph plastered on his broad face. "Our losses?" he asked of the glowing Gymm.

"Four brave warriors will never fight again." Gymm smiled sadly. "And we have ten men who have suffered some cuts and bruises but nothing that cannot be mended," he said with a momentary gleam of optimism as he looked over at Thara. She had done well in the first skirmish against the enemy and had earned a measure of respect from the warriors of her tribe. During the hectic fracas, she stayed back as Jayas ordered, but from behind the advancing warriors she had loosened her deadly arrows with a ruthless efficiency, and now, all were glad for her company.

All in all, Jayas was pleased with the battle. Though the death of even one warrior was cause for lament, the manner in which these men died would live on in song, and their deaths would not go unavenged, of that he was sure. Nevertheless, amidst the air of excitement and victory, a sense of discontent hovered between the warriors and was reluctantly voiced by Gymm.

Clearing his throat, he brought his mount closer to Jayas, not bothering to lower his voice. "Why are we moving away from the Romans? Why are we not attacking still?" Like most of the young men, Gymm wanted to rush the village, and others riding close by echoed his sentiment. "We had them on their heels. We killed at least a couple dozen of them. A stronger push and we would have overrun them." Gymm was confident of this, and still amped up from the rush of battle, he looked around at the supportive nods of his retainers. He stopped the incessant questioning when his friend and cousin fixed him with an icy glare.

Jayas then returned to reconnoitering the path and cuffed his comrade on the shoulder. "I agree and that's a fair question," he said, just ever so slightly raising his voice. "But I have listened to the warriors who have battled these Romans before us. I spoke with Cassivellaunus' men and with Bran. You've heard the same stories that I have. We are much better warriors than these foreigners. The Romans make poor soldiers and do not hold up well in single combat. We know this, but if we make wild charges, what do they do?" he asked, looking hard at Gymm and his nearby retainers. "What happens next, I ask you?" he said forcefully. He pulled his horse off the path, the men following near, straining to hear his words. Before anyone answered, he continued. "The strength of these Romans lies in their unity. Together, they are strong, and when they form up into ranks, they trample their enemy. Their battle order is always the same: throw javelins, hoist shields up, and thrust away in unison with those short ugly blades. Why would we hasten to throw ourselves upon their iron?" He paused, combating the mounting anger that threatened to erupt from him and required a moment to recede. He did not trust his mouth to obey the thin veneer of self-control that had heretofore successfully kept the beast at bay.

It was obvious to him that traditional tactics of tribal warfare would fail if used against the Romans. For battle, the tribes tended to band together in a motley assembly, quite in the open and with minimal forethought to the position of the enemy. For any chance of success, the old way of fighting had to fade and be replaced with mobility, with hit and run attacks. He was determined to see this foray through, and he hoped the results would speak for themselves.

Loudly sighing, Thara slid off her horse, easing into the circle of conferencing warriors. She ignored the curious stares of the warriors and deftly maneuvered herself nearer. She heard Jayas' defense of his strategy and could not resist jumping in and explaining what she found to be obvious. She'd had enough of protocol and they would hear her out.

"Do you not like success?" she asked tartly, not caring that she was treading into matters usually reserved for the men folk. "Would you not rather fight the enemy on your terms rather than his?" She said this last bit to a consensus of murmurs and nods. She pointed at a young warrior she knew to be a fine hunter. "You, Liam. Let me ask you. Would you not prefer to stab a wild boar in the flank rather than its head where its sharp tusks could gore you?" He shrugged in the affirmative but she was not done. "When a pack of wolves hunts, does it not seek to separate its prey from the protection of the sharp hooves of the herd?" Again Liam nodded his assent, this time in communion with the grunts and assents of the others. "So must we, when dealing with our enemies." This claim was met by stony silence as the men tried to digest what she just offered, indeed to digest that it was a woman offering battle strategy that was sound. Jayas could not have said it better.

"We did well tonight," Jayas said. Many of the enemy were slain to four of our warriors, but this was only a raiding party. Our scouts report that a large Roman cavalry force is pressing this way, pillaging villages and taking slaves. Another Roman force is on foot paralleling the river Temes. I would like to see these two forces splintered into smaller groups as well. If we can continue to isolate and destroy the smaller units, ultimately we can destroy the whole." His eyes strayed and caught the light in Thara's. Imperceptibly, he nodded his head and winked in silent thanks. Ever so slightly, she smiled before dashing off to tend to the wounded.

CHAPTER SIXTEEN

WITH THE EYES of a hawk, Cussius gazed across the broad shallow valley littered with bent scrub grass and scattered thistle, the saving grace a silver trickling stream snaking through its center. The color of the fading summer showed everywhere. The eternal green, the mighty oaks, the flowers blowing gently in the humid breeze were giving way to the withering effect of autumn's wind and rain. Where farmers had not yet harvested the wheat, the fields lay flattened as if a great foot had stomped down in anger. Crab apples were red on the trees, some already on the ground, soft, brown and mushy where the sun and bugs feasted on the fruit.

"We make camp here," he said to the Trinovante noble. "Before you complain, Kren, mind you that we are on campaign and not every night can be spent in the comfortable confines of a toasty cabin." In return, Kren flashed his gap-toothed smile because he knew full well that he would be kept fine company by the two slave girls traveling with him. "Graze the horses, water them, and be careful to not let them gorge on those apples. It might put a bit more kick in their piss, but it could also sour their stomachs and lame them for a while," Cussius said to his orderly, who relayed the orders to the officers. Like any good cavalryman, his mount came first, and only after the horse was well cared for could his own comforts be attended to.

With vigor the Trinovante barked orders to his retainers while the Romans went about their business of setting up a proper *castra*. The same basic plan designed years ago by Roman military engineers for efficiency served well for both a mobile army camp and permanent frontier fortification. All over the world, the camps were the same. Each soldier knew his job and went about his duties. Some dug a ditch around the outside of the camp and piled up the earth on the camp enclosure side to make an embankment that was topped with sharpened poles to make a palisade wall. Two main roads led into the camp. One was called the *Via Principia* and the other, *Via Praetoria*. The legionary headquarters were at the center of the *castra'* enclosure. The crossing avenues were then ringed by the large tents housing the Roman contingents. His Celtic allies were eschewing such comforts as tents, instead choosing austere pelts as bedrolls or using their broad and colorful cloaks as shelter. Cussius grinned to himself. If only his mother could see him now. Despite the downturn in her family's fortune, her perfectly Roman sensibilities would be offended to no end. His retinue had grown in the past month, his ranks swelling by ones, twos and threes as disaffected nobles and unattached young warriors sought employment in his growing army. She would be hard pressed to see whether he was romanizing the Celts or they were tribalizing him, but it mattered little. He could care less whether or not he ever set his eyes upon the land of his birth, the seven hills of old that had been replaced by the growing mystique and wealth of this unknown province. He knew that he could not deny destiny, and that no matter what fate had in store for him, it was to be found here. So here he would plant his flag, and he would either have his way with fortune or it with him. The winds of fate were blowing, and he would be sure to have his sail unfurled to catch it regardless where it took him.

He dispatched riders to Marcus, who was floundering along behind him, his infantry pulling security for the growing supply train of cattle, grain, and slaves. Days earlier, he had received word that Marcus had sustained a wound in a hotly contested battle that started out as a simple cattle raid. Pity he is such a quick healer, he mused to himself. Cussius had ridden to his relief, however, and the embarrassment that Marcus suffered was well worth the ride. Marcus had lost face in the eyes of his scouts and men. More than thirty had died and none received a decent Roman burial until Cussius arrived in force and ran off the pestering tribesmen who had harried and sniped at earlier relief efforts.

"Kren, dear comrade," he said slowly to the Trinovante war chief. Having learned more than a smattering of the Gallic language while campaigning with Caesar, Cussius had doubled his efforts in learning the language of the native Britons. Blessedly, the Briton's dialect was similar enough to that which was spoken on the mainland. He continued in Kren's native tongue.

"Tell me again who it was that busted up Marcus' raiding party?" Though he didn't mind Marcus getting humbled in battle, appearances had to be upheld and retaliation was a must or he too risked losing respect. "And don't just conveniently blame it on one of your enemies whose land or cattle you want. I need to know who was responsible for this," he said, his gray eyes flashing in the firelight, reflecting a molten silver. This harassment is getting to be more than a little bothersome, he thought as he chewed the baked hardtack, socking it in the pouch of his cheek to soften before swallowing it whole. Sentries and wood cutting parties were always at risk of not coming back. Groups of men, two or three at a time, were found dead, their bodies mutilated and their heads removed. Whispers and rumors were rampant, the men blaming everything from foreign gods and ghosts to the more real and dangerous specters of lurking Celtic warriors. Roman retribution for Marcus' losses and the ongoing raids needed to be brutal and swift.

His legs stretched out before him, Kren let out a great satisfying belch and repositioned his ample belly to allow for the beefsteak hanging from the tip of his blade. He did not have the patience to pause to blow on it before working the still sizzling strips between his jaws and swallowing, his throat bobbing up and down. "It's the Coritani," he said between gulps. "We're riding close to their lands. They are a jealous lot and I can't imagine them backing down a single bit."

Cussius liked the smell of the cooking fires, a far cry from the stuffy little anterooms that dominated his early childhood in Rome. He could remember the boredom, leaning on soft pillows while reciting the epics of the great Greek philosophers and examining the heroic exploits of Alexander the Great. Though he had to admit he did find the military expeditions of the great ancients fascinating at times, he did not miss the inane rants of the temple priests who would often prostitute their beliefs to curry political favor. He basked in the simple life of a soldier and the rewards won by strength and the will to see it through.

"Won't they?" Cussius leaned up, his attention focused on Kren. "Impertinent! Are they a prosperous bunch? Did they not fight us along with Cassivellaunus? Are they in breach of the terms?" he demanded. Cussius had studiously observed Caesar over the years and consequently gained a wide respect for accurate intelligence concerning any foe, current or potential, and he needed to learn as much as possible about these new belligerents. It dawned on him that these new enemies were of his making, but that was to be expected and of no consequence, unless he failed to address it. Addressing these barbarians in a most vigorous fashion would be the proper course.

"The Coritani did not fight, even though Cassivellaunus..." Kren paused to spit on the ground at the mention of his enemy's name, "sought their assistance. They preferred to see their hated rival take the brunt of the punishment, but now we have their attention--the scum," he said, shrugging as if what he said was widely known and an accepted fact of life. Kren continued, his voice heavy with spite and leaden with hatred. "For years they have raided our cattle, stolen our women and children and torched any farm within the reach of their vile horsemen. They are as backward and treacherous as Cassivellaunus, if not more," he said, the contempt springing forth into the night air as his voice rose in remembrance of perceived slights, insults and offenses perpetrated by the Coritani on his people.

"I see they are warlike. But do they truly like war?" mused Cussius, the hidden philosopher in him fusing with the warrior.

During his years with Caesar he had fought hard campaigns all over Gaul and Spain, and he had seen many warlike tribes reduced to ghosts of their former selves. Peoples who prided themselves on long established traditions of warrior culture were oftentimes found wanting as warriors when Rome flexed her muscle and reduced these brave but wayward barbarians to ruin. The pattern repeated from campaign to campaign, proud tribal warriors charging madly in quests for glory only to be impaled on the swords of rampaging legions. He sighed as he recounted the available forces at his disposal. He did not even have the luxury of a full legion, and Marcus' earlier warnings echoed in his head like a dull headache.

"What is the strength of these Coritani?" he asked, his interest piquing and his keen intellect already doing calculations. "How many warriors could they muster to oppose us and where are their principle towns and villages? More important, are they wealthy?" he asked, knowing that it was much easier to motivate his men to fight when they were assured of the opportunity to loot and plunder.

Kren watched him with one eyebrow arched high in question and smelling an opportunity to pay his old enemies back. "They could call upon a good number of warriors, almost equal to what we have assembled here, and riches they do have — many sheep and cattle and herds of fine horses that graze on some of the sweetest grasses in the land." He paused for effect, noting the rapt attention shown toward his words by the other warriors. Even the Roman general seemed to lean forward in anticipation of the furtherance of his tale. A natural storyteller, Kren appreciated the efficacy of a dramatic pause and took a long draught of mead, wiped his mouth with the back of his scarred and brawny hand, sighing in satisfaction and smacking his lips before continuing. "Their nobles hoard stashes of gold and precious jewels fit for kings. And their women are renowned for their beauty. Any warrior would be pleased to take one of them to his bedroll," he said to a chorus of rough laughter from the nobles and Roman officers clustered about.

"I have fought them as have others of my tribe, and I know much about them," he said before pointing to the young woman sitting cross-legged at the entrance of Cussius' tent. "But she would know better than anyone." The men turned their attention to the black-haired beauty Cussius kept as his own.

Surprising even himself, Cussius retorted, "It is not your men's concern what she knows or may not know." Tossing his empty cup to his orderly, he set his leonine gaze upon the feline girl.

"That's fine with me," said Kren in concert with mumbled words of agreement from the others. "She's your sorceress," he said, fingers forked to ward off the evil eye, emphasizing the gesture with another hearty belch.

Cussius laughed heartily and rose, walking back toward his tent. "That she is, men," he said, still chuckling. "That she is."

CHAPTER SEVENTEEN

HE TOOK THE girl's hand in his and led her into his tent, dismissing his orderly with an impatient wave of his hand. She had fine features and a soft, inviting face. Her features were strong and clear, and she had large brown eyes, the irises liquid black like shale. Her hair was a midnight shade, as if some Persian noble had left his mark amongst her ancestors. Inhaling her scent, he enjoyed the earthy hardiness that filled his nostrils. It took him back to the foraging expedition of a couple of weeks earlier when she first became his own.

He waited for a moment, appreciating the simple beauty of her presence in his brutal world. "Are you of this Coritani tribe of which Kren speaks?" he asked her softly, much more softly then he usually would in any situation where he wanted intelligence. He knew the men whispered amongst themselves that she was a sorceress and that he had fallen under her spell. He found it all rather amusing and simple minded, but the Celts seemed to be respectfully wary of her. Cussius thought she just might be worth exploiting in some fashion, aside from the carnal.

"I am," she said firmly, with no hint of alarm or concern. She is indeed bold, he thought, as she merely stared right back at him, her small show of defiance causing a slight smile to crease his patrician veneer.

"Beautiful night," he said softly, changing the subject but watching her delicate, upturned face. "Would you like to take a walk around the camp?" He reached out to take her by the hand again, and to his surprise, she took it without complaint but remained unmoving, her legs planted stubbornly.

"Not particularly. You did not bring me here to walk about the camp. You brought me here to talk about the Coritani," she said, to his surprise. "And if it's the Coritani you wish to talk about, that is a fine subject and one with which, you will be pleased to know, I'm well acquainted."

Cussius was a bit shocked at this explosion of wordiness coming from the girl, for she had not said more than a dozen words to him since he took her. "Please do tell," he said, surprisingly void of the condescending tone he usually reserved for a subordinate. He held up one hand, a long calloused index finger extended. "Wait. What is your name? A dialogue is always much smoother and more intimate if the parties are familiar with one another's name." He flashed the smile that had won him the companionship of many a fine lady in the more civilized confines of Rome. "You know who I am, and I know where you're from, but what are you called?" He didn't have long to wait, as she seemed eager to return the small flirtations, looking coy and sensual without trying to be so.

She allowed a smile as she warmed to his charm offensive. "I have always been called Lana." She had a subtle defiance within her, a heated energy that seemed to dwell within the depths of her eyes and welled up when summoned.

He bowed his head quickly in a symbol of acknowledgment. "And?" he asked, prodding her to elaborate and fill in some of the blanks.

"I am one of two daughters. My father betrothed me to a clan chief," she said wistfully, her voice thick with regret. "You remember him, do you not, the one you had beaten and killed?" She hesitated, moving her eyes from his to the trampled crabgrass that served as the floor.

He shrugged his shoulders nonchalantly and strode to a small table cleverly designed to fold up. It folded in half twice, one fold for the top and one fold for the legs. Some master craftsman in Rome had designed it, and Cussius had allowed it to travel with him as one small token of luxury. He filled two cups from the decanter of mead and offered her one, which she gratefully accepted and held in both hands before returning her gaze to its former location. "This is a tasty brew you Celts have mastered, but I can't see it replacing a properly distilled and aged cask of fine wine," he said as he drained half the cup, enjoying the small burn in the back of his throat and in his stomach. "As to your late husband, I don't recall making his acquaintance, but I will take your word for it. Please, be on with it," he gently urged. Though his exhibition of patience surprised him, he knew his limits.

Abruptly she shifted her gaze from the floor to his eyes again, a fiery hardness replacing the soft, deep pools of brown. "Well, I won't cry for him. He deserved that beating and more. He was a drunken lout and a poor lover, and he lacked any sort of ambition. He was quite satisfied with that heap of a village he lorded over," she said, contempt evident in her voice. "And that was to be my lot as well. I would have raised pigs and children and seen nothing more than the muddy creek and fields outside the broken-down gate." The hard look in her eyes lingered until the fire ebbed and the warm pool flowed back in with feminine ease, with grace. Finally, she tasted the drink, her eyes delighting in its simple but full taste.

Cussius' smile beamed again, and he tilted his head slightly. "Then I'm glad we could be of service to you, Lana. Perhaps you can be of further service to me; we have much to discuss, you and I," he said conspiratorially while he leaned in closer to breathe in her intoxicating scent. Her allure was magnetic, and he was certain that if they were back in Rome, her intoxicating beauty would surely work its charm on its denizens, evoking jealousy and envy from the powerful and wealthy who would vigorously scheme to secure her attentions. Of course, not one of them would have the audacity, indeed the courage, to lift her too far above her status as a slave. She might be a privileged concubine or mistress, but absolute freedom would be a fruitless dream for her.

Her eyes met his evenly and coolly. "I know we do. My dreams, the signs, the auguries — all pointed to your arrival," she said knowingly. "We have so much to discuss," she said to his knowing grin.

LANA BRACED HER back against the steeply tilted slab of granite and slid along it. She dislodged some stones that crumbled downward to the water below. She edged closer until she was perched along the precipice. She sat on the mossy outcrop of a great granite behemoth overlooking the sprawling mass of trees. Moonbeams bounced off the jumbled gray rocks piled in the ravine below. Trees grudgingly parted to give way to the twisting silver stream reflecting in the luminous light of the moon. Birds and bats rose, dipped, shrilled and skimmed over the water. Shivering in the cool of the autumn night, her heart warmed when her gaze rose to the heavenly bodies, the stars blinking in their mysterious pattern, rapping coded messages to the moon. She wondered if Jayas and Thara were looking at these very same stars, sharing a desperate embrace that only young lovers who are sure of themselves and their destiny have the audacity to enjoy. With considerable effort, she shunted the unwelcome vision aside, placing it in the corner of her spirit where the pain and sorrow would fester and tear at her soul with icy claws of envy sharp as any dagger.

She forced herself to say the prayers that had always brought her comfort. The rivers and creeks, the stars and moon she had always intimately known and embraced, and they embraced her in return. The night was clear, and the moon, a few hours up, could not have lit up the sky any brighter. She sat on the precipice until the moon neared the end of its forlorn journey across the western sky, its glow lording over creation in all its magnificence. Her concentration was great as she listened to the whispers of the wind, picking up its secrets and folding them within herself. Her slumbers of late had been troubled by spiteful spirits and looming dreams that were sinister and bloody, but her dreams were not empty of comfort. Through smoke, carnage and chaos she could detect the unfulfilled possibilities and paths not taken, but she could not shake the melancholy that filled her soul. Sadness was the thread that wove her life into a single piece. In spite of it, in spite of her immeasurable loss, destiny beckoned, for fate was the loom upon which life, the precious newly shorn wool ripe for weaving, was spun. She knew that she would ultimately rise above her current condition and triumph. She would not succumb to despair, and she knew this with clarity of determination not unknown to her line. As the earth yet turned and the heavenly constellations danced to their own music, so too would she bend the cosmos to her frolics.

Lana's dreams were not only as real as life itself; they were not distinctly apart from life in fact but intricately woven into the very fabric of reality. Her dreams were as familiar to her as the pattern of the checkered tunic wrapped around her body. Her faith had been rewarded, and for that she murmured prayers of gratitude, for she had found the instrument to bridge the gap between desolation and sorrow in the Roman who took her as his mistress. She could sense a cold-blooded absence in his psyche, but there was no denying that their destinies were intertwined. Together they would storm the gates of fate, where they would either scale its walls or perish in the attempt. She smiled as an eerie calm took hold of her being. Satisfied with what had been revealed to her, she made the walk back in the comfort of the early morning sun. She would slide into bed before the Roman knew she was gone.

CUSSIUS WOKE TO the dawn, the reddish glow of its insistent light creeping through the folds of the tent entrance, shining its warming rays on his raised bedroll. Lana lay curled beside him, her head resting atop her arm and her dark hair taking on an amber tint where the morning streaks of light found pause to rest. He studied the contours of her body, marveling at the gentle curves of her thighs that gracefully lengthened into finely shaped calves. For a moment he almost regretted the manner in which they met, but regrets were not his forte, and he would not give that a second thought — neither would Lana for that matter. She had talked much the previous night, and to his surprise he had listened patiently, gleaning much information that could prove quite useful if used cleverly.

Though Kren and his other Celtic allies were invaluable with their intimate knowledge of the land and the people, Lana actually hailed from the tribe he meant to teach a lesson for their treacherous attacks on his army. She talked half the night, at times falling into short trances, staring out the portal of the tent and swaying in a strange rhythmic motion, transfixed by the gibbous moon as she related the symbols and figures that stalked her slumbers. She said she was a seer, a prophetess of sorts, who could interpret dreams and read what the skies portended. She had talked of her home, the great village that nurtured her tender years, under the dominion and protection of a Lord Toge. She spoke of love lost and her girlish infatuation with a young warlord of the Coritani named Jayas. She spoke bitterly of his rejection, and she raged as she recounted how he rebuffed her interest in him and turned to the charms of her sister. Her misery was compounded and her fate sealed with her betrothal to her late husband, that is, until Cussius liberated her from this plight.

Cussius was truly intrigued. She reminded him of the feminine oracles spoken of in the stories his Greek tutor read to him when he was a child. The wizened tutor Milos enthralled the youngster with visions of beautiful temptresses steeped in mystical divination who had prophesied the course of heroes of yore, like Achilles and Alexander. Seated outside the gymnasium with other young Roman nobles as the stories were recounted, Cussius could not help but wonder why the great leaders and warriors would show so much deference to these seers. Battle plans and all matters of state, great and small, were subject to their interpretation and subsequent blessings or condemnation. It always seemed to him that a prophet or an oracle's prediction could easily be influenced by a generous offering to the temple's coffers. But Lana was different. She bore no resemblance to the temple priestesses of Rome he scorned as frauds and prostitutes. Her faith was fresh and pristine, void of contrivance or false piety that accompanied the great religions of Rome. Her belief brought her dreams, and her faith fortified her spirit to receive them. There was a refreshing lack of guile in her straightforward interpretation of her visions and he listened.

Dressing briskly, he breathed in the cool morning air and hurriedly gulped down a piece of flat bread and cold beefsteak. He shunned the mead poured into his cup and opted for the water freshly drawn from the nearby stream. His head was already swirling a bit from a combination of the hardy drink and Lana's mystical labors, and he wanted it clear and sharp for the day's endeavors. As he walked out of his tent, he was greeted by two of his longest serving officers, who proceeded to brief him on the state of the troops. He demanded to be provided with this report daily, as he liked to know the state of his forces, including the number wounded, sick, lame or otherwise shirking. Satisfied that his legionaries and cavalry were in order, he began a brisk walk through the encampment with his horse in tow.

Though it was the first hour of dawn, vermillion grudgingly giving way in the face of the ascending orb, the camp already bustled with disciplined activity as his men attended their duties. Horses neighed in anticipation of being watered and fed a rationed portion of oats. Latrine ditches were covered over and bedrolls secured. Weapons were checked, repaired and ground on whetstones if found dull. The smell of cooking victuals delicately mixed with the foggy mist and the night guards came in after being relieved by fresh patrols to warm themselves by the coals of small cooking fires, enjoying a simple breakfast of bacon and bread with their comrades. He was pleased to see the good humor and high morale displayed by his troops as he passed, returning their salutes with a confident grin and surety of purpose.

"Busy up boys," he shouted for their benefit. "Things are about to get interesting." Indeed they are, he thought, as he rode off with his two aides to seek out Marcus and hold council. Fate had carried him a long way, and he intended to ride it as long as he could.

CHAPTER EIGHTEEN

MARCUS WINCED AT the stab of pain that shot through his left arm. A large contusion, approximating a plum in color and size, gave him the appearance of having two elbows. He had just the remedy. He reached over and unslung the leather bag hanging from the pommel of his saddle. It was of Celt design and make, thinly worked leather capable of holding a modest amount of liquid. He unscrewed the wax cork and took a swig of the bitterly hot liquid, wincing as it burned his throat and warmed his stomach. He rubbed his elbow gently and shrugged it off, placing the pain out of his mind and no longer heeding its throb. He slung the bag back into place and resisted the urge to have another go of it. It's for the pain in my body, my elbow, Marcus assured himself. It is not near the pain that Cussius is proving himself to be, he thought grimly. Recently, the two had met in the early morn, and over a breakfast of bread and cold bacon, Cussius artfully revealed his plans for punishing the tribe that attacked Marcus' foraging party. In truth, he was all in favor of punishing those responsible for the killing of his men. He knew it must be done just as sure as an unruly child must be punished, but Cussius wanted to make all out war on this offending tribe that called themselves the Coritani, which was not within their mandate or their means. After much heated debate, including the insinuation that his manhood lacked the space for innovation, Marcus reluctantly relented to his superior officer's plans. Now, seated on his horse, he could not help but think it to be a good day for a reckoning despite his deep-rooted distrust of Cussius. Sighing in exasperation, he stole a glance at the rising sun.

"At least the signs are good," he said aloud. The deities of war were gleefully at work, and Ares and Mars were wreaking their own mischief, for the sun-bled streaks of crimson as it struggled to scuttle the night.

"What's that, sir?" asked Leko. He was busy brushing the horse he had swiped from the supply train, and from the looks of the beast, it was thoroughly enjoying the attention. Leko was proud of his acquisition and glad to be rid of the old, lop-eared mule.

"Never mind. Follow me." They rode the short distance to where the men had mustered. Assembled on the dew-laden hayfield the men patiently awaited the order to move out, their bellies full with breakfast. Low murmurs coursed through the ranks. The men knew that when Marcus ordered the camp cooks to stoke the cooking fires and serve the soldiers up proper before moving out, hard and trying times were soon to follow. Not waiting for his horse to complete its stop, he jumped off the beast and Leko quickly took the reins, the horse obedient to his gentle commands and keeping pace with Marcus' steady stroll. Walking the line, he looked his men in the eyes as he passed, sensing the pent-up aggression within his recently humbled troops. He welcomed the sensation and encouraged his troops with exhortations of his faith in them. All straightened further at his passing, their backs just a little stiffer with pride, their resolve supplemented by his calm, purposeful demeanor.

Remounting, Marcus gave the order to move out, and then he rode at the front with the ever-present Leko beside him. The journey was leisurely and uneventful despite the deadliness of their intent, and he found joy in the simple beauty of the countryside. Neat farms with tended fields gave way to rolling hills thick with forest and dotted with grassy pastures. Once in a while, they would pass a cluster of farms where whole families would sullenly glare at his troops, their daily routines thrown askew with the appearance of his professionals on the steps of war. In return, the legionaries would flash their fiercest grins in the direction of the farmers, but none dared to defy his earlier directive to leave them unmolested. Marcus was surprised to find that the sight of the women and children conjured up possibilities he knew were lost for all time, leaving his heart heavy with regret. At times, his mind would wander thus to scenes he could never enter, and in those moments, his memory would defy his self-discipline, exposing a weakness he preferred buried and eternally unacknowledged.

Looking over at Leko, he realized that he was about the young man's same age when he took to the army, and he wondered where the time had gone. It seemed not so long ago that he was the earnest bright-eyed youngster who yearned for adventure and lusted to carve a name for himself. Marcus was proud of the way the boy had handled himself in the vicious ambush. He had stood his ground and followed Marcus' orders precisely. He had the markings of a quality soldier in the making, and Marcus could not help but feel a touch of pride at the strides the boy had made. The boy even stood straighter now.

Marcus chuckled at the manner in which the boy rode the swaybacked bag of bones. The beast was barely an upgrade from the stubborn mule that had vexed Leko on a daily basis. "Hey boy. You ride that pack nag as if it were a Scythian purebred," he said. He smiled again as the orderly straightened in the saddle in response to his teasing. Even the servile manner that Leko usually adopted in the presence of other Romans had dissipated until it was all but negligible. In turn, the legionaries saw Leko in a different light. Many of the men had taken a liking to him, offering him advice, sparring with him, and teaching him the cadence of their maneuvers. They good-naturedly teased him about his wispy facial hair that yielded its meager fare every few days. They would call him over to their fires, never hesitating to share a ration of beef or to break bread with the youngster, and Leko had warmed to their bawdy jokes and listened rapturously to the tales, some tall and some true, of past campaigns full of bravery, glory and of bounty taken and fortunes lost. He became interested in their tawdry tales of lusts quenched on proper Roman prostitutes too, and of the vice and intrigue of the numerous women who followed a Roman camp. He listened late at night when a cask of wine was passed around the fire while the few married men worried about their loved ones, praying their wives and children were safe in their faraway homeland. He also watched closely as Pharmacon, their Greek physician, wrote letters home for the soldiers. Nothing avoided his attention. For him, it was all part of the adventure.

Spoken with typical Gallic aplomb, the boy merely shrugged. "It is the rider that makes the horse, not the other way around. I can get more out of this nag than a novice can the most fleet of horses. Anyhow, I would not complain. This beast's back surely beats stomping around the countryside on foot." He twisted behind and glimpsed the trudging soldiers moving under the strain of the heavy packs and weapons each bore, and he silently mouthed a prayer of thanks to the gods and to Marcus for the mount he rode. He had the typical Gallic disdain for walking, and though he could never doubt the bravery and abilities of the legionaries, he determined he would always ride to a fight if at all possible.

Marcus smiled warmly. "Well, my young friend, I have a feeling your prowess as a horseman will be roundly tested in the days to come." Thereafter conversation sputtered to a halt as the two wheeled their horses and forded the small stream where they were to regroup with a contingent of Cussius' cavalry. Atop a small grassy knoll in the near distance, Marcus could see two horsemen sitting idly on their mounts, nonchalantly watching the slow procession advance. Squinting in the bright midday sun, he barely made out the riders whirling their horses about and disappearing behind the green descent of the knob. "What did I tell you?" he said to Leko as he motioned for his outriders to close in on the vanishing horsemen. "I would bet a year's wages those are enemy scouts."

"And you'd win too," Leko replied, more sure of his eyesight than Marcus.

CHAPTER NINETEEN

Gymm sat comfortably atop his horse watching the bobbing motion of his scouts on the move. Flies buzzed around his mount, tormenting the rider as much as his horse. One landed atop Gymm's nose, and he angrily brushed it aside. The two riders came at a gallop, whipping their horses in the flanks. Sweat flew from the blows and the horses' eyes bulged in strenuous effort. The riders brought their mounts to a rude stop before dismounting and immediately heading toward Gymm.

"What of it?" he asked the two panting scouts. He could feel the excitement building in his stomach. He had been itching to get another crack at these Romans since the first battle.

If he had been leading that day, the attack would have been pressed and the enemy destroyed, and many of the men were beginning to whisper the same thing, with the subtle encouragement of some of his more conniving retainers. The warriors were tired of avoiding these Roman pigs, running scared of their blades as if they did not bleed and die as other men. He knew they did, for his sword had tasted Roman blood and thirsted for more.

Daren, the elder of the two riders, spoke first, and Gymm gave silent thanks, as the man was notorious for his brevity. "Romans, my Lord. About 400 or so on foot, some mounted, with 30 or more Bibroci scouts on the flanks." Finished, he stared blankly at Gymm.

Gymm waved them off with a nod and thought for a moment. He untied the water bag from his saddle and took a drink. For a moment, habit nearly forced him to send for Jayas, but he caught it in a net of resentment that sent flames up his cheeks in waves of searing humiliation. He would not depend on Jayas making all the decisions. He was a noble in his own right, and no warrior could boast more bravery. Gymm's thoughts wandered to the three hundred warriors his father had placed under his command. The crafty old king wanted to see if he sank or swam. If he failed, his father would probably anoint Jayas, his nephew, as heir to the kingship. Gymm understood his birthright teetered on the precipice of rescission, and he swore silently that he would not be the instrument of his own undoing. He had spied on the enemy camp, avoiding their sentries and roving patrols of horsemen, and now he would attack and prove his worthiness.

DESPITE THE RELATIVE coolness of the day, Marcus was uncomfortable. Sweat streamed underneath his armor, soaking his wool tunic and seemingly adding weight to the already considerable heft of his armor. Inexorably, the tightly packed legionaries moved forward as one. The stomp of their leather-soled feet beat a rhythm that never failed to send a shiver of purpose through his spine. The loud clank of metal and the assertive commands of the officers cascaded down the ranks. Usually, Marcus would have deployed his junior troops in the front ranks, the veterans solidly moving forward from the rear. That measure usually shored up the greener troops and kept them driving forward as trained. Such discretion proved superfluous in the matter at hand, however, as every man in the ranks was a veteran of ten or more battles. Nonetheless, he would command the center block and lead from the front, as was his duty.

Marcus chuckled to himself. If Cussius ran any later, he would miss the coming battle, but it would be immensely helpful if Cussius' cavalry were here to ride around the flanks of the enemy. The ground chosen by the enemy could not have been more to Marcus' liking, however, and upon the hasty withdrawal of the enemy scouts, Marcus moved his troops to the recently abandoned knoll. Now standing amongst the rocks, mosses and liverworts, he coolly surveyed the prospective field of battle.

The knoll itself was a decent observation point from which to survey the countryside, including the surrounding hills. The hill slanted down gently and opened up into a small valley through which the stream they had crossed earlier meandered. The wheat in the fields had already been threshed and was now winnowing. In other fields, farmers had stripped the pastureland of its bounty, and all that remained was a thick carpet of waist-high grasses that swayed uneasily in the westerly wind.

"Enemy!" screamed an alert troop. Marcus pivoted in the direction of the pointing legionary. A short distance away, a figure emerged from the fading green of the forest. Behind the figure, mild hills sloped upward to verdant woods, deep with oak and ash. Marcus smiled grimly, for he knew the forest awaited the opportunity to spew forth its content of warriors.

The solitary figure stared upward toward the waiting Romans. Marcus could just barely make out the warrior's features. He appeared to be very tall, with rippling muscles under clear white skin striped with woad. His hair glowed blond but not unnaturally so, and was thick and shaggy like a horse's mane. He had a cloak fastened at the shoulder with a brooch that reflected brightly in the sun. He rode perpendicular to the forest edge, brandishing his sword and bellowing loudly, banging shield and sword together, his voice reverberating roughly within the natural acoustics of the small valley.

"He seems quite belligerent and full of himself now, doesn't he?" said Marcus, eyebrow raised in calculation. "I can't make out what he's yelling. Is he directing that noise toward us?" he facetiously asked Leko, a playful smile on his lips.

Leko shrugged at the spectacle. "He's putting forth his bona fides. He is Gymm of the Coritani, son of the King, and he's boasting of the enemies he's bested in combat," he said for Marcus' benefit. "He's also challenging you to come out and fight him man to man, in single combat to the death." He turned to Marcus, eager to see whether or not he would accept the challenge.

Marcus gritted his teeth and a predatory grin spread across his lips. Every fiber of his being tensed as the challenge branched its taunting tentacles deep within his spirit and a primeval surge hotly coursed his veins. Though just as enthusiastic to meet the challenge issued by the boisterous enemy warrior, he maintained the stony discipline emblematic of his rank.

"Nonsense," he said to the skeptical Leko. "We fight together." He noticed Leko's expression of questioning disappointment. "I have greater responsibilities than charging out at a silly challenge issued by a half-naked barbarian. We will accept his challenge to fight, however," he said. "Tell him so, but first offer him the opportunity to surrender. Promise him he will be treated fairly."

Leko took a deep breath, filling his lungs as full as possible before yelling in the direction of the raging warrior. "My commander accepts your offer of battle, but he would rather not see brave warriors die needlessly. In an offer of friendship, he asks that you consider surrendering. No harm will befall you, and your warriors will be treated with honor. This my master has promised." As Leko finished, he stole a glance at Marcus to see if anything further should be added.

The strutting warrior leapt off his horse, again clanging his sword and shield together loudly. Jeering, he pulled down his leather trousers, grabbed his privities and gesticulated crudely in the direction of the bemused Roman ranks. Marcus shrugged. He needed no interpreter to get the gist of that response.

He tethered his horse and strode to the fore of his troops. "Sergeants! Prepare to meet the enemy! Pass the word, men, and heed it well: no one, and I mean no one, is to pursue the enemy into the forest," Marcus bellowed, his eyes furrowed menacingly. If he were the enemy warlord, he would want to draw the legionaries into the thick undergrowth in an attempt to turn the battle into a chaotic melee where Roman formations and tactics were negated.

"Advance!" Marcus yelled, the order echoing up and down the line. Suddenly, deep guttural shouts, wild screams and screeches filled the air. Horns and drums sounded behind the shrub curtain. The cacophony made the short hairs on the nape of his neck bristle as his eyes scanned the tree line for movement. He checked the ranks, and it pleased him to see his legionaries' jaws set, their eyes filled with silent determination as they methodically closed the ground. A ragged line of blue-striped warriors burst out of the bushes and dashed across the ground.

"Third and fourth ranks! Javelins!" Marcus ordered at the top of his lungs. He and the first two ranks brought their shields up as the javelins of their comrades sailed over their heads to land amongst the rapidly approaching Coritani. Most of the missiles sailed high, but enough found their mark to leave a few gaps in the line. Another warrior sprang forward, however, to fill each new space and to close up the line.

Marcus picked his first fight with a charging, wild-haired warrior. Naked aside from the blue paint, the barbarian whirled a long sword above his head, a look of furious murder mixed with glory-seeking confidence in his eyes. Marcus smiled mirthlessly, and as the warrior slashed downward, the Roman brought his shield up to deflect the strike aimed at his neck and then drove his short sword into the exposed ribs where the keen blade popped the lungs. The man gurgled, a defiant scream escaping his tortured lips. As the man crumpled to the ground, Marcus swiped his sword across the throat, severing it to the bone and silencing him forever.

The front ranks impaled their foes without mercy. Swiftly and cruelly they bludgeoned with their blades and shields and a small clot of corpses began to pile up. Leko ventured behind the first rank with his sword gripped tightly. He swiveled his head in all directions, then stuck a squalling blue-skinned youth center mass, his frenzy carrying him sheer through until the hilt of the sword rested against the warrior's ruptured chest. The youth dropped his sword in silent agony and clawed at Leko' eyes, leaving a motley collection of thick welts on his cheekbones. Leko worked the sword back out, and with it, plump tubular intestines spilled unceremoniously onto the ground. Striding forward, he discovered the ground was slick with a visceral mess of blood, organs, urine and fecal matter where dying men had lost control of bodily functions as the last of their strength ebbed helplessly into the mire. His head spinning, Leko felt sick in the gut, an uncontrollable nausea exploding up his craw until he vomited bile and coughed up clots of greenish phlegm that splashed on the twisted legs of a fallen warrior. He staggered toward the sound of more fighting, his eyes brimming involuntarily with tears, his stomach still sour, and his heart beating heavily in his throat. He could no longer see Marcus, but the agonized screams that competed with the shouts of exultation directed him to the source of the fiercely contested scrimmage. Onward he struggled, stumbling through the desperately groping hands of the wounded, battering his way in a panic- tinged hatred.

In his frenzied state, he stumbled into a knot of enemy warriors, and at the sight of him, their eyes lit up and their cruel mouths twisted in matching sneers. His chest burned with an icy heat that could only be fear as a familiar voice rose above the others.

"Grab him!" shouted the giant warrior whose earlier strutting and challenging insults precipitated the battle with the Romans. In quick bounds belying his bulk, the warrior gave chase like a wolf on the trail of a wayward lamb.

Leko immediately reversed directions and ran with all his might, unwilling to obey the spurring fear of death at the hands of the enemy warrior, until his legs felt heavy with exhaustion. He turned and vainly raised his shield, shouting defiance into the face of sure death as the flat of a sword smacked him in the back of the head, bringing him a welcome cool stillness, enveloping him in comforting silence.

CHAPTER TWENTY

A PATTERING akin to a light rain reached his ears, and a warm liquid splashed his face, rudely drawing him from his involuntary slumber. Leko tried to open his eyes, but one was swollen shut and throbbed uncontrollably in a dull pain, matching the intensity of the ache in the back of his head. Lying on his side, his shoulders pulsated in waves of pain. His arms were pulled back and tightly clasped with rough leather straps that absorbed his sweat, and he knew they would tighten further when dry. Lifting his head, his one good eye spotted the source of his misery. Standing above him, his face contorted in cruel concentration, his captor grinned as he emptied his bladder onto Leko. Leko rolled out of the path of the oncoming liquid. His tormentor laughed cruelly at the boy's evasive attempt and kicked him in the side before returning to the fire.

Leko cursed the blue-painted warrior. "You dog. If Centurion Marcus had accepted your challenge, we would be dancing on your head now." He knew he was talking to the emptiness of the night air, for the men seated around the flames paid him no heed. He struggled to find a position that would allow him some respite from his pain, but it was no use. After what seemed like hours of being unable to get comfortable, his mind sought sleep, a hidden oasis free of the pain and hunger. Oblivion proved evasive and his attempt to squelch the various sensations was laughable in the face of his disgrace. Then sleep escaped him altogether as the shame of being taken captive for the second time in his life proved more painful than the myriad cuts and bruises. Wounds of the flesh I can endure, he thought to himself. The thought that he failed in his duty to Marcus and his new band of comrades was unbearable, and a groan of despair escaped his bruised lips.

A tear squeezed itself from the corner of his eye and rolled over the contour of his swollen cheekbone, coming to rest at the corner of his mouth. As his dry tongue cleansed this salty evidence of his vanishing boyishness, a great anger coursed his soul. He struggled against his bonds, gaining nothing from his efforts aside from raw wrists. Resigned, he rolled onto his back once more, his vision fixed on the sky. The moon drifted lazily, as if it begrudged its nightly duty to traverse the heavens through the worrisome clusters of grayish clouds. The sound of many hooves approaching raised a faint hope it was Roman cavalry come to mete out righteous punishment, but as he strained into the night, he could hear the sounds of many voices, none speaking Latin, and his short-lived anticipation of rescue quickly died within his yearning chest.

ONLY THE hollow clopping of unshod hooves announced his arrival, and those around the fires leapt to their feet in unison, looking at one another uneasily. Jayas and a hundred of his sworn warriors dismounted, walking quickly to the object of their search. Every inch of Jayas's being vibrated with barely suppressed anger. His careful planning, aimed at reducing the risk to his warriors, was proving fruitful until the debacle at hand. His strategy of bleeding the invaders slowly, using ambushes and hit-and-run tactics, was now at severe risk because of Gymm's near catastrophic battle with the Romans. Out of the corner of his eye, he caught a glimpse of Thara determinedly keeping step. She had insisted on riding along, and he was actually quite relieved she was at his side. Her calm demeanor was a counterweight to his passion, and he found himself more apt to think before speaking in her presence.

The light from a ring of fires revealed a dozen wounded warriors lying on wool tunics and ox-hide pallets. Anxious warriors attended to them as best they could, dripping water into their mouths and wiping feverish foreheads with strips of damp cloth. Moss poultices mixed with spider webs were plugged into wounds torn open by sharp Roman blades. In varying states of delirium, the wounded groaned hoarsely as restless sleep competed with dark dreams, which were interrupted by spasms of pain and cries of anguish. The stench of burning flesh caused Jayas' nostrils to close instinctively as if the disgusting odor were thick, like water, and capable of the same effect, of drowning him. He looked in sympathy at a man whose left arm hung loosely from the shoulder, the elbow cauterized to close the gap his forearm formerly occupied. Ahead, pacing like a cornered wolf, his friend and cousin stood waiting to receive him.

Jayas glared at the sheepish warriors surrounding his cousin. "Leave us," he ordered. They hastened to obey, and the peripheral fires grew crowded as more warriors scurried to get out of the way of the stalking Jayas.

"Gymm. Why? Why did you do it?" he pleaded, his expression containing more hurt than rage. "How many men perished today because of your stupidity?" he asked bluntly.

"One hundred dead, and many more wounded or missing," Gymm replied, his face darkening with stubborn insolence.

Jayas recoiled at the number and closed his eyes. When he opened them again, he fixed Gymm with a look of disappointment beyond description. Nearly one third of the warriors under Gymm's command were lost. Trained warriors were not a readily available resource and this blow to their army put the tribe in mortal jeopardy.

"That's a hundred newly made widows. One hundred mothers and fathers lost their sons. One hundred brothers and sisters lost their siblings this day; and it was all completely avoidable!" He shook his head in disappointment, his anger mounting in the face of the blank look on Gymm's face. "Why!" he demanded. The urge to strike Gymm was never stronger, but he fought the impulse.

"This is not our way!" he shouted, edging closer to Gymm, who stood still as if planted in the ground. "You were not to directly engage the invaders, but to ambush them, wound them and retreat," he said. Veins bulged on the swollen cords of his neck, and little specks of spittle accompanied his words, finding roost in his untamed whiskers. The sight of his cousin sickened him at this moment, and he cringed to think the fate of the tribe could rest with him. "Did you at least manage to hurt them?" he asked, hopeful to salvage something from the day's conflict.

Embarrassed, Gymm tried to defend himself. "I chose the spot, the one we call Valley Knoll. We attempted to lure them into the forest, but the warriors could not contain themselves. They just threw themselves at the Romans," Gymm said as if events were beyond his control.

Fool, Jayas thought. "That's the precise reason we are not to battle them in the open," he said aloud, exasperation oozing from every syllable. "Why didn't you dispatch a rider to let me know? I could have brought reinforcements, helped plan this foray." Wilting under the questioning, Gymm averted his eyes, preferring to settle his gaze on the more welcoming shadows of the night.

"We could have regrouped after they broke our first charge, but their cavalry was on the way and so we retreated," Gymm said by way of explanation. Suddenly, his eyes lit up in remembrance. "But we have a valuable captive," he said triumphantly, as if this small token of recompense were a suitable salve to his previous blunders. "The personal slave of the Roman commander lies right over there," he said, pointing beyond the active light of the fires to a crumpled form lying in the shadows. "Maybe he can give us some information that we can use," Gymm said, moving in the direction of the prone boy and glad of the distraction.

THE SOUND OF HEAVY FOOTSTEPS snapped Leko out of his stupor. Walking toward him were three figures, their features obscured by the dark shadows. With the hood of their tunics pulled over their heads and the clanking of their metal weapons, Leko was reminded of the tale of the reapers. He knew that his fate could easily be sealed by a swing of their swords, and anxiety overcame him. Their gate was purposeful and his heart sank to the pit of his stomach as the suffocating squeeze of fear flexed its muscles, leaving him breathless. Bitterly, he readied himself for death, muttering the prayers his mother had taught him as a babe. Strangely, he found comfort in the rote entreaties to the unseen spirits he beseeched for succor and deliverance.

When he had regulated his breathing, Leko surveyed the trio. The earlier arrogance of the giant had been replaced by a barely contained brooding. For a second, Leko thought his mind was playing tricks with his one good eye, for another giant flanked the first. The thought crossed his mind that they must be brothers. What caught and kept his attention, however, was a distinctly female form that seemed to delicately glide upon the ground rather than walk. An open gentleness drew his hopes to fix her with his eye, silently pleading for mercy. Thankfully, this unspoken sentiment found a welcome home in her visage and he immediately relaxed to the degree possible given his circumstances.

"So this is our valued captive?" asked the newcomer, his voice full of contempt. The looking over he gave Leko was equally contemptuous, as if Leko were little more than a donkey pilfered from an enemy supply line. "What are we to do with this boy? Is this really the one you were referring to?" he asked the captor, his tone incredulous. The man chuckled meanly and shook his head, a long scar staring menacingly at the boy's open eye. "He doesn't look like a Roman. Boy, what are you?" His icy blue eyes were void of warmth and held a keen curiosity. A long scar reached down his face and traced his jaw, but it did not disfigure the man's handsome features, but rather, only served to make his features more strong and stern.

Leko decided to be truthful. He kept an eye on his captor, ready to duck any blow sent his direction, and addressed the scarred one, whom he guessed to be the leader despite the other's protestations. "I'm from the land the Romans call Gaul, across the channel," he said gesturing eastward with his head. He continued, feeling as if he had nothing to lose. "About a year ago, I was captured, taken as a slave by the commander of the Romans you fought. My father was put to the sword for the insurrection he led against the one they call Caesar," he said, his voice sad but the touch of pride still apparent.

"I was lucky. Others were sold off and transported to parts unknown, maybe to Rome or Africa. I don't know. My master, his name is Marcus, took me as his orderly, and he was teaching me how to fight," he added, straightening up as best as he could. "I was fighting when he captured me." Leko nodded in Gymm's direction.

"And?" asked the newcomer, who was bull-shouldered and thick of chest but moved lightly as though he walked on the balls of his feet. Leko privately named him Scar.

"He didn't teach you well enough, now did he?" laughed the one who had captured him, a cold sneer rapidly boring into Leko, but the big warrior stopped talking as the other shot him a disapproving look. The two men stared at one another strangely and Leko could sense the tension between them.

Abruptly, before he could continue, the beautiful woman spoke up, stepping between the two warriors and fixing Leko with a look of bemused annoyance. Youthful she was. She had fine, high cheekbones and long, dark eyelashes that curled around soft eyes. She had good white teeth that shone brightly in the mix of moonlight and flickering shadows of the many fires.

"You're the luckiest lad I know — the gods apparently favor you much. In the end, whether you are free or dead, we seem to have liberated you from your bondage," she said, turning from him to fix her fellow tribesmen with questioning glances, seeking out and finding agreement in the eyes of the scarred one. She turned back to Leko and addressed him simply. "My name is Thara. What is yours?" As she spoke, an elegant dagger appeared in her hand. Its hilt worked in equal parts iron and bronze and complimented by a small slice of amber set in the base of the blade. He felt no fear at the sight of the knife, but relief cascaded through his body as she deftly severed the leather straps binding his hands. Limbs free, he rubbed them vigorously together, noting the resurgent warmth as the numbness receded. She reached into a pouch secured to her waist and tossed him a sliver of dry stringy beef.

Taken aback by his sudden freedom and the offer of victuals, Leko asked, "Why do you offer me food?" He looked around suspiciously, sniffing the chunk of meat but finding no odor aside from the expected. Scar indifferently stared at him while the brutish one glowered as if a prized hawk had evaded a cleverly laid snare.

"Because you're hungry," replied the woman, her eyes soft and absent of guile. "Go ahead," she gently urged, "eat and regain your strength." She gestured, miming the taking of food and placing it in her mouth and chewing, smiling all the while.

Leko, unused to such temperance following the rough handling of his capture and subsequent transport, was not quick to relax, but he was truly famished. Needing no further urging, he tore into the tough jerky, and around a mouthful of partially chewed meat, he managed, "They call me Leko."

CHAPTER TWENTY-ONE

HE FELT THE dew soak into the edges of his tunic, leaving the hair on his legs matted and itchy. The earthy smell of bracken and the tang of death were heavy in his nostrils. Wafting over Marcus' face and along the undulating expanse of the hard-packed earth, a feathery vapor hovered above the stiff and tumbled bodies. The early morning sun burned off the last of the mist, which had acted as a shroud for the many dead lying about the field, and the prior day's grisly reward lay open and ripe. Blue-faced tribesmen littered the ground, their only company the ravenous hordes of flies buzzing anxiously about, descending as one in great clouds and settling upon exposed flesh like a thick black beard. Judging by the condition of the bodies, they were not the first ones to return to the scene of the battle.

Throughout the night, scavenging predators had sampled the fare and taken their due, leaving bones gleaming white and jagged, gnawed in two by snarling dogs and rutting hogs that competed with the pillaging efforts of the legionaries. Marcus expertly picked his way through the morass, stepping over the gore, uncovering a hidden face here and there in his search for the boy. He stopped a moment to evaluate the bloody mound of weapons, a jumbled assortment of shields and pieces of armor the troops had heaped together. All the corpses had already been picked clean of gold, silver and other precious objects, but that was of little concern to him.

He walked on, secure in the knowledge that all would be divided evenly, no man willing to risk the brutal punishment Marcus reserved for hording. In the confusion and chaos of yesterday's fracas, he had lost sight of Leko, and worry for the boy's possible plight gnawed at his gut. A brief glimmer of hope remained as he considered the possibility that the boy had been captured. At least he's not lying dead amongst these other poor souls, he thought grimly. Walking through the killing field, he reconstructed the battle within his mind, examining clues gleaned from the angle of the bodies.

Excluding the loss of Leko, the battle was a resounding success by any measure, he thought as he neared the edge of the darkened forest. The shrubs were torn and saplings bent with branches astray, evidence of the rough passage of many men. The charging tribesmen were cut down in waves as they wildly railed at the ranks and finally sent retreating when the sudden emergence of Cussius' cavalry smashed into their right flank. Only the thick forest and brushy undergrowth kept the pursuit from turning into a complete rout. Marcus' earlier directive barring the men from entering the forest helped maintain order among the ranks, but some of the men, probably Leko included, had entered its murky depths. In their frenzy, they had lost discipline and left the ranks, plunging into the forest after the fleeing enemy. Their bodies, around 10 so far, were found gutted and headless, left to rot by the roots of massive trees. Others were strung upside down, heads lopped off and tied between their legs, grinning in horror, open- mouthed and silent forever. Such displays of barbarity were not unknown to seasoned Roman legionnaires, and the enemy would be disappointed in these displays' lack of effect. A small part of him delighted in not discovering the boy's headless body amongst the more foolish legionnaires who had lost their lives in the wood. That much he was thankful for.

"We've checked everywhere sir," said a tired and bedraggled legionary tasked with locating Leko. "If he were killed and left on the field, we would've found him by now. He may have been captured," the soldier offered hopefully. He was just as fond of the boy as the others and had diligently attended to his search. "Don't worry, sir. The boy is so ornery that the barbarians will probably send him back. Besides, he eats so much, they won't be able to afford to keep him. The blue-faced beasts will come begging us to resupply them so they don't starve." His attempt at levity fell on deaf ears.

"Very well," Marcus said, his expression dour. The campaign must continue, he thought. "Have the men form up."

A WARM DAWN haze lifted over the field, but the moon was still out, dimly lighting a cluster of bodies in the distance that looked like clumps of shadows against the dark, trampled landscape. Cussius controlled his eager mount with his knees, nudging it forward, keeping his hands free so that he could eat his breakfast as he rode. Putting the beast at an easy canter, he reached the top of the small hill. From this vantage, he had an excellent view, and he methodically studied the terrain. He swallowed a mouthful of doughy bread whole, feeling it slide down as a slow moving lump. His attention was drawn to movement on the pasture below, and he watched as Marcus moved about the field, apparently searching for something or someone. The man looked completely at ease amongst the dividends of war, that much was evident, and he crept about the field like a specter, his hulking shadow alive in the chaos. Cussius admired the older man's attention to detail as he noted the terrain Marcus used to his advantage during the previous day's fray.

The ranks of legionaries had marched on the downward slope, and the uphill charge of the barbarians from the cover of the forest had lent a devastating advantage to the Romans. He nodded in silent salute to the distant figure. Marcus had redeemed himself, and a new confidence in his abilities was actually a boon to the troops. The man will have to be controlled, of course, like one of those ferocious Celt war dogs released to wreak havoc when necessary, he thought with a laugh.

The songs of the chirping birds filled the air, strangely out of place with the grisly scene on the valley floor. Despite the many bodies polluting the grounds, here would be as fine a place as any to camp and he meant to build here, to construct a base of operations. A more permanent symbol of his presence on this land was obligatory and should be started as soon as possible, he decided. He thought of the seven ancient hills of Rome, and his mind wandered to the great founding families and the winding streets and many coves of the city, the meandering ways and broad avenues of the Palatine where lived the old families — such as the Julii, and the Brutii, and not least of all Romulus — who had dominated the ancient realty by right of conquest. These families had built their estates and palaces in the most desirable locales, strategically positioned for maximum grandeur, symbols of power impossible to ignore. None of this was lost on him as he surveyed the gore-stained valley floor.

In his experience, the location of a man's house was a direct reflection of his prominence and wealth. For a moment his ears burned at memories of other times, times before he was in control of his destiny. He could still feel the scorn and hear the rumors and cruel jokes other youngsters poured on him after his father's death, and the near destitute state in which he and his mother found themselves. His father's many creditors had laid claim to much of his property, leaving his widow and young Cussius little better than country squires squatting in a smallish estate, yielding only an education and an appointment in the army. Even the appointment had seemed out of reach, however, and his mother had to grovel and beg, scrape together every denarri and jewel in her name to secure his position as ensign to his older and thrice-removed cousin, Julius Caesar. In a detached sense, he now understood. The right of power was as true for the pompous senators back home as it was for the tanners and drovers who dwelled in much less opulence than their betters — the less power you had the less easy your route to a better life. For Cussius, the whole issue resolved to where a man's house was situated, and he surmised the notion to be universal. Even the barbarian peoples of this island wisely chose geographically advantageous positions upon which to settle. Breathing deeply, he inhaled the smell of the earth, which was tantalizingly different from the frequent stenches of the city. The stink seemed to devise new methods of evading the cleverest attempts of the city engineers to eradicate it.

"This is it," he said aloud. His eyes were aglow with the thrill of possibility, and a restless energy kept his mind busy. Roman and Celt shall meet here, he determined. The knoll was wide and large, naturally sloping downward to the edge of the forests and split by the winding creek to form a small valley that, in most other times he thought, must be beautiful in its natural state. Here, he could forge his legacy. These immediate surroundings would form the backbone of his holdings, he determined with growing certainty. The various shades of greenery were in stark contrast to his memories of a more arid Rome, and it was evident the grounds produced ample bounty and the fields would be all the more fertile with the blood spilled on it, he thought grimly but with no remorse. His practiced eye calculated the resources of the immediate vicinity, and he easily envisioned the changes a little Roman sweat and industry could bring. Plentiful wood could be harvested from the surrounding forest for construction projects, and it pleased him that logistics would not be a problem. The thinning of the forests would also serve to deprive the creeping enemy tribesman cover, affording a little more protection from the raids he was sure would come. The clear running stream provided a fresh water supply, and wells could be dug farther out. He was satisfied with his conclusion.

"Do you see what I see?" he asked, turning his attention to his companion who, wrapped in a tunic against the chill of the early morn, sat silently on a small brown pony.

The voice resonated, borne aloft melodically in reply. "I see the proud laid low. I see waste where there should be plenty." There was sadness in the face and tone of the speaker that betrayed the outward look of satisfaction, which gave Cussius slight pause.

Suddenly, he snorted in amusement. "Oh, I agree wholeheartedly," he said with a wicked grin. "But worry not. Waste will not be an issue, and you are correct in presuming that this is a land of plenty, for those with the right and the might to make it so." He kicked his horse and rode down the hill to counsel with Marcus.

CHAPTER TWENTY-TWO

Thara looked down into the dusky valley at the sparkle of the swiftly flowing stream behind the gently waving shrubs dotting the banks. She walked with her head lowered, weary and bone tired from the constant movement and stress of the war campaign. Her clothes were caked stiff with days-old sweat, and a rank mustiness accompanied her movements. She pined for the hearth, the stone dugout lined with hot rocks and the warm refreshing water of her home. She needed a bath and ached to scrub her flesh clean. She yearned to wash and dry her hair properly. Kicking off her boots, she laid aside her bundle and bow as she approached the small but fast-flowing creek. She silently debated disrobing completely but decided to kill two birds with one stone and jumped in, clothes and all, for a speedy scrub job. She felt the slick, rounded stones with her bare feet and probed ahead for depth. Then grabbing handfuls of sand and small river pebbles, she rubbed them vigorously over her body in quick brushing motions, kneading the clothes empty of filth. She then laid down in the current and allowed its swiftness to carry the dirt and grime from her body and clothes, enjoying the cleansing sensation but gritting her teeth against the chill of the stream. With strong, sure, overhand strokes, she swam to the eastern bank of the stream, her soaked clothing now a burden, and floated in a small eddy where the current was weak. Spotting a long smooth rock, she slid upon its surface to allow the sun and breeze to dry her sore and tired body.

She had just started to doze when two powerful arms wrapped around her, lifting her gently and setting her on her feet. Her eyes sprung open, and the smiling face of Jayas met her gaze. She was glad to see a hint of the boyishness remained in him, and she returned his scolding smile with one of her own.

"Why would you wander off from camp without letting us know? I could have been one of those nasty Romans, and then where would you be," he teased, his eyes twinkling mischievously. He looked at her differently since they had entered this campaign together, seeing someone with fire in her heart and lucidity in her thoughts.

She crinkled her nose in mock disgust. "I'm sorry to say it, but your smell betrayed you. I'm sure no Roman would smell like an old musty goat hide. It could only have been you," she exclaimed as she playfully slapped his meaty arm.

Laughing heartily, he bowed in a gesture of respect. "You have a point. But I would rather think that I smell more like a horse than an old goat," he retorted, sniffing himself in feigned concern.

He then stopped laughing and cleared his throat, his tone turning serious. "I speak of the boy. What do you make of all this? I mean, you've spent three days talking with this Roman servant boy. Has anything useful come of it?" he asked. He gestured for her to walk with him. Desiring to be helpful and somewhat atone for his intrusion on her nap, he handed her boots to her. He wanted to talk and he always felt more comfortable while in motion and was already moving from the creek bed. The weight of the past few days' events had shaken his confidence but not his resolve, and he liked the quiet of the forest when mulling over a serious issue.

"He's taken the name of Leko, and he is not Roman. He's Gallic, which means a Celt in his own right, and you were the same age, I do believe, when you considered yourself a man," she said, smiling at the memory of a younger Jayas feeling his oats and strutting about after his first raid. Actually, it wasn't that long ago, she thought. "But he has a strange sense of allegiance to his Roman master, the one they call Marcus." She pulled on her boots and secured her quiver and pouch before catching up the few steps between them.

Jayas was keenly interested, and his eyes narrowed as a name finally attached to the man who was proving to be a bane to the welfare of his people. "What of him?" he impatiently asked of her, ducking under a low-hanging branch and lifting it to allow her easier passage.

She reached up and plucked an apple, looking it over for weevils and worms before tossing it to Jayas, who caught it and nodded his thanks. She grabbed another and repeated the process before taking a bite and sucking on the sweet juice of the sticky pulp. With her throat soothed, she continued. "He says the man is honest and merciful, but that he is ruthless when necessary. This Marcus has survived many battles in many wars, and according to the boy, he is a master of war. Interesting mix of traits when you think of it." She had her own doubts at the veracity of all Leko had told her, but she did not doubt his account of the Roman, which could not all be boyish fascination because events to date proved otherwise.

Jayas shrugged. "Interesting traits. Another warlord is all. Just what our fair island needs," he said sarcastically in an attempt to ward off the uneasiness settling in his stomach. The loss of lives at Gymm's disastrous endeavor deepened his sense of worry, and a frown punched its way to the fore. He said nothing further and waited for her to continue, a little ashamed that his nervousness was laid bare for her to witness.

"According to Leko, Marcus is subordinate to another Roman, the one who leads the Roman cavalry. He is called Cussius," she said, doing her best to mimic the name as pronounced by Leko.

Jayas' eyes opened in surprise at this bit of news. He knew of the cavalry force and had scrimmaged here and there with its patrols, careful to keep the bulk of his troops from between the Roman foot and horse forces. "Are their politics anything similar to ours?" he wondered aloud as he finished the apple and tossed the whittled core into the brush. A part of him still hurt from Gymm's betrayal. Only pride and envy could have forced his cousin to act without even consulting him. A tension had simmered under the surface for the past few years, but he always held out hope that, somehow, they were special and would not succumb to the seemingly inevitable jealousies that pitted family against family. Their fathers had managed to avoid it, so why couldn't they?

"Is that all? What about numbers, supplies, their intentions and long term goals? Could you wring any of that out of the slave?" Jayas asked.

"He doesn't elaborate and I don't press him. I figure if he wants to tell me, he's going to in his own time. He's confused. As I said before, he's quite fond of the Roman, named Marcus."

"I have ways of making him talk," Jayas said ominously.

Thara slapped his arm. "As do I. Now leave it alone," she said playfully.

Through a break in the trees he spotted curling tendrils of smoke from the camp. There was a silhouette of dark gray against a canopy of blue and white, and it stubbornly persisted until the crosswinds gusted and erased its passage. He slowed his walk, thankful for the silence and enjoying the company and counsel of the strange Thara. He was baffled at how she always used to make him nervous and bumble about like an awkward young stallion approaching a watchful mare for the first time. The irony was not lost upon him that he now found thoughtfulness and calm to be the foremost of her laudable qualities.

He could always count on her to get to the heart of the matter. "We need to know everything about these people. The more we know of them, the better the chance their weaknesses will be exposed."

The shadow of a hawk swooped over the two, and Jayas swore he could almost feel the air move with the beat of its wings. Thara noticed it too. It was a powerful symbol. He made his decision.

"I will send word of my intentions to Father and the king, but I think it's time we got much closer to these Romans," he said. He shook his head in her direction. "Not in the manner you're thinking. I know I have no mandate to commit our tribe to anything." Thara just stared, the expression on her face still questioning. "Ok. I will need to meet both my father and the king in council, but I think we must send some sort of emissary to these invaders and it must be soon. We must at least stall them so that we can continue to strengthen ourselves. I need to get up close and gain the measure of these fellows for myself."

Thara nodded, pleased with his analysis and restraint.

With his clarity of purpose renewed, the rejuvenated Jayas grabbed her hand and playfully jogged the last few yards to the edge of the camp. Now to make it happen, he thought.

JAYAS LEANED HEAVILY against the thick wooden post, patiently waiting for the obligatory pomp and niceties to be exchanged. The smell coming from the cooking fires cramped his belly painfully, and for a quick moment, the smell of the rich food almost made him nauseous. He struggled to gain control of his racing thoughts and rumbling stomach, uncomfortable with the damp heat of the council room. The crowd excitedly thronged its walls, and rough voices of varying pitch competed with each other, shouts, accusations and theories bantered back and forth in a disorganized fashion that made it difficult to hear any of the speakers. Slaves moved to and fro busily attending to the ample thirsts of the men, filling cups to the brim with copious amounts of mead and ale. Jayas held his hand over the rim of his cup, waving off an attendant who tried to fill it, signaling that he would take water instead. Though he would have welcomed the mead's calming effect, he wanted a clear head for what was to come, preferring to be unsullied in thought and tongue.

Despite the belligerent hunger pangs, he would gladly have foregone the luxuries of the fare being prepared in exchange for being out of the presence of the bickering and scheming nobles. It was at times such as these that he longed for the feel of the wind in his face and the muscled mobility of a horse ranging on the open lands. He was all too familiar with his naivety and simpleminded approach to complex tribal issues, and with every passing day he gained an appreciation for the depth of Thara's understanding of these issues, but he had little patience for the games and grand-standing beloved by the nobles. He strived to listen rather than speak, to reveal little in the presence of so many with dubious agendas.

He let his gaze roam about the large room. Two extra tables abutted the feasting table, gobbling up much of the available space. The scent of spilled ale and roasting meat hung in the air, noticeable despite the musty odors of so many in such a confined space. The highest-ranking nobles were in attendance, their eyes mocking in silent laughter despite the gravity of the moment. His father was seated next to the king, and Gymm sat brooding at his side. A trusted adviser or the first-borne son accompanied every other dignitary, all adorned in their finest attire, their golden torcs polished and gleaming in the firelight, their leather breastplates freshly shined and oiled. Jayas had barely time to splash some water on his face and wipe his hands clean, let alone seek out finer attire for this council business. He looked down at his trousers and frowned. They were filthy with dirt, dried blood and the salty staleness of his sweat. His frown grew as he glimpsed his faded boots, the sides coated with a drying layer of bog mud. He shrugged. At least my mind is clear, and my conscience is free of complicated entwinements, he thought.

A servant passed by bearing roasted mutton and game bird seared on a slender stick, their tips blackened by the fire. Jayas hungrily plucked one and nodded his thanks. He chewed and swallowed the tender morsels in two huge bites. When the food hit the table, there was scant attention paid to decorum, but the nobles waited until the king took his selection before they descended upon the spread as if the famine spirits were on their tails. Jayas chuckled. The feasting table was more like a raiding party swooping down on an unsuspecting farmstead than a council taking its repast. These were men of vast appetites.

Conversation slowed as mouths were stuffed full with salted meats, pickled fish, roasted beef shanks simmered in their own broth and boiled turnips. Hot loaves of wheat bread were torn in two and passed amongst the feasting men. Occasional grunts were interrupted by belches and gratified sighs of the nobles who, when sated, leaned back with sword belts a little more snug than before. Suddenly, the king stood up and the room came quickly to a respectful silence, all eyes on their declared leader.

Despite his years, the King was still broad of shoulder and thick around the chest. His waist had not yet taken too much of a liking to his ample diet, and his eyes still held the keen, calculating wit that had borne him to the fore amongst equals. Five years senior to Lord Toge, his head was massive and covered with long gray hair streaked with black and plaited into what looked very much like twisted twin horse manes. He wore a loose fitting wool shirt of diamond twill weave with the sleeves rolled up and finely woven wool trousers tucked loosely into the tops of elegant leather boots stained a rustic brown. His bare arms, still muscular, bore scars from knife and club, and his fingers were twisted from breaks that never healed straight. For ten years he had led the tribe, ruling the confederated clans and ensuring peace and justice within the ranks. He kept the outlander tribes from trespassing and raiding his people, and he was respected for his iron will, his good sense and the fact that the folk had undoubtedly prospered under his helm.

He smiled, showing a full set of teeth uncommon for a man of his years. "Friends. Clansmen. Welcome," he said, his voice laden with phlegm. He hacked and coughed, pulling a rag from his belt and spitting a wad of reddish mucous into its folds. He waved off the concerned looks of the others. "The changing seasons, my boys!" he roared. "I wish we were meeting under different circumstances, but the winds of want are a fickle master." He sighed. Clasping a hand on Gymm's shoulder, he gave it a squeeze and searched the room until locking his gaze on that of Jayas.

"Our warriors have been busy, engaging these Romans and their Celtic lapdogs. I hear they have been brave in the face of the enemy and have many new boasts to make." The nobles banged their cups on the table and many shouts of approval rang out. The king raised his arms for silence.

"I also hear that many warriors did not make it home," he said questioningly, staring straight at Jayas. His eyes flashed. "We do not waste the lives of our warriors! How many have we lost so far? Somebody tell me," he demanded, looking around the room at the silent nobles who struggled to avoid his glare.

Jayas did not shrink back into the recesses of the fire's shadow. He met the king's ire and returned it with equal fervor in his own glare. "One hundred and twenty have perished, my Lord. I'm sure you have already seen the wounded. I am not a healer so I cannot say how they will turn out. We have acquitted ourselves, though. We have done our duty and did so with honor. We have not shirked our tasks, but good plans sometimes meet with disapproval by the enemy." He had rehearsed these words and was glad of it, for his confident delivery made him seem more poised than he actually felt. Gymm sat sullenly next to the king, his eyes flickering back and forth between his father and Jayas.

Quiet murmurs and stares met these words. Jayas began to think he had said the wrong thing. The Coritani believed luck played a role in everything, particularly war. Being lucky was one of the most important virtues of being a war leader. His face began to burn, but he managed to control his outrage at the accusatory looks shooting in his direction. He wanted to blurt out that Gymm had led the disastrous expedition against the Romans, but he was sure that was common knowledge. It would only sound like he was ducking responsibility, and so he let the thought drop. Lord Toge stared ahead impassively, his jaw set and eyes unreadable, watching the exchange between his son and elder brother.

"You are quite right, nephew. You can make every preparation for success, but in the chaos of war, the best plans fall apart; and more times than not, victory or defeat depend on chance," the King said, once again clapping Gymm on the back. The mood of the room lightened a bit at the change in the king's demeanor.

He continued, his tone grave and voice raspy. "In all my time as your chief, your king, we have never faced a threat as grave as this. I remember my father's father telling us stories when we were wee boys," he said gesturing to Lord Toge. "Stories of the times our clan fought the invaders from the Isle of Eyre. The pale, reddish fiends stormed our fair lands while the women and children cowered in their huts, took refuge in the caves and forests, and scampered about in fear at the mention of these invaders, who were many and fierce and came to take what was ours." He paused, closing his fist and pressing it against his chest before pointing at the listening nobles. "And you know what? We're still here. That was the moral of the story. And still we shall be here after these Romans," he said, pounding his fist into his open palm in emphasis. Again the room erupted in cheers and shouts of agreement.

He gestured toward Jayas, beckoning him to come forward and take his seat at the table. "Nephew, I have already spoken with my son, Gymm, on these matters. What say you? What have you learned of the enemy? How may we defeat them?" He paid Jayas a great honor by this request, and the gesture was not lost on those assembled. Gymm's eyes narrowed a bit, however, and Jayas noticed a few others stiffened at this query, as well.

"The stories you have heard are true, my Lord. The Romans excel at warfare." Hoots of derision sounded and others hushed them so they could hear Jayas out.

"It's true. They are organized and work together as one. Rarely will a warrior find himself in single combat against them. They march and fight in ranks, with one man's shield covering themselves and the others. Their swords are shorter than ours, and they thrust and stab rather than slashing and battering as we fight with a blade." These keen observations caught their attention. Though all were seasoned warriors and leaders of their own retinue, none had yet fought the invaders, and they now hung on every word as Jayas described the enemy. "They use spears, throwing them as one so that a great shadow crosses the sky with their flight." He paused a second. It was here where he would make his pitch for a little restraint and gain permission to seek a parley. He gathered himself and continued, his confidence on the rise.

"We know the names of their commanders. We know they are warriors and leaders who are not easily deterred, and their intent seems obvious. Before I left to hasten to this meeting, my scouts informed me of curious developments at the Valley Knoll." He looked at Gymm and saw him wince slightly at the mention of the name.

"The report baffled me, and so I went to investigate for myself. Myself and…" Jayas stopped, catching himself before he blurted out the fact that Thara accompanied him. "Myself and another rode through the forest. We left our horses tied in a shallow cave under the creek bank and made the rest of the way on foot. We eluded their patrols and crept to the edge of the wood."

The king looked impatient, and so Jayas got to the point. "They are building. Trees are being felled and ditches dug. The houses being erected are made of wood but built like a block. I saw many boards being pared, and sections of fence were being laid out between these houses." The nobles exchanged worried looks. More and more the Roman presence on their lands sounded like invasion and settlement and less and less like a transitory war.

The king exploded in fury. "We have not been defeated and yet they dare to build and settle on our lands. Arrogant bastards!" he fumed, the color returning to his cheeks in a furious rush of anger. "This new battlement will burn to the ground. I swear it." His eyes contained a deadly glint, and the force of his will was felt by all.

"That is my fervent prayer," Jayas added, nodding respectfully to his uncle. "But before we burn this new fortification, should we not make our own preparations? Should we not improve the defenses of our own hillforts, fortify our farmsteads and hoard our foodstuffs and livestock? For this, we need more time."

The king still stood in place, his hand stroking his peppered moustache, curling the ends of it absentmindedly, mulling over the position. "Time is a luxury for certain, and we have not sat idly by while you and your young warriors harried the invaders," he said pointedly. "But wouldn't a delay play into the hands of the Romans? Shouldn't we bring the full weight of our forces against them now before they become too entrenched?"

"The timing is not right, my Lord. If you would see fit to send an emissary to these invaders, maybe we can maneuver the time and place of our meeting in battle to our advantage. What would it hurt to seek an audience with their leaders? We might seek to lull them, to probe their weaknesses and then strike when they are least prepared." Jayas and Thara had worked over the plan, and he silently thanked the gods for her insight as he awaited a response.

The nobles talked amongst themselves and arguments for and against his proposition were put forth in equal passion. Finally, the king called for silence. "You show maturity of vision, young Jayas, son of my brother, so I will you grant you this wish. You shall approach these Romans under protection of truce. Discover what you will." The king had spoken, and it was decided.

Jayas felt a small thrill and his pulse quickened. Some of the nobles exchanged troubled glances, their envy evident, and signs of distrust lurked behind their guarded eyes. Jayas bowed. "Your will be done, my Lord," he said. He took his leave, the eyes of Gymm and others boring into his departing back as he exited the council.

CHAPTER TWENTY-THREE

HE STOOD IN the middle of the tree-lined path, wholly unconcerned with the oncoming rush of man and horse, his thin frame silhouetted in the moonlight, his dark eyes glinting like a cat. "Whoa!" Alarmed, Jayas yelled to his mount as he rounded the curve and spotted the man. He yanked hard on the reigns and swerved around the obstacle. Leaping off, he ran back, his eyes wide in puzzled anger as he recognized the cause of his unexpected detour.

He threw up his hands. "Are you trying to get killed? Are you finally too old and tired to stay in this world any longer?" he asked Rhu, flabbergasted but relieved at his horse's sensitivity to his commands. "Are you now an ancient old man who has seen too much of life?"

Rhu shrugged as if it were of no consequence. His eyes were warm and friendly and beheld Jayas calmly. "The answer to your first question is no. As for the second, I do find myself tiring easier these days, but these old legs keep taking me around this life." Again he shrugged. "Who am I to question what the gods have ordained? If I was no longer needed in this world, you would have trampled me to death, but your mount swerved, and here we are." He smiled and patted the warrior on the arm, finished with the subject.

Instantly, the old man's visage changed and his eyes hardened — the warmth vanished. "You go to the invaders, do you not?" Rhu asked flatly. He walked past Jayas in quick shuffling strides, heading toward the disinterested steed patiently awaiting its rider's return. He took hold of the sensitive ear and whispered for a moment before grabbing the horse by its strong jaws and bringing the equine face to his own. He laughed at some unseen folly and turned to the young man. "Good horse," he said appreciatively.

Jayas nodded his agreement. "He is, and I am going to meet with the Romans. It has been decided. I have the king's instructions." Jayas awaited the druid's response while intently watching the strange interaction between horse and priest.

The priest's face contorted in pain as if an invisible blade had sliced into his stomach. "The stench of their presence befouls the spirits of our land, and every minute it remains is an insult, an offense of the highest order. This plague must be eliminated lest it overcome us all," he warned, his eyes boring through Jayas.

Again Jayas nodded. "I agree." He felt privileged to see Rhu giving frequent thought to their previous visit together. He often wondered what became of him after the priest left abruptly in his peculiar fashion of coming and going without warning. He thought of camp. Thara would be pleased to see her great-uncle in good health. He was pleased as well.

Rhu returned his attention to the steed, stroking its muscular shoulders and rubbing its neck softly. "Beware of the men you meet. Beware of the men you know. Both conceal dual certainties that are contrary to our people's wellbeing. Study the heart of your enemy so that you may know his mind. Some of these hearts you already know and others you have yet to discover," he said. Rhu walked over to a moss-covered oak, carefully taking hold of a snippet of mistletoe that had leached upon the trunk. He smiled, grunting happily at his discovery, and carefully stowed it in an old floppy pouch tied around his waist.

Jayas was more than a bit puzzled. The old man spoke in riddles and though he thought he got the gist of what he had just said, one could never be sure. "I shall be wary."

Rhu snorted. "You better be more than wary. You must be clever like the fox and as cunning as a wolf, which is what you are," he said assuredly. "I see it in you, as do others. My niece serves with you, does she not? She is a special one, that girl. She and her sister are both gifted," he said forlornly, a trace of worry wrinkling the timeless face. The memory of the ruined village and his missing niece was reawakened and the pang of loss tightened his chest.

Jayas allowed a smile. "Thara is indeed with us. A willful woman she is, and gifted for sure. I have found myself coming to rely on her more and more," he said unashamedly. Staring at the man's profile, he examined it closely in the soft light of the moon, peeling away the layer of years and sighting the familial resemblance. "They both favor you in a way," Jayas thought out loud.

Rhu chuckled and mumbled something that Jayas didn't quite catch. "Ah, that is good. If she were born under a different star, who knows? She may have risen to be king or a great leader of men. Alas, it was not to be, as the heavens do not always heed the whims of folk," the old man said. He pointed to the sky. "The moon-father hurries, and so must we." He waited by the horse, looking expectantly at the warrior.

Jayas mounted the animal, and leaning over, he strongly grasped the old man's bony arm and brought the priest effortlessly aboard. "Yah!" he commanded, and the horse and its riders put to gallop, intent on covering the remaining distance to the camp before the first pink streaks of light crept across the eastern horizon.

SHE WOKE FROM her slumber early, her sleep uneasy and fitful ever since Jayas left to seek counsel with the King. In the pink-silver light before dawn, the camp was still asleep, but she busied herself stoking the cooking fires, fetching water from the nearby stream and checking on the wounded. She changed dressings on sutured wounds and sniffed purplish-looking flesh to check for the rotting spirit that could sweep through a man in mere days, killing the victim in feverish anguish if not checked. She woke Leko early as well, his grumbles at being awakened before the sun emerged falling on unsympathetic ears.

She stood with one hand on her hip and with the other splashed water on the boy's face. All the swelling had subsided from his eye, a remnant of purple the only reminder of his wound. She nudged him with her foot. "No wonder you Gauls were whipped by the Romans. You probably slept right through the battles," she teased the grousing youth. "Come on now. Jayas returns today, and he won't be pleased with any dawdling."

The youth feigned an expression of hurt, his mouth pouting. "I was up late, helping you with the wounded, cutting your wood and dragging around buckets of water, remember? For the love of the gods, we just went to sleep." Leko bit his lip as if embarrassed. His complaints actually lacked merit, for the youth more than willingly mirrored her movements as she ventured about the camp. Some of the warriors took to teasing him, bestowing upon him the pet name of Shadow.

Thara noticed the wisps of hair sprouting above his top lip. "You've stopped scraping your whole face clean. I like it. Before you know it, you'll remember who you are." She could tell he had taken to her, but she was not yet convinced his loyalty spread to the tribe as a whole. It had only been two weeks since his capture, and she could sense his distraction at times, and she assumed he was thinking of his master and his former comrades in arms. Of course, he was not allowed to carry a weapon, and she noticed frequent glances of envy he shot at the finer blades some of the better-heeled warriors wore. She was pleased he had not attempted to escape, and it was not for want of opportunity either. He enjoyed freedom of movement about the camp and could have stolen away at any moment unnoticed. She liked him and hoped he would stay with the tribe of his own volition.

A familiar voice rang out behind her. "Too much sleep may lay you deep. I wouldn't loaf too much, youngster. If you do, you may miss your fortune." The old man smiled deeply, his willowy arms held wide.

She whirled around. "Uncle Rhu!" Thara exclaimed, a smile as bright as the emerging sun fixed upon her delicate face. She dropped the goatskin water bag on top of Leko and ran into her uncle's arms. She pressed her cheek into his chest and squeezed him tightly. "I've missed you. Why didn't you say goodbye your last visit?" She grinned at him, fully aware of his impulsive nature and knowing that he answered to no one.

"Easy my dear, easy. I'm an old man. These old bones can't take a mobbing from a spry lass such as you." He smiled at her gently while patting her softly on the head.

He appeared ageless, his deep-set eyes peering from under shaggy brows. Crows' feet danced around his eyes, mapping his face with trails of worry and wonder. His unflappable manner, his worn and tattered tunic and its myriad stains, and his enigmatic patterns of speech remained unchanged throughout the years, and that comforted her. His beard flew in all directions, wonderfully wild and bushy like a duck's nest. As children, she and Lana were convinced that a colony of shoats took up residence in its tangled confines, and they would giggle uncontrollably as he threatened to shake it out.

She beamed. "Uncle, it is so good to see you. Come, please have a seat." She shooed Leko out of the way with a wave of her hands, and the youth stumbled nervously over the water bag, nearly upending himself in the process. She grabbed the softened ox hide cover that Leko slept on and placed it near the fire pit, smoothing it out on the hard-packed ground.

"Let me prepare you something to eat while you warm yourself by the fire." She ladled a cup of ale, dark and sweet, and pressed it into his hand. "Are you hungry? I have some young goat, killed and grilled just yesterday," she asked hopefully, familiar with his liking of the tender meat.

He smiled, his few teeth showing white from beneath the mess of hair. "I must decline," Rhu replied, his gaze returning to fix upon the open mouthed youth who had risen hurriedly to his feet. "I am fasting."

"Fasting!" she exclaimed. "At your age? You can't weigh much more than me." She looked at him with an expression of concern on her face. She knew better than to argue with him. Though at times his whims and actions seemed random, he knew and saw things she was not yet privy to.

"The body needs cleansed," he said simply. "Deprivation strengthens the spirit and prepares the mind and body for the rigors ahead. You know this." He pointed at the youth silently watching from the side of the fire and beckoned him with a gnarled finger. "Come here."

Leko approached as directed but apprehensively. As dark eyes under beetling brows bored into him, Leko blinked and tried to look away, but the eyes held him motionless. He was riveted by the ancient one who moved so deftly despite the apparent cloak of many years he wore. The old one had the bearing of a healer or a holy man, and he reminded Leko of old Alen, the priest who conducted his people's ancient rites at the festival of the summer solstice. He hastened to obey, not willing to risk the ire of those glinting eyes. He bent at the waist in respectful greeting, straightening and willing himself to meet the mysterious gaze of Thara's uncle.

"You are not of this land, but you have the look of the people," Rhu stated flatly. He critically searched the youth's face, like one would when seeking out a long lost friend from a crowded marketplace.

Leko nodded, nervousness causing him to grunt in reply. He felt as though he had swallowed an apple whole, and the fruit had lodged in his throat and refused to come up or go down. "The land of my birth is across the great water," he managed.

Rhu reached out and took Leko' wrists in a surprisingly strong grip. The old man turned Leko' hands over, palms up. "The rhythm of life beats strong in this one," he said to Thara. Staring into the youth's eyes, he continued. "To which drum does it beat? Listen to your heart boy. It will lead you to the right path as surely as the great star in the northern skies leads the hunter at night."

Leko' confusion deepened and he stammered, "I w-w-ill," not sure of what else to say.

"Good," the uncle said briskly. "He shall accompany Jayas to meet the invaders," he said, turning once again to his niece.

At the mention of meeting the "invaders," Leko's heart leapt in nervous anticipation. "The Romans? When?" He croaked. His mouth immediately dried out and his tongue clung to the roof of his mouth.

"Today of course," said Rhu.

CHAPTER TWENTY-FOUR

THE SKY GLOWED orange under the press of the twilight sun, and the tireless energy on which he always counted started to wane. Still Cussius moved about the large enclosure, bouncing from project to project. He checked on the masons to ensure they had rock, mortar and straw and he then spoke with the blacksmiths, commenting on the quality of their work. He slapped backs and shouted words of encouragement as he strode determinedly from station to station. Leading by example, he stripped off his shirt and jumped in the work line, passing stones and pales of dirt from man to man. He dove into the work and worked up a lather of sweat.

Pausing for a moment, he wiped the sweat from his face and took a swig of water offered by the attentive orderly. It had been a long day, and yet the camp still bustled with activity. The men hurried about, some furiously digging the forward trench deeper while others hauled the newly dug dirt to add to the rising ramparts. The sounds of saw and axe cutting into thick round trunks brought him satisfaction, and he made a mental note to reward the men for their efforts.

"Remo," Cussius said, grabbing the burly orderly hauling fresh water to the work crews. The young legionary stopped, still holding the two wooden pales, his meaty arms straining at the effort and the water dangerously close to spilling over the edges with his abrupt halt.

"Yes, General?" His tone was respectful despite the weight of his load, but the pull of the water was finally too much and he gently lowered the buckets, careful not to spill the contents.

"Pass the order on to the quartermaster: All men on the work crews are to draw double rations. Tell him not to skimp on the ale either. The men have more than earned it." A grin split Remo's face as he saluted. He then rushed off to finish his circuit and locate the quartermaster.

The past week and a half had sped by with alarming alacrity, but it had been well spent. Four blockhouses were finished, complete with fighting platforms from which squads of men could rally to repel climbers. Two-thirds of the wall neared completion, with twenty-foot tall oaks providing the impressive sections. He found it surprising that the Coritani had not launched a major assault on his position, but he was nonetheless relieved they contained their troublesome meddling to accosting his patrols.

"General!" a voice shouted above the racket. He tried to ignore it, absorbed as he was in his labors, but he knew he had to answer. Showing his irritation, Cussius swiveled his head in the direction of the cry. Kren was briskly walking his way leading a heavily lathered mount by the reins.

"What of it, man? Speak your mind. We have a lot still to do and little light left to us," Cussius watched a team of packhorses haul another large trunk into place as a hustling squad slopped a thick layer of plaster on the finished section that, when hardened, would make it more difficult for an enemy to set the walls ablaze with flaming projectiles.

"We have company," Kren stated, his mood gloomy. "We were patrolling only about a mile distant from here when contact was made."

Cussius raised his brows in mock alarm. "We shall sound the horn then. Rally a force and send it out," he said, looking around for an orderly.

Kren shook his head. "Not a war band. There was no fight. A holy man sought me out. A druid." Kren was noticeably bothered, and Cussius felt like rolling his eyes at this primitive superstition but restrained himself as he thought of Lana and her visions.

He nodded sagely. "A holy man. Interesting. And what did this holy man want?"

Kren looked around nervously. "He said two men seek to parley with you, and he asks you to grant them safe passage according to the ancient customs." Kren's heart contained a great hatred for the Coritani, but he paled at the thought of violating a truce council. "It is the way of the tribes for parleys to be honored, most especially when a druid requests it."

Cussius was unimpressed. "It is the custom of all noble people to grant safe ingress and egress for any party traveling under a flag of truce," he said diplomatically. "No harm will befall these emissaries, on my honor. When can we expect our fellow combatants?" he asked.

"They are already here." Kren pointed to the edges of the forest, now farther away after the troops cut a considerable number of trees for building material.

Surprised at this revelation, Cussius strained his eyes as he tried to make out what Kren was pointing at. Seeing nothing but smoothly shorn stumps and the brushy thickness of the spreading forest, he turned back to face his barbarian ally and sighed in exasperation. He wished he were fresher and not bleary eyed and tired from all the distractions and demands of his position. No matter, he thought. In truth, he looked forward to meeting his foes in a more congenial setting. There would be ample opportunity for the opposing forces to fight it out pending the outcome of the parley. He was reminded of his younger years, and through the web of memories the words of his old tutor came to him as he briefly reminisced. His face craggy and eyes perpetually squinting from a lifetime of studying scrolls by candlelight, old Milos would recall the tales of the ancients, the conquerors of old and their paths to greatness. These lessons in history and the martial arts were the only saving grace of his studies, and Cussius had sat enthralled, listening and asking questions of the old Greek. He discovered a common theme ran throughout, and its import did not evade him. The greatness of the heroes of old lay in that of their adversaries, he thought.

"So be it." He looked around for his messenger and spotted him near the horses swinging a large maul, the impact sending the wooden post down a few inches. "Magnus!" he yelled, his voice carrying wide. The young legionary came at a sprint, pulling up and saluting sharply, his face shiny with sweat from his labors. "Locate Primus Ordines Marcus and have him report to me immediately," he ordered.

THE SUN WAS FADING AND he moved confidently through the shadows, taking purposeful strides. His head held straight, he paid scant attention to the curious onlookers who paused from their labors just long enough to cast questioning glares. He carried himself like a warrior in the dawn of his prime, eyes alert and appraising. His sword swayed comfortably at his belt and had been freshly oiled to stay loose in its scabbard. His trousers were fine, cleaned and embroidered with intricate swirling patterns. He wore no armor, only a loose fitting wool shirt with sleeves that stopped below his elbows, revealing the muscled cords and tanned sinew of his powerful forearms. His blond hair was plaited in one thick braid and fell past his full shoulders. His companion was more youthful and wore simpler garb and no sword belt, his face lacking the full moustache of the larger man. Unlike the large warrior, the youth appeared pensive and uneasy, his head turning left and right, scanning the troops as if searching for a waiting face.

The sentries on duty watched them approach, and most of them stiffened uneasily, forming a rough line across the lane as the two moved into their midst. One legionary, tall and with broad shoulders and a course head of hair, stood in the center of the lane, directly in the duo's path. The guard stared, his jeering, challenging sneer revealing an alternating row of jagged teeth. The others nudged one another and made crude jokes accompanied by course laughter meant to provoke the barbarian warrior. A laugh boomed from the mouth of the jagged-tooth guard as he caught the end of one of the malicious jibes.

The guard's head was cocked in challenge. "I don't know. How 'bout I just ask him?" he said, his eyes narrowing cruelly. He was almost as tall as the Celt standing before him and more than dwarfed the youth. "That's quite a scar you have there. What happened? Did the goat you were buggering turn around and horn you? Or maybe it was that pretty young thing there?" he said, pointing to the youth. He laughed meanly, the merriment not mirrored in his piggish eyes.

The big warrior turned to his companion, questioning and murmuring something in Celt. After the youth finished the translation, redness began to spread on the Celt's face, but his tongue remained steadfastly held. He made to walk past the soldier but stopped abruptly when the beefy soldier drew his sword, placing his other hand on the chest of the Celt.

The guard smiled evilly, his mouth curled in a sneer. "Where do you think you're going? This is Roman ground. You just don't go gallivanting in here as if you own it." He laughed at this, appreciating the irony.

His eyes now turned cold as a winter night, the Celt waited, his thick legs slightly bent, arms loose, a strange determined smile playing on his lips as he looked down at the splayed hand touching his body. Suddenly, he twisted and grabbed the guard's wrist with his left hand and with his right he delivered a bruising blow to the jutting jaw of the soldier followed by a looping uppercut into the man's beefy gut. A loud *swoosh* of air exploded from stunned lips as the man gasped and then looked skyward, his eyes rolling wildly. The sword slipped from his grasp and fell to the ground with a thud. Then he was at his knees, pitching facedown into the muck, silent and still. All of the Romans stood planted, mouths open, their eyes locked on the man an instant before shields were grabbed and swords drawn and the guards fanned out in a closing semi-circle. They approached him as they would when nearing a rabid dog. Their eyes narrowed with murderous intent, they slowed their cautious stalk.

"Halt!" a commanding voice called out. "Don't move!" The Celt swung his head in the direction of the voice, spotting the speaker at the entrance of a central building of simple construction.

"Not you," the man said gesturing in his direction. "Sheathe your weapons this instant!" he commanded the soldiers. "Whoever fails to do so dies right here, right now." The confused legionaries looked at one another but none ventured to disobey the order. Obviously disappointed but without any grumbling, the soldiers slid their blades into their scabbards.

ALL WAS UTTERLY still as she peered from the recesses of the darkened room, taking in the scene unfolding a short distance away in the failing light of the day. She gasped as the face turned in her direction, the scar visible even at this distance. As Jayas strode toward the central blockhouse in the company of Roman soldiers, Lana warily eyed his every step. She locked eyes with him, and like embers smoldering too long under ash, the flame of yesteryear was reawakened by the winds of chance. She silenced the pain, forcing a guarded look upon her face and revealing nothing. He nodded in recognition, the look of baffled surprise plastered on his face quickly fading to a blank stare.

Lana hurriedly scurried further into the shadows, a small bit of panic rising within. She looked around the austere room, the wood still green and smelling strongly of fresh-cut oak. Torches were lit and the flames crackled, casting flickering light that competed with the encroaching stealth of darkness. Jayas and the Romans accompanying him were almost at the doorway, and she whirled about, throwing aside the canvas curtain dividing the spacious dwelling. Ever so delicately, she pulled aside a small corner of the divider, peering out from the darkened confines of the uninhabited room.

CHAPTER TWENTY-FIVE

THE ROMANS STOOD, arms crossed, their faces inscrutable, flanked by two Celtic clan leaders, their eyes flashing in the light cast by the torches. They paused in their glaring at Jayas only long enough to speak with one another and then to whisper in the ear of the taller of the two Romans. Jayas ignored their accusatory glares and looked around the room instead, taking in the sturdy log construction that was much different from the round design favored by his people. He found it rather interesting. Instead of thinner lengths of wood meant to bend, the Romans used logs stacked on top of each other and placed in snug precut notches. The gaps in the logs were filled with a hardened substance that dried a dirty white. The structure was large and airy and scarcely furnished with fires burning on opposite sides of the room. A clever, sensible design, he thought.

There was minimal smoke, and the scent of the freshly hewed wood overpowered all other odors. He noticed the canvas hide pulled down, sectioning off a portion that he presumed to be private quarters. Leko stood next to him, his nervousness revealing itself as he shifted from foot to foot, cleared his throat and refused to meet the eyes of the Romans.

The tall one spoke first and with little ceremony. "Welcome to my home. I am Cussius Caesar of the Julii, commander of the forces of Rome in Britannia," he said, smiling and raising his hand in greeting. Jayas was surprised but managed to contain it. The man's accent was thick but he spoke a passable version of his language. The speaker was tall and rangy with a stringy muscularity and could not have been much more than five years his senior. His eyes were void of malice, but they held something he could not quite put his finger on. They were neither hot nor cold, but merely appraising, as he peered with obvious interest at him.

Jayas bristled at the Roman's audacity of calling this his home, but he held his anger at bay and met the Roman's gaze evenly, nodding and grunting something he hoped sounded like a greeting. He realized that Cussius was studying him with the same care used when one reaches out to pet a strange dog.

The man smiled brightly. "I apologize. I have studied your language and am beginning to process it quite nicely, though some of the nuances elude me. I am usually a quick study, but I did not quite catch what you said," Cussius stated before changing subjects midstride. "I almost forgot. This is Marcus Rulus, Centurion of the Highest Order," he said grandly and with a sweeping gesture of the hand. The man named Marcus nodded curtly and did not speak.

"And my tongue-tied friend, you must be Jayas of the Coritani. I have heard much about you." Cussius moved toward Jayas, hands out, showing that he had no weapon, and as he did so he turned to a waiting orderly standing at parade rest, arms folded in the small of his back, head straight and unmoving. "Bring us wine. We must receive our distinguished guests in proper fashion. I've been saving this cask for a special occasion, and this most assuredly qualifies. Hurry now. Our guests must be thirsty after their travels. I would not like to think myself a poor host," he said in magnanimous fashion.

The orderly hastened to comply, expertly filling brass cups with a dark red liquid and serving each present. Cussius raised his in silent salute, sipping it first and then swigging it back. "If there's anything I regret about this land it is the lack of quality wine. Ah, in España some of the finest grapes are grown, and from them masters of the noble craft come up with this devilish concoction." He smacked his lips appreciatively. "The soil of Gaul seems to support its growth as well. Here, I'm not so sure. Time will tell." He smiled matter-of-factly.

Jayas stood rooted, appreciating the import of the seemingly innocuous statement. "This is not my favorite drink. I prefer the simple stoutness of a dark ale, more bitter than sweet, though no doubt you are right in one respect: this soil is not suited for the introduction of strange plant forms. Forgive me if I spoke too quickly. You are correct in that I am Jayas of the Coritani, son of Lord Toge and nephew to the king. I bring you tidings from the king. He wishes you good health and a long life," he lied with a straight face.

The general had a pretty good imitation of concern on his face. "Likewise, and I hope I find you just as well. Outside, earlier, my men meant no offense. The troops, in their zeal to carry out their duty, sometimes fail to stop and think. Please be assured the culprits will be punished accordingly," he said, sighing in resignation. "Well, you sought this truce, so custom dictates you state your purpose. Wait a second. Who is your young friend there? That face looks familiar." Cussius leaned in, his eyes intensely studying the boy as Marcus took three long strides and whispered furiously in his commander's ear. "Yes. I remember now," he said. "Your slave, the orderly." The Centurion backed away.

Jayas spoke quickly. "My king desires to know your intent. He asks why you invade lands that have long known peace. He asks why you kill his people and steal from him. Why do you take our women and children, and finally, why do you build here?" It was a mouthful, and at first he thought the Roman did not catch all of it.

One of the Celts could not hold his tongue. His face reddened significantly from the combined effects of the wine and Jayas' words, he stepped forward. "Lands that have known peace? Hah! That's some nerve you have. You talk about peace while your tribe has raided, killed, and stolen from my people for generations. The nerve..." He stopped when he noticed Cussius' stony glare and stepped back reluctantly, his jaw set firmly and his neck taut.

"He speaks out of turn, and it won't happen again," Cussius said coldly, pointing to a round wooden stool. "Please, sit. Not you, slave. You can stand or sit on the floor for all I care, but only free men of good birth sit at this table." That was a far stretch of the truth as he and Lana dined nightly at the table. The boy glared in return, his cheeks crimson and eyes unblinking.

Cussius looked around impatiently. "Bring us food! I find it vulgar and uncivilized to conduct diplomacy on an empty stomach, don't you agree?"

Jayas remained unperturbed. He was not hungry, but it would be impolite to refuse. Neither could he be sure that poison did not dwell in the drink and food, however. Rhu had warned him of such treachery, but he discounted the notion when he remembered that Lana was here. He had spotted her inside this very building, and if such treacherous deeds were afoot, she would surely alert him somehow. He shook his head in agreement. "A man could do worse, I suppose. If you are offering dinner, then I accept." He pointed a beefy arm behind him. "My companion would be hungry and we ask that your generosity extend to him as well."

Addressing his commander but looking at Leko, Marcus spoke up. "He will eat. He has the appetite of two legionaries, but the blessings of youth leave none of its trace upon him. You look well Leko," he said, his voice neutral and baritone flat. He took his seat at the table, the stool disappearing under his bulk.

Leko nodded, his gaze locked on the floor.

The two Celts followed suit, introducing themselves and sitting down ready to eat. "Kegan of the Bibroci," said the one guilty of the earlier outburst. "That is Kren of the Trinovante," he said, nodding toward the burly, squarely built clan leader to his left.

Jayas smiled thinly. "I know of you. I believe we have crossed paths in the past, and here we are once again."

"We eat," Cussius said as two sweating orderlies laid out a simple meal of leavened bread and beefsteak. "Forgive the simplicity of the meal. We are but simple soldiers and your unexpected arrival did not allow time for the preparation of a suitable feast." He smiled behind hooded eyes, reached in the basket and took a loaf. After splitting it in half, he tossed one section to Jayas.

The strange-smelling bread made Jayas' moustache twitch as he shifted slightly in his seat. The Roman beef and bread were almost as good as the versions that came out of his mother's kitchen. His earlier reluctance aside, he tore into the meal with the same fervor as his hosts. Around a mouthful of beef, Jayas probed. "How far is your homeland from here, and where are the many soldiers with whom you fought the Catuvellauni? It would seem you are here alone, in a strange land inhabited by a people unlike you, people who did not invite you. Neither did you enter our lands seeking friendship. No, you came but to take and leave blood, it seems."

Jayas had thought he was stating the obvious, but the silence that greeted his words made him realize his simplistic approach may not have been the best. He could remember watching the nobles speak with one another, exchanging greetings, tales and debates, all jockeying for positions of wealth and influence; and rarely during one of these spirited skirmishes of council did any party reveal the depth and breadth of his knowledge of the other. Jayas wished he could take back what he had said, but his words were as surely gone as an arrow shot from a drawn bow. Oh well, he thought, I must be true to my nature. He wondered if Cussius and the others would do likewise.

A murmur went through the watching men, and their eyes glittered like those of wolves watching at the edge of sight around a campfire. Cussius smiled, a tight controlled curve of the lip. "My homeland, you ask? Rome is the center of the world, the place where all the nations of the known world do business and to which all nations pay homage," he said grandly. "And we are not alone. Delude yourself at your own peril, but do you so easily discount the brave and loyal Trinovante and Bibroci warriors who have united under my banner?" He spoke slowly from behind an impassive front, the challenge accepted. "We are not so different, you and I. Our people are not so different. Human nature, despite the wearing upon it of literacy, religion and the like, remains consistent. I have seen this as a child in my native Rome. I have seen it in España and Gaul, and I embrace the notion once again on this soil — we are here because of our strength of arms. It is as simple as that. If you and your tribe were able, you would evict us accordingly and this would be a moot exercise." He smiled wolfishly, his canines glinting in the light of the flames, shrugged and leaned back.

Jayas took a moment to digest what was said. Inwardly he boiled. His anger stemmed from the truth in the man's words, and he fought to keep his expression blank. "You may be here, but we control the countryside," he said defiantly. He recognized how weak that sounded and opted for silence. Behind him, he could hear Leko swallowing hard and shifting from foot to foot, his meal completed and his nervousness rushing back.

This must have touched a nerve with Marcus, for he sat forward abruptly and stared hard at Jayas. For a moment there was utter silence in the room. It was broken by the gruff voice of Cussius. "Do you?" he snorted. "How so? We go where we will, and none have had the stones to stand in our way aside from the energetic effort you have put forth on this very spot." This last remark he said to gall and provoke, and from the way that Jayas' body stiffened, he knew the effort was rewarded. "But must we be enemies? I think not," he acceded with a nod of his head.

It was Jayas' turn to snort. "Friends? Friends do not treat one another so. Friends exchange gifts in respect and do not offer half-truths and trickery with words." He bit his tongue and his face reddened in embarrassment. He knew he had jumped at the goading and the Roman was now needling him. "What kind of friendship? How would either of us benefit from such an association?" Jayas then asked in his straightforward fashion.

"Isn't peace a reward unto itself?" Cussius asked in reply. He took a hard swallow from his cup and rose from the table. Jayas watched his every move, as did the rest of the men in the room. The torches were burning low and the shadows danced on the men's faces, mixing with the slice of moonlight that crept through the open door. Cussius paced the shadows as he spoke. "You benefit by living peacefully, without fear of marauding savages bent on killing and enslaving your people. Your children can play in the meadows and swim in the streams without fear. Your cattle, goats and sheep can grow fat without fear of the skulking wolf. You will reap the harvest from your fields of wheat and hay without concern that malicious parties are stalking about. That is the benefit of peace with Rome, peace with us." Cussius' face showed nothing save what he wished.

Jayas was appalled at the audacity of the Roman, but he responded with slow, careful calm. "We appreciate your concern for the welfare of our young ones, for our crops and herds, but do not worry yourself about them for they are well tended. My king and his warriors ensure the safety and security of the folk." Jayas drew a deep breath and continued, knowing that what he would say would be laughed off or taken as a challenge. Either way, they would know where he stood. "Please be assured. If you were to leave, we would guarantee that no harm befell you in your journey to the coast or back to the lands of your Celtic allies. We will even provide an escort, if you so desire." Jayas took another bite of bread and chewed as he waited for a response from the staring faces.

Leaning forward on a beefy elbow, Marcus gained the floor with the force of his presence. His face worked into a sour sneer, and the man bristled with hostility despite his apparent attempt to be civil. He began to speak but finally leaned over and whispered intensely into the angled ear of Cussius.

Cussius nodded and murmured to the squarely built Roman, encouraging him to voice his idea. "Words are empty without some action lending them import. You are a man of action, that much I can tell. I admire and respect that, but I am not a diplomat, merely an old soldier of Rome. My commanding officer is the warrior and diplomat," he said without any hint of condescension in his tone. "However, I proffer this: How can we trust your goodwill without any assurances you would see them through? Why not show us? For instance, why not return the boy as a sign of your good will?" he said, nodding in the direction of Leko, who remained standing behind the seated Jayas. Marcus continued. "Make the first gesture. Let us gauge the sincerity of your actions as opposed to your words." Marcus stood, his bushy eyebrows furrowed intently as he studied Jayas and Leko.

There was a long pause. For his part, Leko stood uncomfortably still, trying to avoid eye contact with any and all in the room. A look of confused distraction came upon his youthful face.

Jayas turned his focus to Marcus, his brow drawn in an expression of suspicion. The man had the bulging shoulders and thick wrists indicative of a soldier who wielded shield and sword as a way of life. His hair was cropped short, his eyes sharp and dark brown, and his blocky face was clean-shaven. Jayas stared into Marcus' black pupils. He responded, "One gesture would beget a reciprocal gesture on your part, I presume. In the spirit of compromise and mutual goodwill, we would entertain the return of the youth. However, we would ask the same of you. Return the one called Lana." He knew he was gambling with the facts as he was not absolutely certain that the face peering at him previously had been Lana's, but this was surely a way to flush out the truth.

He noticed Cussius react with a slight hitch at the mention of Lana, but the Roman quickly regained his composure before answering. "Such gestures render a bounteous harvest without the necessity of tilling the soil and planting the seed. The exchange of prisoners and taking of hostages are time honored customs, albeit customs that usually culminate the terms and conditions of a negotiation. I'm afraid we have not worked out any such, and hence, it would be premature to even bandy about such terms." His eyes sought those of Marcus and the message was conveyed: stay silent. The big man pressed his lips together as if his words were bitter on his tongue, and Jayas thought he detected a slight rise in the man's ruddiness. He pressed further, his earlier suspicion confirmed.

"So the one we call Lana is here," he said while taking a closer look around the spacious room. Once again his eyes were drawn to the canvas room divider.

Cussius remained unmoved, his face as blank as a writing slate set in front of an unlettered man. Suddenly he moved, stepping closer to Jayas, pausing to give Leko a thorough examination like a Syrian horse trader gauging the value of a breed with questionable bloodlines. "You presuppose many things, and you forget one important facet of negotiation. You can only ask for concessions from a position of strength." He jabbed the air as if he were an orator pounding home the last few nails in the coffin of an overmatched opponent.

His grin feral, Cussius continued. "As a practical matter, the results of any negotiation are practically preordained, or at the least predictable, based on the polar opposite situations of the aggrieved parties. Negotiation is not as difficult as reading the stars or deciphering mathematical formulas like Pythagoras' theorem. Quite simply and most important, one must know where one stands in the equation. You see, if you failed to realize this fact during the course of our advance, let me remind you. We are in the position of strength and you are not. Therefore, you do not dictate terms and you do not toss speculation around as if it's a child's doll." He smiled coldly, any vestige of the warmth and charm he earlier exuded vanishing like the hastily consumed meal set before them moments before.

Marcus' hard dark eyes met Jayas' gaze for a moment, and then darted away in the studied disinterest of a man insulting another in the most civil of fashions.

Jayas bristled. "It would seem our conference is concluded. I believe we will take our leave," he said over his shoulder to the youth standing behind him. Now was the moment of truth. They could kill him and take the youth, or they could hold Jayas hostage, which was not an unheard of practice. He and the boy could also walk out with honor, as befits emissaries. All these thoughts competed for validity in the span of a heartbeat. He stood up from the table and bowed respectfully, his back rigid. He half expected a sword blow to his neck, but the moment passed and he silently let a sigh of relief pass his lips.

Though he felt like a bear must when cornered by a hunter's hounds, a sense of curious anticipation materialized beneath his anxiety. He stopped at the door and turned to face his enemies. "Next time we meet there will be no flag of truce."

Malicious smiles and glowering looks met his words before Cussius spoke one last time. "*Veritas*," he said in his native tongue. "The next time we meet, it will not be the hand of friendship that is extended. You have been witness to the warmth and generosity of the Roman heart. But that is past for you. Hence you will receive the cold, indifferent edge of the blade. That much I promise you, and I am a man of my word."

The two warriors merely glared at one another with the understanding that an unspoken pact was brokered. "Go now. This is the last time you come or go in peace," Cussius said with eerie finality. No further prodding needed, Jayas and Leko slipped out the door under the translucent glow of the moon.

CHAPTER TWENTY-SIX

"LANA!" CUSSIUS YELLED. It had not been more than thirty heartbeats since the emissaries left. Marcus looked up, startled by the suddenness of the cry. Marcus saw the canvas curtain part and a vision as pure and stunning as the statuesque Aphrodite met his eyes. Her beauty was raw and untainted, her smooth skin drawn over high cheekbones, and her voluminous eyes reflected in the muted torches like obsidian. Her dress was simple but well maintained, and her hair gleamed with the strange oils she worked into it. A gentle pink shone upon her cheekbones and her long black eye lashes framed sparkling almond-colored eyes. Her small, slightly tilted nose was lifted proudly, accentuating the daintiness of her jaw line. She was not smiling, but neither was there any trace of sadness. This was the one the troops were whispering about, the Celtic sorceress who supposedly had an uncanny hold on their commander.

He watched as she gracefully entered and weaved her way through the shadows, and Marcus noted the fearful glances nevertheless filled with lust shot her direction by the men. Cussius held out his hand and took hers in his. He kicked a chair out and pulled it closer to the table, lowering the beauty onto the stool. After a brief pause in thought, Cussius looked up.

"Kren and Kegan, please retire for the evening. Check on your men. Get some rest. You're going to need it," Cussius said in his dismissive tone.

The two Celts needed no prodding. They entertained a healthy fear of Lana, wholeheartedly believing her to be a bewitcher of some kind. They hastily stood up and bowed deeply to both Cussius and Lana before turning on their heels and disappearing through the door and into the night.

These gestures did not sit well with Marcus. She was a mere slave, and yet the men scraped and groveled as if she were Helen of Troy and neglected to even venture a salute in his direction. He sighed. Evidence of the breakdown of Roman ethos, he thought, a reversion to barbarism. He shuddered to think of the possibilities.

"Marcus, you may stay," Cussius subtly demanded while pointing to the stool. "Sit. We have much to discuss." But his gaze seemed to find only the girl, and Marcus was a mere afterthought.

His eyes dancing merrily, Cussius fully turned his attention to Lana. "What did you think of our emissaries? Will they attack? Did you sense a weakness in the man?" Cussius asked. He reached for the amphora of wine, poured a hearty portion in a cup and passed it to the woman. He then piled a plate high with bread and beef and slid it in front of her, encouraging her to eat.

Marcus was fascinated and mildly repulsed by the spectacle at the same instant. It did not sit well that the commander of the Roman forces was cavorting intimately with a native barbarian woman. Worse still, it appeared as if he actually sought the counsel of the woman. This blatant display left him flabbergasted. He fully expected to be asked his opinion on the parley, but here he found himself subjected to watching his commander serve the woman and seek her advice.

Marcus fought to keep his face expressionless and decided to play along. "Why yes. Please tell us," he added politely. Uncomfortable, he drained the sweet wine and waited for its dulling effects to take hold. He expected some sort of shenanigans, perhaps chants or prayers, but he was disappointed.

The woman was contentedly chewing on a piece of beef placed between two slices of clay oven-baked bread. She swallowed hard and took a drink of the wine. She cleared her throat, oblivious to the waiting Romans. She drank again, this time much deeper.

Suddenly she spoke. "He is as I remember him: haughty, arrogant and full of pride. He contained much of what he wished to display, though at times he struggled like a caged wolf in order to retain control. He is quickly learning to be a leader, and he believes in himself. More than that, his warriors believe in him. Men like that are a dangerous lot, but fate dogs them indiscriminately." She was speaking directly to Cussius though occasionally she would venture a short glance in Marcus' direction to include him in the conversation.

Her voice low, she continued. "His greatest strength may also be his greatest weakness," she said mysteriously before taking another bite, easily tearing the morsel with straight, even teeth. She chewed methodically, like the cattle seen grazing the plains.

Cussius was intrigued. Marcus could tell the man was almost intoxicated with the experience, and he wondered if he had been into his cups before the parlay. She continued, breaking him from his reverie. "The last battle was not led by Jayas. Did you know that, Marcus?" She turned and addressed Marcus directly, capturing his gaze with a serenity that seemed to mine the depths of his spirit.

Marcus took a moment to slake his thirst. He shared a private laugh as he thought of Cussius bribing Caesar's quartermaster for the wagonload of wine. The finest example of leadership the man has displayed thus far, he thought with a half-grin. The woman's voice snapped him to and brought him back to the subject at hand. "Is that so? This Jayas looked awfully like the belligerent fellow who roused the whole ruckus in the first place," he replied, knowing this Jayas held himself differently than the warrior who challenged him at the battle of Valley Knoll. Both were tall and strongly built with bright yellow hair, but this one had a distinctive scar that the warrior at the second battle did not have. A flicker of memory brought Marcus back to the raid of a few weeks ago. Yes, he thought. Jayas is probably the big one who started that ambush. "Eerie resemblance then," he added.

Lana continued as if he had not spoken. "Gymm was the warleader who opposed you here. He is the king's son, heir apparent to the throne — if it were not for Jayas, that is." She smiled and returned to her food. Meticulously picking at the beef, she left the fat untouched with her measured nibbles.

Cussius stood up, a hard edge in his voice and a malicious glint ricocheting off the waning light cast by the dimming torches. "So our native hero would be King if this and if that..." Cussius paused to imbibe the sweet violet wine, swishing it in his mouth appreciatively before swallowing. "Is there bad blood between the two?" he asked brusquely, holding up the decanter and gesturing toward Marcus with it.

Marcus thought Lana seemed to be enjoying herself, toying with them as she did the food. "Jayas is a natural leader of warriors. He has always excelled and Gymm has not. They act like best friends, the closest of cousins, but I know better. A dark and bitter seed was swallowed by Gymm, his pride, wounded many times throughout the years by the adoration Jayas received while Gymm wallowed in his shadow. The battle between your foot soldiers and Gymm will most likely be the last he leads. Gymm has much shame, and now he has cause to hate you Romans and Jayas as well. The implications are obvious." Her cold matter-of-fact delivery made the hair stand up on the back of Marcus' neck.

Marcus looked over at Cussius. He was now stroking his chin, his eyes alight with a faraway gaze, one that could seemingly peer through the sturdy log walls and penetrate the depths of the forest.

Cussius leaned in. "Marcus," he said, reaching over and grabbing him by the shoulders. "Find this Gymm for me. Have Kren and Kegan bring him to me, but tell them not to ruffle him too badly. Appeal to his vanity. Lie, but get him to me somehow. Do it quickly." He released his grip on Marcus' shoulders.

"You are dismissed," Cussius said with a flip of his hand, dismissing Marcus as if he warranted nothing more.

The dupe's attention is already back on that slave whore of his, thought Marcus. Magic and spirit talk could all rot in Hades. He immediately wanted to take back the thought. To insult the native gods in their own lands meant certain ill luck. He warily watched the sorceress as he backed out of the building and into the moonlight.

Stepping into the cool night air, Marcus was glad to leave the company of his commander and the strange woman who made him feel wildly attracted and repulsed simultaneously. He walked around the rapidly growing fort, and then he climbed to the highest rampart, which faced northwesterly and afforded a view of the valley slope and the edge of the inhospitable forest. He saw what probably was a red deer on the edge of the forest, but he found himself wondering if it might really be Jayas and the boy crawling on the edges, prying with spying eyes. He looked up at the stars and knew they provided sufficient light for the boy on his path through the dark forest. He grimaced. During the parley the boy made no indication whatsoever as to his wishes. He couldn't tell whether he wanted to come back or stay with the barbarians. He was unreadable, which both bothered Marcus and made him proud. No matter, he thought. He would kill Jayas and Leko would return. They would collect the tribute from Cassivellaunus and return to Rome. "Or maybe not," he thought aloud to the dark of night. Maybe Cussius is on to something.

He walked the perimeter of the fort and checked on the sentries. As he ensured torches were lit and that fire guards patrolled the makeshift barracks, he thought of Rome. It had been ten long years since he stepped foot on its hallowed ground, ten years since he walked amongst its people, strolled the markets, attended the theaters and conducted business in the forum. Not that he had much occasion or means to do so. His brothers and sisters long ago stopped answering his letters, and he felt out of step with Rome itself. The long gap in communication with his loved ones troubled him. Maybe they died of the plague or the pox. Maybe they moved away. Perhaps they thought him dead and buried on some faraway battlefield. Who knew? His parents were long dead as he was informed in the last letter received from his brother Altos, five years ago. The others? Maybe they just didn't care and had forgotten about him. He had been gone for a long time. He shrugged and continued the walking. His solitary walk was the simplest of pleasures, and he enjoyed the briskness of the air on his exposed skin and how it cleared his head after the warm stuffiness of the cabin.

Marcus climbed a tower parapet and spoke briefly with the legionary on duty who kept look on the recently completed bridge overland. He then made his way to the very top and gazed down into the curving stream. The moonlight was a dazzling silver streak on the water as it drifted slowly onward. Staring into the sky he could see the same stars he would gaze at as the son of a cattle drover on their simple stead on the outskirts of Rome a lifetime ago. The memory was almost unreal, as if it never really happened. The moon was halfway out but brightened the cloudless sky nonetheless. He sighed. He was tired. For the first time in his life, he thought of retirement, but the thought left him anxious and unsure. He thought of all the promises, of how Caesar had promised him, campaign after campaign and battle after battle, fertile lands of his choosing. He said he would raise us up, Marcus thought bitterly.

"And now I have nothing," he said to the riverbed below. He unslung the goatskin flask nestled on his side, unscrewed the cap, and took a long, hearty draught of the fiery liquid as he said a silent blessing for the Celtic stiller who stoked this firewater. He drank deeply, and the more he drank, the stronger his melancholy took root.

The back of his throat burned and the liquid warmth spread throughout his body like a welcome old friend. It was a rare occasion when he would unhinge his iron discipline and truly dip into the cups, but when he did, he did it right. Unfortunately, this gloomy island had a way of gouging away at him and the cups had been pouring at an alarming rate as a result. It was usually better if he were alone, for experience taught, always through hindsight, that he did not make a jolly inebriant.

He inhaled deeply through his mouth, tasting the crisp moistness of the island air. Why can't this be home, he thought shamefully. I fought for it, bled for it, and suffered loss on this grim island. Good comrades lay buried in the ground and the ashes of others spread into the soil. Though the place was settled, it wasn't overly so. This land was as good as any he'd seen in Africa, Greece,

Spain or Gaul. This whole expedition had made little sense thus far, but he started to warm to the concept of staying put. After all, what do I have to return to, he thought as he climbed back down? He found himself walking behind the main lodge where earlier the parley had taken place. He stopped, for he felt a bit lightheaded, and he shook his head to clear it. Pressed against the building, deep in the shadows cast by the lone standing giant oak, a figure could be made out. Distinctly, he could make out the outline of a person, slight in stature, with a face partially covered by a hood. He walked on the balls of his feet, carefully placing one foot in front of another, much like a cat would when stalking a mouse. He closed the distance.

LANA ENJOYED THE crispness of the night-chilled air. She stood tucked in the shadows, finding warmth in their dark embrace. She had witnessed the entire parley, studying the profile of the arrogant young noble as he did his best to keep up with Cussius. Her anger ran hot as she thought of his audacity to request her in a prisoner exchange. How dare he, she thought. It was another slap in the face, another example of someone else trying to dictate her future. Never again would she be shuttled off to some swineherd's so-called estates to serve as a docile handmaiden to a greasy and foul sub-chief. Those days were behind her. No, she thought, I dreamed them.

She stared up at the Great Hunter in the sky asking him that the spears of the Roman army fly true. She prayed for drought in spring, for a cold winter in which the drifts would be twice the height of a sizable man. She longed to see her enemies humbled, their abodes burned and violated. She would only be satisfied when they suffered the same indignities she did when they shunted her away to the frontier. She wanted to see them come crawling back, seeking surrender and begging for mercy. She wanted to see the looks on their faces and witness their sneers of derision give way to mingled fear and respect before they supplicated themselves. This she dreamed as well, for her eyes could see far. They always could.

Her uncle said she had been touched by the gods and he had fretted about it for as long as she could remember. He would caution her and urge restraint, patience, torturing her with tales of woe associated with acting otherwise, as if her gifts were a detriment. It was obvious he did not want her to develop them, but that only served to make her strive all the harder. Her sister Thara could see too, and her gift was nurtured and coaxed like a spring bulb reluctant to blossom. While her family doted on her sister and entertained her fancies, Lana was forgotten, an outcast in her own home, the echoes of Rhu's warnings filling her heart with anxieties. She began taking to the woods at night, hiking the deep hollows that were pitch dark, massive oaks forming a tightly weaved roof. The tribe whispered of strange beings lurking in their depths, of troubled spirits wandering the steep crevasses, and foragers spoke hauntingly of the screams from past sacrifices that still lingered. Shepherds would avoid these places, their livestock gladly veering away from the clutches of the dark that lurked there. It was rare for birds to nest amongst the twisted limbs of the hollows, except for the crows and ravens. The deepest part of the woods was full of mystery and wonder, an enchanted place if there ever were one. Young men would dare one another to probe its recesses and stay the night. Few tried and fewer succeeded.

Lana had been but thirteen when she determined to do what the warriors had not the stomach for. She remembered the first night as if it were only yesterday. She ate with her family as usual, and she listened patiently while her father told a tale from long ago around the fire. The sun went down, the moon appeared in its usual gait, and her parents finally shooed Lana and Thara off to bed. An hour ticked by as the moon rose brightly. In the loft above, she could hear the gentle rhythmic snores of her father and mother, and she could hear the steady breathing and sleepy sighs of her sister on the pallet next to her. When all was quiet, she stole past the gentle old hound flopped disinterestedly in front of the hearth and out the door into the night.

The mysteries of the dark called to her like a mother calls for a lost child. It was as if the darkness and the damp, musty smell of rotting vegetation in the deep woods were proof that the forest expected her. In the treetops, the caw of a raven and the crow's squawk announced her arrival into the shadowy midst of the forest where time stood still. She could hear the secrets of the ancient trees as they sighed and whispered with the shifting of the winds. She walked where giant ferns grew sparsely amongst the tiny areas where sunlight barely reached the floor. Rare herbs and mushrooms with strange powers grew freely and undisturbed here, and she took attentive notice. She stalked the narrow paths lining the hill-side, evidence of the comings and goings of deer and other trail animals. Caves were a sanctuary for wolves, and she would come upon their patrols and listen to their howls as they walked parallel to her path. It was there where she realized the power and value of fear.

In the midst of the towering oaks and the deep, crevasse-ridden hollows, with the shadows her only companions, she also discovered her authority over fear. She would sit all night with her legs crossed under an especially towering specimen that afforded her a view of the moon through its gaping branches. There, she would sing the songs of old, the melodic chants she learned from Uncle Rhu; and she made good use of them, honing her craft in the dark of the night. The spirits of the forest and the branches of the trees would sway and bend to her chants, adding their harmony to hers. Her spiritual transformation was proceeding nicely in those dark nights in the woods, and her hopes and dreams were on the rise. But the thrill and pride she experienced was short lived. Her uncle was not pleased with her learning, with her growth. He feared exposure to uninvited spirits, and he sniffed about, sampling the herbs with practiced fingers, looking for traces of soul.

She sighed now under the moonlight in the Roman encampment, her eyes closed in fond remembrance. It was determined. When the time was right, she would lead the Romans through the dark hollows and come up behind the hillfort of her youth. The thought warmed her and brought a strange, weary smile to her lips.

Her thoughts were shattered when two powerful arms gripped her from behind, roughly handling her as though she were a doll stuffed with winter straw. She stiffened her body and dropped her weight, making it more difficult for her assaulter to grapple with her. She pivoted before he caught her by the waist and pinned her in place. She fended off sloppy pelvic thrusts and slapped at the hands that reached teasingly around her body. Then she pushed away from her attacker and looked up into an accusing face behind glossy red-tinted eyes.

Her tone left no doubt. "Marcus. Leave me be! This is not welcome!" Her eyes were commanding and she could see the doubt flash behind his red-streaked orbs. He breathed heavily and the smell of sour plums came off his words in a slur of tongue- twisting queries.

His mouth curled into a sneer. "Slave woman, or are you a witch, or is it harlot provocateur? What are you doing lurking about the camp this hour of night? I know what it is. You're still with them, aren't you? Tell me. Are you a spy for your tribe? Maybe you are," he said, eyes squinting as he examined her, almost leering at her, his face so close to hers she could almost drink the smell coming out his pores.

He made a crude clucking of the tongue. "Here you are, out here alone in the pitch dark, sneaking around, perhaps trying to pass off messages. What are you doing out here? Does Cussius know you steal away in the dark of night?" He spoke fast, as if the quicker he said it the truer his accusations might become. He seemed desperate and a wild-eyed abandon clung to him thickly.

Her eyes held his for a moment, the truth conveyed but unsaid. Sheepishly, he relinquished his grip on her and he seemed to shrink inside himself. "Forget this happened. I meant no harm. I can see where your heart lies, and I see it is true and straight." He paused for a moment and backed farther away, as if afraid that she would change her mind and not forgive him before he could scurry off. Nervously, he continued to talk.

"I just don't understand. This is your land. You were here first…" He didn't finish the thought. Instead he reached over his shoulder for his flask and uncorked the top and let the last small dribbles of the sour mash splash on his tongue. He shook the flask and frowned before continuing. "Do you have any idea who we are? If you did, I doubt you would be so friendly," he slurred. "It's what we do. We are here to dominate your people. To kill them, crush them if they dare raise a hand against us. Yet you help us. You help Cussius. I don't understand." He sighed deeply, rubbed his eyes, and gave a great yawn before continuing. "And yet the boy... He made no move to come back. Gave me no signal, no indication of up or down. It looks like he wants to stay with your people and I have been more than civil to the lad. I treated him like a son, but yet... All this boggles my head." He shook his head as if trying to loosen the enigma from his mind. He had the natural distrust of a soldier for a turncoat, and it was a hard sentiment to shake, having been drilled into him for the better part of twenty years.

She stepped away from the building and out of the shadows, the moonlight shining brightly upon the raven-colored hair that cascaded from under her hood and spilled unabashedly into the night's breeze. Marcus was unsteady, swaying like a sapling in a strong westerly wind. The stink of sour, rotten plums pursued her doggedly, and she crinkled her nose in distaste. She could answer him truthfully, but she wasn't sure he would understand. She stepped past him and strode to the base of a massive oak, feeling secure with its living trunk pressed against her back. The familiar padding of green, spongy moss provided a suitable cushion.

She eyed the drunken Roman sub commander. "My conscience is clear, if that is what you refer to. As far as the boy is concerned, his motives and fate I cannot ascertain. I haven't looked into his heart. I simply follow what the gods have chosen to reveal to me. Nothing more, nothing less. Anyway, how can you be wrong when fate wills your every move?" She leaned with her arms crossed and slender brow arched slightly.

Marcus scoffed loudly, his face twisted in a drunken sneer. "You speak of fate. I piss on fate. Curse it all and this accursed island of yours. The gods can have it."

She smiled and nodded sanguinely at the curt and sullen Roman. "The works of the gods combined with the efforts of us folk dictate our respective fates. Worry not, for yours is still unwritten." She paused as he pondered this. "Of course, this island could very well be the slate upon which you will etch your destiny. It is up to you and none other." She turned and left Marcus openmouthed and reeling, her sandaled feet making little sound on the soft clay surface of the recently turned path.

CHAPTER TWENTY-SEVEN

THE WIND BLEW mild from the north over leagues of mist-laden grasses dotted with brush and copses of trees. They rode through the bracken and the wind stung their ruddy and chaffed faces, leaving moustaches plastered tight against their cheeks. They rode fast for the hills. At the foot of the wide slope, a forest of oak and ash spread before them, dazzling the riders with its russet-reds, greens, oranges and yellows of the changing seasons. Thicker portions of the forest contained trees twenty to thirty feet in diameter, their limbs stretching to shield the forest floor from the rays of the sun.

The rainy season was upon them, however, and it had poured steady the past two days. The horses slid on their haunches as much as they walked the descent. The grass was sodden and swollen with dew and runoff, leaving crags dripping with water and causing rivulets to form, the footing treacherous for man and beast. The riders picked their way carefully, leaning back in the saddle with their legs tightly squeezing their mounts. In places, the slope and meadow still glowed a lustrous blue-green that interwove with the yellowing heather.

The riders skirted the edge of the forest, staying within the friendly confines of the vast shadows cast by the ancient behemoth oaks. They were dogging the trail of an enemy troop and had wagered this shortcut would put them in the path of the raiders. A force of forty to fifty enemy horses had cut a swath of rapine and pillaging on the far southwest borders of their lands. Stragglers and refugees were pouring in from the countryside, seeking shelter and protection from their lord and his brother the king. Only the calm, steadying hand of the lord and king kept the people together and focused.

After Jayas returned from the parley, the Council decided to split the army despite impassioned arguments to the contrary. In the end, they had sided with Jayas. The strategy was to keep forces deployed in the field, making good use of their knowledge and intimacy of the land to harry the Romans, ambush them and retreat. Jayas sent his warriors out in bands of thirty to make it difficult for the Romans to work or to communicate and travel. So far there were mixed results. Their patrols skirmished almost daily with the Romans, and he could sense the eager aggressiveness behind the feints and shows of force the Romans liked to stage.

Jayas kept his warriors to the forests and moved their camp every few days deeper and deeper into the fold of the trees and ravines. He made use of hidden clearings and meadows sheltered by massive oaks and unknown to all but the most able hunters. Resources and supplies were ample as the women and children in the rear were busy drying and smoking meats, and the bows of the warriors invariably brought down fresh game from the abundance of the woods. Still, it was hard not to worry about how things were going back in the villages. Often, his thoughts were of his cousin and his abrupt change in attitude toward him. At other times, Thara dominated his mind and he would feel a strong yearning that left him tired and weary. Thankfully, he was always within one or two days' ride of either.

Unbelievably, Gymm retained joint control with Lord Toge of the forces arrayed around the two main hillforts. So far, he had to admit that Gymm had delved into the task with good cheer and a fierce energy, apparently to work off the taint of his earlier failure. He kept work crews busily harvesting the orchards of apples and plums, and the smaller hands were set to plucking the ripened berries that would later be transformed into sweet jams and ciders and the remainder cut and dried for later consumption. The wheat and barley stood golden and high in the fields, and the young were kept busy stripping the stalks bare of the plump yellow-brown grains and scything the stalks to churned earth. Much of it was stored in vast pits dug out of limestone that were dry and cool, but some of the barley and oats were stored with the wheat in tough burlap bags that were then stacked away in anticipation of hungrier times. Hay and straw were put up and the field chaff and stalks laid aside for the swineherds. Extra corrals were being constructed to house horses and cattle. Sheep pens were extended and the surrounding fields were stripped bare of anything useful. At Lord Toge' behest, Gymm even met with crews of tribal artisans — stonemasons, carpenters, and woodcutters — and put them to work shoring up the meager perimeter defenses. After what Jayas saw at the Roman camp, the inadequacies of the tribe's fortifications screamed for attention and he was pleased the fortifications were being put in good order. Just as important, the tribe's smithies were hard at work after he and his father harangued them into grasping the immediacy of the problem.

When Jayas left the rapidly transforming hillfort, the pressing ring of hammer on anvil and the churning sounds of barrow loads of raw ore and charcoal being hauled were constant. Nicked, docked and bent blades were heated, and then subjected to a series of short, powerful blows all along the heated edge of the blade. The smithy would repeat the process two to three times before he or his apprentice would rush the red-hot blade into a waiting barrel of water and remove it only after they heard a certain echo of sizzle only they recognized. The blade would then be set upon by a skilled sharpener and once again sing with deadliness, the edge capable of slicing through the neck of a bull.

As Jayas rode, his thoughts were continuously drawn elsewhere. He was particularly troubled by reports coming from Cassivellaunus and the tribes under his confederation. Emissaries from the Coritani were again treated coolly, Cassivellaunus' representatives merely shrugging noncommittally at the king's overtures of an alliance. They cited their own recently completed war, the need to recuperate and set in for the winter. There was one complication, though, and all three sides knew of it.

Cassivellaunus was due to deliver the tribute demanded by Caesar, and Cussius, the Roman overlord, was ready to receive it. Jayas did not want it delivered. Rumor had it that it was a massive amount of cattle, sheep and slaves; and wagons of grain and precious metals were sure to follow. The Coritani could ill afford their enemies receiving an influx of supplies that would sustain them through the hard winter. On the other hand, Cassivellaunus was not in a terrible hurry to cripple his treasury in that fashion, and to date, had not begun the trip.

Jayas grimaced and his stomach grumbled uncomfortably. Tough decisions and even tougher times lay ahead. He did not see an easy answer, but his will and desire to resist the Romans could not and would not dampen, and the will of his warriors was undaunted, as well. The scent of smoke reached his nostrils, causing him to raise his head and sniff the air carefully. It smelled of new smoke. His shoulders slumped. They were too late.

Suddenly, a fox's bark pierced the dusk air, snapping him back to attention. His eyes roved the trees and bushes for the source. His horse's ears twitched and the beast shifted from hoof to hoof, all the while swishing its tail at the occasional green fly. Jayas tugged his mount off the faint trail that led over the ridge and down to the creek where it finally adjoined a small village. He strained his head and listened. He could make out the pounding of what sounded like two horses approaching, no more than three, making straight at him. He motioned to the others, and as one, they melted into the brush and waited.

Lann galloped up, the thin warrior's youthful face painted a fiercely brilliant blue, making the whites of his eyes shine brighter in the waning moments of the day. Next to him on a smallish pony was a tall man, his tunic and trousers too large and engulfing his slight figure. His skin was pale and marked with freckles that stretched taut over raised cheekbones. He had a feral look with large darting blue eyes that seemed to miss nothing. He tightly clutched a mean-looking spear and a small oval shield.

The young Coritani warrior began to make the bark again, but Jayas saved him the trouble by stepping out of the brush, his hand raised for silence. Lann swung out of the saddle and walked forward, the thin clansman following close.

He leaned in and whispered quietly. "My Lord, the enemy is encamped on the other side of the village. Mostly Bibroci and Trinovante tribesmen with 15 to 20 Romans. They're drinking mead, laughing and joking around the fire and having their way with the women." He looked away when he said this, his tone disgusted and unforgiving.

He gestured toward his tall companion. "He and some others were watching the trail," he said by way of explanation. "His name is Bryn, the clan leader of the village. He and three others are the only warriors to escape. I'll let him tell you."

Jayas nodded to the man. He could see the seething mixture of pure hatred and grief etched in the man's lean features as he related his tale.

"The fault is mine, my Lord. I delayed answering the call to arms because I wanted to see the harvest in and gather the flocks and herds. We were going to come as soon as we had finished," the tall warrior said, dipping his head respectfully, his remorse evident.

Jayas looked stern. "There is no time for this. Go on."

"I had two riders posted but they were killed before they could raise the alarm. The outlanders breached the gate and rode through the hamlet before we could organize a defense. They rode through, spearing and slashing and throwing torches, and seeking out women for capture. A few of my men were able to join forces and we fought our way through to the creek. Most of the women and children...." He paused, his shoulders bowed slightly, the stench of failure almost engulfing the man in his grief.

Jayas understood his pain and could see it in his mind's eye, but he needed the information and had no time for theatrics, no matter how deeply the man might ache. "Hurry, man. Time is of the essence."

The man took a deep breath and gathered himself. "We were only able to bring out four of the women and six of the children.

They now huddle in a cavern under the lip of the creek bed. May the gods not allow it to rain again." The man pointed behind and then looked up in prayer. The threat of flash floods was an ever-present threat, especially considering the precarious location of the women and young. Any further rainfall and a torrent of muddy water would sweep them to oblivion.

Jayas' eyes glinted like those of a wolf and his scar was drawn tight in a mirthless smile. "So they get lazy and fat while they plunder our lands. They murder and commit mayhem and then sit down to enjoy the spoils at the tables of their victims," he muttered. "It will not stand. Tell me, what of their guards and where are they posted? Can we get to them undetected? I'm not simply talking about the sentries, but the whole lot of them. I want them all. Their heads will be yours, clansman." He fought to keep his anger under control, running the options through his head as the men supplied him with the information.

Jayas spread the word down the ranks. They were outnumbered by twenty or so, but that was of no matter. On the other side of the hill, not more than half an hour away, the unsuspecting enemy was reveling in its bloody deeds. They would rue this day.

CHAPTER TWENTY-EIGHT

Grinning, Kegan rose unsteadily to his feet, his head and body reeling from the raw bliss he had just reaped from the naked woman who squirmed and kicked underneath him. He allowed himself a satisfied sigh and tucked his blouse back into the band of his trousers. Stepping over her and breathing deeply, he took a long pull on the sheepskin jug, trying to slow the beating of his heart after the tumultuous row with the Coritani wench. She was spirited and had fought him tooth and claw for every pleasure he took.

He felt the side of his neck, which stung and was running red with blood where she had clawed at his face. Well worth the effort, he thought. Shrugging on his mail, he clasped his leather breastplate overhead and slid it down his shoulders, marveling at the design that protected him and yet allowed him freedom of movement. He was glad to have it. Marcus gave it to him after he commented on how he liked it, and he grunted in approval as he rotated and stretched his aching shoulders.

Looking around the remains of the village, he was extremely displeased. His Bibroci warriors were getting as lazy and shiftless as the Trinovante, and the Romans who came along for the raid were not acting within their usual disciplined reserve. He watched as two drunken legionaries tugged a half-conscious woman by her hair while a Trinovante scout leered and hooted. He was sure Marcus would not approve of their antics, scowling stern bastard that he was. Under ordinary circumstances, he could care less and would probably lead the excesses himself. He expected the rapes and beatings of the captives during the course of war, but the timing was all wrong. They should have retreated with their booty and slaves, putting some distance behind them and this village and not lingered, just as Marcus had ordered. He was afraid they were too late as it was. Already they had been here for half the day.

The mist had begun to settle in with the coming moon. The village was nestled between two gradual slopes that stretched up from cleared pastures, adjoining a forest from whence a stream flowed. The enclave was little more than a semi-circle of roundhouses, small hovels that abutted a ramshackle collection of wooden boards doubling as a palisade. It boasted a tannery, now aflame. The low acrid smell of smoke and the pungent stench of flesh and death were an affront to his senses, and he wanted to get out to farther environs where he could breathe clean, cool air. The smoke rolled off thick and black into the darkening sky, and he knew it was a beacon that would not be ignored. A Coritani reprisal could almost be counted on.

"Form up, you scoundrels! Bibroci, on your ponies! Magnus! You best get your Romans in order. You know Marcus would not approve." That was an understatement. The more time on the trail he spent with the implacable Roman, the better understanding he had of the Roman's mind. On the other hand, he knew the exchange was mutual, as the Bibroci tendencies were being impressed upon the Romans too. The Romans went about their business with a certain professional zeal, which left Kegan nodding in respect most of the time but scratching it in bewilderment at others. He would have chuckled if not for the gravity of the moment. This was a head-scratching moment.

The Romans scowled and cussed, waving him off with drunken sneers. The flames sent dancing shadows across faces shiny with soot and sweat. "We deserve a taste ol' boy," one particularly energetic soldier growled at Kegan. He pawed a grubby hand over the sobbing Coritani girl, her eyes swollen with tears and resignation.

Kegan shrugged. "Suit yourselves. But we will be leaving." He took his horse by the neck and grabbed a handful of the mane, leaping atop the animal easily. "If I were you, I would be too. Take the slaves with you. They will still be slaves when we are miles from here and you can still do with them what you wish. Stay here and… and it's too dangerous. I don't trust the feeling of this place anymore. Let's be away." He shrugged in the saddle, already turning his horse to round up his straggling warriors.

They jeered him. One Roman loosened the straps of his trousers while tightening the grip on the lass's hair. "Easy for you to say, ol' chap. You've already had your fun. We educated Romans call that hypocrisy, a concept I believe you to have roundly mastered," he exclaimed to the guffaws of his compatriots as they backslapped one another.

Kegan' horse looked away. Slightly startled, its ears pricked up. "Wait, wait. Silence!" urged Kegan with a wave of his arm. He thought he heard something as well. It was hard to tell with the cacophony sent up by the looting warriors and legionaries, but those near obeyed. All squinted with eyes red from fatigue, smoke and drink. They turned as one in the direction of the forest, now difficult to see because of the seeping blanket of mist and the hazy screen of smoke adrift on the valley floor. His horse stood breathing in snorts, its ears now pinned back, its front legs pawing nervously at the cracked mud.

The laughter abruptly stopped, replaced entirely by stunned silence and bulging eyeballs. The Romans dropped their squirming prey to the ground with a thud where she scrambled to her feet and scurried away. Everyone then moved at once. They stumbled into one another, exchanging curses and shoves as they scuttled over the muddy ground and frantically searched the shadows for their shields and helmets. The Roman sergeant was screaming for his unit to form, and answering shouts could be heard as confusion threatened to morph into chaos. Warriors and soldiers alike rushed back and forth, calling and cursing. Somewhere, a captive shrieked in hopeful anguish.

Kegan spurred his mount and drew his sword in a singular motion. He whirled to meet the threat he knew would be upon them in an instant. "To arms! Bibroci, to arms!" His horse stamped nervously, tossing its head and snorting loudly. To his right and left he could see some of his warriors quickly slicing the tethers that hobbled their ponies. He hoped the Romans could form up, but he didn't have the luxury to wait, for bursting out of the shroud of fog and smoke were the ghostly shapes of men and beasts in full motion. Fleetingly, through the smoky gloom, he thought he recognized the scarred and angry face outlined by streaming white hair. Riding a muscular beast, the warrior loomed before the others and bent low on his mount with his javelin extended afore, its sharp iron head glinting malevolently.

Kegan briefly looked around and took stock of a bad situation. He saw the confusion in his warriors' eyes as they hastily scampered aboard skittish mounts. There was no other choice but to shout his own challenge and charge into the gloom.

JAYAS ROARED WITH savage glee. His every muscle was alive and tingling with malice as his eyes bored through the haze and locked onto the Bibroci turncoat, Kegan. He kicked his strong mount, and just as eager for battle as his master, it surged the remaining distance. Jayas' horsemen were aligned in a wedge formation like the head of an arrow, and he was the deadly sharp tip. They aimed straight for the greatest concentration of the milling enemy and meant to crash right through them, breaking any hint of resistance with the speed and ferocity of their charge. To his left and right he could see forms breaking for freedom as others stood to fight, all of them cut down to earth again. A pair of enemy warriors threw down their weapons and bolted from the fray, but they were easily surrounded by horsemen. Coritani men swung their swords and jabbed downward with javelins until their enemies fell, their blood and urine soaking the ground and drowning their frantic cries for mercy.

Ahead, Kegan whirled in a circle, swinging his sword wildly at the passing Coritani. Jayas hacked his way through the melee, his horse barreling into Kegan'. Shoulder to shoulder the two beasts met, the reckless impact sending the smaller pony onto its haunches and throwing the Bibroci war leader violently from the saddle. Instinctively, Jayas slid from the saddle and his legs hit the ground running. He pursued the dazed Bibroci further into the gloom, where the flames from the dwindling fires ended.

Kegan tried to duck but Jayas was too quick; he lunged with the javelin and the thick wet sound of cloven muscle was audible as the point tore through his enemy's neck. Jayas ripped out the spear and tossed it to the side where it clattered on the stones. Straddling Kegan, he unsheathed his sword and the man's gurgling shriek was followed by the crack of splitting bones. He had no time to take the traitor's head.

Out of the corner of his eye, Jayas caught a red blur of movement and brought his shield up in time to catch the wild-eyed lunge of a panicked Roman. He swept his sword under the brute's legs and slashed behind the knee, the hapless victim collapsing weakly on the muddy path, his blood gushing hard. Jayas whirled around and crashed into a body and felt himself stumble, his legs tripped up by kicking feet and hard knees that were searching for vulnerable soft spots. A heavy body landed atop him, stunning him and causing him to lose his grip on his sword. The man's fetid breath reeked of stale mead and the more sour and gut-wrenching stench of fear. Jayas rolled swiftly and rose in a crouch, swinging at the unseen warrior. The man's hands wrenched savagely at his neck and face with the wiry strength of a desperate man. As Jayas grasped the man's wrist, he barely managed to get hold of his bone-handled boot-knife, secured mid-calf with a leather tie. He brought it up savagely, the point easing between the man's ribs with a wet sucking sound. Again he thrust the blade upward, the iron point puncturing the Roman's life center. The man screamed once, a shrill, curdled sound cut-off in mid-breath, and then fell with a graceless thud and lay thrashing and moaning.

Jayas gasped as air flooded back into his lungs. His eyes stung from the smoke and he needed to get back in the fight, but by the sound of it, things were unfolding as planned. Back in the center where first contact was made, he could see no imminent threats remaining. His immediate vicinity was cleared of the enemy, and riderless horses bore mute witness to the downfall of their previous owners as they nervously milled amidst the waning chaos. His own horse stood impatiently by, uneasily eyeing the new additions and shying at their strange smells, nipping at any beast's flanks that came close enough as it shouldered its way toward its master.

In the firelight cast by a discarded torch, a gleam caught Jayas' eye, the sword and shield he lost in the melee, and he scooped them up. He ran out of the shadows and in the direction of the shouting. His warriors were now riding back and forth, cutting down any remaining enemy. He leaped over the bodies of some Romans who were in a neat little pile where they had circled defensively back to back, their bodies forever caught in a grotesque pose of loyalty.

The ground was slippery under the crust of dried mud and congealing blood, and he skidded to a halt as he reached for his willing mount. He climbed aboard his horse, glad to feel the sound platform of his steed. The horse broke into a canter and Jayas rode through the village, which was now beyond repair and would have to be rebuilt. The villagers' belongings were strewn about, hurriedly abandoned by the panicking enemy as Jayas and his warriors swept through. Piles of skins and furs were dragged from the fires; that much was salvageable. Jayas could see villagers poking through the ruins and relieving the dead of their weapons and armor, and he rode into their midst.

Bryn, the village elder, was the first to greet him. The man looked restored, the light of vengeance shining brightly in his eyes. His fallen men could not be replaced, but the retaking of his village and the reunion with the women and children strengthened him greatly. He fell to his knees as Jayas rode up.

"May the gods give you a thousand thanks for every one of mine. Thank you!" he cried from his knees.

Jayas stayed on his horse and did not smile as he eyed the man. "Get up, man! You fought like a warrior; now stand as one. This is not nearly over, so gather your people and bury your dead. My warriors will deal with the enemy dead so you need not worry about them. Grab the food, seed and livestock; and take whatever else you can — leave by first light. Take word of this battle to the rest. Let them gain heart by your brave actions today."

"Aye, Lord," the man said as he scurried to his feet and rushed away to gather what his people would need for the retreat to the hillforts.

Lann reined in hard next to Jayas and his horse pranced. "There you are. We were a bit worried. What happened to all that talk of caution and whatnot?" He smiled, the curled edges of his mouth revealing large teeth hidden under a droopy moustache. "It's a great victory, my Lord. Two or three got away, but the bulk of them..." He smiled and ran his thumb in a slashing motion across the stubble on his throat.

Jayas allowed a small cold smile to play at the corner of his lips. "Take their heads and leave the bodies for the scavengers," he ordered. "And hurry. We have ground to cover."

CHAPTER TWENTY-NINE

GYMM LOOKED AROUND uneasily. He put the cup to his lips, draining the contents in nervous gulps. He was not comfortable, and the Roman made him nervous in a way he could not quite put his finger on. Despite his smiling exterior, the Roman had an icy demeanor about him, and Gymm did not detect any true warmth meant for him. He shifted in his chair and tried to keep his focus on Lana, though that did little to ease his discomfort. She sat next to the tall foreigner and looked all the happier for it. She had changed very little since he last saw her, except the wild glint in her eyes seemed to have grown smokier, as if their murky depths shielded grim secrets. She is still beautiful and forever touched by the spirits, he thought. He shook his head as if these two before him were a mirage. Lana and her enemy escort had appeared as if out of nowhere.

It had been like any other day of late. He was early to rise, seeing to the work crews, checking supplies, and helping the lord devise a rationing system. It was quite a challenge since he had not mastered his figures when the druid tutor used to try to drum them into his head as a boy. After the morning's duties he decided to take a break and clear his head, so he did what he always did: He grabbed his bow and went hunting. A couple of birds or a fat deer always made a welcome addition to the table, and he liked the stalk and hunt. When he was only a couple miles out and had barely begun to beat the bush, Lana had stepped from the forest like a specter from the past and called to him.

Gymm now eyed the container wherein resided the sweet drink he found to his liking. The Roman was smiling, but the steadiness of his gaze never faltered, and Gymm could feel it like a burn on the side of his face. "More wine?" the Roman asked in Gymm's language but with an accent.

Gymm grunted his assent and greedily gulped another cupful, the warmth spreading from his stomach and into his temples. The Roman refilled his cup and returned the decanter to the table.

"Thank you for agreeing to this meeting. I am Cussius, commander of the Roman forces. You must be Gymm, I presume. I have already met your cousin. Your king sent him as an emissary under a flag of truce," he said while carefully studying Gymm.

Gymm scowled. "So what do you want with me? Jayas spoke for the king, for my father." He mumbled the words as if he spoke of something foul or unpleasant.

Cussius grinned, his teeth gleaming in the torchlight. "Precisely put. I wanted to make the acquaintance of the prince."

Gymm was irritated and it showed. "I will not be king. Thanks to you Romans," he spat. "By the way, where and how did you learn our language?" he asked irritably.

Cussius leaned forward and spoke in a voice barely above a whisper. "I listen and learn. Now back to the subject at hand. If you are not to be king, then who will be? Not your cousin. That could not be." He scrunched his eyes and canted his head as if seriously evaluating Gymm. Finally he sighed as if stymied by a puzzle he could not decipher. "What does he have that you do not? Look, I'm sorry. I get ahead of myself and it's really none of my business." He paused and took a sip of his wine.

He now spoke as if to a child. His voice was crisp with certainty, allowing no room for the slightest doubt. "It is not my desire to see eternal enmity between our two peoples. It profits neither of us. You are a warrior who is strong and brave, and so are the other warriors of your people. But I am strong too. If only a leader among the Coritani could see the potential of our armies as one... Nothing on this island could stand against us." His voice grew husky with conviction. "If only your tribe had a strong leader, one who could see the value of friendship with us. That man would be free to lead his people and live according to his own ways, only for agreeing to answer when called and to work together with me militarily. I would support a Coritani king like that." Cussius leaned back and placed a hand on Lana's leg as he waited for some response.

Gymm was beginning to feel better. The Roman was making a lot of sense, and the wine made him warm and lessened his earlier misgivings. He shot a glance at the door, where one of the Roman's orderlies waited with his arms crossed over his chest. Beyond the attendant, the sun had dipped below the break of the wall, and shadows had begun to infiltrate the outer edges. Gymm had to get back soon, for he knew the others would fret to the point of sending out riders to look for him. Hesitantly, he answered. "Maybe my father could be convinced as to the wisdom in your words. We will see." He shrugged, his eyes lidded and heavy by the effect of the drink.

Emboldened by the wine, he turned to Lana. "Why are you here and not with your family?" he asked while stealing a quick glance at Cussius.

Cussius made no move to hush her as she leaned across the table and grabbed Gymm by the wrists in a surprisingly tight grip. "I will ask you and maybe you will understand. Why go back to a people who have overlooked me and moved on, back to the people who ignore the signs of their own destiny?" She paused and her eyes burned red with an intensity so hot that Gymm did not dare look away. "Besides, fate willed my being here. It was ordained long ago. This is the path to the future, the only path upon which our peoples will survive. But not only will we survive if we take this new path. No, we will thrive. Now, when you go back, are you meekly going to accept a false destiny ordained by a shortsighted people? I think not, for I have seen the way of the future. Can't you see it?" she pleaded. "Within you is the blood of a noble king. You cannot deny what you are, for if you do, you chip away at your spirit. Every minute you grovel at the foot of Jayas and the others is another minute you deny who you are. Every time you are thus cowed, your spirit is further weakened. Your spirit will eventually wither and spoil like unharvested corn left on the stalk. Your very being will be shattered, leaving you hollow where nothing will ever be the same. The pleasures of a willing woman will leave you unsatisfied, and the taste of your food will be bland — even your mead will taste too bitter to enjoy." She relaxed her grip and his hands dropped to the table with a *thunk*.

Gymm tensed, and he tried to cast his mind more widely. His face twitched and he looked rattled, the way he always looked when he was unsure of himself. Unsteadily, he stood up, readying himself to leave. The room felt warmer, as if someone had added logs to the fire and stoked the coals. He was a bit baffled by what Lana said, but the way she said it made the small hairs on the back of his neck stand straight. He felt goose bumps and reflexively shrunk away from the fiery intensity of her eyes.

He cleared his throat and felt himself stutter something, the truth of her words distracting him. "Thank you for the drink. I must return to my people. I will think long and hard on what you have spoken of. That's all I can say for now." He shook his head as if somehow the motion of it could dispel the low *thrum* coursing through his mind.

"Remember what we talked about, and until then..." Cussius allowed the sentence to die. He watched as Gymm bowed simply, nodded at Lana, and hurriedly stalked out of the hall.

Cussius walked to the door and watched the Coritani mount his horse and ride toward the gate. He waved off the orderly and had the night guard posted before turning to Lana. "You have quite the passion within you. Do you know the effect you have on others? I watch them when they are around you, and it's quite the spectacle. They look at you as if they fear you. Maybe they fear what you can see more than they actually fear you. Nonetheless, what a pair we are, you and I. You are as wily as a red fox. Olympius, the mother of Alexander the Great, would even have to respect your presence. You are a natural, that's for certain," he said while eyeing the raven-haired beauty. "Come here." He patted his knee.

She obeyed, lithely sliding on his thigh and laying an arm across his shoulder where she ran her fingertips through his short-cropped hair. "There is nothing wily about the truth. And all people nurse a fear of the unknown. We, you and I, do not fear because we have fate by the tail and will not let go." She leaned over and kissed him on the mouth. "Shall we go to bed? We have dreams to induce." She led him by the hand to the makeshift cot and wool quilt they shared.

CHAPTER THIRTY

It was nearing dusk, and the tiring sun blinked behind drifting patches of white rimmed with red. The cold wind was rising, keen edged and whistling in the branches of the oak trees. In the waning light that meandered through the changing leaves, Leko searched the spongy ground below a thicket of large oaks for branches the size of a large man's wrist. That was the perfect size for the cooking fire Thara wanted stoked, and he went about his task in earnest. He couldn't help himself. While he worked he cast quick glances her way.

On the far side of the massive clearing, she playfully stalked two deer that ambled up the ridge and then abruptly vanished into the wood. He waved to get her attention and motioned in the direction the deer had bolted with their tails held high in alarm. She grinned and shrugged. Even at this distance he thought he could see the rising pink in her high cheeks. He returned her smile, and for a split second, he allowed his mind to take him to a world where it was just the two of them, a world where they could hunt the woods in peace and tend to their herds of horses and cattle, a world where Thara would bear his children. He laughed at the idea, but the noise that came out of him lacked mirth and tasted bitter in his mouth as though he had just eaten an acorn.

Something was poking at the edge of his mind, creeping along inside his head, persistent like a worm on an ear of corn. He knew

Jayas was enamored with Thara. It was obvious he doted on her and relied upon her greatly, but every moment Jayas spent sniffing around her made Leko burn with envy and such feelings only left him ashamed. Jayas was nobility and a renowned war leader, and Leko was little better than a servant despite the protestations of this tribe of warriors to the contrary. Leko knew that Jayas lusted for Thara. He had seen the looks and knew them for what they were. Worse, he had seen Thara return them as if the two spoke a secret language that he was not privy to. It drove him crazy and he dreamed of the day when he could match Jayas, size on size, sword for sword, blow for blow. He enjoyed the victory in his mind's eye as he imagined winning the hand of Thara. A rash of falling acorns dropped to the leafy ground and wrenched him from his thoughts. He glanced down at his waist, and for a moment, he imagined that he again had his sword. He felt incomplete without his sword, and its absence nagged at him — another symbol of his reduced status and another reminder that his fantasy that included Thara was futile.

It began to rain, and Leko wondered how he had managed to miss the dark gray clouds that were now dumping fat wet drops onto the earth. Thara sauntered over, and he couldn't help but stare at the beautiful apparition as she moved through the tall grass. It was as if she appeared from the mist like a golden goddess of the oak. Apparently, the rain did little to stifle her spirits, and her mood appeared high despite the dampness of the darkening day. She smiled from underneath hair plastered against her head and nodded at Leko as she navigated the fallen timbers and clusters of turning brush.

"Spot any berries? You know, you should always be alert for forage opportunities. Berries, roots and nuts. The earth provides for us, but of course, we must be open to its generosity. The berries ripen quickly this time of year and you have to get them before the first frost." She paused and sniffed the air. "And that shouldn't be too far off at all." Poking around the bushes, she let out a squeal of delight at her easy find. Squirrels chattered angrily from high in the branches, their evening dinner disrupted by the foragers below.

Most of the foliage was a fast fading green interspersed with a yellowing hue. Here and there were boughs of red and purple foliage, a display of nature's creativity. Thara held aloft a round purplish berry and took a bite. "See, they're all around. We must hurry. It's getting dark fast," she said with a glance at the sky before tossing him a small leather tote and gesturing toward the wood.

Leko felt frustrated. He wanted to tell her how much he loved her. He wanted to marry her and run away from all this, maybe all the way back home to his village in Gaul. He tried to keep his spirits aloft, and it was easy to get caught up in Thara's cheery optimism, but he couldn't quite shake the doldrums as he followed. He mostly listened to her stories and smiled, seldom offering much in the way of conversation. He found berries and gathered nuts as he went along, placing both inside the tote, but he was still on the lookout for dry wood. Snatching an especially jagged piece of wood from the ground, he examined it before tossing it to the side as too wet. He suppressed a shiver and looked over at Thara, who appeared none the worse from the pattering of cold rain that soaked her skin and turned the forest floor into a soft mush. He drifted closer to the base of the tree and was rewarded with a large branch that appeared relatively dry. Thankful for the find, he dragged it to the edge of the clearing where he pulled a small axe from the leather belt cinched around his waist and cracked it in three pieces of equal size. He leaned over and tied the wood in a bundle and slung it over his shoulder.

Thara stood staring at him. A quizzical smile played on her lips, but her eyes held more concern than merriment. "What troubles you?" she asked as she laid a warm hand on his arm.

The feeling was electric, and Leko felt a surge within him. Blushing, he looked aside. "I don't know," he stammered. He risked a look at her, feeling warm and flushed despite the coolness of the autumn drizzle that worked its way through the leaves.

"Don't tell me that. All you've done the last few days is mope around all glum and without humor. That's not a way to meet the days you are granted on this earth," she scolded. "Look at me."

With a cupped palm, she gently lifted his chin until he raised his face and met her eyes. She held his gaze, and as he was drawn into the liquid depths of her eyes, he realized she already knew where his heart lay. Strangely, he felt liberated, for just a moment before shame threatened to overwhelm him, causing him once again to avert his gaze.

She smiled gently, a hint of flattery playing in her eyes. "It's okay. I know what you're feeling, and it's natural for a young man of your age. Well, I am not a man, so I can't venture to know exactly how you are feeling. Your own father would have spoken about this to you, and I'm sure you had a rough education about the relations of men and women when you were with the Romans, but I suspect such things are a bit more complex among the Romans than what you or I are accustomed to — but don't fret over such matters. We have bigger things to attend to. Besides, you know me well enough by now to understand that I'm spoken for," she quipped.

Her eyes never once faltered, and Leko took heart in the fact that she did not laugh at him in scorn for his boyish fascination. He straightened a bit, his back and neck rigid as the import of her last sentence finally sank in. He played it off as though she had never said it. "You say 'we'. What do you mean by that? The Romans took me as a slave. They even killed my father and many of my tribesmen, but yet they spared me. I served them, but they also trusted me to carry a sword and taught me about soldiering. I truly felt wanted despite the path I took to get there." He paused, not knowing which way to continue the conversation. "Here with your people, all I do are menial chores. Don't get me wrong. I love every minute I spend in your company, but how can you ever respect me if…" He didn't finish the thought, for his mind was racing and his tongue felt thick and unwieldy, making it a struggle to convey his meaning.

She reached out her other hand and ran it over his cheek, the sensation thrilling him to no end. Her touch was light and delicate and seemed to radiate heat. "Do not worry about such things. There is a season for everything. Besides, you are what and who you are regardless of your circumstances. Performing menial chores merely shows you are a humble young man. My Uncle Rhu says that humility is next to godliness. He would say, 'Having a spirit to serve manifests itself in many capacities' and then would rattle off example after example. And by the great gods of old, don't get him started on all the perceived depravities of humanity. By the gods, help us all if he did."

She chuckled at some memory of her uncle before continuing. "'Pride!' he would shout with disgust. Uncle would then proceed to tell the tale of the proud wolf, leaving me and my sister fighting and arguing over what it all really meant." She paused again, lost in private memories of long ago. "Come. Let's head back." Thara motioned for him to join her as she made her way back to the lightly traveled trail that crossed the wood.

Leko perked up in interest as he adjusted his tote. "What wolf tale?" he asked as he hustled to catch up. When he moved, the bundle of wood he toted bounced upon his shoulder blades painfully but he disregarded the discomfort and matched her stride.

"Come now, Thara. What was the wolf story?" he asked, smiling in encouragement and happy to have her attentions, fleeting and temporary as it was. Besides, he found anything having to do with her Uncle Rhu worth listening to, and he couldn't stifle the boyish curiosity that welled up within.

THEY CROSSED a corner of the grassy plain that glowed translucent silver in the moonlight. Spurred by hunger and the growing chill, Thara and Leko made it back to camp just in time for the cold had begun to bite. The little bit of fog that gathered along the edges of the forest seemed reluctant to leave. It settled over the ground to compete with the soft glow of the ebbing embers. Exhausted, Thara directed Leko to add a log to the fire and stir the coals before plopping down within arms' reach of the resurgent blaze.

She held her hands out, rubbed them together and then blew on them, thankful for the returning warmth. She did not sit in place too long, for the wet chill of the earth seeped into her bones, sending a shiver throughout her being. She watched Leko as he busied himself roasting a small hare over the pit. She truly liked him and enjoyed his company, but not in the same fashion that he fancied her. There was nothing ugly or boorish about the youth, and she was fond of his openness. His hair was in the fashion of the folk, long and swept back off his forehead where it lay curling on his shoulders. His eyes were wide set with thin brows that curved finely to whatever mood he wore. His mouth was wide, the lips covering strong, white teeth. He was boyishly handsome and slavishly attentive to her, but she could not envision returning the same feelings. She sighed, her breath misty in the cool night air. There was room for only one suitor in her life, and at present, he was loose in the countryside, countering the Roman incursion.

Leko brought over the steaming rabbit leg, its juices running along the length of the stick upon which it was impaled. She smiled her thanks and blew on the chunk before biting into the hot meat. She longed for sea salt sprinkles, but the natural juices flavored the tender morsel just fine. The burst of flavor playfully teased her palate until the need for salt was forgotten.

A loud cough and clearing of the throat drew her attention across the flames. Leko finally broke the silence, his voice thick with hesitation and regret. "I miss home. I miss it more and more with each passing day. The weather, the food, the people — my people. Life was so much more simple there. I knew my role, my place and what my future held." He sighed loudly, and the boyish wistfulness of his pose tugged at the chords of Thara's heart, but he continued before she could respond. "At least I thought I knew. Now, I have... I just don't know anymore. Some of my family has to be alive. My eldest brother was away when the Romans struck, and so he's probably still alive. My oldest sister was long married and I didn't hear whether or not her village was destroyed, so it's possible she and her children survived. I even miss Marcus. I've been with him and the legion for over a year and he's never done me a bad turn, caring for me in his own rough way. He took an interest and if he hadn't, I would have been killed or sold into slavery with the others. He taught me about soldiering and about honor." His voice hitched as he continued. "Yes, even slaves have honor." Leko paused again, and she could see the moistness seeping into his eyes. His jaw, not yet blue with beard shadow, quivered as he struggled to contend with his sadness. He shrugged as if it were no great matter and chewed at the leg of rabbit with a nervous quickness.

Her voice was soft but clear and void of regrets. "I too have experienced loss. My own sister, Lana, has been taken from us and enslaved by the Romans. Her husband was murdered, her village destroyed, and now she is the property of some foreign pigs. Our fates may yet be more similar than you think. I pray not and have great faith that we shall turn the invaders back, but fate is a tricky master and one must be quick enough to see the options it affords." Her voice had taken a determined turn, and the hurt momentarily overtook her cool.

Leko looked up at her words and wiped the grease from his mouth and fledgling moustache with the back of his hand. "Your sister is not a slave," he said with a queer look. "She is the lover of the Roman commander, Cussius. I've seen her myself. You two are definitely sisters." He took another bite of the meat and chewed slowly.

Thara was stunned, and a look of disbelief stole over her face. "Lover? What would you know about that? She was forcibly taken. You can't tell me she wasn't. Is she free to leave?" she asked, a look of triumph on her face.

He shook his head and shrugged his shoulders. "I don't know. I don't think she wants to anyhow."

Thara's eyes narrowed. "How would you know this?"

Leko shrugged again, his hooded eyes guileless. "Everyone knew of it. She's his witch." He cast the sign to ward off any unwelcome spirits and looked hard into the dark of the night as if expecting wild ghosts to burst out at any moment. "Besides, I've seen her walk about the camp and into the countryside at any moment of her choosing. If she had a mind to leave, I suppose she would have. You already know that, I'm sure," Leko added before once again keeping vigil on the shadows of the night.

A look of understanding crept around the edges of Thara's mouth before disintegrating in doubt. She was unsure of herself and felt like a small child, her legs straight in front, arms crossed in hugging, and her lower lip pushed out. "Maybe her predicament is not too unlike yours. But still, it wouldn't make sense for her to stay of her own accord." Deep within her she knew the truth, however, and cold grief filled her belly. Her appetite gone, she tossed the remainder of her meal to Leko, who eagerly accepted the boon of meat and tore into it with the zeal of youthful hunger.

Suddenly Thara felt exhausted. She dropped her gaze and listened to the faraway sounds of the night as her mind struggled to put things in perspective. She bid Leko goodnight and curled up on her ox-hide mat, pulling her thick wool robe around her form before drifting into a fitful sleep.

CHAPTER THIRTY-ONE

In no mood to wait, Cussius stalked the long room from hearth to hearth. With four or five full strides he could cover the entire distance before he was forced to pivot and reverse direction. It was not lost on him that he stalked about like one of the caged lions he once saw as a boy when his father took him to the coliseum on a day trip. His lips drew back in a sneer as he imagined his canines glinting like the lion's that day as it peered out hungrily from behind the iron bars. His head ached dully so he was unable to enjoy the vision for as long as he preferred.

Bad news had arrived earlier. The courier of the Catuvellauni tribe arrived just as the sun reached its zenith. Bravely and without hesitation, the tribesman relayed his master's message. Apparently, Cassivellaunus was unable to deliver the tribute. Unable or unwilling, wondered Cussius? It mattered very little. This was a clear breach of terms and tantamount to a declaration of war. Cussius had listened intently as the Catuvellauni nobleman tried to smooth the news over with promises of the spring. He had made excuses and declared his people poor and near to destitution.

"If it weren't for the ruin that the superb forces under command of your Caesar inflicted upon us, we would be able to comply more quickly. Be that as it may, we need more time to gather what you demand," the Catuvellauni nobleman had sniffed.

Cussius had closed the distance between the two in a swift bound. His body was tense and his neck rigid with anger as he glared into the nobleman's face. "You have breached the terms of the surrender!" he had shouted, partly in joy and partially in apprehensive anxiety. "What does your master offer in return if we were to...ah...overlook this egregious breach of faith? Are you to be taken hostage as a guarantee of your people's faithfulness to any possible renegotiation?" At these words, the nobleman, despite being of considerable height, seemed to shrink and his cheeks lost their color. His lack of courage only served to infuriate Cussius, and he spun away disinterestedly as if the man deserved no further attention. Eventually, he had tired of the matter and had the guards drag him off. Even now the man sat in the stockade.

Cussius stopped his pacing when the canvas partition lifted to the side and Lana ducked in carrying a loaf of bread and a platter of steaming pork chops. The smell brought him to the table where she placed the scrumptious smelling food in the center. With a smile, she gestured for him to sit.

"Where's Marcus?" he growled. "He's supposed to dine with us. We have much to discuss."

Lana smiled knowingly as she took her own seat. She looked up at the doorway. "Someone is here," she said.

Cussius turned around and saw that a sentry was opening the door for Marcus. The man was dripping wet and his short hair was matted to his head. The fall rains were relentless of late, and the walk from his lodging was just enough for a man to get drenched.

Cussius stood up from the table but did not leave it. "Do come in, Centurion Marcus. Please have a cup of wine and help yourself to the hot chow. It looks like you might need it." Marcus shook himself, much like a bear would when emerging from a mountain lake. Cussius chuckled at his private vision. "Have a seat," he ordered.

Marcus walked to the table and plopped down on a stool, his legs making a wet, slapping sound. He nodded to Lana respectfully before addressing his commander. "Thank you, sir." Marcus reached over and grabbed a wineskin, pouring the amber liquid until it came close to spilling over. He gulped it down and took a large bite of pork. "This is delicious. The cook should be promoted. Mmm---succulent," Marcus said before chewing once again.

"I'm glad you like it." Cussius wolfed his meat down and did not really take the time to savor it. "Did you hear?" Cussius asked.

"About Cassivellaunus not following through with his end of the bargain?" Marcus asked rhetorically. "Yes, I have heard about it. Complicates matters, doesn't it?" He slathered some fresh butter on the bread and ate it in one bite.

"It does make things a sight more interesting, that much I will allow." Cussius stood up from the table. The restless energy was back and he could not sit still. "I knew that old war lord would go back on his word as soon as he could. Truth be told, I would bet he never intended to come up with the tribute. Cagey bastard. Chief Mandubrac knew as much. Remember? He warned us a couple months back, not long after we took on this mission." He sighed, and all of a sudden the veil was lifted and he could clearly see. Caesar himself saw this was coming. No matter, he thought. "This certainly does leave us with room to be creative. Whichever route we take, it must be decisively done."

"We can't afford to fight the Coritani and Cassivellaunus at the same time. We don't have the manpower for a two-front war," said Marcus.

Cussius was back to pacing the length of the room. Marcus has a keen grasp of the obvious, he thought. "You are quite right. We have 2000 fighting men and that's not something to sniff about." Actually, he still smarted from a blow his forces had recently suffered. A fast-moving mixed force of Bibroci, Trinovante and Roman horsemen were demolished by Coritani forces at a backwater village. But still, his confidence and belief in his abilities and that of his men remained undaunted. "We are a force to be reckoned with. So they must know something we don't, or else, why risk our ire? That's easy. Precisely because they believe we won't risk fighting them both simultaneously." Cussius found it therapeutic to think out loud. He spoke rapidly, his words keeping pace with his mind. "We will deal with them one at a time." Looking at Lana, he asked, "Would the Coritani and Cassivellaunus ally against us?" He paused long enough in his pacing to take a cup of warm wine and held it with both hands, appreciative of its warmth.

Lana sat at ease, her hands folded before her and resting on the oak tabletop. "It's possible. I'm sure overtures have been made," she said thoughtfully. "The Coritani have already sought Cassivellaunus' help. On the other hand, Cassivellaunus sought the aid of the Coritani when he was fighting your Caesar. The Coritani did little aside from sending a few head of cattle. Traditionally, our tribes have been rivals, and old grudges have been difficult to put aside. There have been border raids here and there throughout the years as we've tested each other's strength, but in my memory, they have never fought a major war against one another." Lana had gleaned this information from listening quietly while her father discussed business with the many traders and artisans who passed through the village. Her uncle was another source. He was keen on learning and delighted in word play. She enjoyed the storytelling and absorbed it all. Even her late husband, as dull as he was, occasionally spoke of the comings and goings of the tribal conflicts, further expanding her limited education.

Lana paused, frowned and stared into the fire as if deep in thought. Cussius waited intently, oblivious, or maybe purposely immune to others witnessing his attention to the woman's thoughts. "Maybe overtures should be made to both. I suspect Cassivellaunus will be the more eager partner."

Cussius continued stalking as he considered her words. His moving shadow flickered on the walls like a host of dark clouds moving across a dawn sky. She was shrewd and prone to examining issues from a broad platform, and if he were honest with himself, he had to admit that she could possibly be in tune with the gods. He was prone to agree with her assessment. "Either way, our Celtic allies will have to adjust," he said thoughtfully. He knew the Bibroci were still smarting from the death of one of their clan chiefs, Kegan, at the hands of the Coritani. On the other hand, Chief Mandubrac and his second, Kren, of the Trinovante nursed an equally scorching hatred for Cassivellaunus and the Coritani. He smiled grimly as he thought of the finagling ahead. You can't please everyone all of the time, he thought. He had made his decision.

"I believe that in exchange for the delinquent status of their tribute payment and for their grievous breach of the treaty terms dictated by Caesar, this warlord, Cassivellaunus, shall enjoy the glory of an alliance with us, with the Romans." He smiled mirthlessly.

Marcus raised his cup in salute. "To new alliances and the destruction of our enemies," he toasted. His lips drew back from his teeth, revealing the long and sharply pointed canines.

All three raised their cups and drained the contents. "Prepare the men. We move out two days from now," Cussius ordered.

CHAPTER THIRTY-TWO

EARLY IN THE morning, before the sun had risen, Cussius and Marcus headed out in strength. Cussius was pleased. Half a cohort of his finest battle-hardened cavalry led a winding column of three centuries of Marcus' infantry. Ahead of the main body and on both flanks, roving bands of Bibroci and Trinovante horsemen acted as a security screen. If necessary, they would skirmish with any raiders and alert the main body of the dangers ahead, but he didn't anticipate running into any roving Catuvellauni patrols. If they did, the element of surprise would be surrendered and events could get away from him fast. He had issued orders, particularly to the allied tribesmen that contact with the enemy was to be avoided at all costs. Such an order was always unpopular with the barbarians, but their clan leaders knew the value of stealth. In truth, he wanted nothing more than an undetected and uninterrupted march. If necessary, there would be plenty of opportunity for battle, but he would prefer it to be at his instigation and on his terms.

Behind them, the sun was creeping over the skyline. Turning in his saddle, the last thing he saw was Lana standing on the western parapet and perfectly silhouetted by the emerging rays of the dawn. The sight of her sent a sharp pang like a needle pushing its way into his chest. She was looking in his direction, and she raised her arm and waved. For a second, he imagined her looking at him and him alone, and he returned the stare as intensely as possible; but conscious of his image, he did not wave back. Instead, he turned toward their destination and disappeared into the depths of the forest.

The Romans rode and marched northwest, following ridge trails and creek beds, sometimes losing sight of the river for an hour or so. Cussius increased the pace to a steady trot. They checked direction by the sun and by watching which side of the trees the moss grew on. He enjoyed picking up on the native woodcraft and paid close attention to the ways of the tribal horsemen. He was impressed with the respectful ease with which they moved through the forest. It seemed as if they were careful to leave as little trace of their passing as possible, but Cussius thought it wasted effort as the passing of six hundred men was impossible to conceal. Nevertheless, he was pleased the scouts took his earlier directive to heart. As he rode, he envisioned what a little Roman engineering could make of this rough path, which was really little more than a widened game trail and barely sufficient to accommodate four mounts riding abreast. He determined to develop this roadway once an alliance was secured with Cassivellaunus. It would make sense to have a road capable of supporting heavier transport to make things easier militarily and commercially, and such a project would further bolster any potential alliance. The easier two peoples could travel and trade with one another, the greater the likelihood of good relations.

The day was cold, but the streams flowed smoothly, unimpeded by ice as the autumn season had heretofore refused to give way to winter. Throughout the day, riders came in with reports. So far, no Coritani horsemen had accosted the column. Neither did the scouts report any recent trace of the enemy. Old fires were investigated but found to be at least two days old. The longer they rode the farther away from Coritani lands they traveled. Finally, Kren rode back and announced they were in Catuvellauni territory.

Cussius climbed from his mount and began checking the shoes of his horse. He lifted the foreleg and ran his hand over the hoof to ensure the small iron nails were flush against the shoe. Around him, other cavalrymen did the same.

"Shall we camp here?" asked Marcus.

Not taking his eyes from his work, Cussius shrugged. Then, turning to Kren, who leaned against a tree beside him, he asked, "How much farther to Cassivellaunus' main village?" They had traveled at least twenty miles, and he figured the infantry to be only five miles behind.

"Not much farther. Maybe five miles," Kren replied.

"Marcus." Cussius looked to his left where his second rigidly sat in the saddle. He could tell the man was more comfortable on his feet than in the saddle, but that was not his concern. "How far back are your troops and how long until they arrive?" Speed and timing were critical. He wanted the arrival of his forces to be a complete surprise and catch the old bastard unaware.

Marcus glanced up at the sky and noted the long shadows. It was maybe one more hour before the sun disappeared for the day. "They won't be here until two or maybe three hours after dark. They will be tired but will do what is demanded of them," he assured his commander.

Cussius had his mind made up. "Strike camp here. Half of my cavalry will remain to await your infantry. I will take the remainder and half of the Celtic scouts ahead. I'm anxious to make this warlord's acquaintance." He began to ride forward even as his orders made their way to his troops. Half of them disembarked and began preparing camp. Cussius turned in his saddle, his cavalry picking its way around him.

"Marcus, you are in charge. If we have not returned by sunrise, follow us and burn the place to the ground." He kicked his mount and trotted away.

THE CLOUDS HAD passed and the night sky was clear when the Romans emerged from the dark woods. Cussius and his horsemen closed the distance to the hillfort. The ground was covered with a mist that rose to the shoulders of the horses and gave the men the appearance of walking on misty waves of gray. He could hear the calls of alarm echo up and down the length of the palisade wall. The peculiar luminosity the moon occasionally favors provided ample light, and the fort rose up as if it sprung from the night. He could see the heads of men bobbing up and down over the picket wall as they sought a better view of the oncoming riders. Cussius decided to throw caution to the wind and boldly rode up to the main gate. He hailed the sentries in a loud and confident voice.

"Cassivellaunus!" he shouted. "It is I, Cussius Caesar. Commander of the Roman forces of Britannia, and I demand an audience!" His horse snorted and danced nervously. The strange smells did not sit well with him, and the animal, a gelded war mount trained for battle and excitable at the smell of blood, pawed at the ground in a bad temper. He never failed to obey Cussius' commands and always charged into the hottest of frays with hooves slashing and teeth nipping and biting. Cussius leaned over and cooed gently into his mount's ear. He was a bit nervous himself. There was no guarantee an enemy bowman would not simply lean over and unloose an arrow into his chest, but he trusted his bravado. A show of confidence should sew confusion and the enemy would comply with his demands out of sheer disorganization and surprise.

His answer came in the form of the thick oak gate swinging on its iron hinges. Anticipating action, his horse just barely stepped forward, and Cussius grinned fiercely at its display of pent-up aggression. Behind him, he could hear the fifty men who composed his escort spread out in expectation of trouble. It was unnecessary.

An older man stepped out. He was accompanied by two rough-looking warriors bearing torches, and each one led a very large dog of identical breed. The moonlight shone upon the attack beasts' shaggy heads and their red eyes glared behind large powerful jaws set on thick necks. On command, the animals sat obediently, with only their black lips quivering as they slid backward to reveal long sharp teeth slick with saliva. A low, steady growl escaped their throats, but they did not attack.

Cussius nodded and was met with silent glowers. He had observed the warlord at the parley where Cassivellaunus had agreed upon the terms that ended hostilities between his people and Caesar. He had to admit the man was no coward. It took courage to step out in the dark to face an unknown number of men with dubious intentions. Yet Cussius exalted within. His gamble of quickly re-acting to Cassivellaunus' refusal to deliver the tribute had paid dividends. If only the remainder were to unfold as nicely, he thought as he measured up his foe and perhaps soon-to-be erstwhile ally.

Cassivellaunus was very tall and grim. Even in the moonlight, his gaze was penetrating and his voice harsh. His long graying but still auburn hair fell to his shoulders. Despite his age, his hair was like a mane, full and wild, with no hint of thinning. From under his nose sprouted a finely tended moustache surprisingly void of the gray hairs that peppered his head. He wore a large golden torc and a voluminous patterned cloak with a thick plaid fastened over it. His eyes were beady and swept over the ad hoc gathering as if he expected them. All the while, his arms remained crossed over his chest and the fine example of a sword that hung from his belt re-mained sheathed.

The Celtic warlord did not mince words as he spoke directly to Cussius. "What brings you here? Your behavior is bold, sir. It bor-ders upon rude." Cassivellaunus spoke in heavily accented Latin, but his grasp of the language was more than adequate. "You barge upon the walls of my peaceful village when I am in the midst of din-ner with the mother of my children. What should stop me from ordering the archers that are manning the walls to pour down ar-rows upon you? Can you tell me? What could be of such importance that you barge in unannounced and risk retaliation?"

Cussius smiled in return, but his eyes lacked any merriment. He enjoyed the cagey warlord's attempt at subterfuge, but he would not be fooled. "I agree it is bold. You speak a passable version of our language, and so you must have received some rudimentary educa-tion in the past. Let this moment serve as another education. We have a saying that roughly translates to 'seize the day.' Can't you see?" He pointed to his surrounding troopers who sat silently and watched the encounter closely. "That is precisely what is happening. The day has been seized — by us. And besides, if you had a hun-dred archers walking the walls as you claim---well, let's just say my welcome would have been a bit pricklier than it was. Now, shall we sit outside all night in the chill, or shall we convene in more appropriate environs where we can discuss our business in proper fashion?" Cussius maintained his grinning façade. Inside, his belly was cold and his heart beat rapidly as he waited to see if he had correctly called the warlord's bluff.

For a moment, Cassivellaunus kept his hooded eyes on those of Cussius. He did not blink, and the stillness of the man and the night was unnerving. Finally, he ventured a forced smile. "Not all of your men can come in. It would be unseemly for so many to enter these walls." He waved at the watching cavalry and left his true thoughts unsaid.

Cussius rushed to assure him. "Worry not. Not all of my men will come in. I would not dare impose such demands on a loyal friend and ally. Impose upon a partner in peace? Never. That just wouldn't do. Only my escort will accompany me inside the walls. The others will remain at the edge of the forest," Cussius said innocently. He enjoyed the look of consternation creeping into the warlord's face as the beady eyes strained to see into the night beyond Cussius' horsemen. It was proof the man's confidence was further shaken. Like a wolf with the smell of blood in his nose, Cussius continued the press.

He leapt off his mount, oblivious to the snapping teeth of the war dogs that strained at their leashes in quick lunges. "Control those animals or I will hack the jaws off their heads!" he ordered. He stood unblinking, his only movement that of drawing his sword. The two bodyguards strained with their charges, their arms bulging with their efforts to restrain the beasts. Behind him, Cussius could hear swords sliding free from their oiled scabbards. While Cassivellaunus remained motionless and unperturbed, the bodyguards exchanged twin looks of rising panic. Finally, a series of desperate, hard jerks on the leash brought the dogs to heel. Sheathing his sword, Cussius calmly motioned the remainder of his troopers to follow suit.

He waited until Cassivellaunus passed the threshold before he loudly announced, "Antonius! You are in command of the troops while I'm inside. Notify Marcus. And allow no riders to leave the village. No one is to leave. If I'm not out by midnight, you know what to do." He was sure Antonius would follow the order to the letter. He also knew the message and its intent did not go unnoticed by Cassivellaunus. In twos, Cussius and his attendants followed their newly gracious host inside.

CUSSIUS DRANK IN the smell of the warlord's lodge. He was used to the scent of smoked meats and soured ales and had begun to welcome these odors. By tribal standards, the man dwelled in relative opulence. The lodge was of the standard conical design, but on a much grander scale than Cussius had seen to date. It looked to be of recent construction, and he thought he could smell the freshly limed wattle and daub that brightly coated the walls.

He scanned the interior of the lodge and noted the limited number of nobles in attendance. Any elder or noble within village limits were roused from their slumbers and had gathered within the lodge. Their retainers ringed the seats with daggers as their only arms. Most stood directly behind their lords, literally minding their backs. To a man, they gawked at the Romans in disbelief. Some rubbed their eyes sleepily and shook their heads as if they were dreaming.

Cussius accepted the hastily poured mead and nodded his thanks to the shapely servant. The girl bowed and then tossed her hair provocatively before attending to the cups of her master. Cussius rose and took command of the floor.

"To Cassivellaunus." He raised his cup toward the ceiling. "To our eternal friendship, I propose a toast, and I would like to thank you noblemen and fine fighting men of the Catuvellauni for your gracious hospitality. To friendship and good health," said Cussius. He sipped his brew and watched the nobles over the rim of his cup. Their looks of bewilderment were utterly enjoyable for him. Some raised their cups tentatively, but others anxiously watched their king for some sort of indication. Cussius turned his stare upon him as well. Finally, Cassivellaunus raised his cup to the ceiling.

"To friendship," he said. He tipped the cup and drank deeply. He burped and wiped his dripping moustache with the back of his hand. An audible sigh of relief swept through the assembled noble-men, and the tension dissipated like a retreating fog in the face of the morning sun. The sight of the fully armed Romans was unnerv-ing, but the nobles were now in familiar territory and knew that terms were sure to follow. They leaned in, eager to hear him out.

Cussius plowed on. "A short time ago, our peoples were at war with one another. Terms were agreed upon and peace ensued. Host-ages were taken and tribute demanded by Caesar." He paused a moment and looked about the room. "In short, you have failed to live up to the terms. I was most distressed to learn of your tribe's re-fusal to abide by the treaty and deliver the promised tribute. I thought to myself, surely this cannot be. An honorable fighting man, of renowned nobility such as Cassivellaunus would never renege on a treaty so recently penned in blood. With a heart full of sadness I had to come here and address you personally," Cussius said, a look of contrived sadness framing his face. The gathered nobles stared at him impassively, but behind their blank stares he could smell their collective guilt and pressed on.

"Your emissary has pleaded your cause. He speaks of times be-ing lean and the inability to procure the tribute because of the recent war. I understand your plight, and that is why the terms of Caesar's treaty will change as thus; five hundred of your best warriors will be serving under my command." He waited, giving the startled nobles a moment to digest what he demanded and was pleased with the response. He could see their collective calculating wits at play, the nobles whispering and nodding amongst themselves.

They probably think this is an opportunity to pawn off five hundred mouths they won't have to feed, thought Cussius. Dashing their hopes he hastily added the caveat, "The men serving under my command are put to the task and are in need of a lot of food and material to serve at their best. Therefore, due to the high demands upon my soldiers, you will cause to be delivered double their winter rations." The nobles exchanged worried looks and sought the eye of their king. For his part, Cassivellaunus maintained a steady stare at the floor before finally looking up.

"You fight the Coritani? We will fight them with you. But..." He held up one hand, the index finger extended. "We expect to reap the harvest of our efforts as well. That is not too much to ask?" Cassivellaunus was perking up. His beady eyes gleamed with calculating greed.

Cussius recognized the symptoms. Self-preservation stoked fiery hot with greed was etched in the warlord's face. "All men who ride under my banner are amply rewarded," Cussius said loudly. He was sure to make eye contact with as many of the nobles as possible. He wanted to bind them to him. "I'm sure some of those Coritani farmlands, rich with rolling fields of sweet grass and wheat, will be in need of new masters," he suggested, pausing a moment as the nobles murmured amongst themselves with furtive hand gestures and sharp nods.

Cassivellaunus rose from his seat and walked to Cussius. He extended a burly arm and Cussius clasped it in return, sealing the deal.

"It is good." The warlord grinned.

"Indeed it is," Cussius said. He bowed deeply and announced his leave, and as quickly as they arrived, the Romans filed out and melted into the surrounding countryside.

CHAPTER THIRTY-THREE

THE NEXT THREE days sped by, and Marcus was kept busy inspecting the Catuvellauni warriors who swelled the Roman ranks. They were a rough lot, and many of them had borne arms against and clashed with the very Romans they now considered allies. The irony was not lost on any of those assembled, and many jokes were made in an attempt to defuse the tension. Inevitably, occasional fistfights broke out around the campfires, and it was particularly contentious wherever Trinovante and Catuvellauni warriors crossed paths. Insults flew and anger spilled out of control until flailing warriors rolled around in the mud, swinging and kicking madly at one another. No serious injuries had resulted from these fisticuffs, but if it continued, it would only be a matter of time before blades were drawn and blood spilled and Marcus had seen enough. He formed a squad of the meanest and ugliest legionaries he could muster who roamed the camp and responded brutally to any shows of aggression by the rival warriors. Heads were thumped and order soon prevailed. The word quickly traveled that hooliganism would not be tolerated. Discipline demanded, the native troops toed the line.

Cassivellaunus had made good on his pledge and then some. In addition to five hundred warriors on foot, he attached a force of ten chariots along with a contingent of fifty mounted scouts. He also forwarded the winter's worth of double rations demanded in the negotiations. As Marcus took stock and marked the inventory scroll, his attention was drawn away by the sound of legionaries shouting, "Salute!"

Riding his magnificent charger at a trot and jauntily returning the salutes, Cussius drew up alongside the provisions. He did not dismount.

"Not too bad a haul. Caesar's tribute may well be gone, but our army grows by 600 warriors with provisions to feed double that over the winter. Our prospects are looking up." He grinned.

Marcus failed to find the humor in the statement but still managed a weak smile in return. He began to shout for Leko to bring his horse but then remembered the boy was captured. The fact only served to darken his mood further.

"May I ride with you? I have some things I would like to discuss." Marcus was already walking the short distance to his mount. He clambered up and deftly maneuvered the bay mare alongside Cussius.

Cussius eyed him casually. "I guess you may. Our exchange has to be quick, as we both have much to do. But before our business, let's stretch the legs of these beasts. Yah!" With a sudden explosion of muscle, Cussius' charger bolted into a full gallop in the twinkling of an eye.

Marcus put his mare to a gallop but the charger was too fast and powerful and he had no chance of closing the gap. As trees sped by and men scattered, they neared the edge of the camp. Cussius reined in hard and circled his beast as he waited a few brief seconds for Marcus to catch up.

"You don't ride too bad for someone who earns his bread fighting on his feet," Cussius allowed. Marcus was red faced and appeared as aggravated as his horse was fatigued.

"I prefer to lead my men from the ground and from in front. I will leave the cavalry to you, sir." Marcus hesitated. The men dipped their heads low as they rode underneath a beech with low-hanging limbs.

"What is the reason for this impromptu meeting, centurion?" Cussius asked. His slate gray eyes dwelled shrewdly upon Marcus' square face.

Marcus eyed his commander thoughtfully. Cussius appeared calm, content, almost catlike as he waited for Marcus to get to his point.

Marcus took a deep breath and exhaled. "What are we really doing here? We have overstepped our bounds. I mean, we have gone far beyond our orders from Caesar. We were to establish a garrison at the confluence of the rivers. Remember? We were then to meet with Cassivellaunus and take the tribute back to the coast for shipment to Gaul. We are doing neither. Instead, we are in a war with blood oath implications," exclaimed Marcus. "Well? Did I forget to add that it looks more like we are here to conquer and settle this land than to merely take tribute? We do not have a mandate for any such actions, and even if we do conquer these barbarians, we don't have any colonists on the way to settle it, which also means we have to occupy this place. Occupation garrisons need resupply and a rotation of troops." He sighed loudly. His blocky face was etched with worried resignation. "Don't forget we would surely face charges of treason and desertion if Caesar knew of our actions." His brown eyes locked onto Cussius, and he was surprised to see that the man maintained his studied reserve.

It was Cussius' turn for quiet. He rode his horse forward and led them to a clearing behind a stand of scrub oaks. Eerie and odd for the season, the air hung in leaden layers, not a breeze stirring. He dismounted and waved for Marcus to follow him to the cover of a big oak tree with gnarled roots bulging from the ground. Cussius reached down and grabbed a handful of the loamy soil, mixing it with the year's batch of fallen leaves. He closed his eyes and brought the mixture to his nose and breathed in deeply.

He opened his eyes and fixed Marcus with a stare. "It smells like home to me. Do you get that feeling? I do," he said with a faraway look in his eye before his energy-driven intensity returned. He stood up hastily.

"We can never return to Rome. Why should we want to anyhow?" He said this in a soft whisper, almost as if he were speaking more to himself than to Marcus. "You know that I am of the family Julii, do you not? Does it truly matter to have a shiny old name such as that? I allow that it did at times, but that time is past for me. Rome does not have a hold on me any longer. It is a city teeming with petty patrician squabbles and senatorial hypocrites who send out their most ambitious to win new riches for themselves. You know that my name is not enough to secure my appointment as senator. That is all well and good and is the way it should be, but neither is my military service to the republic of any value. Of course, it helps immensely if there is military success but those chapters remain unwritten. My name and service would not suffice regardless of how meritorious my petition may be. Land and estates is how they measure wealth. If I had enough land, I could buy my seat in the Senate. Do you see anything peculiar about that?" He cocked his head to the side.

Marcus shrugged. "I never had cause to think about a Senate seat and appointments and such. I just followed orders."

Cussius returned to his mount and grabbed a water skin hanging from the pommel of his saddle. Cussius then walked to where Marcus sat and peered down at him, hand extended with the skin offered to Marcus. "Here, take it. I've noticed your growing fondness for this stuff. It doesn't suit me, so here," Cussius said with a smile and nod. "I digress. Is that not problematic in itself? Is that not the natural order of things, or is it merely the enforced order? Does it not bother you that you could never be considered for the Senate? Or for tribune? Any high office would be unattainable for you, and all due to the station of your birth, I might add. The Greeks would argue that such a system is unjust and does not afford good, quality men true freedom. What say you?"

The barrage of questions on unfamiliar subjects startled Marcus. He scrambled for words. "The legion is my home," Marcus said. "It has been good to me. I have moved up the ranks, and I believe I deserved it. All of my promotions were due to the strength of my arm and my dedication to the life." Marcus scrambled to his feet and stretched his legs. He uncorked the bag and took a sniff. The stench of fermentation assailed his senses. He took a cautious sip, the liquid burning his gums and tongue as it slid around and down his throat. He took another drink and closed his eyes as a fire took hold in the depths of his stomach.

Marcus offered the skin to Cussius who declined with a curt wave of his hand. Marcus pursed his lips and growled, "Well, it seems that the system worked in your favor now didn't it? Look at us for example. While an important promotion seemed beyond me, it fell into your lap like a scrambling pup. You and I both know that I should have been given command of this mission. I have served longer than you. I never shirk a task and I always rate successful," Marcus boasted truthfully.

Cussius' eyes lit up and he smiled. "Exactly my point!" he cried excitedly. "I agree wholeheartedly. You earned those promotions through the sweat of your brow and the blood you shed. You have learned your craft and excel at it. Life in the legion is simpler than the goings on at the Forum and the Palatine. Are you blinded to the familiar? Your not being promoted is merely symptomatic of the ailments besieging our wayward homeland. But out here, battle is life or death, a very simple formula to grasp and to implement. The strong and cunning survive while the weak and unimaginative die, and yet Rome itself does not embrace these ideals. There, the opposite rules. The weak are cunning and the strong are sacrificed for the benefit of the weak. Our ethics — strong wills, hard work and innovation — would be mocked. In Rome, money and land and title outweigh talent and drive. The well-to-do would crinkle their noses at the likes of us. Well, I say let them. We start over right here. We build our own state, our own country. The land is here for the taking and is a new beginning, a new slate awaiting the carver to make his mark. Look around you. This island is wealthy. And women! They are beautiful, are they not? You could find yourself a choice virgin and start yourself a family if that's what you desire. The point is, here, you can make that choice and then do what is necessary to nurture that choice into reality. Can't you see it? Join me. Let's build this together, here, starting all over," Cussius pleaded.

Marcus was taken back and he stood blinking for a moment as he digested all that was said. Another swig of the plum liquor broke him from his silence. "What about Caesar? Do you think he's going to let a renegade legion run amok and essentially desert on a mass scale? He will return and make war upon us. We would end up like any others who have resisted him — dead or captured but ultimately dead regardless. And for what? A dream? I do not fancy marching Roman legion against Roman legion. It is not right."

Despite his reservations, what Cussius said appealed to Marcus. When he thought about it, there really was not much worth going back for. The small family farm was probably ground to dust or swallowed up by the very senators and forces of corruption that Cussius railed against at this very moment. Vaguely, through the fog of jumbled thoughts, Lana's earlier words came to mind. A clean slate sounded good to Marcus. Maybe he could find a place to call home. Perhaps he too could experience the warmth and commitment of family, a family outside of the legion.

Cussius whirled and spoke excitedly. "What does Caesar care? We are but a thousand Romans. He has over seven legions to play with and a rebellion to defeat. Don't forget the Senate will recall him as soon as he's finished in Gaul. You see, he is just the sort that makes them nervous. So, fortune smiles upon us, as Caesar is too busy fighting his own wars to bother with us." Cussius appeared confident and a slight smile creased its way to the fore.

"Besides, are our actions really that far off from our orders? If Caesar were to return today, what would he see? I will tell you. He would see a fort built, roughly halfway between the Coritani and the Catuvellauni, which is close enough to approximate his original orders. He would see us adjusting, innovating and adapting to the realities of this island with regard to the tribute. By allying themselves with us and providing troops and supplies, Cassivellaunus is paying homage to Rome. So you see, we have been consistently following orders the whole time."

Marcus thought he looked smug in his defense of their actions, but he had to admit that what Cussius said made a lot of sense. "We will see." He still harbored a deep distrust of the patrician despite all the heady talk of equality and freedom. He did not even notice as another drink stole past his lips.

Cussius leapt atop his mount with remarkable ease, much like other men take to their favorite chair. "Let's go. We have a war to conduct." They made the short ride back and readied the troops for the march. It was a good day to set out. The sunlight was pale and the air had a chilly edge.

CHAPTER THIRTY-FOUR

JAYAS WAS ANTSY with anticipation. Every part of him was alert. His eyes slanted meanly and his head was cocked with shoulders rigid. He had one hand on his reins and the other clutched his spear. Satisfied they had not been spotted, Jayas and Lann watched the column slither its way up the wooded slope. From deep within the tightly woven branches of the massive willow tree, they observed their quarry plod toward the ground he had chosen, the perfect terrain, a u-shaped ridge not easily flanked, with an impassable marsh to the right and a precipitous ravine on the left. He wagered the Roman supply train would choose the ridge as its camping spot because of its seemingly defensible position. His wolfish grin showed white in his blue-painted face. He had other plans.

Early that morning, before the first pink streaks of dawn appeared, two hundred of his warriors had secreted themselves along the length of the ridge and spread out. They were now cleverly concealed on the conical hill amongst its jutting crown of rocky ledges, silent and still, enduring the cold for almost twelve hours. Now he and another one hundred warriors were shadowing the slow-moving column but did not risk contact. His eyes narrowed in recognition as he made out the squarely built figure striding in front of the supply train's infantry escort. Jayas watched the man keep a ground-eating pace and obviously expecting the same of those who followed.

"Marcus," Jayas whispered in a tight hiss. Even at this distance, he recognized the dour face. "Where's your commander?" he wondered to himself, his breath becoming a dull gray spurt in the cold air.

Jayas patiently stalked his prey, silently encouraging it to take the path he had foreordained. So far, his prey had listened to his fervent urgings and was climbing the stairs of destiny. He was nervous despite the blessings he received from Rhu before departing, and cold claws of doubt gripped his chest. Fighting the sensation, his mind flickered with days-old memories that might as well have been nonexistent, as tough as they were now to recall.

The strange ceremony Rhu put him through before departing for this battle had left him tired and watchful. He remembered Rhu advising him: "Beware of the Romans. They are like the sun, the wind, and the rain. In the end they wear everything down to sand." Stranger still was the sensation that Thara did more than watch the ritual. Through the haze of the tea-induced fog, he made out her presence. Her scent was intoxicating and her supple willingness enveloped him whole. Suddenly, and without reason, she pulled away without a word. Then she turned and left the smoky lodge, leaving him to his dreams. He still didn't know what to make of the ceremony or her actions, let alone his dreams. He wasn't even sure any of the experience had been real.

The shouting of the drovers and the cracking of whips from the Roman column floated to his ears and drew him back to the present. His heartbeat sped up once again and kept a steady *thrum*. Despite the cold, a warm feeling began spreading throughout his body. The Romans were stopping for the night.

MARCUS STALKED THE length of the wagons. He was not happy with the sloppiness of the march and the subsequent attempt at setting up camp. "Get those wagons up here and in line! Now!" he screamed in exasperation.

His sergeants came to life and found their voices. "Dig in, men! We aren't on holiday! No one sups until you finish!" they warned in unison.

Marcus came upon a group of wagoneers, Catuvellauni by the looks of them, huddled around a recently sparked fire warming their hands over the flames. Some enterprising soul had procured spirits and they were energetically passing the jug of liquor around. Marcus shot them a look of loathing he reserved for shirkers. "Hey you! You lot of loafers aren't paralyzed, are you? If not, get off your lazy asses and help dig in!" The barbarians made ready to give him some lip, but something in his bearing led them to leave it alone and they skulked off muttering to one another.

Taking a quick glance around, Marcus sneaked a drink from the abandoned jug. He welcomed the burning sensation and savored the hot streak it left from throat to belly. Marcus shook his head in self-admonishment. He was into his cups earlier and more often than usual. What does it hurt, he thought? He was still on top of the job, and besides, drink took the edge off. He took another swig and looked heavenward, swirling the sharply biting drink around his palate before swallowing greedily. The sky began to darken as the sun retired to its post for the night. A sliver of moon hung shyly as stars approached, blinking and shooting across the sky. Somewhere, a night bird called out with a warbling, melodic sound. He listened as an owl answered with a hooting call of its own. He tipped the jug in salute to the singing creatures and enjoyed the moment he had to himself. He thought of what he and Cussius had spoken of a couple days earlier. It could work. He could make a go of it here on this island.

He took a drink and held the jug aloft once again. "Here's to home, to wherever we may find it," he whispered hopefully.

Nearby, a horse nickered and another snorted wetly. He thought it probably the result of nothing more than a lone starving wolf braving the smell of man in exchange for sneaking off with a scrap or two. Off to his left, the camp cooks were adding logs to their low smoky fire. Throughout the length of the camp, fires were beginning to glow as duties were finished and the men warmed water for cleaning, shaving and drinking. The cooking fires lit up their faces as tired men sat with their arms slumped over their knees and stared out into the darkness as if they could see their own deaths or the shadows of comrades long gone to earth. Others leaned back on their rolls, their tired feet soaking up the feeble warmth given of the fires stoked with green wood.

Marcus heard something out of place, like the shuffling of feet, or perhaps it was only the flutter of wings. He kept his neck craned until it ached. His hair stood up as his ears detected what sounded like wrestling and the wet sound of punches meeting flesh. His temper flared. It had been difficult putting an end to the jealousies and hatred that plagued the shaky alliance between the Romans, the Trinovante, Bibroci and the Catuvellauni tribes. Obviously, they hadn't completely learned. Irritated, he stood up with a slight wobble in his legs. The potent drink must have worked its dark magic in a hurry. In the darkness, the struggle amplified with desperate grunts. He jogged toward the sound.

He came to an abrupt stop, his mind scarcely registering what his eyes were witnessing. A naked Celt, painted and shining in the moonlight, crouched over a motionless legionary, chopping into his head. The war axe was shiny and bright with new blood. Marcus shook his head violently to clear it. Blurs of motion in the darkness kept his attention from focusing on any particular area. Blue-painted savages were running, crouched and swift, toward every fire in the camp. The bitter stench of mortality was heavy in the air.

A shout of alarm burst from Marcus' throat and he jumped the short distance to where the Celt was sawing at his grisly trophy to kick the snarling warrior in the throat. He skidded to a halt and swung his steel, which sang like a sizzling flame as it cut through the air and cleanly sliced through the blue-painted neck. He then ran to where the wagons were drawn. From the corner of his eye, he glimpsed five figures sprinting to cut him off, and he doubled his efforts.

He began shouting loudly and waving his sword. "To arms! To arms! Enemy within the camp!" He hurried to the wagon where he had left his shield. Answering shouts were heard amidst screams of pain and confusion. Two wild-eyed Celts rushed him, their blades held high. He hurled the shield at the closest one and grinned wickedly when the warrior slammed to the ground, his momentum viciously interrupted by the spinning iron. The other screamed his challenge and vaulted over his tribesman, eager to sink the edge of the blade into soft flesh. Still howling, he aimed a strike at Marcus' head. Marcus parried the blow, slashed and thrust his blade into the warrior's shoulder. Blood spurted wildly and coated the length of the blade before he yanked it free.

Marcus scrambled to get his shield, only pausing long enough to stick the tip of his short sword into the bulge of the fallen warrior's throat. As he felt the tip grind into the rocky soil, he looked up in time to meet another frantic rush. He grunted and swung the sword backhanded. It came around with a hum and smashed into the foremost warrior's elbow. The warrior sagged and the sword swished again. His painted head rolled onto the soiled ground.

Two more longhaired barbarians moved in deadly concert. Their blue-painted bodies glowed in the moonlight. Marcus slowly backpedaled as he kept his adversaries to his front. Behind him, he could hear the wild yelps of the Coritani mingling with the cruder hoarseness of Latin curses. He was sure pockets of his men were rallying, and he meant to fight his way through the barbarian forces to reach them. He eyeballed his stalking pursuers. There was no wild rush. They did not waste their breath on war cries. These are more mature warriors, he determined with respect, warriors not prone to rashness. They approached with their long shields to the fore, eyes peeking over the edge of the iron-rimmed wood. Marcus knew his window of opportunity was closing.

JAYAS FELT HIS HAND tighten instinctively on the shaft of his spear as he inched his way closer. He approached quietly, as if stalking a grazing herd of deer through the tall grass. He leaned forward over his horse until his chest lay flat against the mane. He saw that the Romans were breaking into smaller groups as they huddled around their fires, preparing for their evening meal and a night of rest. At the fire he stalked toward, two of the Romans had raised their heads and were staring across the fog trying to see with their eyes what their ears could barely detect.

The moon was an orb casting a flood of light atop the leafless trees. A gust of wind swept over the ridge, rustling limbs and scattering fallen leaves. The Romans were alert but paid the sounds no further attention, attributing any noise to the fickle wind. Around Jayas, his painted warriors stalked in deadly silence. He straightened in the saddle and raised his spear before putting his horse to a gallop. He rode boldly into the midst of the Romans, his horse leaping and kicking, its hooves catching one slow moving legionary in the side of the head. The trampled legionary lay silent and unmoving. Jayas hurled his javelin and grinned as he watched it cut an arc through the air. A fleeing Roman caught it between the shoulder blades and flopped to the ground with great bellows of pain and outrage before ceasing to move.

Jayas drew his sword and kicked his horse toward a group of Romans scrambling for their shields. They scattered at his approach, and he struck several sharp, cutting blows against bare heads too panicked to duck. All around, his leaping, yipping warriors wreaked murderous havoc on the unprepared Romans. It was as if the night itself had birthed them.

He rallied a group of warriors who were taking heads and poking around the Roman packs. "Leave them be for now! No looting until the fight is over!" he screamed. "Attack! Follow me!" He spurred his horse toward the wagons where a round of fierce fighting ensued. Shouting war cries, the Coritani moved like a blue wave over the crest of the ridge as they rushed the wagon train. Jayas dismounted on the run and leapt atop a wagon where a drover had taken refuge. The man jabbed at Jayas with a spear. He easily sidestepped the attempt and crushed the man's skull with a hack of his sword. He paused and stood on the wagon seat. From this vantage point he could better see how the battle was unfolding. He noted that small pockets of Romans were forming. He could not afford to let these smaller units coalesce into one and then counterattack. They had to be shattered.

At the fore of one of these pockets of resistance was a familiar figure. With leaping warriors all around, the Roman slashed, parried and thrust his sword, striking and hacking at the warriors. Jayas watched as Marcus used his shield as a battering ram, smashing aside the clumsy attempts at skewering him with spears. "Bastard!" Jayas yelled. He leapt off the wagon and sprinted toward Marcus. He slipped on the soft ground but caught himself and moved on. Wet and pliant from the season's rain, the ground easily gave under the weight of his churning legs, but his boots dug in and he gained traction. His scar drew back into a tight, white line that creased his blue dyed face in a nasty sneer as he closed the distance in swift bounds.

He batted two of his warriors out of the way. He wanted to kill the man and would allow no others to share in the glory of the deed. He crouched low and began slinking forward, every muscle in his thick body tensed and ready. "Look around and listen, you Roman dog," he cursed. "You hear that? That's the sound of your men begging and crying for their lives."

Marcus appeared unafraid as Jayas snarled and shook his shaggy head. They charged at the same time and collided shield to shield with an impact that seemed to jolt the air. Marcus slashed wildly and violently, yet with a precision. Over and over the short sword sought Jayas' bowels, but his shield absorbed the impact of the thrusts and his flesh stayed whole. Marcus was much fatigued and his face was red and damp with exertion. Jayas went on the offensive, driving Marcus backward with powerful battering strokes. His arm fatigued and bruised from the incessant blows, Marcus dropped his shield. Before he could bring it back up, Jayas sprang at the creased opening. Swift and true, his sword sliced through the leather breastplate and bounced along the ribs. Marcus did not let out a sound but withstood the wound with a grimace and desperately lunged and thrust his blade at Jayas, who easily turned the blade with a flick of his wrist before forcefully swinging the hilt of his sword and connecting with the man's temple in a sickening thud. Marcus dropped his sword and his knees buckled. He tumbled like a great oak felled by a terrible wind.

Jayas stood with his boot on the chest of the slumped Roman, whose breathing was ragged and shallow. A clipped lung most likely, thought Jayas. He crouched down and grabbed the Roman by the head.

"Open your eyes," he said, shaking Marcus' head violently. The Roman's eyes sped in response, finally opening after a series of winces and flutters. "Look at me," he ordered, smacking the Roman in the mouth for good measure.

Marcus closed his eyes and spat a glob of bloodied spittle. "Go bugger a goat, you barbarian bastard," he spat, his voice raspy and weak.

Jayas didn't respond. He drew a dagger from his belt and slid it between Marcus' ribs, slaying the Roman with a thrust to the heart. He died without making a sound. With little ceremony, Jayas raised his sword skyward and brought it down in a ferociously quick stroke. The keen edged blade sliced through the Roman's bull-like neck with surprising ease. Smeared with blood, the head rolled away and stared back with lifeless, accusing eyes. Jayas tied the Roman's head to the mane of his horse. He took the man's short sword as well, wrapped it in a wool blanket and tucked it in his saddle.

A lanky warrior approached, leading a dozen heavily armed Coritani. Their faces and arms were streaked with smoky soot and blood, their long hair matted with sweat, grime, and dried flecks of blood. Blue paint ran in rivulets where the salt of their sweat worked its corrosive effect.

By a small miracle, Jayas remembered the warrior's name, Devon. Devon led a small retinue of warriors and had answered the call when the word went out to muster. "My Lord," he said with a slight bow of respect. "The Romans are in disarray. They flee down the ravine and back up the road from whence they came. They left everything in their haste. It is a great victory, my Lord." Devon smiled brightly, but his expression seemed out of place with the butchery and stench of death.

Suddenly, Jayas was tired, but he knew there was much more to be done before they rested. He issued orders before the men became complacent in victory. "Round them up," Jayas said, leaning over his horse's neck to speak to Devon. "Herd them like cattle and swine if you must, and kill any who resist. Gather their horses and oxen. Load all the food and weapons in the wagons and burn the remainder. Looting and trophies of the enemy dead are allowed, and leave their plucked bodies unburied. Let the wolves feed."

CHAPTER THIRTY-FIVE

HE WAS AN OLD man, his hair and moustache whiter than a senator's toga and his face like sun-worn leather. He did not look or act like the priests of Rome, who were smooth-skinned and sallow of complexion, their nails manicured. Neither was he oily and plump from the riches supplicants offered. He was gaunt and hungry looking. The ridges of his brows were so prominent that his eyes seemed buried deep in his face. His eyes blazed with a subtle intensity and intelligence, and Cussius had the feeling he had seen those eyes before. The old one did not get up, nor did he speak. He merely stared at Cussius, like one would when first glimpsing a long-sought prize.

Lana made the introduction. "Cussius. This is my Uncle Rhu. Remember? I have spoken of him in the recent past," she said in hopes of jarring his memory before burying her glance in the hard-packed earthen floor.

He did remember. He returned the Druid's stare with a smile and a bow. "It is an honor to finally make your acquaintance," Cussius said by way of greeting. He felt the intensity of the Druid's eyes upon his face like a blast from a well-fed stove. The man's hatred was evident and he made no attempt at concealing it. The man bowed curtly, as though the very motion was beneath his dignity. Cussius walked to the hearth and waved his hands through the low flames, enjoying the sear of heat.

"Lana. I am hungry. I trust we dine soon?" he asked. "It will be nightfall before long, and since the sun rose, nothing has passed these lips but water." He glanced up. Pale skylight filtered down into the smoky gloom through a series of smoke holes in the roof.

"We do. The orderlies have seen to it. The meal should arrive shortly," she said, moving toward him with a cup of his favorite wine. He nodded his thanks as he took the cup and tasted its contents. It was warm but acted as a salve on his dry throat.

"It has been a momentous few days. If you hadn't noticed, our forces have grown. Cassivellaunus has joined us." As he said this, he turned so as to keep the old man where he could see him. The man went still and his eyes rolled up as if he were afflicted with the sleep-shakes. Cussius took a step closer.

The man's eyes flew open and fixed Cussius with a cold glare. "Cassivellaunus is a fool. He claimed to be a defender of freedom, of the old ways. Instead, he defends treachery. He has proven that greed can tarnish the heart of any man, be his renown great or small. In the end, he is merely a man who cares nothing for the people he is charged to keep. Since he cares not, I do not recognize his authority," the old man said in a deep, clear voice. With his left hand, he pulled at his moustache and frowned. With his right hand, he plucked violently at his tunic while his eyes cast about with painful intensity.

Lana spoke before Cussius could reply. "Uncle, you have taught me that people are want to change like the seasons. You were also fond of saying, 'A man's mind is as fickle as the leaves on a tree.' You, above all, should not be surprised by this new alliance," she said in a voice barely above a whisper.

"I haven't begun to address your whims, girl. In time, I will. Right now, I have things to discuss with this Roman," her uncle said, with a dismissive wave of his bone-thin arm as he sought the gaze of Cussius. "Your subordinates and allies will desert you and disappear. It has already begun." The old man smiled, revealing missing teeth and puckered gums.

One brow raised, Cussius let his gaze settle. The old man was an oddity for certain. "You are mistaken, old man. My army does not merely grow by the moment but grows more disciplined, as well. Even today, I rode at the head of a thousand troops. My second follows with the supplies given by our Catuvellauni allies. We only grow in strength." He grew animated with the words and spilled the wine in his zeal. He did not like the priest's attitude. It was unapologetically frank and too self-assured to suit him. "I guess this is where you tell me something I could not have known," he said sarcastically.

The old man shook his head. "Not unless you already knew that your second will never arrive, and neither will your supplies. His head belongs to Jayas, and the supplies will feed the people." The Druid straightened, his bony frame leaning forward. He shuffled closer to Lana. "You should come back to your people where you belong." He reached out to take her arm, but she pulled away.

Cussius took her hand in his and brought her close. He could smell her fear and its scent, foreign and offensive, angered him. For a fleeting moment he wondered at the source of her anxiety. "What do you mean? Marcus is escorting the supply train and will be here tomorrow at the latest," Cussius said incredulously. "You have quite the mouth on you. You should be more respectful in your tone and in your choice of words, priest. You cannot command Lana to go anywhere." Cussius felt the blood thumping at his temples and he restrained the urge to grab that skinny, wrinkled neck and twist until his tongue stuck out. He smiled at the image. Stepping around the druid, he led Lana to a seat at the table and helped her to it.

Rhu was unfazed. "I only speak the truth. Your man is dead as surely as you are alive. And in her heart, Lana knows to which beat it strums," he said, unfurling a long finger and pointing in the direction of his niece.

"But even if what you say about Marcus is true, it doesn't change a thing." A small knot of anxiety took root in the pit of his stomach. Though the man initially ground at his nerves, he had grown to depend on him because he knew the old centurion would follow his orders and see to it that others did the same. He thought of the loss of Roman infantry and he groaned inwardly, but he controlled the flinching in his stomach. Roman infantry was not easily replaced. He still had two hundred of the Roman infantry under garrison here, but he would be hard pressed to absorb such a blow. The impact on morale would be great amongst the remaining infantry, but that could be changed. His Roman cavalry would be relatively unaffected, but the native allies would surely take notice of what happened.

Rhu scoffed. "It changes everything and you know it. You have no future here and should return to the land that is yours. This is an ancient land where ancient spirits are at work and play. It is very serious business and they will not rest with your presence befouling the lands. Your fate here is decided by greater things than you or I." Rhu shrugged his shoulders, and Cussius could imagine the bones loosely jumbling around inside the thin limp clothing.

Lana suddenly stood. Her lips were pressed tightly and her dark eyes sparkled defiantly. "No, Uncle. You are the one who is mistaken. I have seen something very different. The gods are ancient, true enough. They are a jealous lot as well. But they care not who pays them respect as long as it is respect that is paid," she said confidently.

Rhu let out a raspy laugh followed by a fit of coughing and hacking. "You're quite the pupil, I must say. You speak of respecting the gods but have paid no homage to the old ways. These foreigners care nothing for our ways or our people. They come but to take. What could displease the gods more than that?"

It was her turn to scoff and laugh. "Uncle, you can't be serious. Our lands see constant strife. Two out of four seasons our young men spend more time raiding and warring than tending to fields and herds. Constant bloodletting, tribe against tribe, has been the way of these lands. It's rarely safe and only a druid can wander from tribe to tribe and remain unmolested. Do the Romans engage in any behavior different from our own?"

Cussius could tell she was enjoying herself. For a moment he was once again the bored pupil rising to the challenge of the old Greek tutor's rhetorical baiting. Rhetoric and debate he had found a tiresome but necessary part of any young Roman noble's education, and so he had paid attention and learned enough to know that he was now witnessing two who grasped the finer points of the art.

"An astute observation and a more salient point I could not have authored myself," Cussius said while clapping his hands in soft applause. "Uncle, I am not a religious man. The gods of Rome have no hold on me. I bow my knee to none of the so-called deities. All religion seems a bunch of rubbish to me. Think of it. A carved figure of wood or stone someone like you claims to be divine and attentive to the needs and wants of humanity? Such a concept has never appealed to my sensibilities. So rest assured that I have no designs on subverting the tenets of your religion."

Rhu's brow furrowed and the wrinkles deepened until shadows filled the long, thin cavities. "The gods do not exist to serve the whims of mankind. Mankind exists to serve the whims of the gods." Rhu crossed his arms as he studied Cussius.

"No one under my command would thwart the Coritani tribe's right to serve their gods. Again, my concerns are not religious in the least." It was true. He could care less if the ignorant wretches worshiped the rump of an ass or Jupiter himself. It was all mythology in his estimation. But if the people rallied against him under the banner and leadership of their religion, then he would begin to care.

Rhu shook his head. "Maybe your indifference is what offends the gods."

Again Lana spoke up. "You have always fondly spoken of the importance and inevitability of fate, Uncle. Fate has opened another path. I know this because I have seen it." No other explanation was necessary, for her uncle knew of her intimate familiarity with the dream world.

For the first time, despite his apparently aged condition, the old man looked truly haggard. He met the challenging stare of his niece with a look of pity. "All paths lead to the same place. Don't you know that? The twists and turns life takes are merely occasions that strengthen your sense of identity and etch the story of your life's actions in the wrinkles and folds of your skin. Character some call it. Some refer to it as the soul or the spirit." He sighed and his thin chest rose and fell with the exhalation. "Believe what you will, for determined stubbornness is your true master. I leave you with one last warning. Leave these lands. This island is not yours to take. We are proud people who uphold ancient traditions. Leave while you can."

Without as much as another glance, the old druid made for the door and walked out. And just like that, he was gone as quickly and as without reason as he had appeared.

CHAPTER THIRTY-SIX

GYMM WATCHED THE procession from atop the newly built rampart. At his side stood one of his more loyal retainers, Roc. They watched Jayas enter the gates at the head of his victorious warriors. Gymm was in a particularly foul mood, a condition in which he found himself more often of late, and Jayas' victory did nothing but make it gloomier. He could see there were gaps in the columns where fallen warriors would never again ride, but the losses were acceptable when offset against the damage inflicted on the enemy. Huddled in the middle of the horsemen and stumbling along at a miserable half jog was an assortment of Roman prisoners.

The women and children lined the way and heaped abuse on the broken enemy. Instead of the haughtiness characteristic of every other Roman Gymm had seen, these looked no different from any slave or prisoner that passed through. Dejected and downcast, the Roman soldiers kept their eyes glued to the ground and ignored the curses and insults showered upon them. Gymm watched as one enterprising lad darted into the group and broke his stick over the back of a prisoner. Another towheaded boy used a small shovel to fling horse dung at them. A grieving widow flung herself at a large prisoner and began clawing at his eyes with her long nails. Before a warrior could dismount and escort her back to the others, she had dug in and managed to rip an eye from the Roman's socket. He shrieked in agony and fell to his knees. His comrades lifted the maimed prisoner by the arms and tramped through the muck. The woman held her bloody trophy aloft and shook it as she scurried back to the howling mass of folk.

The blood of the people was up. There was an air of anxiety that had morphed into angry frustration, as the people got a fresh look at the bogeymen who had turned over their lives the last few months. Roc howled with laughter as a couple of village mutts scrambled toward the column, barking and snapping at the bared legs of the prisoners. Even the dogs can feel it, he thought. Gymm slapped Roc on the back and motioned for him to follow. He and his band had not been in the field since the disastrous battle at Valley Knoll, and he wanted a closer look at the rabble Jayas had captured.

The day was overcast and the ground remained soft from the fall rains. Navigating the many puddles and thick mud, Gymm and Roc walked down to where the prisoners were being held. Gymm kicked an overly energetic cur and it scuttled away with a yelp.

"Gymm!" boomed Jayas as he sat astride his horse. The voice grated on his every nerve and Gymm ground his teeth and clenched his fists at his sides. Sometimes his anger was such that he couldn't concentrate. At other times it was such that his sleep would be interrupted by odd dreams that made his head throb dully. Jayas had made sure that no one forgot who was really responsible for the early defeat by the Romans at the Valley Knoll and everywhere Gymm went whispers and snickers followed. Most of it could be traced back to Jayas, he thought bitterly.

He looked up and caught his cousin's eye. Gymm tried to look happy at his cousin's victory and he spoke in a light tone. "Praises, Jayas. You must be proud with all the prisoners and booty you return with. I'm sure the bards will sing of your exploits. You have much reason to be proud." Gymm saluted. At his side, Roc gave an exaggerated bow.

Jayas smiled broadly and gestured to the sulking prisoners. The Romans were a sorry lot. Their faces were gray and defeated and their eyes were locked on the ground. Their tunics had been appropriated and not yet returned, and the prisoners shivered from the cold dampness. Jayas reached into a rough burlap sack and pulled out a head. "Here. I thought you might want to see it first."

Gymm glared at the decomposing Roman face. "Congratulations," he allowed.

Jayas nodded and tossed the head back in the sack. "We hold council tonight. I hope you attend. Maybe we can catch up." His smile was clean and unassuming.

Probably just wants to brag, thought Gymm bitterly. "Thank you for the invitation, cousin. If my duties do not detain me, I will be there," he lied.

With a wink and a nod, Jayas rode off to see his father. Gymm watched him go and nudged Roc.

"There is no telling how powerful he will become, maybe even king," Roc offered in his gravelly voice. He nursed his own misgivings about Jayas and was a willing accomplice to whatever Gymm plotted. The gold coins and casks of ale and mead are awfully convincing in and of themselves, he thought. His benefactor was generous, so Roc was loyal.

Gymm's eyes narrowed menacingly at this. "If he keeps returning victorious, the king and the people will be blinded to his true aims," Gymm said. "That mustn't happen."

They skulked off and made their way through the crowd to their horses. With all the excitement surrounding the triumphant return of Jayas, no one noticed them slip out the rear of the walled compound and into the surrounding wood.

THARA'S VOICE WAS full of breath as they crept into the large and surprisingly airy kitchen. Jayas shooed the servants and cooks out, telling them to take an early night off. They did not complain and retired as hastily as their tired legs could carry them. Patiently, he had suffered through the meal just finished. Niceties and debriefings followed before the men's attentions shifted to the plentiful drink and willing maidens. He and Thara had silently appraised one another from across the table as their fathers spoke of tribal business. He had gotten up to leave and his heart fluttered like a trapped bird when he noticed she followed. Now, he gently tugged at her arm and led her into the small cold room off the rear where sundry items were stored for coolness. Thara giggled and he could tell she was taken with their little adventure. Many voices could still be heard in the great room, laughing, shouting, cursing and singing in rhythm to the flutes and drum. They ignored it all. They only had eyes for each other.

Jayas smiled softly and wondered at the delicate creature at his side. He loved to just look at her when she was preoccupied with something. He liked the way she bit her lip when deep in thought, or how she never failed to place a delicate fist atop her rounded hip when her ire was raised. He enjoyed the smell of her long dark hair and the way it laid along her gracefully slender neck. He liked everything about her lithe and slender strength and how her beauty concealed it at first glimpse. He tenderly patted her hair, which was silky smooth, and he knew she must have braved the cold waters of the river to wash it, for it gleamed in the soft glow of the torchlight.

Nothing was said. There was nothing to say. He was not given to idle chatter and a comfortable silence hung in the air and washed over the duo like a soothing rush of reassurance. Her eyes drifted off as if she were looking at a man she knew but couldn't name, and he made a fierce face before relenting and offering her an open smile. Their eyes locked and Jayas quivered with excitement. Thara giggled softly, her cheeks aglow with the effects of the wine that Jayas provided from the plundered Roman supplies.

He knew he was loosened from the drink and took liberties he usually would not have the courage to broach with the object of his fascination. Casting chance to the wind, he covered her hand with his, slipped his other arm around her waist, and drew her into an embrace. She looked up at him in expectation.

Such longing filled Jayas that his vision clouded over and he stumbled over his words. "I want you to be my wife. I would risk all for you," he managed before desire choked off his voice.

She placed an index finger over his lips. "It is enough that you risk all for the people." She rose on her toes and brought his massively shaggy head downward. Her lips found his and they kissed hungrily. Her breathing was quick and hot. She let her hand come to rest on the flat of his stomach and she melted against him. He opened his eyes and saw that hers were wanton and filled with playful wickedness. Their thoughts and desires were left unsaid as they sneaked past their drinking and reveling clansmen to make their way to Jayas' private quarters. He led her to his mattress filled with raw wool and a world opened up that heretofore had remained hidden from ordinary view. When their passions were spent, they reveled in the restful pleasure of love.

CHAPTER THIRTY-SEVEN

LEKO SNATCHED A glance at the darkening sky and continued toward the stables. He wanted to finish the chores before the sky opened up and its contents gushed on his head. He was sick and tired of fetching water, emptying slop buckets, chopping wood and grinding flour. With every passing day, his patience had lost another thread until it threatened to unravel completely. Nearing the intersection, he stopped and stared openmouthed at a decomposing head hanging from the top of the post at the entrance of the main council house. Hollow sockets stared accusingly where the crows and ravens had pecked out the eyes. The blanched gray of the ragged face sagged weakly and the hair, dull and lank, had begun to slip. When the wind blew, gray-brown clumps floated in the air. Around the severed neck, jagged pieces of flesh had putrefied and withered with the blood dried a rusty brown. An icy wind, pungent with decay and animal and human refuse assailed his senses. He recognized the man to whom the head had belonged, and he felt sick.

Leko felt a pain starting deep within his ribcage, and his heart raced as if threatening to tear apart. He realized another part of his life was gone to never appear again. A searing rage filled his heart and he could feel the blood pounding in his ears. For a moment, he considered scaling the pole and removing the grisly trophy from its perch. He deserves a proper, honorable burial, he thought, fuming. With considerable effort, he choked down the sobs and restrained the tears. He would not be seen as weak, not ever again, he determined. It was at that moment that Leko truly felt as if manhood was his to take.

He straightened his shoulders and walked on, lost in his thoughts. His tunic, a brown checkered pattern, flittered and flapped about him with each step. Everywhere there were throngs of people. He avoided their gaze and ignored their greetings and attempts at small talk as he walked through the muddy streets. The image of Marcus's head, dead and staring emptily, weighed heavily on his mind.

A knot of people were gathered around a large supply wagon on the main thoroughfare bogged to its hubs in the thick gummy mud. He thought about lending a hand, but then he thought better of it when a low moaning caught his attention. Urgent whispers quickly followed and cut through the varied sounds of the village. He looked around for its source. Over by the cattle pens, between the sheep and milk cows, the Roman prisoners stared out from the fencing. One was gesturing in his direction and whispering loudly in Latin. He looked as miserable as a wet dog on a cold day and as hungry as a fasting Druid.

"Leko! Leko," he hissed in a hoarse voice. "Is that you, boy? We thought you were dead."

Leko recognized the sergeant who always had a kind word or suggestion for him and never treated him poorly. Once he even took the time to show Leko how to properly thrust and parry with an economy of motion. Marcus had called it skimping on technique, but the sergeant said it saved energy in a fierce fight. Leko practiced his swordsmanship both ways. Nowadays, he mimed the techniques and performed the exercises Marcus had taught him, using his body weight as resistance. If they would not trust him with a weapon, his mind was powerful enough to supply the necessary tools, and thereby, he stayed sharp.

"Sergeant?" Leko asked. He looked around to see if anyone was watching. The warrior posted to guard the prisoners was by the well flirting with a couple of buxom village girls and could care less about the prisoners, absorbed as he was in the girls' charms. So

Leko stepped a bit closer and pretended to strap his boots. "What happened?" he asked in Latin. The words felt fuzzy in his mouth and his tongue struggled awkwardly, as he hadn't spoken Latin in over a month. "I saw…my master…First Centurion Marcus, uh, he is dead. They took his head." A cold drizzle began and the wind increased in chilly gusts. He pulled his tunic over his head.

The sergeant looked down for a moment, his eyes glued to the muddy wallow. The driven raindrops stung like sleet, but he ignored it as if this were a spring day. "Aye. Caught us unawares, they did. Those that could scattered and got away. Those that stayed and fought are dead or here." He pointed to the others. "I imagine the ones lucky enough to flee have already made it back to the fort. Our comrades won't let us waste away here. The general will demand our release. I'm sure of it." Crowded around the sergeant, more Roman faces stared out at him. They murmured their agreement, gaining snippets of hope from his words.

Leko risked a small smile. "That may be so. You all look cold. I will see if I can get you some firewood and some blankets. I will see about some food too, if I can." He started off.

"Weapons!" hissed the sergeant to Leko' back.

Leko ignored the plea and walked on. He passed the guard whose amorous pursuits were interrupted by the elements. "Get moving, you whelp!" he ordered.

Leko scowled in return and did not bother answering. He concentrated on the ground and avoided the ankle-deep mud. He did not want to ruin the new boots Thara had procured for him by carelessly stomping around in the muck. She would give him a scolding for sure if that were the case. The words of the sergeant still echoed in his ears as he crossed the remaining distance to where he was billeted. He could not shake the doldrums and his mood threatened to grow as dark as the clouds storming across the sky. He knew what needed to be done. Honor demanded it.

CHAPTER THIRTY-EIGHT

A SERVANT APPROACHED the table. In his hands was a steaming platter of meat, hot from the coals of the cooking fire. Lana placed two wooden bowls and ladled a thick meaty broth into both. She turned to the meat and helped herself, then loaded Cussius' plate. He had worked up a ravenous appetite with his demanding schedule of meetings and councils, and he worked the plate like a sow would a trough, slurping the broth loudly, the steam leaving his face moist. As he ate he reflected on the past forty-eight hours and its implications, and it left him mildly melancholic. By nightfall yesterday, everyone in the camp had heard of Marcus' death. He had moved swiftly to quell any defeatist talk and set the men to training to keep their minds and bodies occupied. He had seen to the reorganization of his troops and had consolidated some units to make up for losses. This past day, seventy-five surviving infantry-men had made the safety of the fort in straggling groups, and Cussius had gleaned the details of the well planned ambush. It was just as Lana's uncle had related. All told, at least one hundred and fifty Roman legionaries and many tribal warriors had met their end. The remainder of the Legionaries, around seventy as far as he could guess, were presently the reluctant guests of the Coritani.

His anger ran as hot as the fare set before him. Though confid-ent in his abilities, he felt slightly adrift. He realized that he had grown used to the steady predictability of the old centurion and that his abilities would be sorely missed. He could fill the vacuum with his own leadership, but things were much simpler when he could delegate much, knowing that Marcus would see any task through. His stomach felt a bit sore and he burped sourly. He sighed. His fury would only be satisfied by repaying the Coritani one hundred fold for the massacre of his troops. Instead of dissuading him from further action, the ambush and Rhu's subsequent visit were infuriating, and he was now more determined than ever to see his vision through. He also thought a lot on the encounter with Lana's Uncle Rhu. He marveled at the similarities between uncle and niece. If he were completely honest with himself, he would allow that she possessed a gift and for that he was thankful.

He studied her as she sawed at her food with a knife, the delicate slices cleanly done with her skilled hands before she nibbled them down like a beaver would a stick. Having no patience, she set the knife down and grabbed the chunk, bit off a juicy bite, and chewed it quickly. The fat dripped down her chin. She wiped it off with a grin and continued her assault on the meat. Her beauty was stunning, even as she savaged a meal, and he was elated that she was his.

Cussius maintained a stony silence as he methodically cut his meat into thin slices and ate them with his fingers. Lana had turned her attentions to a bowl of oatmeal mush sweetened with honey. Lately, she had been eating as much as he did, and sometimes, even more. He was amazed at her newfound capacity to ingest vast amounts of food.

Around a mouthful of food, Lana finally broke the silence. "It's going to be a cold winter. I can feel it in my bones. Do we have enough supplies for all?" she asked.

Cussius laid his blade down and pushed the plate away with a grimace. "I'm not one to complain about food, but that is entirely too done for my tastes. I like a little blood in my meat, but the broth was exquisite, my dear. Oh, I'm sorry. Your question, of course. The quartermaster seems to think so." The loss of the supply wagons was a setback, but one that could be overcome with proper planning and rationing. Their lack of stores was another sore spot, and since he had dealt with the matter already, he did not wish to dwell on it.

She smiled and picked at her food. "The winter season will be upon us before you know it. Traditionally, the tribes refrain from raiding and warring during the cold season. Better to stay in the warmth and comfort of the lodges with the women folk and young ones," she said. She crossed her arms and made like she was shivering. "Plus, graves are much more difficult to dig in winter. The ground is frozen," she said in a matter-of-fact tone and with a shake of her head.

Cussius knew something was afoot. Why else would Lana stay fixated on a season of the year? He took a stab at what she was hinting at. "The Coritani will not raid in winter? Can we count on that?" he asked. The makings of an idea began to form as he awaited her answer. Already Kren had broached the subject of slacking off the raiding for the winter season. He had hemmed and hawed and danced all around the issue but never came right out with it. He didn't need to. It was evident his Celtic allies wanted to return to their villages for the winter. Cussius could hardly blame them.

"In the past that has been the case. I doubt they would mount an attack in winter. They will probably harass wood-cutting parties and the like, but nothing more than that," she assured him.

She sounded sure of herself, and Cussius had no reason not to trust her judgment. She was Coritani and knew their ways better than anyone in his camp. Of course, he would not lessen his vigilance or slack on the training regimen merely because of a low probability of attack. On the contrary, he had no reservations whatsoever about warring in the cold months. The corners of his mouth curled up in a cunning smile. "I guess it's time to begin a new tradition then. We Romans burn our dead." He now felt much better.

GYMM WAS DEEP in thought. The wind whistled above and light flurries of snow spun in the air and settled on his horse's neck before slowly dissolving. Branches sawed back and forth with the gusts, groaning and creaking their displeasure at the turn in the weather. The chills settled into his bones, but it wasn't just because of the temperature. He did not trust the Roman general, Cussius. The man made him uneasy. Of course, he doubted the Roman trusted him either. As they rode, he stole a quick glance at the man. Their eyes locked and Gymm's insides quivered. The man's gray eyes seemed bottomless and void of any feeling whatsoever. Gymm realized that power lived in those bottomless pools. Gymm quickly looked away, determined to keep his eyes and thoughts hidden from the always probing Roman.

The forest smelled crisp and pungent, and the frozen leaves crunched loudly as the heavy hooves of their mounts blazed a path. Tendrils of mist crept across the frosty ground and birds hopped from tree limb to tree limb, chirping and singing. Hungry squirrels shuffled through the forest floor in sporadic motions, lifting leaves here and there in a frantic search for stashed nuts. Gymm had no idea why he agreed to join in the hunt. Earlier, he and Roc had approached the Roman garrison under a flag of truce. Cussius had acted as if he expected his arrival all along and welcomed Gymm like a long lost friend. Gymm knew that dealing with the Roman was risky but he saw no other option. He would see what he could get from the Roman. Besides, Gymm thought, we both want the same thing---for Jayas to get out of the way. Now Gymm found himself riding in a hunting group, surrounded by foul smelling Romans and their Trinovante lapdogs.

The sun crested the western horizon through a break in the trees. Colorful daggers of light shot across the sky, lancing the moving clouds and spilling yellow across the rolling hills. Gymm was jumpy, and he was sure the Roman was more than aware of it. He scanned the tree line and tried not to think on it. A movement by the thick brush growing in a stand of oak trees drew his attention. Something flashed amongst the trees. He would like to shoot a fat buck or doe and show these Romans what a marksman he was.

Roc, an experienced hunter as well, needed no prompting. He quietly slid off his mount while Gymm hopped off his horse and whipped his bow around. He drew back and sighted his target along the length of the ash shaft.

A chuckle interrupted his aim. "I dare say you are about to shoot a youth or his mount. A good shot it would be, but I doubt either would make good eating," the Roman general said. The others accompanying the hunt laughed heartily and made disparaging remarks about Gymm's eyesight and hunting abilities. His ears burned hot.

"You there! Come out or we shall run you down like a dog," the general ordered.

From behind the trunk of a large oak tree covered with frozen moss stepped the youth. He waved and approached warily, leading his horse by a tether. He pushed his way through a bramble of shriveled gooseberry patch without taking his eyes off the riders.

"Well, I can hardly believe it. You're the slave boy, Marcus' youth, I do believe. Correct me if I'm wrong," Cussius said with a bemused look.

"It most certainly is, General," piped in another Roman who sat slouched in his saddle.

"I should have drawn and released," growled Gymm. "He can't be left alive. He would tell the others and our plans would be bunk." He walked toward the youth, his manner menacing. The youth stopped, and for a moment it looked like he would make a dash for it. Instead, he pulled the short sword that hung from his belt and waited.

"This time it may be different," Leko said loudly. There was no give in his voice and he stood his ground.

Gymm snarled and drew his own blade. Roc leaped off his mount and circled the youth. He raised his javelin as if to throw.

Gymm's eyes widened in disbelief as he recognized the muscular gray dun. "That's Jayas' charger! Boy! You stole his damn horse!" His eyes narrowed in deadly intent and he hastened his step.

Leko' eyes darted back and forth between the two and he widened his stance — he could either leap aboard his horse or charge one of the menacing warriors.

Cussius laughed and kicked his mount into a charge, coming between the two Coritani warriors and the youth. His horse circled tightly as he addressed them. "How's that for fighting spirit. Give me a hundred like him and I would have this island wrapped up in no time. Gymm, leave him be. Approach, lad."

A cold breeze tousled Leko' long hair and it got in his eyes. He shook his head angrily, sending the unruly stalks back to his shoulders. He would have it plaited. Better to keep it braided and out of the way. No, he decided. In honor of his late master, he would cut it off and wear it as Marcus did. He would shave the scruffs of hair above his lip as well. He would wield his sword as Marcus did too.

He sheathed his sword, and like a spider he sprang onto his mount. He closed with the general and reined in tightly. He bowed his head in respect and responded as he had seen Marcus bow. "Sir! I report for duty!"

For his part, Cussius was grinning broadly. "Welcome." He gestured toward the dun. "You stole the man's horse, and for that alone you are released from any former state of bondage," he said magnanimously. "I hear you fought with us against the Coritani?"

Leko nodded, his boyish face a stern reflection of his resolve. "I did, and yes I was a slave. But I fought with you because I wanted to."

Gymm laughed gutturally, drawing attention to his cause. "Actually, I captured him in battle with your warriors. That would make him mine. Consider this to be a test of our future endeavors together." Gymm shared a grin with the sycophantic Roc. "And since he's mine, he must die — we cannot risk his having another change of heart. Besides, he's been passed back and forth so many times it's too hard to tell where his loyalties lie. He's kind of like a dog without a pack, always lurking about and sniffing for scraps. He's better off dead." Gymm's eyes glinted malevolently. If he could kill the boy and lead the horse back, he would be hailed a hero and raised in esteem. Jayas would suffer shame at being outwitted by a boy and having his prized war horse stolen from under his nose.

Leko stared impassively from atop the charger. He felt he could run over Gymm with a kick of his heels. He tensed his legs, laid his hand atop his blade, and leaned forward slightly in preparation to drive the war horse over this fool who wanted his head.

Cussius waved them off and his Romans circled the contentious trio. "There will not be blood today, not on a day of such momentous occasion." His breath was white and puffy and dissipated like smoke in the wind. He looked at Leko. "Get off the horse." He then whirled to Gymm. "You can take the horse but you do not take him. He has earned his liberty." Cussius recognized the opportunity to weaken Jayas, and he would allow Gymm that much.

Leko burned and he felt the familiar sting of betrayal as he thought of all the trouble that went into swiping the horse. Yesterday, after spending the morning and early afternoon splitting firewood, Leko had returned to Thara's lodge. He immediately spotted the gray charger tied to the post. It chewed at its bit in a bored fashion, barely giving notice of his passing aside from a swish of the tail. He had neared the door and heard muffled sounds coming from within the lodge. His hand on the door, laughter, giggles and moans assaulted his ears. Curious and fearful of what he knew it to be, Leko had slowly opened the door and stepped in. What he saw was seared in his mind in taunting detail. The light from the open door revealed Thara, nude and on her back with an equally unclad Jayas lying atop of her. A look of ecstasy worked Thara's face and it struck his chest cold as ice. Thara let out a startled gasp and shrieked at the sight of the gawking Leko. Then Jayas jumped off Thara and closed the distance, striking Leko in the chest and knocking him back out the door where he tripped over a milk bucket, sending it and himself in a sprawling heap. As the door slammed and he picked himself out of the muck, a white rage overtook him. It was as if a dam had burst and all of the betrayals and loss had come together at once, pushing inexorably until he could take no more. His pride burned like a flame, engulfing him, goading him to unreasonable action. He had backed up and untied the horse, walked it behind the row of lodges all the way down to the livestock gate and out of the compound. No one had paid him a flit of attention, but he knew his death would be the cost if he were discovered. He cared not.

Leko stoically ignored the hot glares that the Coritani warriors were boring into his being and concentrated on Cussius, who had the look of late fall in his eyes, gray and chill. The two glowered at Leko but heeded Cussius. The smallish one stepped forward, and Leko leveled his stare on the man as he approached. Roc wore a sneer like a mask, his animosity oozing from heavy short breaths. The man was exceptionally cruel and had enjoyed having Leko around to dog. At his capture, he had been as ugly and mean as possible. As a matter of fact, Roc was the one who had closed Leko' eyes with overzealous blows to his unprotected face. Leko imagined returning the favor and warmed inside at the prospect. His smile was as the weather — sunny but cold.

He held his hand out with the reins. Without a word, Roc snatched the tether and wheeled about, leading the gray dun away. Gymm smiled coldly and bowed curtly before he rode off with Roc, Jayas' horse in tow.

CHAPTER THIRTY-NINE

The sun was dull and weak and eked its way through the drifting patches of white. It was cold, and the hiker's breaths looked like dissolving shots of smoke as they navigated the little used trail. Thara trudged through the brushy path slick with icy mud that thankfully did not stick to her thick leather-soled boots. Her tunic caught on a thorny bramble and she jerked her arm. She could hear the wool fabric tear and she sighed in exasperation. Careless, she thought. She knew she shouldn't let her mind wander. That was dangerous, thick as the forest was of late with patrolling Romans and enemy tribesmen. She paused a moment to scan the length of the trail. The two youths Jayas assigned to keep her company on her forest jaunts mimicked her actions and peered intently in the direction she faced. They did not seem that enamored with their assigned detail, and Thara was not too keen on the notion of needing an escort either.

She felt flattered and comforted by the fact that Jayas saw fit to keep her safe, but on the other hand, the two boorish youngsters offered nothing in the way of conversation and were exceptionally surly. At times they could be downright uncouth and vile, earning tart rebukes for their crude ways. She looked at the chubbier of the two and scowled in admonishment. The chunkier of the two boys suffered from a rumbling stomach, and as a result, he constantly passed gas. That was understandable, but what wasn't tolerable was the other youth's fascination with his companion's curse. His laughter usually followed the other's foul expulsions. Thara could only shake her head in disbelief at their antics and distance herself from their proximity. Today, she would scour the woods for the root she suspected would cure the chunky youth's ailment. The worst part for her was that these two were poor substitutes for Leko, and his absence gnawed at her.

Leko had been gone for over a couple of weeks now, and she missed his eagerness to help and his timely attentiveness to her comfort. He was unstoppably curious, and Thara had grown used to answering his questions. She even looked forward to those exchanges, imagining herself the druid tutor and Leko her eager pupil. She sighed. She knew the boy had not been happy among her people, and it was hard to blame him for fleeing. She only hoped he had not left because of her and Jayas. If he had, there was little she could do for him in that regard. She looked at the two youths accompanying her and a pang of regret tweaked her tender belly. They were close in age to Leko, barely old enough to scrape their chins smooth and ride with their first raiding parties. They were eager, brave and willing to fight. Leko' earnestness was no different, she thought.

She smiled suddenly and stifled a giggle at the memory of Jayas discovering his treasured gray dun having been artfully removed from his possession. At first she had found it funny, until his rising anger drowned any humor from the situation. She had never seen him in such a frightful state. His face had grown beet red and the scar on his face glowed white hot as he spewed epithets and curses. She knew that the person who stole his horse would surely die a brutal death once Jayas caught the culprit. Now, thanks to Gymm, Jayas had his horse back and knew the identity of the thief. She was relieved to discover that Leko had eluded Gymm, and she wondered if he had returned to the Romans. She had pleaded for clemency if he were caught, entreating Jayas with appeals to the folly of youth. In return, she found Jayas' heart to be as hard and stony as the granite cliffs above the big river. To her dismay, Jayas' desire to have Leko's head had not yet cooled, and he railed that it would soon join that of the ghoulishly decomposing Marcus, which still adorned the post and seemed to leer at those walking beneath its grisly perch. She shivered at the thought and muttered a hasty prayer that Leko would finally find his way home.

She concentrated on the bend in the trail where the way curved and was swallowed by towering beech trees, the overhanging branches still clinging to browned leaves. She strained her eyes, trying to penetrate the shadowy depths of the bend, willing the darkness to peel away and reveal itself. Birds chirped high in the branches, flitting to and from swaying limbs at their whim. At the top of a tall oak, a hawk blinked down at her before turning its attention to the forest floor. Red squirrels poked in the bushes, using their quick little paws to move leaves and twigs as they searched for a nutty morsel. Every so often, they would pause and stand up on their hind legs and survey the landscape before returning to their labors. She considered taking a shot with her bow but ruled against it. She had no hunting arrows in the quiver on her back, only shafts fitted with iron points honed razor sharp. If she hit a squirrel with one, it would pretty much cleave it in half, ruining any chance much meat worth the effort would remain on the carcass.

She sensed nothing amiss and took a deep breath of the cool, clean air and slowly exhaled, watching the stream of hot breath give way to the cold. She continued up the trail, the youths plodding behind. Her mood was lightened by the beautifully crisp day, and she led the way to the little meadow amongst a stand of oaks where she knew she could dig some much needed medicinal roots.

KREN AND ELEVEN of his Trinovante warriors were carefully concealed amongst the brush and fallen timbers overlooking a small clearing. They had taken great pains to hide themselves, some going so far as to heap mounds of brush and dead leaves over their bodies. Kren wanted a better position from which to scout the meadow so he was on his stomach beneath a wide juniper tree, its lower branches hanging to the ground. From this vantage, he could make out the slight bulges in the forest floor that were his men's positions. He was satisfied. A casual bystander would pay no heed whatsoever, so well hidden they were. They had been here since daybreak, and the surrounding wildlife, content that the men posed no harm, gladly went about their daily tasks. The cracking of twigs and the crunch of frozen leaves garnered his attention, but it was a false alarm. Proud and enthused with the energy of the rutting season, a buck deer, his antlers bare of velvet, traipsed into the meadow and circled, tossing his head excitedly. Kren noticed the well used game trail and knew why the buck was feeling the heat. Groups of does would surely frequent the clearing with its secluded bounty available for the taking.

The smell of the passing does was apparently strong in the buck's nostrils, and it blew out white streams that floated away. Kren watched as the buck selected a sapling oak where it proceeded to cock its head and rub its antlers up and down the length of it, the bark peeling with the effort. The animal paused to sniff and scrape at the ground until the leaves and grass were tossed aside and all that remained was bare earth. It ended the ancient ritual by urinating on the scratched ground, ensuring his scent would be a powerful presence in this forest oasis. It then proceeded to nose around, seeking out the high protein nutrition of acorns to gather its strength for the demands of the rutting season.

Kren plucked a dry piece of grass from the ground and chewed the blade. The weather was turning frosty, and his thoughts wandered to home. He would rather be back in his home village, enjoying hot meals cooked by his wife and regaling his youngsters with new tales of daring. He imagined the smell of his wife's hair, the soft smoothness of her skin, and the pliant readiness of her affections as he slid beside her in their comfortable bed piled with wool blankets. He conjured other images of her scurrying about the kitchen, scolding the slaves for their shirking and shooing them away from the food. She trusted no one to cook for her family and took great pride in her culinary abilities. He could almost taste her bread, hot from the stone and clay oven. Almost, he thought bitterly as his mouth watered helplessly. Instead, he was cold and wet and waiting with a hungry belly for a target that may or may not arrive in this particular area of the forest. He sighed a little too loudly, and for a moment the buck took notice, but it returned to the serious business of eating.

Kren cursed his gullibility, and he cursed the Roman general. Cussius could be vexing. Initially, the raiding and taking of slaves and booty were good, and his men were proving themselves brave, and many had enriched themselves at the expense of the hated Coritani. The second humiliation of Cassivellaunus was good to witness, as well. But now, autumn was growing long in the tooth and his men grumbled about home. They had been warring constantly for the past three months and their mounts were tired and thinning. The ponies were a sturdy breed, but the beasts needed rest and good hay and grain. Often these days, warriors sought him out, mumbling about the cook pots of their women and venturing guesses as to how tall their young ones had sprouted. The message was clear. It was time to regroup and fatten up over the winter, time to nurse old wounds to health. He scrunched his brow in thought and chewed on the inside of his lip. He knew he was partially responsible for this situation. He and his king, Mandubrac, had encouraged the Romans. No matter now, he thought.

He sighed once more, wishing he were whittling next to a warm fire with one of the youngsters perched atop his knee. The quicker he and his men got what they came for, the quicker he could be home.

Sunlight dappled the ground, shining on old leaves and twigs. The abrupt pop of acorns falling with a clatter to the old leaves of the forest floor drew his eyes. The buck raised up, its brown eyes glittering and head held stock still. It now stood under a quartet of oak trees, and a splash of late-day sun shone on its sleek coat. Above where Kren lay, the stubborn acorns clinging to the branches had a purplish color. He wished he had his hunting bow with him. The animal, fat as he was, would make a fine meal, and Kren could hardly miss at this distance with a clear field of fire. He watched as the buck tensed and then bolted with its tail held high, the bushy white underside a bobbing marker as it leaped the distance and dove into thicket. Kren swung his head slowly. A shuffling noise came from the forest to the right. Twigs cracked. He tensed and readied himself. He drew in a breath and perfectly mimicked the bark a bitch fox would use to call her pups.

A BREATH OF WIND stirred the trees, loosening the tenuous hold of many acorns and sending them cascading downward with a splash in the leaves. Thara thought of the oncoming winter and her belly convulsed involuntarily. It could prove to be a hungry one if they were not careful. She twirled an oak twig in her finger as she strolled.

She looked at her two companions. "Nym," she addressed the chubby one. "You should make yourself useful and pick up as many acorns as you can." She turned to the other. "You too."

The youths looked dumbstruck. "But we don't like acorns. They sour my belly for one thing, and they taste too bitter. Nasty," Nym said with a pinched face. "And we're your guards, not scavengers."

Thara was not feeling patient. She snapped, "Well, others do like acorns, and besides, everything sours your stomach." She gestured at his belly, a rarity amongst the tribe, as most of the young warriors kept lean and strong by training with their weapons, wrestling, and horseback riding. The rest of the youths were hardy farm boys, their muscles lean and tight from the rigors of hard labor. "Acorns make a passable flour, and if our grain runs low over the winter... Well, let's just say an acorn or two would suit you just fine I suspect." She threw the oak twig down and shook her head at their display of ignorance. Her pace quickened. She was more angered about their shortsightedness than their aversion to labor. She could feel the blood rushing to her cheeks as her patience waned with every step.

Thara stopped and surveyed their faces. Both were ruddy and flushed from the hike and wind. Nym looked dully at her and scratched his nose, further earning her ire. "You are mistaken. You two are not my guards for I need no guarding. You have been detailed to me by Jayas, your war leader, if you need reminding. So, when I ask you to do something, I expect you to do it. Do you understand me?" Thara challenged.

Both looked properly chastised as they murmured their understanding and their consent to her demands. Nym's lips turned up, the resulting grimace approximating a smile like a horse might imitate a dog. Satisfied, Thara spun away and continued along the forest path.

They had almost reached their destination, and her mind began to loosen. The clearing was one of her favorite places, and she tried to make it there at least once a month. She had always found the meadow teeming with herbs and other plants worthy of foraging. Because of the recent fighting, her supply of medicinal roots was rapidly dwindling, and so she would especially be on the scout for those particular pickings. As she walked and thought on the subject of healing, the words of Uncle Rhu came to mind. He would always say, "Cheerfulness, temperance and exercise, are the keys to health." Hard to be cheery and exercise with broken and gashed limbs, she thought. But where prevention did not work, he always managed to heal those in need. He used a motley but exact concoction of plants, herbs and mare's milk — and the effect was invariably therapeutic. She mentally inventoried what was needed: varian, rosemary, wort, valerian or yarrow would be nice, amongst others. She chuckled. Maybe she and Jayas had eaten quite a bit of yarrow and just hadn't realized it. Perhaps it was sprinkled and stirred in our food and drink, she giggled. It could be a powerful love charm if done right. No. No need to resort to that. She laughed out loud and the two youths looked puzzled as they wondered what she found so amusing.

"Never mind," she whispered. "Keep an eye out sharp. We may get a shot at a deer if we're lucky." Invariably, she could count on a deer or two visiting the meadow to sample the brown meadow grasses. A gust of wind made the trees moan.

Ahead, through a break in the trees she could see the small meadow in the fading sun. She held her hand up and all three stopped. She ducked down to one knee and motioned the other two to get down.

She held her hand up and splayed it above her head for the symbol of a buck deer. By the time they swiveled their heads around, the buck had caught sight or scent of them, and their chance for fresh venison took flight and was lost from sight. She shook her head in disappointment. A nice hunk of venison, slow roasted over a spit, would go a long ways to making some folk happy.

"Let's go." She sighed, wiping the mud from her knee with her free hand. Somewhere up ahead, a fox yipped, its bark echoing across the rolling hills.

AT KREN'S SIGNAL, warriors began to emerge from the woods as if the earthy cellar of the forest floor had birthed them. Kren exploded from under the tree and leaped a jagged oak stump as he loped toward his target. He grimaced. His muscles were cold and tight after maintaining the same posture all day. He much preferred a horse.

Ahead, the hiking trio came to a screeching halt at the edge of the meadow and began backpedaling, their eyes grown large as torcs, their mouths open as if a wedge had been inserted, and it struck him as funny. He hoped they stayed and fought. He was not in the mood for a lot of running.

He let out a shrill war cry, and his warriors screamed theirs in answer. The two youths with the target were little better than boys. They inexpertly clutched their spears and swords, unsure of which one to use. Their inexperience was killing them and they didn't even know it. Probably never even saw their first battle, Kren thought — too bad.

"Welcome!" he shouted meanly, his deep baritone coming out breathily and echoing off the trees. His shout mixed with the lusty cries of his warriors who were gaining ground in leg pumping bounds.

The boys kept backpedaling until they realized the woman had not. She drew her bow and loosed an arrow. The missile whirred by Kren' ear and his eyes furrowed menacingly at this unexpected threat. Behind him, a curse split the air as the arrow rammed home followed by the wet thumping sound of a man's body hitting the ground.

"You bitch!" Kren screamed. He doubled his efforts and closed the distance as she nocked another arrow. As he neared, a fleeting thought crossed his mind that he had seen this woman before.

"COME ON. COME ON," Thara muttered under her breath as she fiddled with the arrow. All of a sudden her fingers had become thick and difficult to maneuver. She watched the big enemy warrior close the distance. He was almost upon her and she could see the look of triumph gleam in his eyes. Thara ripped her eyes off the charging warrior and screamed at her erstwhile guards.

"Fight!" In her haste she fumbled the arrow and it slipped off the nock and fell to the ground. She cursed and spun around. Thara tried to sprint but her boots kept slipping in the mud, sucking into it with each step. The youths had a head start, and they veered off the trail and scrambled into the brush in a panic.

"Don't!" she shouted. But it was too late.

The angle for their pursuers was better and the boys' chosen course only made it easier. She stopped and helplessly watched as an enemy warrior tripped Nym, who stumbled to his knees and raised his spear in a wild lunge. The warrior leaped and shattered Nym's spear with a chop of his sword. He then swept through with the blade. She could hear bone grating beneath the blade, severing tendons and ligaments before cleaving through the middle of the shoulder. Nym screamed in horror and pain. He rolled on the ground and wailed loudly, the sound reminding her of the late summer slaughter of the sacrificial cows.

The other youth fared no better. To his credit, he managed to turn around and come to his friend's aid. He screamed and charged the enemy warrior, but now three others had closed, as well. They kicked his spear thrust away and knocked it from his grip. He went to draw his sword, but before he could slide it half way from the sheath, two warriors hit him with their shields. He dropped to his knees, stunned and out of breath. A trickle of blood oozed from a gash on his forehead and into his eyes, blurring his vision. He stumbled to his feet and reached out with both hands, groping like a blind man in strange environs.

"Mercy! Mercy!" Thara shouted as she dropped her bow to the ground with a clatter. She knew resistance was futile. "No need to..." Before she could finish, a heavy fist plowed into the middle of her back, knocking her violently forward and causing her breath to whoosh out. She lay face down in musty-smelling leaves. She struggled to get her breath and finally managed to come to all fours. Vaguely, she could make out the mulish sounds of Nym's pitiful cries of pain.

A strange voice interceded. "I'm not going to knock you senseless because we are not going to carry you to our horses. Get up," the warrior ordered flatly.

Thara got to one knee and looked up at the man. It was a practical demand and it gave her hope that he could be reasonable in other matters. "Don't kill him," she panted. "Please. You have won. We surrender. Don't kill him," she said breathlessly.

The man scoffed. "He's bleeding like a stuck pig and crying worse than one. He didn't fight honorably either. Besides, his wound is fatal. Look for yourself." He coldly pointed to Nym.

Somehow, Nym had managed to prop himself against a tree, his chest heaving in sucking breaths. His cries, still pitiful, were now low as he stared wildly about, heedless of the blood that pumped from the nasty wound. A breeze carried the pungent coppery scent of his blood to her nostrils and Thara saw the truth in the warrior's words. She looked up and sadly shook her head.

"They're just boys. You don't have to kill the other one," she said weakly. He was still lurching about, shoved to and fro by the grinning warriors, who were laughing at him and inflicting further cruelties upon him.

The warrior did not appear convinced. He stared down at her with a questioning look, the depths of his eyes barren and disinterested. Without taking his eyes off her, he addressed his warriors. "Silence that mewling kid!" he ordered, jabbing his sword toward Nym.

A lanky warrior, not much older than Nym, smiled devilishly and strode the short distance to the wounded youth. With no ceremony, he thrust his spear into Nym' chest. The squealing stopped as the sharpened iron point burst through his chest cavity and into the heart. Nym slumped sideways to the ground, his eyes finally lifeless. He would suffer no more, and for that, Thara was thankful.

Thara had fully recovered her wind but her back was sore and she was sure a large, purplish bruise was forming where the beefy warrior had punched her. "Thank you for your kindness," she said. Thara meant it. The boy had lost a lot of blood and would have been dead in minutes. At least now he would feel no more pain.

He laughed mirthlessly. "Don't thank me yet." He turned once again to his warriors who now had the boy on his knees with head bowed.

Thara could hear him crying softly and thought she could see salty tears mixing with the forest debris. She silently pleaded for the boy to show courage. She knew his survival depended on showing a brave face to prove he was worthy of life and of some value to his captors.

The big enemy warrior sneered in disgust. "Warriors do not weep like little children," he said.

She pleaded, "But a slave does. Take him. Make him yours. If you spare his life, he will repay you with loyalty." She was stretching things but had no other course.

He stood silent for a moment, contemplative. "You know our ways. It's up to the warriors who caught him. They may have his head or take him as a slave. It is our way. You know that." He shrugged, knowing there was little he could do. He was right of course. A good war leader allowed his warriors to take heads or captives. It was good for morale.

He grabbed her by the arm, reached to her belt and removed her knife, admiring it for a second before tucking it into his own belt. His grip was tight like a tourniquet and she felt the blood build up in her arm.

"Warriors! Do what you will with that scamp, but we must return."

The warriors shrugged, their fun at the boy's expense beginning to bore them. Finally, a warrior strode forward and grunted at the boy. He grabbed him by the chin and looked him over like he would when deciding on whether to trade a prized goat for a wormy pig. Then he grabbed the youth by the hair and yanked him upright. The boy let out a squeal of pain but bit it off quickly. A warrior yanked his arms backward at an extreme angle and ran a short piece of wood under both shoulders before tying his wrists tightly together. The boy's eyes were a cloudy mixture of relief and pain. Without a further word, captives and captors melted into the wood for the trek to where the horses were hobbled.

CHAPTER FORTY

Picking his way carefully, Leko led four young Bibroci warriors along a seldom used path. A cold mist had obscured their passage but now gave way, fracturing into long, wispy tails before whispering into nothingness. The trail cut a black swathe through tightly grown trees. It was gray now, the darkness receding. A stiff wind blew in, shaking the pine boughs. Huge oaks stretched skyward, their limbs like dark twisted arms.

Leko moved easily in the saddle, thankful for the powerfully muscled animal Cussius had given him. It moved with muscled grace, was quick in a sprint, and most important to Leko, could run all day if need be.

Leko leaned over and patted his black gelding, thankful he no longer had to wrestle with that old lop-eared mule he used to tend. The mere memory of the obnoxious cuss vexed Leko to this day.

He motioned the riders to a halt, reined in his mount and stared at the deep frozen track, trying to separate the frosty sludge from deer, swine, and horse sign. His concentration was interrupted by the low murmuring voices of his squadron.

Except for one, the Bibroci warriors were a year older than him and resented the fact that he was placed in charge of their scout team. Leko thought he had more than earned his leadership role. More important, Cussius agreed. The general had shown great faith in Leko and granted him leeway to raid and scout the Coritani. It was awkward at first but Leko had fallen back into the rhythm of the Roman legion and was putting his familiarity with the enemy to the test. It was a welcome distraction. The harder he worked at soldiering the less he thought of Thara, but the more he kept at training and scouting, the more he obsessed about killing Jayas. As far as he was concerned, he had honorable reasons for seeking Jayas' death.

A flicker of memories worked behind his eyes. The kind and mentoring image of Marcus gave way to that of the rotting skull, the hollowed sockets peering into the void. The memory of the indignities heaped upon his former master burned hot in his chest, demanding action. Marcus would do the same, he thought. He still felt somewhat adrift despite his new responsibilities and the more recent memory of stumbling upon Jayas and Thara engaged mid-coitus threatened to overwhelm his thin veneer of control. Both were images he wished purged forever. Finally, with considerable effort he was able to dispel the dark mood wrought by the memories and concentrate on what he could control.

Leko waved the Bibroci silent and motioned for them to dismount. He tied his horse to a maple sapling, not bothering to hobble his mount. Marcus had told him to never hobble a horse when you may have to mount up in a hot pinch. Tethering will do, he thought. His eyes flitted over the hilltop, skimming the trees and rocks and trailing down to a meadow. He remembered it as a place the Coritani sent woodcutters to harvest firewood, an easy trek of four miles from their stronghold.

The cold morning air smelled like raw bark and wet earth, and his breath condensed into little white clouds as his breathing grew more labored with the climb. Stepping into the damp leaves released the musty fragrance of the forest floor and further heightened his senses. He strained his ears, cautiously stalking until he reached the massive trunk of an old oak. The young Bibroci warriors skidded to a halt beside him, hunkered on their haunches, and looked at Leko questioningly.

"Now what?" asked Kege in a whisper. He was the youngest of the warriors and not prone to patience. He had recently lost his father, Kegan, to the bloodthirsty Coritani, and was anxious to get in the fray. From the boasts Leko had overheard while captive, Jayas had taken Kegan's head before he took Marcus'. Leko knew it to be true as did Kege. It was with good reason that Keges' hatred of the Coritani and Jayas rivaled that of Leko.

Leko smiled at him, his eyes full of mischief. "You guys ready?" he asked with a little more bravado than he actually felt. Leko marveled at Kege's similarity to his father. He was quick to laugh and joke, and he teased Leko but was just as quick to laugh at himself. Leko liked him immediately.

"Of course we are. Where is the enemy? We didn't travel half the night to take a nap under a big oak tree." Kege smiled when he said this.

"Don't worry about naps. We don't nap while on ambush," Leko said seriously. He hoped he sounded more confident than he felt. As if it were mocking him, his stomach began to grumble ominously.

"There's a good chance a woodcutting party will show. He gestured toward the meadow below. "This is a likely spot. Trust me." He grabbed his two javelins and spun away from the group. The others followed.

Something stirred in the forest ahead of them, and they all froze, their heads cocked to the side, some cupping their ears to ease out the wind. The distinct sounds of hooves sinking into leaves and cracking twigs rent the air. Voices could be heard cutting through the forest.

Leko' heart leapt in his chest and began to hammer rapidly. "Cover!" Leko hissed. The youths scattered behind stumps and bushes. One of their number lay down flat and unmoving, his leather-clad body melting into the dead leaves. Leko scrambled low and took cover. He landed on a thick carpet of damp leaves behind a tangled pile of fallen trees.

As he gazed through a weave of deadfall, he noticed that his hand was steaming lightly as the hot sweat mixed with the cold morning air. He concentrated on the meadow below, holding on to a small hope that Jayas would appear, off his guard, calm and relaxed in the security of his lands, oblivious to the secreted threat. His mind took off in different directions as he imagined how the fight would unfold. He would wait until they were within javelin range. Marcus had told him that any fight worth its salt started within javelin shot. He forced his breathing steady, and slowly the hammer blows in his heart began to diminish.

The sounds grew louder and the voices more distinct. Then shapes materialized from the forest. Leko counted six armed and mounted warriors. Behind them, they dragged and half tugged a motley collection of slaves linked to one another with a long rope tied around each man's waist and looped one to the next. A seventh warrior emerged from the forest pulling rear guard. He lazily held a spear across his lap and looked bored and disinterested with his charge. Jayas was not among them and Leko experienced mixed pangs of regret and relief.

The wind gusted across the hilltop and the trees groaned a great sighing cry. Leko squinted and focused on the slaves. He smiled to himself. Despite their dress and poor diet, the slaves were undeniably Roman. Their hair was growing but was so much shorter than that of their captives as to be laughable. Further revealing their identity, short, curly beards sprouted from faces long deprived the sharpened edge of a thin razor.

Leko's heart suddenly leapt alive again, the flutters swimming about as if he had swallowed a handful of minnows. He bit his lip, his confidence waning. He felt like he had to do something, but he didn't quite know what. He had planned to raid, but he hadn't quite thought the how-to part all the way through. He chanced a glance backward at the warriors spread out behind him. He made out wide eyes staring back at him from the sparse foliage.

So far they were undetected and had the element of surprise if they attacked, but with their mounts in the rear, they were on foot and outnumbered. If they attacked, it had better be good and deadly, he thought with a swallow. Hopefully, the Roman slaves would join in.

"Wait on me. Wait on me," he mouthed silently, holding the gaze of each. Almost imperceptibly, nods of understanding returned his plea.

Leko returned to his study of the enemy. He gently picked up a javelin, tightening and relaxing his grip on the deadly missile as four of the Coritani warriors dismounted and tethered their horses before busying the slaves with chopping at a downed oak. While the slaves struck blow after blow upon the giant trunk, all but three of the Coritani started a small fire and sat around it, warming their hands. Shortly thereafter, the smell of roasting meat was borne on the drifting wind. Mumbled conversation came from the direction of the fire as the men enjoyed breaking their morning fast. Leko determined there would be no better time.

He slowly turned again. "We attack the fire first," he conveyed silently, praying they could read his lips.

Leko took a deep breath and held it before exhaling sharply. A Coritani warrior walked his direction and Leko tensed. The warrior stopped at a nearby hazel bush and set his spear to the side, leaning it against a log with its bark peeled off. The man hummed to himself and unbuckled his sword belt, laying it to the side with a clatter. He pulled up his blue-checkered tunic and drew down his course wool trousers, taking a squatting position with his back to Leko.

Leko grabbed the other javelin and crept to the edge of the deadfall as the Coritani warrior went about answering the call of nature. Leko felt hot and his grip on the javelins was damp and slick. The blood pounded in his ears. He took one last deep breath and steadied himself.

He burst into a sprint but did not dare risk a war cry, his throat far too tight with fear and exhilaration for such a display. Leko brought a javelin back as the warrior jerked his head to the side, as if listening. Leko flung his arm and shoulder into the short throw and watched the deadly shaft zip toward its target.

The man was standing and frantically tugging at his trousers when the sharp iron point drove between his shoulder blades and clean through the thin leather armor he wore. A gurgled scream escaped his tormented lips and shattered the rhythm of the axe strokes. Leko had no time to stop.

He felt as if things were moving slowly. He could see the Coritani warriors gathered around the morning fire throw down their food and scramble for weapons. As he had seen Marcus do on multiple occasions, Leko crashed headlong into a thick, squat Coritani warrior who was attempting to rise. He brought his entire weight behind his shield and bashed into the warrior, knocking the man back onto his haunches. The man rolled to his left and tried to tug his sword from its scabbard as Leko flung his remaining javelin, but his shot went wide, striking the enemy warrior in the shoulder. Leko had no time to finish him.

From the corner of his eye, Leko saw the other Coritani in motion, clearly over the initial shock and surprise of Leko's attack. Behind him, the high, guttural war cries of the Bibroci joined that of the shouting Coritani and his heart rose in response.

Leko drew his short sword, thankful he had oiled the scabbard as taught. It slid without a sound and he stood rooted to meet the enemy counterattack. One fierce warrior with a scraggly moustache and yellow teeth yelled his challenge and vaulted the short distance to Leko, who raised his shield to meet the strike and could feel the wild blows vibrate through his shield and into his forearm, numbing it to the bone. The man was strong and wildly desperate. Leko thought to yield and allow the blows to slide by instead of absorbing them. He moved and a backhanded swipe glanced off his shield. He then stepped back quickly and thrust at the vulnerable belly and groin, but the warrior batted the stroke to the side and swung his long blade upward, the tip narrowly missing Leko's jaw as it sliced by with a whiz.

Around him, Leko sensed the battle raging. He thought he saw a Bibroci warrior go down under the hammering blows of an enemy swordsman but could not be sure. He heard a horse whinny loudly and continuously as a Roman prisoner planted his axe in its chest. Leko saw its rider tumble to the ground and disappear under a swarm of flailing axe blows and kicks. He shook his head and moved back once more, his leg entangling with a water bag. He spilled to the ground, his left boot in the fire's edge. The warrior above him grinned fiercely, his eyes mere slits as he moved to take advantage.

Leko kicked violently with both legs, his boots sending a shower of burning wood, coals and ash into the path of the charging enemy warrior. The man dropped his sword and clutched his face, tearing at his skin in an effort to dislodge a flaming piece of kindling that glowed red and sizzled. Leko sprang to his feet and fell upon the staggering warrior, punching the gladius through his side at an upward angle, the sharp steel ripping through leather, flesh, and organs. The warrior buckled to his knees and slumped over dead, the blood dark red, almost purple as it pooled.

Leko felt as if his heart were going to explode. His breathing was quick and short and his vision was blurring slightly. Through the haze he saw Kege and another Bibroci jump on a fleeing enemy. They cut the Coritani down with slashes that cleaved wide sections of flesh from the man's leg and back. The warrior fell to his face and tried to get back up, but he collapsed when Kege used his shield to smash the man's skull with a loud wet thump.

The sound of galloping hooves reminded Leko of the lazy seventh rider he had spotted earlier. The man was now riding pell-mell in short circles, swinging his sword to either side as a Roman prisoner swung around by the horse's tether. The Roman was holding on for dear life to give the other Romans time to encircle the spirited horse as it galloped, turned and jumped in an attempt to find an opening. Finally, the horse reared and threw the Coritani onto his back with a crashing thud. Two Romans descended upon him in a frenzy of hacking and slashing that left the body striped white and red with blood.

Leko's breathing returned to regular and his head cleared of the foggy sensation as he looked around at the scattered fire now smoldering in smoky little piles of leaves damp with blood and earth. Three Bibroci remained alive, the fourth lying in a misshapen pose of death, his sightless eyes empty and unblinking.

Leko was glad to see that four horses remained alive. "Gather the horses!" he hollered. "And help see to the Roman prisoners. We have to move out. Quickly!" He took in the looks of respect and deference the Bibroci now gave him as they hustled to follow his instructions.

CHAPTER FORTY-ONE

Leaving Kege and the others to their own devices, Leko slogged his way across the grounds of the Roman stronghold. He was excited and it felt like fireflies were bouncing around his belly, tickling his heart. It had been weeks since he had seen Thara, busy as he was aggravating her tribesmen with raids and such. He knew of her capture and asked of her often but had yet to pay her a visit. He looked forward to seeing her now, and he whistled a lively tune he knew her to be fond of. He smiled and nodded to the bored legionary pulling guard outside her quarters, knocked the mud off his boots the best he could and shuffled in, quickly shutting the door behind him. Outside, the wind howled and moaned like a hungry wolf, shaking the small wooden structure that was Thara's quarters. He shook off the light dusting of freezing rain that clung to his shoulders and stamped his feet, blowing on his hands and rubbing them together for warmth. A draft fought its way through a crack in the wall near the door and settled along the floor. As his eyes adjusted to the dim interior, he called, "Thara? Thara, it's me, Leko." A small, squarely cut window allowed a faint sliver of gray light and his eyes settled on a rising shadow in the far corner of the poorly ventilated hut.

"It's going to be a mild and short winter season." She broke into a fit of coughing, getting it under control after a moment. "The snow of last week will be the last of it. It's been awhile, Leko. It's good to see you," she said quietly, her voice raspy. She rose and moved wraithlike as the little puffs of frost hung on her words before slipping away. Drawing her arms around herself, she shivered at the cool air, sneezing wetly into her hand. She sounded as if she could hardly breathe, her words coming in spurts. She sneezed and wiped the yellowish mucous on a rag, wadding it up and tossing it in a corner when she finished.

Leko did not need minding of what to do. His brow furrowed in concern, he asked, "Why did you let your fire go out? You know how to start a fire and feed one. Do you want to catch the coughing sickness? You need to stay warm," he said as he shook his head and pointed to the sizable bundle of wood that lay forgotten and unused. He did not wait for her to answer as he grabbed the bundle and tossed it next to the hearth.

He felt the hearth floor. The thin layer of ash was gray and cold. "Look, here's some beech. It burns hot green or seasoned. This will do." Leko got down on his left knee and took the dried pond reeds and split open the tender tops, scraping the dry fluffy white innards into a neat pile. He looked up and pointed toward her cloak, which lay in a crumpled pile beside the bed. "Put that on and get warm."

Thara coughed loudly into her hand and waved his demand away. "If you insist on building a fire, you can cut to the chase and use the oil. No need to toil unnecessarily." She sighed and slowly walked over to a small table with wobbly legs, where a small tin decanter was resting. She held it up for him to see.

He waved it off with a frown. "I know how to start a fire. Thank you," he added before reaching into his pack and pulling out flint and steel. With quick sure strokes he smacked them together until sparks flew and landed on the nest of kindling. When red sparks singed the pile, he held his face close and blew until a tiny flame licked up and the twigs caught. He pulled larger sticks from the bundle and gradually added them until a decent fire blazed. He rose, a broad smile on his face.

"See? Come get warm." His gaze took in the bare room, which was large enough for Thara to walk around a bit and had a cot covered with a thick wool blanket and a length of goat fur. It looked comfortable. It also looked unused.

He crinkled his nose at the scent of wood smoke mixed with the smell of sickness. Sniffing further, the sweet, sickly odor of rotting food assailed his nostrils. He strode over and looked under the bed. A small pile of decomposing food ended his search. He looked up, his eyes wide and questioning. "Thara? You're not eating." It was more a statement than a question. Leko walked toward her as the fire flared brightly and orange sparks rode vectors of warm air toward the ceiling and out the rudimentary smoke hole. The flickering light captured her figure, and for the first time he noticed that her eyes were drowning in hollow, dark circles. She looked pale and waxy, her cheekbones more pronounced and sharper than before. She was almost gaunt. Her hair hung limply, dank and unwashed around her shoulders. She looked bony and raw, with a yellowish tint leaking into the whites of her eyes. Still, she braved a smile.

"I have not had much of an appetite the past two weeks. The food does not suit me," she said while shrugging meekly. She stayed beyond the flames and heat of the fire, sticking to the flickering shadows. "Maybe they'll let me go home to eat," she joked.

Leko moved closer. "If you don't eat, you'll wither away, and then where would we be" he said with a hitch in his voice. He had been very young at the time, but he remembered the winter when a wave of the coughing sickness weaved a deadly path through his village. The healers were helpless to stop it, and with a shudder, he recalled the smell of death and the sounds of mourning. He remembered the cries of the sick and dying and the feverish prayers for those afflicted. In his mind's eye he could still see mothers and fathers scraping shallow graves out of the cold, hard earth and carefully lowering small snuggly wrapped bundles with anguished care. He also remembered how some of the bodies had to be kept until spring, the ground too frozen for proper digging. That was a long winter.

Thara began to speak but broke into a fit of coughing, the deep wet sound of phlegm rattling her chest and causing her eyes to tear up in pain. She panted from the exertion and took a hesitant, stumbling step before leaning over, her stomach heaving dryly.

Leko rushed to her side and took hold of her arms. "Thara!" he cried. She fell against him, and Leko caught her sagging body. He grabbed her under the arms and dragged her to the cot. With little effort he was able to get her on her back and under the cover of the wool blanket and furs. Her teeth chattered and she mumbled incoherently, her body writhing as if a thousand needles pricked her from head to foot. Beads of sweat pooled on her creased brow, and her cheeks burned hot with two matching crimson splotches.

Leko felt as if his heart had leapt into his throat. He shuffled around the room looking for a rag. Finding none, he pulled his knife and sliced a strip from the blanket, dipped it into a water pail, and tenderly dabbed her face. He knew he must get help or Thara would die. "Be strong, Thara. Stay with me," he whispered while gently squeezing her cold, clammy hand with both of his. With one last look over his shoulder, he bolted out the door and ran hard toward the stables. He ignored the shouted salutations of the Roman soldiers and kept at a sprint. Kege and another Bibroci youth looked up at his passing and Leko yelled out, "Kege! Come with me. You!" he shouted at the other youth. "On your life, you care for the prisoner, Thara! On your life!" Kege shrugged and ran after Leko, leaving the other bewildered youth looking around helplessly.

"Where are we going?" Kege asked breathlessly, struggling to keep pace.

"To find a holy man. A healer," Leko said, too rushed to elaborate.

CHAPTER FORTY-TWO

JAYAS LEANED OVER his mount and into the wind, allowing the chill to cleanse his mind and focus his thoughts. He slid behind a screen of tightly grown beech, his movements shielded by the trunks. Moonlight flooded the trail and stars were high and distant. He enjoyed the dark solitude of the forest at night. Some were fearful of the forest, but the notion of evil spirits and ghouls lurking in its depths had no hold on him.

The woods were sodden, the creeks swollen, and the biting wind cold. Far off and high above him, a nighthawk screamed. In the depths of the forest an owl questioned loudly and was answered by the warble of a night bird. He followed another light trail until it opened into a starlit meadow blurred black in the shadows cast by the high- reaching trees surrounding it. A northern wind gusted, picking up the chaff and spinning leaves across the earth. Faintly, the scent of fresh wood smoke turned him in the right direction. He pointed his horse east and rode as the dull waxen moon peered through the forest and lit his way.

He could see the glow of a small fire just ahead, the flames flickering off the great stones arranged in a strange pattern as if the gods had cast them deliberately to baffle mankind. Jayas dismounted and walked the remaining distance, leading his horse by the tether down the narrow trail. Ahead, a shadow moved. A dog grumbled a warning and then fell back asleep, its black muzzle on its paws.

Rhu sat cross-legged before the crackling red flames, and Jayas had a feeling the Druid knew he was there. Rhu's craggy face was set in intent purpose, the lines flushed with shadows by the flickering light of the fire. His eyes fluttered and his mouth moved quickly under the layers of tangled beard. Jayas could hear the rhythmic chants ride the air on whispers, and he waited respectfully. Finally, as if awakening from a nap, Rhu rubbed his eyes with a bony fist and yawned, baring his few remaining teeth before glancing up.

"It's about time," Rhu said.

"What do you mean? I just decided to come," Jayas said.

Rhu shrugged. "I knew you were coming. So did he," Rhu said, pointing to the large dog that snored contentedly by the fire.

"Where did you get him? He looks like one of the king's war dogs," Jayas said.

"He is, or rather, he was. He took a liking to me and followed me here." Rhu shrugged again. "He's fine company and doesn't complain. Plus, he's warm," Rhu said with a grin before the smile dropped like a stone. The old man's eyes faded slightly in the light of the fire. "Sit. Sit down." He gestured toward the fire.

Jayas tied his horse to a crookedly growing young maple, unslung the pack he had tied to the rump of his horse and tossed it next to the fire. He sat down, thankful for the dry warmth, and unrolled the blanket, unveiling the wrapped grub. He took a loaf of bread and split it in half, handing the larger portion to the priest. He also tossed some jerked beef to Rhu before tearing a hunk for himself. Jayas chewed contentedly as he stared into the fire, waiting for the priest to finish. He watched as the big dog, awakened by the smell of food, ambled over to his master and plopped down at his feet, his square head resting atop his forepaws, his eyes imploring. Rhu tossed a piece of jerky into the air and the dog raised up, snatching it midair before returning to its former pose and licking its lips with a wet pink tongue. Jayas could easily imagine it was smiling with sated pleasure at the unexpected treat.

"The struggle continues," Rhu said tiredly. "Push and pull. Equilibrium. Do you know what that is?" He fixed Jayas with a stare and continued before the young warrior could formulate an answer. "Balance. The ancients understood balance. The earth we sit on spins in balance. It gives us night and day. It gives us the tide and surf. Long days of summer give way to the long nights of winter. Balance, equilibrium." He sighed deeply, sounding tired and spent. "Be it sunshine or rain—too little or too much and the effect is much the same. Gradual ruin."

The fire burned low. Jayas placed another log on the coals and blew until the coals flared red hot and flames licked up the sides of the wood. He looked up at Rhu, his brow creased by a frown. "I get it. Love and hate, war and peace, and so on and so on," Jayas said in exasperation. Rhu's eyes flashed angrily and he immediately regretted his tone.

His eyes closed in thought, Rhu spoke forcefully. "I don't think you do. Both my nieces are gone, swallowed by the ravenous beast from across the sea." He looked through the fire and into the night. "And that beast threatens to do worse."

Jayas looked up. "They live," he said lowly. Thara's absence hurt and he was driven to distraction with grief and worry. His mood worsened with every passing day, his attention span grew shorter, and his temper flared at little to no provocation. Worst of all was the guilt. It was his fault, and worse, many of the folk were whispering the same thing, questioning his abilities and faulting him for allowing her to even be outside the hillfort. Most, if not all, had been appalled when they heard Thara had fought the Romans, and worse that Jayas had sanctioned it. He sighed, wishing he could take back time, tell her it was too dangerous and demand she stay where she belonged---out of harm's way with the rest of the women and children. But Thara's charms were not easily dispelled. He barely thought twice when she told him she needed herbs for her healing medicines. Busy seeing to his warriors and holding council after council, he merely made her promise to have an escort accompany her on her foraging mission. He ground his teeth. He should have been with her and not those two weaklings he had tasked for the duty. He felt a pressing need to do something but was at a loss for how to proceed.

"If only Father and the king would sanction it, I would take the warriors and storm that lesion upon our lands. I would burn the Roman fort to the ground and rescue Thara. I can do it," Jayas said with little confidence.

A long sigh erupted from Rhu before he spoke. "Only the folk matter, not affairs of the heart," Rhu answered with a slow moving shrug. "Attacking their fortifications would be folly and you know it. Slow down and think. Anger is little more than a moment of madness, an intentional loosening of control. Untreated, anger turns...turns to lingering insanity. That's something your kinsman Gymm would do. With only your warriors, you cannot hope to attack the fort outright and expect to prevail." He sighed once again, but this time in resignation. "And your motivation for doing so cannot be based upon your love of a single woman. To be a leader, Jayas, is to put the needs of the whole above that of a few. It pounds on the heart like the great stone that grinds our wheat, but it is the way, and the only way if our folk are to survive this blight." Rhu paused long enough to poke the fire with a stick, the coals flaring hotly at the disturbance. "But you are right in one respect. This lesion upon our land must be removed. Yet we need the other tribes for this." Rhu's wizened face, dry and cracked, held bright eyes that penetrated the smoke of the fire and locked onto Jayas.

"Then how? The other tribes are either neutral or aligned with the Romans," Jayas complained. His mood threatened to plummet and he glowered at the fire.

"Yes. They are tentative fools, much like the family of rabbits who welcomed the foxes to build a den in their glen," Rhu said, referring to a tale told by the people. "Greedy appeasers, each and every one, willing to forget who they are and stumbling all over themselves to accept the graft of the corrupter." Rhu clucked his tongue. "The wolf has been allowed in the lodge and now it is sating itself on blood. That's Celtic blood it gorges itself on. We only have to survive and wait for the right time. The day is not too far off when the wolf will become lazy and amicable. When that happens, our trap will spring."

Jayas readied a response but stopped at the sound of cracking twigs that caused his horse to snort in alarm. From somewhere in the dark, a horse whinnied in return, followed by a muffled curse. The dog stood up, a low growl coming from deep within its muscled chest. The hair on its neck bristled and the lips drew back to reveal long canines. Jayas was already on his feet, his sword drawn. He stepped away from the fire and thought to douse it but had nothing handy to do so. He kept to the shadows and motioned at Rhu to follow. The old priest waved him off. The dog stayed by Rhu, its hackles raised, on alert, while Jayas moved in an arc around the fire.

There was a crunch of hooves mixed with the lighter tap of boots in the brush. A voice cut through the night. "I come in peace. I seek Rhu, uncle to Thara of the Coritani," said the slightly accented voice, youthful but obviously in the midst of irrevocable change.

Jayas froze, his eyes searching the area from where the voice and steps came. He caught a glimpse of movement and crouched behind a berry bush, careful not to snag himself on the thorns. The voice was familiar. He clenched his jaw as realization set in. The voice belonged to that damned whelp of a prisoner who stole his horse. He probably even had something to do with Thara's abduction, he thought darkly. His teeth began to grind and the pain focused his concentration.

Once again the voice shattered the night. "Hello. You know me. I come in peace. Trust me. It's important." He stepped onto the trail, not twenty paces away.

"Quit your hollering and present yourself proper!" boomed Rhu's voice from beside the fire.

LEKO WARILY APPROACHED, careful to keep in the shadows. Jayas was here so he couldn't slack his guard. He handed his reins to Kege, who remained behind a screen of oaks, sentry to any flanking attempt. Leko saw the old priest seated by the fire, a huge dog bristling and growling by his side. The dog's beady eyes gleamed yellow and red in the light of the fire and were fixed on his every movement. Leko swallowed hard and emerged, his eyes glued to the holy man. He could feel Jayas slink beside him, the fierce energy burning an itch into the nape of his neck. He shunted aside the nervous flutter of wings that beat in his chest and around his stomach and began to speak but thought better of it. Jayas remained partially concealed by a thick tree heavy with vine and it made him nervous.

"Tell me what brings you to pester me in my winter quarters," the old healer ordered, his eyes lidded as he studied Leko' face.

Leko cast an uneasy glance at Jayas before addressing Rhu. Taking a deep breath, he began. He did not hold back and his words came in a torrent as he detailed what he had seen of Thara. "Her condition is bad enough for me to come seeking your help," he said, desperate for them to believe.

Jayas moved into the light, his sword still unsheathed and held at his side. "Lies! Damnable lies. Thara deathly ill? She was fit as a spring filly before your filthy Roman friends stole her! It's a bundle of lies! The words of a horse-thieving traitor are not worth a damn. He means to lead us into ambush. They could be out there for all we know. And how did you know where to find us? Tell me." Jayas swore under his breath and shook the sword in the youth's direction.

Leko stepped back into the shadows until his haunch brushed roughly against a rock . He gripped the hilt of his sword and silently pulled it free. His heart hammered and his mouth lost any trace of moisture. He licked his lips.

"I do not lie. And why do you insult me? I come here as a free man, seeking assistance for *your* clanswoman and you treat me like I'm nothing. And how did I find you? You left a trail clear enough for any to follow," Leko lied, stifling the urge to scream his hatred and rush Jayas, to see his blade cut into the pompous swine.

Jayas snorted and laughed meanly, his scar dancing in the flickering shadows of the rocks. "A free man followed me? Isn't that something? Well, I ought to…"

"Enough!" Rhu stood up and pointed at Jayas. "Slay not the messenger, for he is merely a vessel bearing tidings upon his lips. He may be confused as to what and who he is, but the truth is planted in his eyes and bare for all to see. I will go with him and heal her. Do not worry. It will be so." He patted the big dog on the head while scratching his scraggly beard in thought. Finally, he turned toward Leko again and said, "Turn around and walk to your horse. Jayas come with me."

Leko's brow furrowed, and then his face reddened, burning hot at the further insults heaped upon him by Jayas. He spun on his heel and made his way back to his mount, taking the reins from Kege with a nod. Through the gloom he glared at Jayas.

"He's coming with us I suspect," he whispered to Kege. The young Bibroci warrior's eyes widened and he made the sign to ward off evil spirits.

"That's the ancient Druid isn't it, the shape-shifter?" Kege whispered back, again casting the symbol.

Leko waved it off. "He's not evil. He's strange like most priests and has powerful medicine, but I don't think he'll hex us." Leko wasn't altogether sure if what he said was true, but he put on a brave face. They were here and that was that. If Thara lived, then it was all worth it, hex or no hex. He clapped a hand on Kege' shoulder and tried his best to appear nonchalant. They watched as Rhu and Jayas spoke animatedly by the glow of the dying fire before Rhu and the dog broke away and headed in their direction.

"Who is the big warrior? It seems like I've seen him before," Kege said, stroking his clean-shaven chin. Then realization set in and his eyes narrowed to deadly slits, venomous in nature and intent.

Leko took a deep breath and exhaled raggedly. "Now is not the time," he said. He stepped in front of Kege, his voice husky and low, warning, "Not the time. We go back with the old man."

Kege nodded and shrugged, a cold smile playing on his lips. "If you say."

CHAPTER FORTY-THREE

CUSSIUS STEPPED FROM the doorway and inhaled the cold, morning air. He filled his chest with its crispness, enjoying the fresh taste as it cooled his mouth and throat. A yawn escaped his mouth, and not bothering to stifle it, he looked up. A cold, light sprinkle began to fall just as the first spurts of dawn finally caught the tail of night. His guards made to follow him, but he waved them off. "Stay back. I want to think for a moment. I doubt a horde of Coritani infiltrated during the night and are buried in the mud, ready to ambush us. Clean yourselves up and get something to eat. Rest if you can," he ordered. The men were grateful and hastily beat a retreat.

He ignored the rain and walked around the fort, the motion helping to steady his thoughts. Muted curses and rough laughter met his ears as he passed the barracks. The curses were followed by dull thuds and scrapes. The winter season was grinding on his nerves, the monotony of garrison life sapping the fiber from his being. He frowned. From the sounds of it, the men were just as eager for the return of spring. Every day was more of the same: receiving nobles from allied tribes, settling petty squabbles amongst them and keeping tabs on supplies. Antonius made sure the Roman fighting men kept trim and fit with drills and by rotating patrols with the Bibroci and the few remaining Trinovante warriors who had not slipped off to their villages for a well-deserved respite. Cussius placated himself by drilling and sparring. It relieved tension and stress and he always felt a bit invigorated after an intense session. Of course, Lana was a welcome distraction, proving herself a quick and observant study and lending a unique voice to events. He wore a smile on his face as his thoughts drifted to the previous evening.

Her hair had shone raven black, and her skin was oiled to a high sheen, her mouth sensuous with her even white teeth artfully revealed in a flash of smile. Dressed in a simple wool robe, she was stunning. Antonius, Kren, and the other officers and nobles who dined with them seemed taken by her charms. A smile here, a touch of the arm there, nuances and nods, she mesmerized them all. Sitting back, sipping his drink and taking it all in, Cussius had marveled at her ability to turn their fear and lust, for that's what it was, into something he could not quite put his finger on. Respect perhaps, but the fear and lust remained despite it. After listening to the same tales, grown larger and more heroic by the telling, he was more than ready to carve out some new ones for himself. He imagined entering the world of Roman politics, a world that was always just out of his reach. How would he be received with Lana on his arm, gliding through noble society with her exquisite and foreign features evident for all. Her wit and raw intelligence would be on display for the civilized world to enjoy and appreciate.

He sighed at the imagery in his head. A bore it would be, a needless gauntlet of intrigue and pitfalls with little hope of gainful return. They would mock her as uncivilized, uneducated, and barbaric. Beautiful, yes, but they would pay no heed to her other, just as obvious, talents. The old families would whisper mockingly, spreading deceit and scorn, driven to undermine her apparent strengths, and relegate her to little more than a used pair of sandals. He would be the recipient of equal amounts of scornful rebukes and mockeries, his old name sullied and smeared with rumor and innuendo. Proper Roman society would never sanction her as his spouse. No matter how humble in riches a Roman noble dwelled, the sanctity of their proud names must be preserved. Marriage to a barbarian woman would not serve that end, at least as far as the descendants of the old families were concerned. His face burned with the realization that his homeland, despite all its strengths, was thus limited.

He squinted into the wind as he walked, returning the salutes of legionaries already up and attending to the morning's first duties. Heavy mist blew into his face and ran down his cheekbones in tiny rivulets.

"General!" a voice thundered from a doorway of the officers' quarters. Cussius looked in time to see a figure break from a small huddle of junior officers clustered around a common water trough.

Cussius greeted them with a slight scowl. "Already, Antonius? I haven't even had my breakfast. What is so pressing that you must howl like a wild Celt to get my attention?" He did not pause in his stroll, and Antonius, a wide-shouldered, burly man with a florid complexion and a fast choppy way of moving, hustled to catch up. He talked fast and worked his hands in rhythm with his words. Cussius knew Antonius wanted to give his morning report, and it was a little game Cussius played to be on the move when he tried to give it.

"Sir! Seven hundred and fifty Roman soldiers battle effective. We have an equal number of allied Celtic troops," Antonius said in a flurry of words.

Cussius cut him short with a look and a single word. "How goes the training?" The Romans had been working the Bibroci and Trinovante in the Roman mode of fighting. Resistant at first, the tribesmen were growing to appreciate the ruthless efficiency of the Roman methodology and now trained in earnest. Initially, the discipline of marching and fighting in ranks was a difficult endeavor for the Celts, but time and pressure was molding them into what he wanted. To further buttress the training and encourage cohesiveness, Cussius had placed a Roman officer in charge of each tribal century with a Roman squad leader for every ten men. So far the strategy had worked, but these Celts had yet to be tried in a major battle.

"The Bibroci are coming along nicely. The young ensign..." Antonius paused as he searched his memory for the name. "Leko, the slave. He must have been paying attention to the old man. He has a knack for soldiering," Antonius said with an approving nod. "He is developing a workable century. They could almost pass for legionaries, but I think they are way too fond of their horses to make a proper marching century. It is probably best to integrate them into our cavalry. All in all, we have lost none and all seem to be well fed and spoiling for spring." Antonius looked satisfied with himself.

"Morale? Any grumblings from within the ranks?" Cussius asked. He was always keen to sniff out any dissension that might be brewing. Bad attitudes and nay-saying were potentially contagious, and Cussius thought it best to keep his finger on the pulse of the men.

Antonius shrugged. "The usual. Some miss home, but the majority have nothing to go back to anyhow. As long as they have access to wine, women and song, they will be fine. And of course, as long as there are potential riches and land to be had," Antonius added quickly.

It was well known that more than a few of the men had taken up with some of the native women. Cussius could have claimed privilege as far his relationship with Lana went, but if his longer--range goals were to have any chance of success, relationships and ties to the land were needed. A breath of wind carried smoke from the cooking fires. Ahead he spotted the source. Ramshackle collections of lean-tos were lined out in tight rows and intersected by muddy paths. The makeshift market stayed crowded with traders hocking goods and foodstuffs, and rough shanties sprang up where camp hangers-on scratched out a living and a place to live. As with every Roman camp of any decent duration and size, houses of ill repute also took root and flourished.

"Of course," Cussius scoffed with a glance at a squat building that boasted two chimneys and sprawled at a ninety-degree angle from the tack barn. The low structure housed thirty slave women who doubled as concubines and prostitutes. An especially brutish Bibroci named Kembell ensured peace and quiet and collected the dues earned from the backs of the slaves. Enterprising man that he was, Kembell would not miss a chance to slake the other thirsts of the parched legionaries and sold mead by the cup and by the jug. Business was crisp. As if on cue, two legionaries stumbled from the entrance, one holding the other up and moving in short, shuffling steps toward the barracks.

Cussius raised an eyebrow as he looked at Antonius. "Care to revise your figures?" he asked with a mean grin and sharp elbow to his subordinate's shoulder.

Antonius knew what to do. "You two! Stop!" he shouted. Turning to Cussius, he said, "Seven hundred and forty eight legionaries fit for battle, sir." Antonius shared a grin of his own while rubbing his smarting shoulder. He was known to take advantage of the generous charms of the slave women himself, but he would not tolerate drunkenness, especially if that drunkenness happened to transpire at the beginning of the day and in view of their commanding officer.

Cussius nodded toward the besotted legionaries now resting against the fence. They wore stupid grins on their faces and swayed slightly before collapsing onto their haunches.

"There is a time as well as a place for frolicking," he barely whispered. "Square those men away, Antonius!" Cussius ordered, the disgust evident in his voice. He raised his voice as a few passing legionaries gathered to gawk at the embarrassed duo and listen in. "I will not tolerate shirkers nor drunkards while duty beckons. There is a time for revelry and a time for attending to the demands of nature, but a man whose mind is muddled with drink is a man not fit to fight. And if a man cannot fight, he is of no use to me. Why is that?" he roared, blood flushing his cheeks red. He whirled and fixed the two miserable looking men with a cold glare. "Because they are void of any meaningful utility to their comrades. That is why." He pointed over the walls. "Let them be the drunkards. Let them sully and dumb themselves down with excesses. Our ability to moderate our behavior is what makes us civilized. Moderation," he muttered for Antonius' sake. The man had a reputation for savagery, and Cussius would not tolerate cruelty to his own troops. He could not afford to alienate them by extreme measures, but neither could he afford to allow wanton drunkenness to go unpunished. "Moderation," he said again, eyebrows raised, the message conveyed. A legionary who suffers a broken body or shattered spirit by the whip is of no use either, he thought.

Antonius looked menacingly at the two drunkards, whose saliva-ridden chins now lolled on their chests. "Aye, sir."

"And Antonius." Cussius stepped into the man and came eye to eye with his second.

"Yes, General?"

"Shave that moustache. You look ridiculous, and standards must be maintained lest the men take to sloth and debauchery," Cussius said with a nod in the direction of the two inebriants. "You do not want to be mistaken for one of these wild Celts, do you? Well, maybe you do. It is an attractive concept to ride like a barbarian, I admit. You are dismissed."

And that was the truth. Cussius admired the fierce individuality of the tribesmen and found their lack of discipline and formality endearing to a certain extent. Like their cousins in Gaul, they had no written word and relied on memorization and singing for their rudimentary education. Particularly fascinating were the bards, who had learned their trade from their Druid mentors and transported the Celtic knowledge from generation to generation. He thought their lack of formal education was an impediment to their development, but that could be remedied.

Lana was a case under study. To pass the time on the long winter nights, she would listen avidly as he related tales in Greek and his native Latin. She especially took to the teachings of Plato, relentlessly questioning him, ensuring that he did not hold back any choice nuggets of wisdom. He humored her and did his best. He took to writing down some of the fanciful stories she related, and the give and take in their private moments was something they both looked forward to. She carefully studied his writings and asked questions, until one day, she shocked him by picking up a scroll containing a scribbled message and read it to him flawlessly. He remembered her simple delight in surprising him with her newfound talent, and his appreciation for her quick wittedness grew.

Absorbed in his thoughts, he hardly noticed Antonius salute and turn his attentions to the two luckless legionaries who resignedly slouched to their fates. Their grins had vanished and their eyes were downcast. Evidently they found the frozen mud more understanding than their comrades' condemning disapproval.

CHAPTER FORTY-FOUR

GYMM WINCED. The day had been promising, crisp and cold but with clear skies. Now, the sleet was driving hard, the small frozen nuggets stinging like angry bees. He lowered his head to avoid the bulk of the abuse and wished he had the foresight to dress appropriately. His horse lowered its head to the ground and walked on by instinct and feel, slogging along the rapidly freezing trail.

Gymm shivered violently in his heavy tunic and brought the hood up over his head. It did little to help. His mood lowered further when Roc nudged his horse closer to Gymm's and peered at him from within the folds of a patchwork of furs. "What?" Gymm shouted above the wind. He was cold, hungry and getting wet and did not fancy exchanging pleasantries for no particular purpose.

Roc raised his arms slightly, his brow scrunched in uneven rolls of skin. He looked none the worse for wear. He was wrapped in a fur he had taken from a dead Brigante warrior two years ago. Gymm remembered the day clearly. They had attacked a poor bunch of Brigante warriors upon discovering them snooping along the edges of their territory. The battle was brief and as far as plunder went, it was lean pickings. Roc hated to come away from a fight with mere noses or heads. He preferred to take something more permanent than rotting flesh, and after picking over the leaking corpses and shaking off the blow flies, he had settled on the fur robe. It was an assortment of squirrel, fox and rabbit stitched with thick uneven lines and one size too large. The garment looked ridiculous, let alone its odd smell, kind of like a favorite pet buried three or four months past. Since that battle, the short noble had worn it at the slightest hint of a cold snap. Now, his eyes and nose were the only parts of his face exposed to the punishing wet wind, while his arms and torso remained dry and warm.

Gymm gave him a hard look. Roc sat on his mount and shrugged as if he were sorry for Gymm's plight but powerless to change it. Aggravated, Gymm looked away and studied the trail. He guided his horse down a slippery embankment, flexing his knees tightly around the beast's torso as it navigated the slope. At the bottom, he gritted his teeth and stole a look at the sky. The snowfall was getting worse.

Blue puffy clouds hovered above, spewing thick veils of snow, the first fat white splotches landing on his shaggy head and atop the dark mane of his horse. It melted quickly but was immediately replaced by an army of others. Gymm sighed and shifted uncomfortably, thankful that his bottom remained dry. The snow was now falling in swirling sheets, blinding in its brightness against the stark gray-brown of the forest trees. He cupped his hand over his eyes to gauge the time of day, but it was useless. It was obviously getting late for the shadows had grown as thick as the driven snow. He settled in for the ride.

Hunched over the horse, his head and neck tucked down into his shoulders for added warmth, he fell into rhythm with his mount and pondered what he had done. Oddly, he felt no guilt over the matter. The betrayal of Thara to the Romans really did not faze him. It suits the little wench, he thought meanly. Of course, her capture suited his purposes as well. She could join her harlot sister, and they could truckle and spread their charms amongst the filthy Romans and their stinking tribal allies for all he cared. He smiled thinly despite the cold and warmed at the recollection. For once he had made things happen instead of letting events unfold however they might.

It wasn't his fault anyhow. "Jayas brought this upon himself," Gymm said to the falling flakes of white. His cousin had schemed and plotted to steal his birthright from under his nose. Gymm boiled. Even Gymm's own father, the king, had fallen victim to his ruse. Gymm grimaced. He never would have seen through this plot without the insight of Roc and his father.

Well, Gymm thought, if everyone believed he would sit idle while his cousin fleeced him of what was rightfully his, they had another thing coming. He would fight for what was his. He sneered in the face of the blowing snow. He knew the nobles believed him stupid, not swift in matters of the mind, but he watched and listened and played along with their games.

He thought of his unlikely alliance with the Roman general, Cussius. It was full of risk but bearing fruit. Thara had been missing for over a month with seemingly no word of her whereabouts. In turn, Jayas' spirits had tumbled to the depths. First his horse was stolen and then his woman disappeared. Gymm grinned from within the folds of his checkered tunic. It was as if the wind had been kicked from Jayas and he was still struggling to regain it. Jayas believed the gods had turned against him, and his warriors were beginning to murmur amongst themselves about his misfortunes. In return, Gymm's own disastrous battle with the Romans at the Valley Knoll was becoming but a distant memory in the shuffle of Jayas' personal setbacks. Now he needed to do something notable to erase the memory, to lead and regain his injured honor.

"How," he wondered aloud as he jerked his mount off the trail. The thought of having to cross Cussius sent a cold shiver down his spine. There was something about the Roman, something about Lana, and indeed, something about the kid, Leko, or whatever his name was. Damn him; I should have gutted that whelp when I had the chance, thought Gymm. It made his head hurt to think on all of this for too long.

The snow began to wane, and much like the beast he rode, Gymm shook his body to remove the light layer from his tunic. He spotted the stream in the distance. From here the Roman fort was a mile through the forest. He became wary.

CHAPTER FORTY-FIVE

THE CRIMSON LAST LIGHT of day rent the heavens like a flaming sword, the sun finally retreating to lick its wounds as it gave way to dusk. Cussius walked the planking, careful of his step, for the planed boards were covered with gobs of slushy mud where boots had carelessly tramped. He shook his head. Predicting the weather patterns of this land was next to impossible. It was mild here in comparison to the mountainous regions of Gaul, but there was always a torrent of snow or ice looming threateningly in the form of fat dark clouds.

"The weather of this land is much like its people," Cussius muttered to himself. He unfurled the letter once more, squinting to catch the words in the lame light cast by a nearby torch. His stomach leapt into his throat and he forced it down. This was unexpected. Caesar had not minced words and the orders were clear. He swallowed hard and rubbed his temples, relieving the pressure building in his head. He was to pull up stakes and make for the coast come spring. In three months time, transport ships would dock to ferry the troops and the tribute to Gaul. Caesar expected the allied Bibroci and Trinovante to follow, their cavalry very much needed on the continent for the spring offensive.

"The situation must be serious," he thought out loud, his mood and spirits paralleling the sinking temperature. The Gauls were apparently more troublesome than expected, not unlike the Celts of

Britannia. He grimaced. Mandubrac and Kren of the Trinovante would not obey this directive. He was quite sure of that. Neither would the Bibroci. Already they had lost their clan leader to the Coritani, and the heir apparent, Kege, was little more than a boy and reliant upon Cussius to help him govern. The order would go unheeded, putting Cussius in an embarrassing predicament, and Caesar would demand to know why. The pressure in his head continued to build, aching in a dull throb. He shook his head at the thought of convincing Mandubrac, Kren and the Bibroci of the legitimacy of Caesar's order. These warriors would not leave their people defenseless in order to sail to Gaul and join up with Caesar to fight their cousins, the Gauls. Cassivellaunus would probably take advantage of the imminent departure of Roman troops and withdraw his tepid support, while the Coritani would step up their endeavors, putting pressure on the allied clans to turn on his isolated Roman legion. The potential mess is controllable but potentially disastrous, he thought with a grimace.

His mind drifted, and with considerable effort, he yanked it back to the present. A strategy came to mind. He looked around. "The precipice beckons," he said aloud. He pulled the torch off its perch and touched the flame to the dry papyrus, the edges turning black with little blue-yellow flames licking the length until the letter was consumed, the ashes crumbling and catching the wind. There was no going back. He sighed deeply. A twinge of guilt rushed over him and then faded by degrees as he realized that Caesar's messenger and his escorts must not return. Maybe they would be offered a chance to change course. At least they would have a choice, he thought grimly. He envied them, for in reality he had no such choice available to him. The weight of responsibility pressed down on him as the import and significance of his act sunk in. He wished his conscience could be as easily dispersed as the weightless ashes of the message that disappeared before his eyes.

He walked the rampart, the footing slick and treacherous. He gained the top and surveyed his holdings in the fading light. As his gaze swept beyond the jagged trenches and onto the rolling fields and forested hills sweeping the horizon, a thrill of pride shimmered through his chest. He had carved out what he surveyed and Caesar would have him leave it. A strange tug of reservation rose within him, sharp pangs of doubt stabbing within his chest where pride had reigned but a moment ago. A sound like sidling feet caught his attention and Cussius came up short, his head snapping alert, then relenting as the familiar face labored toward him.

Lana clambered the remaining distance, her face catching the soft glow of the dying sun and emerging stars. She pulled up and her eyes locked on his. "What troubles you?" she asked softly.

"Nothing," he said, shifting his gaze beyond the walls, his eyes searching for the author of a harsh and resonant cawing. A carrion crow circled the far edges of the dusk sky, flying north, dipping and disappearing behind the dark tree line. A jack snipe called out, its cry like a distant galloping horse.

She remained unconvinced. "The messengers from your Caesar, what do they want? They want you to leave, do they not?" she said calmly, her mouth set.

"What are you talking about?" he asked. He really did not feel like going over the letter or giving thought to the couriers who delivered it at this moment.

Her eyes narrowed. "It's not what I'm talking about but what those messengers are talking about amongst themselves. They speak to one another as if I'm not even there, as if I'm invisible. They have said nary a word to me, but blab to one another like traders at the market discussing spring wool. Not that I'm bothered. It's an opportunity to listen and learn." She smiled.

Cussius shared the grin. "Of course." He grabbed her around the waist and drew her to him, sweeping some careless ropes of her hair back over her shoulder. "How can anyone ignore a vision like you? I'm not complaining, mind you. What are they saying?" he asked.

"Not much else besides the order to leave. They plan to stay here to see your departure through, traveling to the coast with your legion in the spring. They also speak of cold and pressing times across the water. Hunger and famine reign; the people and land are tired. The Gauls are united and pushing against your armies, then retreating and burning foodstuffs or taking all supplies with them. Caesar winters and is gathering his armies. At least that is what they say." She pulled back and looked at him. "Well?" she asked.

"Do you want to leave here, leave the only place you have known as home? Even if you did, Caesar would not allow you to travel with me, and you would have to bunk and travel with the camp followers." He stopped himself. He knew he was only trying to justify the decision he had already made. Besides, Lana needed no explanation. She seemed to expect him to do whatever he did as if she knew before he knew.

"The answer is no. We are not leaving. Look, if I refuse the order, I will be a rebel and treated like one by any citizen of Rome. Caesar is proconsul-general. His word is the same as Rome's. If I defy his order, I become an enemy of Rome and could die a traitor's death." He felt a great weight lift, breathing as if for the first time, upon speaking these words aloud. For some reason, he thought of Spartacus. Did the Thracian slave feel such exhilaration when he tore off the shackles of slavery and dared to be free? Cussius was a mere child at the time, but he clearly remembered the panic and fear that gripped Rome when the slave rebellion erupted. Spartacus' slave army grew in numbers and in proficiency, rampaging across the peninsula and back, until finally it was crushed by Crassus and Pompey and the majority put to the sword or crucified en masse. Any who remained alive were returned to slavery, often under the cruelest conditions, such as in the faraway mines of Spain.

"Will Caesar return to make war on you? On us? Will he be able? The tribes will hear how the war over the sea is going. Word always travels. Traders trade in gossip as well as goods," she said.

"Good point." He did not need to be reminded that the tribes could be emboldened by word of their Gallic cousins' successes across the water. If the tribes here united because of that news, as the tribes had apparently done in Gaul, the consequences would be bloody ruinous. Options are sorely limited, he thought.

The sun was gone now, leaving only a thin haze of purple over the hills. Suddenly, Lana walked by him, her haste causing him to turn quickly. He stopped, a new frown working its way to the fore. He did a double take as his eyes locked on the main gate.

Grabbing a passing legionary by the nape of the neck, he ordered, "Come with me." His eyes narrowed as he watched. Unchallenged and trudging through the opened gate were three familiar figures.

"What are you doing here?" he yelled, his long legs covering the distance in determined strides. Legionaries gathered round, and the guards, who had just seconds ago greeted the trio like long lost comrades, now ringed them, their glances hostile and questioning.

He pointed to Leko and asked the obvious. "Are you party to this?"

Leko slouched on the mount, the old man's bony arms wrapped around his waist.

Cussius cocked an eyebrow, an uncomfortable knot forming in his stomach. He looked into that familiar face, the face of a man who knew his worth. A wealth of flat, white hair cascaded around his thin neck, framing an angular bearded face shrouded in craggy wrinkles. The old one's eyes had his attention, though. They bored into him, peeling away his carefully constructed façade of confidence. A large black dog loped behind the horses, its pink tongue lolling, panting from its arduous journey.

Leko brought his mount to a halt. "I had no choice, General. Thara is deathly ill, and Rhu is a healer of great renown." He shrugged unapologetically.

Angry, Cussius waved the explanation away. "We have healers here. All you had to do was let one know. Her own sister is quite adept at healing. And you," he said accusingly, "you have quite the nerve, old man, to show your face here, invited by a well-meaning youth or otherwise." He shifted his glare from Rhu's unreadable face to the guileless face of Leko. An idea began forming like an itch in the back of his head. He remained silent, smiling a fresh welcome.

Lana stepped forward. "Uncle, I had no idea she was ill." She gave no further explanation and kept her head up, holding the intense gaze of the priest.

Surprisingly spry, Rhu slid off the rear haunch of the horse and fell into step with the big black dog. As he walked, he held a hand out for the dog to sniff and nuzzle. The beast instantly shifted its attention, alertly raising its muzzle and moving ahead with its eyes slit and ears pulled back. Rhu barked a command, and the beast slowed its stalk and stopped, its mouth open and teeth bared, occasionally loosening a rumbling growl in protest. Rhu stopped and rubbed its head thoughtfully, the growls receding to complete silence.

"Show me to her."

CHAPTER FORTY-SIX

The round pocked moon floated silently through the night sky, traveling alone in its quest to cover the horizon. Gymm sat with his shoulders hunched and his head up, absorbed by the glittering sky as the stars waved the moon on its journey. He felt a kinship with the moon, for its inexorable march to its destination was always the same. Gymm broke his stare and sighed a last time as he took a tighter hold on the reins. He shook off the dusting of snow and squared his shoulders with a great shiver. He sorely missed the chirping of crickets and the grumble of faraway frogs — spring could not come quickly enough to suit him.

He turned to Roc. "There is no turning back. It's me and you and a few others, and this is a gamble." His mind wandered to the many bad wagers he had laid in the past, and his mood sank low. Cursed luck, he thought. Gambling was never his strong point and it nagged him that he was about to cast the bones with a foreigner who might not honor his end of the bargain.

Roc shrugged from under his fur, his smile dissolving into a thin sneer. "It is to save our people. If our people are to be saved from certain doom, you must lead them in these times of uncertainty, and you cannot lead as long as Jayas presumes your rightful place."

Gymm shook his head in disgust and spat. "If I didn't know that, would I be here?" he snapped.

Roc's smile vanished and he nodded thoughtfully. "Of course not. No worries. My father will delay Jayas long enough." He retracted his head back into his fur like a turtle into its shell.

Gymm nodded toward the Roman fortress. "Let's go." He kneed his mount in the ribs and lurched in the saddle as his mount started from the wood.

THE FIRE CAST A FLICKERING amber light over the shadows of the faces gathered around the low burning fire. He stared into the inferno, watching the orange tongues of flame licking up the length of the split wood. Sparks flitted and popped as the fire battled to overcome pockets of moisture left from the recent snow. Jayas much preferred the sudden pops and snaps of the fire to the arguments flying around like so many busy fireflies. To Jayas, the sounds of the bickering men were much like the noise of the cicadas of summer and he paid them as much mind. He sighed. He knew he could not ignore those raucous voices as much as he would like to. He was in a sour mood and the sniveling entreaties for caution pricked his pride as if he had stumbled into a patch of nettles. The loudest voice was that of Roc's father, Bret, a nobleman of some note whom Gymm had taken up with of late.

Jayas eyed the man. He was about the age of his father, give or take a couple of years, and short like his son, his red hair flecked with streaks of gray along the temples. His plaid tunic was thick and effective against the elements, but it was clear to see that his shoulders still bulged with muscle and his midsection had yet to go soft.

Jayas stood up, the leather of his boots squeaking loudly with the motion. "And what would you have us do, Lord Bret? Our army is here," he said, pointing to the leaf-sodden ground and sweeping the length of the wooded valley with his gaze. His eyes settled momentarily upon the shadows moving in dark clumps as horses and men stamped around the darkness to keep warm. "The enemy is five miles from here, tucked in snugly like sleeping babes. They think their tall walls will keep them safe." He gestured toward the unseen distance. "If we are ever to surprise them, it is now. Not later, now!" He sat back down to a chorus of shouts and nods of approval.

Bret waved at the air with both hands and called for silence. He smiled widely from under an iron-gray moustache. "You have a point. But I ask you in return: How safe are the Romans? I too have seen their defenses, and they are formidable. Their walls are high and thick." He held his arms out as wide as he could. "And they have dug trenches like large funnel traps used to catch game, except we would be the game," he said, looking around at the clan chiefs and nobles of the war council. His smile vanished as he continued. "How do we get in? I am not a spider. I cannot climb those walls. Look." He waved his arms in a deep flapping motion, miming a lake swan. "Neither can I fly over them. Can you, Jayas?" His tone was full of challenge.

The warriors and nobles shifted their attentions to Jayas. His anger mounted and he fought to keep his tongue and sword in check. "I cannot fly or climb like a spider, but perhaps the Druid Rhu can," he said. Those around the fire quieted down and whispered amongst themselves. "Rhu is already inside the walls, and he will find a way to open the gates. We will spill in like a great flood of retribution and sweep the invaders from our land, cleansing it. Then we shall return our land to the way it was before they arrived, to the way it has always been." He kept his stare upon Bret and continued, more for the benefit of those assembled than for the contrarian nobleman. "Lord Bret, Rhu has said it will be so. If you had these doubts in your head, you should have raised them with the king and Lord Toge. On the trail of war is not the time for second guessing and hesitance. We have kept the Romans and their allies at bay through our boldness of action. To wilt now like late season violets will leave our forces broken and scatter them to the wind. We have our orders. The king and gods have spoken." He turned once again to Bret, his challenge plain for all to see.

Jayas studied the man's face. It was flushed and dirty and the corners of his mouth twitched as if he had an itch he could not scratch. Jayas continued in the face of the man's sneer. "If the plan of action does not suit your tastes, Lord Bret, ride back and convey your doubts to the king. Convince him of his folly, but be warned, the time for debate has passed. The time for action is nigh and we will not wait for you."

Bret blew a deep braying breath. "Boldness of action?" he scoffed with a grunt. "Would your newfound plan of action have anything to do with the pretty young thing being held captive by the Romans?" Low chuckles and murmurs of innuendo swept through those within earshot.

His face flushed crimson in the light of the fire, Jayas sprang to his feet again. Lips quivering, he pointed a finger at Bret. "Thara plays no part in this," he said heatedly between clenched teeth. He stole a look at the men. His lie was reflected in their hooded eyes and hidden smirks.

For his part, Bret merely stared back expectantly, a faint smile threatening to break to the fore, but he settled for maintaining Jayas' glare. Choosing his words carefully, Bret broke his silence. "Is there no better plan? Can we not draw the Romans out of their shell like a hunter draws the wolves from their dens?" He then folded his beefy arms upon his chest and sat down amongst his clansmen. They clapped him on the back and barked their agreement.

Jayas' ears burned, and despite the frigid temperature, sweat formed in the middle of his back and on his forehead. He resisted the urge to wipe his face. What Bret said was true and the men around him knew it as well. Bret was mouthing the same strategy he had formulated, the same that he and Thara had so strenuously put to Gymm and the others after the first battle with the Romans. He searched his mind and settled upon the familiar. "Not every battle calls for the same plan, but Rhu wills it as does the king. Are you to defy the gods and the king both?" Silence followed. Warriors shifted uncomfortably as they suddenly found the burning logs more interesting than his intense glare. Even Bret dropped his gaze, studying his blocky hands as they grew and shrank in the flickering shadows of the fire.

Jayas looked around and caught the eye of Lann. The man nodded grimly and clapped his hands together. "For the king! For the

Coritani!" Lann shouted. Others beside him picked it up and the sound flowed over Jayas like a welcome breeze of relief.

He did not wait to hear anything further from Bret. "We move out!" Jayas commanded. He gestured toward Lann. "Scouts ahead and on the flanks. Clan chiefs — we crawl through the trenches. Silence! Silence until I say the word! Put the fire out," he muttered to a warrior hastening to mount up. Another warrior stopped to help, and in a flurry of scattered dirt and fresh snow, the flames sizzled and wilted until all that remained were steaming logs, charred black and smoldering. Jayas stalked away glaring angrily and snapping orders in a clipped, hushed tone.

The scouts surged forward and around him, melting into the forested backdrop. Hushed commands reverberated down the gulley as clan chiefs barked orders and warriors hastened to comply. Horses sensed the excitement of their masters and whinnied and snorted their assent. The war dogs growled and snarled a low rumbling akin to faraway thunder. Jayas' dark grin showed white teeth in the shadows.

"We're coming," he whispered as he leapt atop his dun.

CHAPTER FORTY-SEVEN

LEKO PEERED OVER the old Druid's shoulder, wondering what it was he was looking for as he hovered over Thara's body like a fisherman would his catch. The priest leaned close, his ear pressed upon her chest as he listened to Thara's labored breaths. He returned upright and shook his head. He mumbled something that Leko did not catch.

Rhu spun on Leko. "I will need some things," he muttered.

Before Leko could respond, Cussius spoke. "And you shall have them." Beside him, Lana's brow furrowed deeply and she wrung her hands.

Rhu nodded and addressed Leko. "She's going to need to eat. Some pottage would be a good start." Rhu paused in thought, his eyes speeding about the room and people.

Leko's stomach rumbled at the mention of food, and in particular, pottage. His mouth watered involuntarily as he thought of filling his pinched belly with the stew of oats, beans, peas, leeks and turnips simmered in hog fat. He snapped to, realizing Rhu had spoken.

"And violet petals. Get going now. No time to waste," Rhu said with a flip of his gnarled hand.

Leko caught nothing of what came before "violet petals" and he silently cursed himself for his ever-wandering mind. He scratched his head, casting about for a question that would not make him sound the fool. "And where would I look for those?" he finally asked.

"A small leather satchel in my quarters," Lana said. She glanced at Cussius from the corner of her eye. "Our quarters. Look under the extra blanket at the foot of the bed. Cussius opened his mouth as if to speak but stopped when she laid a hand upon his arm.

Leko nodded his thanks and made his way out the door.

Cussius stepped forward. "Any way I could be of service?" he inquired with a courteous nod of his head.

Rhu fixed him with a stare. His hair straggled across his forehead but he made no move to brush it away. The old man's head slowly canted to the side and he paused, the strain palpable with the cords of his scrawny neck visible under the mangy beard. He reminded Cussius of the beggars who pawed passersby up and down the length of the Palatine, their eyes as searching and desperate as their hands.

A sneer emerged from the sunken folds of his grimy beard and moustache. "I don't see how," Rhu said suddenly. A dark frown passed over his face as he stepped into the shadows, and the visage took Cussius back. His face looked sunken and weary, the skin over his cheeks so taut it seemed close to ripping. The old man sat down on a stool at the foot of the bed and ran a wet cloth over the woman's face.

Cussius smiled flatly and rubbed his hand over his chin. His unshaven face felt as if it were pricked by nettles. "To the point. Though I would have to disagree with your premise." Cussius stepped beside the old man and stared down at Lana's sister. She looked pale and shrunken, her features bonier than when he had last seen her. He took a step backward as she suddenly began to writhe and convulse, her face scrunching in a twist, the muscles of her jaws bulging with the tension. The spasm stopped after a moment. Her hair lay damp and matted to her head and small beads of sweat pooled on her smooth brow.

Cussius turned away. "You are a man who likes to think, to consider possibilities and probabilities. I am of the same mind." Cussius was not trying to flatter the man, though it did not hurt to pay respect to his knowledge. Classical and literate it was not, but in this land, he possessed the highest levels of knowledge the place offered.

"You want nothing of me. You profess as much. You wish to purge this land of my presence---of the Roman presence. But listen and take to heart that, if it is not me, it will be Caesar. If it is not Caesar, it will be another, and so on. This incursion into your land will not stop, for Rome knows this land exists and its curiosity will not cease. It's a universal concept really, one that all people share to a certain extent and often from opposite sides of a battlefield. It is destiny I speak of, a fickle master prone to following only its own dictates. Rome believes in its destiny, and Roman destiny is to conquer and rule, to spread peace through civilization and trade." It was the old noble line, the dictate of the Republic born of a pure and noble belief in its superiority and hence the obligation to share itself with the world. Cussius chanced a glance at the priest's face. He looked tired, his bony face pale and he sat so still that he appeared to be nearly lifeless.

Rhu's face sagged to his chest and his eyes closed. Cussius frowned. The man was sleeping. Cussius turned on his heel and exchanged a puzzled shrug with Lana before they walked to the door. The old one's voice brought them back.

"You Romans are an odd lot. So fond of your long speeches, so fond of the complex. Boiled down, all I hear are threats. Threats of further invasion, of war, of conquering...and yet you dare speak of peace and trade?" Rhu's eyes were still closed but his head followed the sound of Cussius' nailed boots.

Cussius had turned back, and here came the big gamble. "I do. It is peace that I desire. Can you envision a peace that includes us staying here? What if that peace were to include an alliance dedicated to thwarting any further invader of these fair lands? I can help you turn back the rising tide," Cussius said evenly.

The old man's eyes flew open. "Would the sheep invite the wolf into the heart of the flock to have it nuzzle and caress its members? I have not seen the day when the wolf can lie with the lamb. Would not the wolf still be a wolf?"

Cussius raised his eyebrows. "A bit chilly is it not?" He walked to the fire and fed it a couple of logs, stirring the coals with his sword to reposition the red-hot ashes with the fresh wood. He continued. "But this pack of wolves is unlike any you have encountered before. You have seen this with your own eyes, yes? You witnessed how easily Caesar rolled up your lines and made the allied tribes capitulate, and with my limited numbers, I have thwarted your every effort. Now, imagine. That was only the tip of the Roman spear. To beat them, you need someone who knows them. It is as simple as that." Cussius stopped. His explanation was elementary but sufficient. He had cast his lot.

Rhu stood up and laughed, a sound somewhere between a coughing fit and a cackle. "Do hearts change that easily? I think not."

"I think a man is within his right to choose his own destiny. I have chosen mine. That's a lot more than most people can boast," Cussius said defensively.

Lana cleared her throat. "I have chosen mine as well, Uncle," Lana said. She smiled easily at Cussius and stepped toward the old man, took his hands in hers and met his quizzical gaze.

Rhu cocked a bushy eyebrow until it disappeared into the unruly straggles of his tangled hair. "You have chosen what, exactly?" Rhu asked.

Eyes softened, her jaw unyielding, Lana continued. "My destiny and that of the folk are the same. He…" She gestured toward Cussius. "He is the one who is to set us upon our course. Fate has brought our two peoples together. We now have the chance to choose a course that will serve us well in the coming conflict. I have seen it. Please, believe me," she pleaded. Her thoughts drifted to the last few nights' sleep. Her dreams were blurry and ran together unfocused and spasmodic but they always ended with her teetering and scrambling up a rocky incline, thick roots dotting the way and tugging at her ankles and feet. At the top she would find herself clothed in a finely designed tri-colored dress and wrapped snug in a flowing red tunic. From this vantage point she could survey the forested hills where the trees suddenly bent and cracked as if a giant unseen hand had given them a twist. Lightning and thunder streaked across the wind-lashed landscape, striking the earth in powerful spasms that left the rocks and trees covered in fine powdery dust. A great wind gushed and scattered the thick acrid smoke only for it to come together and solidify and take form right before her eyes. A sleek muscular charger with flashing smoke-colored eyes rippled and twitched as it waited for her to climb atop.

Rhu tightened his grip, his intense stare unnerving. After a few tense moments, he relented and dropped her hands. "It's the twisting of our culture, of our heritage that I fear more than a spear thrust to the belly, more than a sword chop to the neck. For without our heritage, we would be hollow and unable to withstand the fury of time," he said softly. He walked about the room. The big black dog woke from its nap and followed on his heels, sniffing at the priest's hands and casting an occasional flick of its pink tongue. Cussius eyed the beast uneasily.

The door opened and a gust of cold air entered with Leko as he hustled to the wobbly table and tossed the satchel, sending it sliding across and into the waiting hands of Rhu.

Rhu opened it and examined the contents. "Ah, you have paid attention," he said. The corners of his mouth lifted as he delved into the bag and spilled its contents onto a torn piece of tunic. He gingerly fingered strings of herbs, inhaling their scents and sampling with his tongue before discarding them. Finally a murmur of delight signaled his discovery, his hands emerging holding roasted eggshell, dried marigold petals, white root, and juniper needles. He pulled a knife and chopped it all together in quick, precise slices, then paused long enough to evaluate his work. Unsatisfied, he grabbed a rock from near the fire and ground the ingredients into a powder before mixing it with heated ale. From his own pack he added a greenish substance that had the consistency of ash. Satisfied, he turned to Thara.

"Thara," he said loudly. "Thara. Wake. You must drink," he said as he shook her shoulder.

Her eyelids flickered and she struggled to open her eyes. She cringed from him, making pitiful noises like an animal caught in a trap as Rhu propped Thara's head up and her mouth open and began spooning the dark liquid in while she sputtered and swallowed.

He looked up at the three spectators and shrugged. "Time will tell."

Creaking on its hinges, the door swept open once more. A young orderly nervously shuffled his feet and chewed his lip until waved over by Cussius. "Excuse me for a moment," he said, breaking from the huddled group and striding to meet the orderly. He leaned in, listening to the young man's urgent whispers.

When he straightened up, he said simply, "Dinner is prepared. I will have it delivered promptly. I will leave you in the good hands of my legionaries. You will want for nothing. Good evening."

CHAPTER FORTY-EIGHT

The smell of freshly baked bread permeated the room, mixing easily with the light smell of burning beech wood. Torches on the wall provided ample light, casting flickering shadows that danced and jumped from face to face of those gathered to sup. Gymm nodded agreeably, his mouth working itself into a suitable imitation of a smile. He tore the bread, cramming it into his mouth and chasing it down with a healthy swallow of the thickly brewed ale. He was hungry and dove into the blood pudding, savoring the lingering taste of onion that remained long after his plate was scraped empty. He refilled his cup and drained it, welcoming the lofty tingling that filled his head and warmed his belly. He thought to stop until he dealt with the Roman, but a quick look around spawned an uneasiness that only heightened his thirst and he helped himself to more ale, slopping the drink down the side of his cup where it pooled in a tiny eddy until finally dripping off the table and soaking into his tunic.

The Roman general chuckled. "The Bibroci are fine brewers, I must admit, but I do not think it was the stout ale and Lana's blood pudding that brought you here. Are you in need of your uncle's remedies as well? You appear to be healthy, aside from the obvious excesses," said Cussius as he examined Gymm from across the table.

Gymm scrunched his face at the jibe. He was already nervous, and the circular fashion in which the Roman spoke was aggravating. Sometimes he wished the man would just get to the point. He took another long pull on his cup, drained the contents and wiped his moustache dry with the edge of his tunic. "My uncle?" he croaked.

Cussius shrugged. "Sure. Yours, Lana', Thara'. You know, Rhu." Cussius leaned back.

"My Uncle Rhu is here," Lana said to Gymm, casting a sideways glance at Cussius.

Gymm felt the beginnings of dread fill his belly. The blood pudding and bread now conspired to form a knot in his stomach and his head throbbed dully. His lips felt thick and numb, and his tongue felt as if it were glued to the roof of his mouth. The thought of crossing the Druid sent a shiver down his spine and his mind came alive with all the rumors of magical capabilities attributed to the old priest. "He cannot know we are here," he hissed, nodding toward Roc, who shifted nervously in his seat and ate as quickly as he could move his hands to his mouth.

Cussius set his cup down and stood up. "And he will not. Now, to what do I owe this honor?"

Gymm swallowed hard and coughed into his hand. Beads of sweat sprouted like morning dew, and all of a sudden the room grew inward, leaving him small and exposed. Lana was nodding as if she knew what he had to say and all that remained was for him to prove her right. He took a deep breath and blew it out slowly. He licked his lips and smoothed out his bristling moustache. "We have an understanding, you and I?" Gymm asked. He picked up his knife and used its sharp tip to pick at wedged snips of food. He did not trust the Roman, but he needed his help if he were to keep Jayas from snatching what was not his to take. His eyes followed the Roman as he repeated the question, adding, "Do we not?"

Smiling, Cussius nodded and said, "I am certain of it. Honor demands it," he said, clutching his hand to his chest. "I would have it no other way. We have an understanding and appreciation of each other's talents, and we can envision what those talents can accomplish with the proper amount of collaboration. Do not fret, Gymm. Our futures are entwined as the stars are to the night. Now, I ask you again, why the unexpected visit?" He asked the question sharply, the gray of his eyes swimming like molten silver in the glare cast by the torches.

The Roman stopped in front of a low, burning torch, his shadow enveloping Gymm like a flock of ravens. Gymm swallowed hard and held the Roman's gaze. Here was his gamble. If he succeeded, Jayas would be humiliated, maybe even captured or killed. For a moment, a twinge of guilt washed over him as boyhood memories of Jayas and him flooded his mind's eye. A strange smile played on his lips as he remembered their early rivalries, always friendly but aggressively pursued, the wrestling and swordplay and the long summer days spent on horseback racing through forest and over plains with the hot sun beating on their necks. His smile melted away. "Tonight, Jayas and the army are on the move. They come here," he added sullenly. He did not feel any relief. If anything, the knot in his stomach grew, its tentacles reaching up and tickling his chest, causing it to leap and kick like a young colt on its first spring day. Seated beside him, Roc nodded solemnly between mouthfuls of bread and blood pudding.

The Roman's eyes narrowed and his smile melted away to be replaced by the makings of a frown.

He tramped to the door and whispered into the ear of the sentry. The man saluted and turned on his heel, scurrying down the steps and into the night. Antonius, who was nearby awaiting any orders, finished his drink and was up fidgeting with his sword belt, all the while studying the face of his general.

Cussius stopped his pacing. "Antonius, put half the garrison on alert and in position to repel an enemy attack. I want scouts on horseback dispatched now, small elusive patrols wary of ambush. Send Leko and his cadre of Bibroci scouts out on the perimeter scouting. I want a captive or two for good measure. A little more detail of the enemies' plans would be a plus. Dispatch riders to Mandubrac and Kren. Our allies are to push their mounts as hard as possible and hit the enemy where it hurts the most---their homes," said Cussius.

Antonius saluted. "It will be done, Sir!"

Cussius waved him away and walked the length of the table. He stopped behind Lana and rubbed her shoulders in firm, circular squeezes. He leaned down close to her ear, his breath hot. "Fate would force our hand," he muttered in a low whisper. Lana stiffened, the color rising to fill her cheeks. Cussius patted her shoulders reassuringly.

Gymm's jaw dropped open and he made to speak, but he clamped it tight when Cussius cut him off with a raised hand. "Gymm, worry not. We will not destroy your people. However, we shall clear the way for your assumption of the crown, as we have agreed. Until then, security risks must be addressed, and trust me on this — our actions are for your own good."

Stunned and momentarily wordless, Gymm watched as Cussius made for the thick wooden door and flung it open, allowing a gust of cold air to burst in, carrying with it tiny frozen specks of snow that quickly melted in the cozy gloom.

Holding the door open, Cussius leveled his gaze on Gymm and yelled, "Guards!"

Heavy footfalls tramped in step and four fully armed legionaries burst in, their swords drawn and glinting a brilliant red in the flickering torchlight.

"Remo," said Cussius pointing, "there are your charges." He stepped aside, making room for the quartet of legionaries, who stalked the length of the room, cornering their quarry by the table.

The legionary named Remo was brutish, appearing more than capable of extreme violence at any moment of his choosing. His protruding brow ran together in a continuous line of bushy hair, curving down and over the bridge of his nose. He stepped forward and kicked the stool from under Roc who, yelping like a kicked pup, fell to the ground with a grunt as the air whooshed from his full stomach. He scrambled to all fours and sucked in gulps of air, grasping for the sword dangling at his side.

"Up, you scoundrel!" the guard shouted threateningly as Roc rose unsteadily to his feet.

Gymm sprang from his stool, his face the color of fresh beets. "Treacherous bastards!" he spat. He glared down at the shorter guards, his hand clutching the hilt of his sword, the blade halfway out of the scabbard. He gripped the blade so tightly that his hands shook and his knuckles changed from red to pink to white.

"Don't do it, Gymm! Remo, step back!" Cussius snapped, his own blade sliding silently within the greased scabbard. "Everyone calm down! No harm. No blood," he ordered with his own sword drawn. "Think! Rhu is already confined and you are to be as well. You have been captured and no one will believe otherwise. It's for your own good. Understand?" Cussius asked, his tone suggesting he cared not if Gymm failed to do so.

Lana stood up and slinked away from the table, careful to keep the table and stools between her and the drawn swords. She held her hands up and massaged the air as if her hands could allay the situation. "Do as he says, Gymm. How would it look if you are discovered roaming about the fort, free as a bird? Rhu could see you, and he is no fool," she said impatiently. "I want what you want, Gymm. Cussius wants what you want. Just do what you have to do and it will work out. Trust me, trust us." Sighing, she tossed up her hands and threw back the canvas divider, leaving the men behind.

"Okay," Gymm muttered. He relented his grip on the blade and it slid with a smooth metallic whisper into the snugness of the scabbard. He attempted a smile, clapping Roc on the back in the process. It was a measure aimed more to calm himself than for Roc's sake, but his muscles stayed rigid nonetheless. Gymm turned toward the Roman brute who had accosted Roc, his lips now quivering in poorly disguised rage, "Where to?"

CHAPTER FORTY-NINE

IT HAD GROWN bitterly cold and dismal. Every man straggled shivering and stumbling through thick powder. The freezing sleet had drifted away only to be replaced by an onslaught of countless white crystals. The snow was upon them suddenly, pouring down as if the gods were dumping huge buckets of it merely to foil the plans of man. Jayas felt his teeth chatter. It angered him and he clenched his jaws tight until he had the sensation under control. Jayas blew on his fingers and rubbed them together in a futile attempt to warm them. He cursed. Thus far, Jayas thought, things were off to an auspicious start. He plowed forward, hunched against the wind. They needed to get to the creek where its angular banks could provide some shelter against the fierce gusts of snow-laden wind.

Jayas paused and turned his back to the fierce gusts. He scanned the night for his men. He covered his brow with his hand and finally made out a stumbling group of warriors emerge from the swirling storm, their heads canted downward or tucked tightly to their necks like a pod of startled turtles. He waved them forward and absorbed their hostile and sullen glares. If he could endure, then they could endure it as well, Jayas thought. He ignored them and leaned into the gusts, his eyes squinting and blinking. He again took the lead, one hand in front of him like a blind man groping for the walls in a strange room. He stumbled into a large rock, jarring his knee, and knew he was close to the creek. He felt the incline with his boot and slid down an embankment. Shadowy snow covered figures stumbled behind him, some landing in a tangled, grunting heap of muffled curses and clanking metal.

There was no path so Jayas blazed one, his boots sinking in and out of the ankle deep snow. They followed the narrow bed of the creek. The ravine was strewn with sharp, ice-covered boulders and he picked his way, cautious to keep his footing. Behind him, a shout was followed by a loud cracking sound. He grimaced. Some careless warrior would soon be walking on frozen feet. Moisture was an enemy. Getting drenched was worse. In this weather it could lead to frostbite, amputation and death.

Jayas sensed they were close. The Roman fortress was within bowshot. He was sure of it. Jayas scuttled to the west bank and collapsed behind a row of thorny bracken shiny and heavy with fresh snow. A figure materialized next to him. The wind blew so hard that his eyes watered and he strained to see who it was.

"What do we do now?" asked Lann in a voice interrupted by the chattering of teeth. Other clansmen moseyed over and hunkered down, their backs to the twisting rows of spiny bracken, thankful for any buffer that could provide some small respite from the snow-filled gale. Jayas could sense their unease. They all looked cold, wet and miserable and stared at him as if he were the sole cause of their current discomforts.

"What?" Jayas shouted. He leaned in closer. Lann looked miserable, his body quaking and shivering, his teeth chattering like the steady hollow thunk of a woodpecker. Jayas looked Lann over in the weak light afforded by a break in the gusting snow. His hair was askew and his tunic, doused in the creek earlier by Lann's misstep, was frozen stiff. Little wonder, Jayas thought.

The gathering grew as Lord Bret pushed his way through and plopped down on one knee. Despite the nagging elements, Lord Bret looked comfortable and gave no sign that the weather was any more bothersome than a swarm of late summer fruit flies. Jayas eyed Bret's long-sleeved tunic worn under a woolen cloak, a plain twill with a blue checkered pattern fastened with a metal clasp. The man wore thick wool trousers, an undyed diamond twill weave made with belt loops, tucked into the lips of soft leather boots.

Lord Bret nodded. "It may be time to head back. Nothing good can come of this," he shrugged and pointed up at the sky.

Jayas fought his natural urge to lash out at the interfering noble. His jaw jutted forward and his brow furrowed as he chewed over Bret's comments. "Just a little bit farther," Jayas bristled in return. The thought of Thara spending another minute with the filthy Roman invaders sullied his mind. In a detached sense, he knew his obsession with Thara was affecting the way he commanded, but then again, this foray was Rhu's idea.

A strong wind bore a curtain of snow and it left everyone, already stretched to their limits, feeling more tetchy and short-tempered than before. Jayas took stock. The men were gathered in uneasy clusters, their ears and noses reddened by the cold. Hunched over and crouched close together, wearing leather armor under tunics and furs, they talked in hushed whispers, their breath billowing into the frigid air. Jayas caught nothing of what they said as the tone and content of their hushed conversations were drowned out by the howling wind.

"I am not giving up. Maybe Rhu has devised a way for us. We are almost there," he pointed toward hills hidden by swirls of snow. Farther out in the darkness a wolf sang its deep, mournful song. The cry rose, a pitiful howl that fell upon the ice encrusted lands until matched and finally drowned out by the rising wind. "We should at the very least creep up and see if Rhu has found a way to open the gates for us. I will go first and if the way is clear I will signal." For a moment his mind wandered to his previous visit to the Roman fortress. His hopes sank as low as the temperature as he tried to imagine Rhu's scrawny arms tugging and pushing on the large oak logs used to bar the main gate. A near impossibility, he determined. The vision did little to inspire confidence, but Jayas was determined to see it through. He would take even the slightest opportunity if that meant he and his warriors could have a go at the Romans within their camp. His feral grin returned.

Skeptical murmurs and nodding heads under the cover of hooded cloaks were his answer.

"Good. You," Jayas said as he pointed at Lann, "will stay here. I'll take ten of your scouts and see what I find. I will be back," he said, seeking out and holding the gaze of Bret, "and you will be following behind me and into the soft Roman belly. The gods are with us. Look for yourselves. The snowstorm is giving us the cover we need to sneak right in on them." Then he and the selected scouts scaled the icy bank and set out.

CHAPTER FIFTY

The heat hit Cussius and Antonius like a wave and sweat immediately began to form in the small of Cussius' back. On his orders both fire pits were roaring full bore. Flames licked the length of the stone chimney, sucked upward by the promise of fresh air. Antonius headed for the bucket of ale, stripping his tunic off and tossing it on a stool in passing. It slid off its perch and lay in a crumpled pile under the table. Cussius peeled off his red tunic and shook it dry the best he could. He found a wooden peg and hung the garment, brushing bits of frozen mud with swipes of his hand. He frowned as dirty brown pools formed where he had flung the icy chaff to the floor. Forgetting the minor nuisance, he eyeballed his captives.

Jayas still wore his leather armor and heavy plaid tunic draped over his shoulders. At the sight of Cussius Jayas twisted his body, sucking in great breaths of air and exhaling slowly, which had no noticeable effect on the ropes looping his frame. They had not budged. He panted from the effort and sweat streamed down his face. His hair lay matted on his head, dirty and lank. Cussius walked over, cupped the man's chin and lifted his head — eyes like blue flame shot into his. From a seated position the man lunged and kicked out with his boots, striking nothing but air as Cussius dodged the poorly aimed blow. Scowling guards moved forward to rebuke the unruly prisoner. Jayas bit at reckless hands and a yelp escaped the lips of a careless guard. A vengeful guard smacked Jayas openhanded, leaving red welts splayed across his cheek. The squad leader shot a looping punch, and a sickening crunch signaled cartilage and bone splitting on impact. Blood trickled from both nostrils and a split upper lip.

Jayas spit blood at his tormentors. Remo hauled back for another blow.

"Enough, Remo! He forgets his manners." Cussius left unsaid whose manners it was to which he referred. He walked toward Remo, his eyes lit in anger. He gripped his sword.

"Did I order you to strike the prisoner? That's rhetorical. Let it suffice to say you are a brute with no tact. Since when do we torment bound captives?" he demanded. Puzzled faces exchanged glances. Even Leko looked at him strangely, for violence inflicted upon prisoners and captives was commonplace.

Remo backed away. "But General, he bit..."

"I don't care a whit if you've been gored by the man. You managed to get stung by the only weapon he had available — his teeth. Shame on you, Remo," Cussius stared the man down. He briefly considered walking over and smacking Remo a few times for good measure but let it pass. No need to humiliate the man further, for his words had bitten as deep as any blow.

Cussius glared into the eyes of the bound Coritani. He studied Jayas. The man was a fighter. He was bound tight like a hog for the slaughter and yet he fought. He was not unlike the many other clan chiefs and so-called kings littering Rome's path. Caesar was masterful in his handling of the Celts and Gauls. Cussius had seen firsthand how Caesar cajoled, threatened and flattered the chieftains by turns playing off tribal jealousies and exploiting family feuds. He supported clans and leaders friendly to Rome's aims and subverted those who did not. If none of that worked, brute force would convey any message diplomacy failed to translate clearly. Cussius wondered if Jayas appreciated any of this. No matter, he thought.

For his part, the warrior was tight-lipped and watched his every move like a snake would a curious dog, ready to strike if opportunity presented itself.

Antonius spoke up. "I don't think he's fond of you, General. It looks like he wants to carve your liver. Well, yours or maybe his," he said, jerking his head toward Leko. He continued, "I told you the slave was paying attention to what the old man was doing." He winked at Leko, a small but much deserved token of respect.

Leko did not look amused but nodded in reply and took a drink of ale. He appeared more interested in studying Rhu and wasn't paying anyone much mind.

Cussius grinned, thin eyebrows arched. "The great Jayas, bested by a whelp." He turned toward Leko, his smile growing wider and genuine. "No offense, my boy. Great work." He walked behind the prisoner, grabbed Jayas by the shoulders and patted him reassuringly. It had the opposite effect. Cussius could feel goose pimples rising on the back of the warrior's neck.

Cussius sighed deeply. "So hostile. Is that all you're capable of? If so, I'm quite capable of reciprocating. In fact, my men are begging for your blood, Jayas. They would like nothing more than to see your head lodged on a pole in the center of the fort. Some would like to see you and the woman you're fond of sold off into slavery on the continent — far from here; you in the salt mines of Spain and her off to Africa. But unlike you weaklings, I'm an honorable man. Perhaps your luck may have turned. Just maybe you were born under the right star." He nodded toward Leko where he was leaning against the wall, immobile and silent. "As a matter of fact, I'm sure Leko or Kege would like another go of all this. Maybe next time." Cussius wondered how Leko or Kege had refrained from slaying Jayas, but he was not complaining. He had not yet received a full briefing on the scuffle that resulted in Jayas' capture. In brief snatches of conversation with Antonius, he had learned that the fierce snow storm recently blanketing the land contributed to Jayas' demise. Blinded by the blizzard, confusion took hold in the Coritani advance and Jayas was separated from the main body of his warriors. Thanks to Gymm's warning, Leko and the other Bibroci scouts were circling the Roman holdings when the two groups slammed into one another. Rendered unconscious in the ensuing melee, Jayas' inert body was slung across the back of Leko' horse and then the scouts beat a hasty retreat. To hear it told by Antonius, Leko had no clue that the limp form slumped over the rump of his mount was the young Coritani war leader. Once Leko was safely inside of the palisade walls, he discovered the captive's identity and had been morose and sullen ever since. Cussius could not suppress a grin. The deliverance of Jayas to his keep was a boon he intended to maximize.

Jayas canted his head and blew his nose. Clots of blood dotted the floor. He spat.

"Silent? Nothing to say?" Cussius walked to the table and poured a cup of ale. He drained the cup, dragged a seat over and set it within a couple arms' length of Jayas, then slid onto the stool. They faced one another.

"What do you gain by not speaking? If I were in a similar predicament, I think I would reconsider the tactic. As a stratagem, silence leaves much to be desired, especially with so much at stake. If you opt to stay silent, you have no say in your future or that of your tribe." Cussius paused. He wanted to smirk, but instead he returned Jayas' deadpan stare.

"But that depends on you. In with the new and out with the…" his voice trailed off and he glanced about the room for the old man. "It's time for you to face the bare facts. Rhu, you can help in this," Cussius shouted over his shoulder. He was surprised the priest had not said a word since he entered.

Rhu did not bat an eye or give any indication he heard Cussius. The old man's back was turned to him and he made no effort to be included. Cussius was in an expansive mood and ignored Rhu's disrespect. Why not give them the illusion of freedom and self-determination, he thought. He cleared his throat and spoke clearly. "Choose a leader from amongst yourselves with whom I can negotiate. Keep in mind that all things must come to an end. Progress is inevitable, progress of the mind and spirit. You can be pious but be smart, be realistic. The realities on the ground dictate the avenues you can take. Not vice-versa."

Cussius barked a command. There was the tramp of nailed boots on the wooden floor and the thick canvas divider parted. With a rough shove, Gymm was brought in the room. His hands were bound behind his back and he looked angry, glowering at any who met his eye. Cussius motioned to his seat and gave it up. Gymm sat opposite Jayas and the two locked stares. Neither blinked.

Cussius sat at the table. He grabbed a piece of bread and ate. It was dry and hard. Rhu was now studying Gymm, his eyes slits and mouth working silently. Cussius was thrilled with this outcome, and he strived to remain aloof. It was a demeanor that came to him naturally so it wasn't too difficult. He had them all here, the two young leaders of the Coritani and their priest, under his control and at his mercy. Meanwhile, their army was rudderless and scattered around the fortress, impotent and exhausted. He took another bite, chewing slowly as he observed his captives.

The hatred between the tribesmen was palpable and the tension was stifling. They didn't get it. He aimed to take advantage, but it wasn't that easy. The messengers from Caesar were snooping around. It would be difficult to convince Maximus in particular that he was proceeding as was necessary, he could be sure of that. So far he had managed to avoid them because of all the excitement, but his excuses were running thin.

Rhu stood up, his knee bones crackling and snapping in protest. He was not tied or shackled, and he shuffled toward the fire and held his bone-thin hands near the flames. He rubbed them together. He spoke low. "We may have to think the unthinkable. A test of wills may not be the wisest of courses." Rhu sounded tired.

Rhu had the room's attention. Gymm and Jayas watched the old priest most intently, waiting. The air in the room grew heavier. Under the drying blood, Jayas' face took on a deeper shade of crimson.

Jayas exploded with no warning. "Quit trying to be clever. Be quiet. You're useless. You've led our forces to ruin and you're over there babbling nonsense. Why don't you just say what needs saying and quit dancing around it."

Rhu waved, an imperious gesture. "What gives you the right? What makes you so certain that you know what it is I have done here?" He stepped from the fire and ambled toward the table. No one made a move to stop him so he helped himself to a cup of ale.

He made to fill another but Antonius growled a warning. Rhu smiled, his eyes sad and forgiving.

Gymm broke his silence. "Do not blame Rhu, Jayas. It was your folly, not his. It was you who led our army to these walls. Your prideful boasts, numerous as the crows of a cocky rooster, peppered the council table until the king believed your nonsense. All along it was your precious pride and your lust for Thara that mattered to you. None of that is the Druid's fault."

Leko perked up at this exchange and mention of Thara, his mouth curled into a mocking sneer. He scratched at a knot in the wooden wall, picking at it nervously as he shot hate-filled glares in Jayas' direction. "A lot of good it did him. You don't deserve a creature such as Thara. To think of it, she hasn't even mentioned your name since she's been here," Leko taunted. He paused and looked around, his eyes lingering for a moment on Cussius, who remained impassive, as he idly sipped the warm wine.

Emboldened, Leko approached Jayas, his eyes wary and searching. Leko settled behind Jayas. All that could be heard was the faint crackle of the low fires. He leaned over and whispered, "Thanks to me and Rhu," he nodded in the old man's direction, "Thara lives and that is all you need to know. But now I'm left to wonder, your life for hers? How about your life for the honor you stole from Marcus?" he hissed lowly before retreating back to the wall, where he fixed Jayas with a scathing look of contempt.

Jayas exploded in a burst of futile energy. He flexed and strained against the ropes. Failing at that, he tried hopping. The motion got the chair rocking but it did not budge an inch. His body quivered in impotent rage.

"You're little more than a mongrel whelp!" Jayas bellowed at Leko. He ripped his reddened eyes away from Leko and leveled Gymm with a glare, his eyes accusing daggers. "And you! Jealousy, envy, and greed! Those are your traits!" Jayas spat. "And where were you? How did you get captured? Now that I think of it, I haven't seen you for two days. You were riding with Lord Bret's retinue, and then, gone. Convenient." Jayas hissed the allegation.

"I would kill you for those words," Gymm said through gritted teeth.

"And I should have killed you when I had you under my knife," Leko bitterly muttered from the wall.

"That was your one and only opportunity, little one," Jayas shouted, his eyes bulging like those of a spooked horse.

"We'll see," Leko said hoarsely.

Straining against the tight cords, Jayas leaned in Gymm's direction, hissing. "You would? Or do you mean, you will? What did your betrayal cost? Tell me what your betrayal has cost you, cost your tribe. Please tell Rhu." Jayas' eyes narrowed to mere slits. His scar was pulled tight and gleamed pink in the flickering shadows.

Gymm gawked, his stupid expression frozen. Despite the heat of the room his face paled. His eyes darted away for a second as if the truth were secreted in the far corner of the room.

"Let's just get this over and done with," Cussius said, his patience waning. He touched his forehead and pain radiated backward and down his neck. He was tight and tiring of the drama. Jayas was smarter than he thought. He had put together what had transpired quickly enough, or maybe he hadn't quite yet, thought Cussius, but he will soon. He could be fishing, dangling bait in front of a confused and defensive Gymm. Cussius shook his head at Gymm's amateurish display. Gymm being tongue-tied and baffled was the same as the fish swallowing and gagging on the bait as the fisherman jerked and set the hook.

"Betrayal? It sounds so nasty, doesn't it? The word leaves a bad taste in your mouth, makes you feel dirty, not worthy." Cussius peered right through Jayas as he spoke. It wasn't a question, and on a subconscious level, it irked him. He knew the taste — bitter like soured wine. He changed the subject.

"Leko, run to the officers' quarters and summon the couriers sent by Caesar. I think they should be present as we broker our agreement with our partners in peace."

CHAPTER FIFTY-ONE

LEKO HURRIED BACK with his charges. Caesar's envoys entered and stood rooted, blinking as their eyes grew accustomed to the dim light.

Maximus, a patrician lackey of Caesar's, was senior. Alert and searching, the man was keen to nuance. He walked the length of the room, his scarlet tunic scraping over his iron breastplate and sweeping along the floor. He was of middling height and spare of heft. Cussius was certain Maximus had volunteered for the mission so he could gather information and gossip, planning to hightail it back to Gaul to cast vile aspersions at the feet of Caesar. If he were allowed to, Cussius thought. The other two Romans were of ensign rank, young and fit, their eyes wary and appraising as they swept the room. Shadowing Maximus' movements was a hulking fellow of great height and girth. He had long, stringy black hair flowing from a wide forehead, and large blue eyes measured those in the room from a heavy cheek-boned face. One of Caesar's personal German bodyguards had accompanied Maximus, which Cussius found interesting.

Cussius took the patrician noble by the elbow and escorted him to the table. A more gracious host would not be found. "So kind of you to make it, Maximus," Cussius said. "Please help yourself to drink. There is plenty. I would like to thank you for your patience.

Events have unfolded so quickly that I've had little time to properly entertain."

Maximus sniffed and nodded toward the captives. His eyes beheld the bloody spectacle of Jayas and his mouth curled downward. "Are you hosting games this evening, Cussius?"

It was Cussius' turn to sniff. "I never treat diplomacy as a game. It's a deadly serious business. Wouldn't you agree?" Cussius asked, his tone fake and jolly.

Maximus grinned, his thin lips parting to reveal remarkably intact teeth. "I would. So it's diplomacy you conduct. Interesting methods. Successful, I presume? Who are these so-called diplomats?" Maximus asked.

"My apologies." Cussius bowed, sweeping his hand in a grand gesture. "This cheeky duo would be Jayas of the Coritani and Gymm of the same. The wizened creature shuffling about is Rhu, their Druid priest." Cussius was certain the names meant nothing to Maximus. Nonetheless, pretenses must be maintained.

"Ah, the hiccups of civilization. Were you in need of assistance? Do these men need further convincing? It seems as if you have things in good order." Maximus looked bored. It was not an unfamiliar scene. If one campaigned with Caesar for any period of time, a legionary of his rank was sure to experience the seedier sides of politics.

Cussius nodded and brought him up to date. "Despite my greatest efforts, they resist an alliance. They seem to believe that, if they defeat me, a legate of Rome and the duly appointed symbol of Roman power and authority, then they will live free of Rome and its influences. Can you imagine?" All he had to do now was button up and let Maximus and his very patrician sensibilities rise to the bait. He was not disappointed.

Maximus laughed, a harsh grating sound he directed toward the "diplomats." "I'm afraid that's typical of the barbarians, the simpleminded approach that is soothing and familiar to the savage mind," Maximus leaned back against the table. A smug expression sat on his close-shaven features. He looked away from the captives.

Scorn dripped from his words. "They think that would be the end of it? Do they think we would not know who was responsible? Rome never forgets. Rome never forgives. Their every night would be sleepless. Every wind would carry the whisper of a Roman blade. It is a brutal lesson — one not easily forgotten." Maximus fixed the captives with a stare. "If you do not believe me, maybe you could ask one of your Gallic cousins. I'm sure they could educate you."

Rhu had fixed Maximus with a curious look and was mumbling something too low for anyone to pick up. Maximus seemed to notice, his eyes sizing up the old man. "I'm not an adherent to your brand of religion, and so any appeals to the will of the gods and so on you can keep to yourself. No Roman worthy of his ancestors is going to bow to your heathen gods, especially to gods whose holy men smell like wooly goat fur and are allergic to the razor." He leaned backward and pinched his nose. His voice was nasal like the honk of a goose as he continued. "I will keep my Roman gods, thank you. Venus and Mars are worthy of proper Roman homage. You can peddle your drivel elsewhere." Maximus folded his arms, his mouth half-cocked in an ugly smirk. "I hope that was instructive."

"Indeed it was. I could not have said it better myself. Wouldn't you agree, Rhu?" Cussius asked.

Understanding washed over Rhu's craggy features, but another glance at Maximus and the old man thought better of talking. The druid fidgeted under his heavy robe. It was more tunic than robe but easily could have been a mix of both judging from the erratic stitch pattern. Holy man, perhaps, handy with a thread and needle he was not, thought Cussius.

"I would call it a load of shallow Roman boasts, little more than offal and hogwash, lies and half-truths to bolster their position. And there is a big dose of arrogance," Jayas shouted, his face full of hatred.

His dark eyes flashing, Maximus shouted back, "Call it what you will as you twist and flop like a fish out of water, helpless as a lamb under the herder's shears. Is your current condition not proof enough? And you call me a liar. A savage of low breeding dares cast doubt on the word of a Roman citizen of good birth?" he demanded, his tone low and menacing. Maximus' hands crept toward his dagger and the muscles in his face twitched. Behind him, the big German shifted his weight and drew his tunic to the side, freeing the path to his sword.

"Are you going to abide this insolence? Are you going to permit an ignorant barbarian to insult a Roman officer — an officer of good birth? Fifty lashes would suffice. He's lucky I don't demand his life in satisfaction for this offense," Maximus said venomously, his dark eyes cold and penetrating.

Cussius ignored him. In Rome or Gaul or anywhere else that Rome's rule extends, such a demand would make sense. The noble's honor would scream for recompense and satisfaction would be had. Usually it was some creature of low birth that overstepped his bounds and paid for it with a bloodied back. Often enough the bloody back would then take a turn for the worse, start stinking with infection, and before the poor sap could bid farewell, he was a burning pile of ash in the city dump. The thought reminded Cussius of the stink of the city and his nostrils clenched.

"Well?" Maximus asked. His two escorts began to stir behind him. The black-haired German remained silent and stationary like a Greek statue, his stare hard as granite.

Cussius took another gulp of ale and tossed his empty cup on the table. Maximus had spoken with utter confidence, and it galled him. Cussius wanted to swipe the smugness from his face and stamp it under the heel of his boot. The man was probably dying to play his trump, to bring up the fact that he bears the will of Caesar, a fact he would use to bully Cussius and get his way. He supposed the big German bodyguard on loan from Caesar was supposed to serve as a reminder of that very fact, or a warning, depending — Cussius was unconcerned.

"It's not a bad life here. It's free of all the pretensions rampant in Rome," Cussius said to no one in particular.

A look of puzzlement worked itself loose from Maximus' usually composed features. "What?" Maximus demanded, pursing his lips in contempt.

"No lashes, no life in return for your wounded honor. My decision," Cussius said flatly, his eyes defiant.

For a moment, Maximus was too flummoxed to answer and he merely ran his tongue over his lips, but his confusion did not last long. "My apologies, but I'm afraid I misunderstood your last statement. Did you just refuse my lawful request for satisfaction? You would take the part of a savage, a barbarian who can think no further than to fornicate, swill ale and war with his own kind over that of your Roman comrades? Do you forget yourself?" Maximus asked, his expression incredulous.

"I forget little and forgive less," Cussius said with a hard edge to his voice. "And what would happen if a Roman legate refused lawful orders? For instance, if a legate would rather retire early and take to parts known and unknown, and what if the legion under his command were of a like mind?"

Maximus laughed again, going so far as to hold his stomach and slap his knee. The laughter tapered off quickly for he realized that no one shared the humor. There was a deadly seriousness in the air. "Laughable and foolish. He and the legion he commands would be declared enemies of Rome. The sentence would be death for all." Maximus reserved his stare for Cussius.

The two men studied each other. Maximus' companions moved just a hair's breadth, their hands inching toward their swords.

Cussius could sense Leko disengaging from the wall he leaned upon, and a cup rattled on the table as Antonius quit his drink and slid off the stool. Jayas quit his muttering and strained to see through blood-encrusted eyelids. Remo stalked around the table, his movement reminiscent of a hound with the scent of fresh blood in his nostrils.

Maximus smiled with the warmth of a winter breeze, snug in the security of Caesar's shadow. "And who would this hypothetical legate be? Are you at liberty to reveal the source of your inquiry?" he challenged.

Cussius did not flinch. Maximus had not gone so far as to outright accuse him of treachery but instead danced around the subject like a cat approaching a body of water. "What are you trying to say, Maximus? Are you accusing me of something?"

"Do I have reason to accuse you?" Behind Maximus, the two ensigns licked their lips and used their shoulders to wipe the sweat from their brows. Only the German remained stock still, his eyes kindled in sullen interest. Leko had inched closer and now stood within ten feet of the young ensigns. A sense of foreboding filled the dry air.

Cussius made no attempt to dispel it. "I think we both know the answer to that. Are you that fond of rhetoric that you phrase the majority of questions in such a fashion?" He sighed, tiring of the verbal gamesmanship. With an eerie finality he muttered, "Yes, you have much reason to accuse."

Maximus jumped at the admission. "Then as the *lawful* representative of Caesar, I urge you to reconsider your position. You have until sunrise tomorrow to give me your answer. Whatever it is, I will make it abundantly clear to Caesar what your sentiments truly are." Maximus stood up, his jaw set. His companions surrounded him, their stony eyes darting.

"Why wait until sunrise? I think you know my answer," Cussius said.

"Is that a road you wish to travel?"

"It is."

"Then we have no further business. My contingent shall return when the weather and other circumstances are amenable to our travel. I take my leave then." Maximus finished with a curt nod.

"Not so fast. Why don't you wait here, Maximus." It wasn't a request and Maximus knew it.

Maximus fixed Cussius with a glare. "I am under no obligation to take orders from a deserter. Your demands lack any authority," Maximus said, his voice rising to a high pitch.

"I'm not claiming the authority of Rome, Maximus," Cussius said as if speaking to a child, his voice even and unthreatening. "You men," Cussius gestured toward the ensigns, "may take your leave. Not you, German. You stay here."

The two young ensigns looked at one another, unsure of what to do. Nothing registered on the face of the German, his face hard and settled like a marble façade.

"They go where I go," Maximus snarled with ultimate conviction.

Cussius shrugged. "Stubborn, aren't we?"

Maximus rose to the challenge. "It is not stubbornness from which I speak, but a little something called fidelity, something your character is deficient in and that's why you are nothing more than a thin, brittle imitation of a man worthy of Rome." Maximus stopped his tirade, the atmosphere having grown chilly despite the efforts of the fires. A cold sullen stillness dominated.

The seconds ticked by and no one moved.

Cussius ran a finger under his nose to suppress a smile. "Very well. You leave me little choice." Without warning, Cussius struck Maximus with the back of his hand.

Maximus reeled from the blow, steadied himself and drew his dagger. "That's twice you insult me. You will die for this. If not here by my hand, then by the long hand of Rome." Maximus sneered as he breathed in heavy spurts, his face red as a beet. Sinister thoughts played behind his cold eyes.

Silence and a defiant sardonic smile were his response, for Cussius already had his blade out. Leko drew beside him, no trace of fear on his face. Cussius was pleased to see that Antonius and Remo were flanking the big German. It would be easy to kill Maximus. He could run him through with the blade and burn his body by nightfall. The man would just disappear. He paused. That would not be good enough. A long death was necessary for the spectators. No clean surgical stroke of the sword for Maximus. His death would be a statement – a death more demonstrative than beheading or stabbing. It was a cruel necessity but a seed well worth planting.

Without a word, Cussius leapt the short distance into Maximus. He swung the flat of his sword as hard as he could, catching Maximus a terrific wallop on the shoulder. A crunching sound like breaking ice rent the air. Maximus screamed and a grunt of pain escaped his lips as his dagger dropped to the floor with a clatter.

Maximus held his shoulder, which drooped limply and his hand dangled close to his knee, with his other arm. He dropped to a knee, his face twisted in pain.

Cussius heard a vicious yell and turned to see Antonius and Remo atop the big German. Remo used a club, wielding it heavily and connecting with wet smacking sounds. The German collapsed under their combined weights, and went down silent and unmoving. Remo and Antonius stood up but kept uneasy watch on the unconscious figure.

The two ensigns backed themselves to the wall and held their hands out. One spoke. "I thought you said we were free to go," he complained, his face taking on a greenish hue.

"Stop your sniveling. Leko, if they make any untoward moves, by all means continue your tutelage and strike them down where they stand," Cussius ordered.

Leko nodded, his eyes never leaving those of the two ensigns. Their early watchful confidence had dissolved and they now looked like frightened virgins on the night of their weddings.

Cussius strode over and gripped Maximus by the hair. He dragged the man to where Rhu stood. Jayas and Gymm craned their necks to follow.

"Well? You have ears. Do we have ourselves a deal?" Cussius asked all three.

"We do," Gymm blurted.

"Silence, Gymm!" Jayas commanded. "You do not speak for the people."

Cussius sighed and shook his head. "Not yet. I'm not finished." Cussius turned his attentions to Maximus, cognizant of the lethal stares stabbing into his back.

"You would see me dead — isn't that what you said? No matter. You will not live to see it through." Cussius sheathed his sword. He cracked his knuckles, loosening the stiff joints for the task at hand.

"Remo," Cussius yelled while nodding toward the kneeling Maximus. Remo hustled over and roughly jerked Maximus' arms behind him, eliciting an anguished howl in return. Tears rolled down Maximus' upturned face. Pitiless eyes surveyed Maximus before Cussius wrapped both of his large hands around the envoy's neck. Cussius could feel the man's jaw bristle against his thumbs and fingers as he squeezed slowly, avoiding Maximus' bulging eyes in favor of those of the Celts. He continued applying pressure, and from the tail of his eye he could see that Maximus' face had turned a deep purple. He doubled his efforts and squeezed harder, and in the back of his mind he was amazed at how long it was taking. He ignored the choking sounds and applied pressure until the body violently convulsed. Finally, he returned his gaze to the newly deceased and released his grip. The man's body slumped to the ground, his head twisted at an extreme angle.

Cussius stepped back and wiped his sweaty hands on his tunic. All eyes were upon him, and that was what he wanted. In the corner, the big German stirred, managing to prop himself up and look around groggily. The two ensigns had not moved, their eyes wide like small moons. Cussius could sense that even the Celts had a different look in their eyes as they followed his every move. He had conveyed the message. It was one thing to order a man's death, and it was also one thing to take a man's head with a sword, but using one's own hands to feel the life drain away was quite another. The significance was in the eyes of those who had beheld this minor spectacle, and Cussius was glad to see it there.

Cussius looked around, his expression grave. "I ask one last time. Are we allies? Do we face the future together?"

Rhu stepped forward, his thin frame stooped. "Together? Or do you expect us to truckle and jump to the Roman way?"

Cussius gestured toward Maximus' body. "That is what the Roman way is to me now, a corpse. I have left that life behind to start anew. You either believe me or you do not. Make up your minds." Cussius made his way to where Maximus had dropped the dagger and picked it up. He bent over and sliced the restraints from Gymm's wrists.

Gymm brought his wrists to the front and rubbed them together to get the blood and feeling flowing through his hands. He looked appreciatively at Cussius.

"We shall be allies," Gymm announced.

Rhu shrugged. "The land needs time to heal, and for that, we need peace." He looked toward Jayas, his stare demanding.

Jayas dropped his head, resting his chin against the ridge of his chest. He finally raised his head, his gaze steady. "Peace it is." His whisper was barely audible.

About the Author

Joe studied history and criminal justice at Marshall University in Huntington, West Virginia, where he also worked as a police officer until leaving to study at Cleveland-Marshall College of Law. Since matriculating from law school Joe has been an associate for a large creditor's rights firm, worked in private practice as a solo-practitioner and sat the bench as a magistrate at the Court of Common Pleas. His passion for books, history, writing, and in particular, historical fiction, led him to writing book and literature reviews at joeunleashed.com. These days you will find Joe polishing the sequel to "A Roman Peace in Briton: Blood on the Stone" and practicing law on a case-by-case basis as necessity and inspiration see fit.

9008598R0

Made in the USA
Charleston, SC
02 August 2011